EUROPA BLUES

A Greek gangster arrives in Stockholm, only to be murdered in a macabre fashion at Skansen zoo, his body consumed by wolverines. As the Intercrime Unit — a team dedicated to solving international violent crime — investigates what brought him to Sweden, eight Eastern European women vanish from a refugee centre outside of the city; while an elderly science professor, the tattooed numbers on his arm hinting at his terrible past, is executed at the Jewish cemetery. Three cases, one team of detectives, and an investigation that will take them across Europe and back through history as they desperately search for answers, and the identities of the killers.

EUROPA BLUES

ARNE DAHL

TRANSLATED FROM THE SWEDISH BY ALICE MENZIES

LARGE
PRINT

First published in Great Britain 2015
by
Harvill Secker
an imprint of Vintage

First Isis Edition
published 2016
by arrangement with
Penguin Random House UK

The moral right of the author has been asserted

Copyright © 2001 by Arne Dahl
English translation copyright © 2015 by Alice Menzies
All rights reserved

A catalogue record for this book is available
from the British Library.

ISBN 978–1–78541–258–5 (hb)
ISBN 978–1–78541–264–6 (pb)

Published by
F. A. Thorpe (Publishing)
Anstey, Leicestershire

Set by Words & Graphics Ltd.
Anstey, Leicestershire
Printed and bound in Great Britain by
T. J. International Ltd., Padstow, Cornwall

This book is printed on acid-free paper

CHAPTER
ONE

It was an evening in early May. It was completely still.

Not the slightest of breezes was blowing in over the waters of Saltsjön. Out on Kastellholm, the castle's flag was hanging limp. The toothed facades of Skeppsbron were like a painted backdrop in the distance. There wasn't a flutter on the flags over on Stadsgården, not a treetop swaying over on Fjällgatan, and up by Mosebacke, not even the leaves were moving an inch. The only thing distinguishing the dark waters of the Beckholmssund from a mirror was a shifting, rainbow-coloured slick of oil.

For a moment, the young man's reflection was framed by a nearly perfect concentric rainbow, *as though through a telescopic sight*, but then the circle dispersed and flowed calmly on towards the Beckholm bridge, its colour changing as it moved. The young man brushed off the momentary unease which passed through him and snorted the first line of coke.

He leaned back on the park bench, extending his arms along the back rest and raising his face to the cloudless sky, which was darkening with discernible speed. He didn't feel any different. Just the same self-assured calmness which had, for that split second, been disturbed. With a defiant smile, he looked down at the playing card lying next to him on the bench. The queen of spades. With a second line of coke waiting for him.

He unrolled the note and licked up the residue of the white powder. Then he held it out and looked at it. One thousand kronor. A Swedish thousand-kronor note. An old man with a beard. He would get bored of the sight of him over the next few months, he knew that much. He rolled the old man back up again and carefully lifted the queen of spades from the bench. He felt doubly brave, doubly strong. To be sitting on a public bench after just a few weeks in a new town — in a new country, at that — and snorting cocaine was ballsy enough, but it was doubly so with the risk of a sudden breeze blowing away his entire high.

Though the evening was completely still.

These days, it took two lines for him to feel anything. He didn't care that it would soon take three, then four, then five, and he held the rolled-up old bloke above the delights of the queen of spades and snorted his way to paradise.

He could feel it now. Though not with the same kind of force as before, that baseball bat to the jaw, it was more creeping; an immediate, insatiable desire for more.

The high grew slowly but surely, twisting his field of vision sideways, leaning slightly, but not producing any gusts of wind. The dusky city was still completely still, it looked more like a postcard. Lights had started to come on in some of the buildings here and there, the

2

headlights of cars slipping silently by in the distance, and the slightly decayed smell of early spring suddenly grew stronger until it became a sewer, the dung of a couple of enormous giraffes looming over him amid the distorted sound of the piercing, echoing shrieks of children. He hated animals. They scared him; ever since he was a child he had hated them. And now these monstrous, stinking, braying giraffes — like something from a nightmare. A brief wave of panic rushed through him before he realised that the giraffes were nothing more than a couple of large shipyard cranes and that the sound of children was coming from the nearby amusement park. The stench of giraffe dung receded; the air smelled like early spring once more.

Time passed. A lot of time. Unknown time. He was elsewhere, in another time. The high's time. An unknown prehistoric time.

It was starting to rumble within him. He stood up and regarded the city the same way he would an enemy. Stockholm, he thought, clenching his fist. You ruthlessly beautiful dwarf of a big city. It would be so easy to conquer, he thought, raising his fist towards the capital, as though he was the first ever to have done so.

He turned around in the ever deepening twilight. His vision was still slightly askew, the sounds and smells still slightly warped. Not a person in sight. He hadn't seen a single person the entire time he had been there. But, despite that, he could feel a kind of presence. Faint, like a mirage. Something that seemed to be moving just outside of his field of vision. He shook off the feeling. Those weren't the thoughts of a man about to conquer a city.

He picked up the queen of spades from the bench, took pleasure in licking her clean, and then placed her in his inner pocket, closest to his heart. He patted the chest of his thin, pale pink jacket. He unrolled the thousand-kronor note which had been glued to his hand during the immeasurable period of his high. Again, he licked up the last of the white powder and then demonstratively ripped the note into long tendrils which he dropped to the ground. They didn't move an inch. The night was completely still.

When he started moving, he made a clinking sound. He always did. For him, wealth was still measured by the thickness of the gold chain around his neck. People should be able to *hear* his success.

He was surprised to find Vattugränd, whose name he strenuously spelled his way through from the street sign, completely deserted. Didn't the Swedes go out at night? It was then he felt how cold it was. And almost pitch black. Completely quiet. Not a single joyful shout from the children in the amusement park.

How long had he been sitting down there by the water, lost deep within his high?

Something swept past his feet. For a moment, he thought they were snakes slinking by. Animals. A brief panic.

Then he saw what it was.

Strips of a thousand-kronor note.

He turned around. There were geese on Saltsjön. The ice-cold wind swept straight through him. The

4

thousand-kronor snakes rushed off towards Djurgårdsstaden.

That was when he felt the strange presence again. It was nothing. Nothing at all. And yet there it was. An ice-cold presence. An icy wind straight through the soul. And yet not at all. As though it was always hovering at the precise point where his vision didn't reach.

He came up onto the main road. Still not a person in sight. Not a vehicle. He crossed the street and entered the forest. It felt like a forest, anyway. Trees everywhere. And the presence was suddenly much stronger. An owl hooted.

An owl? Animals, he thought.

And then, out of the corner of his eye, he saw a shadow move behind a tree. Followed by another.

He stood still. The owl hooted again. Minerva, he thought. Ancient mythology which had been drummed into him during his childhood in the poor quarter of Athens.

Minerva, the goddess of wisdom. Athena's name once she had been stolen by the Romans.

He paused for a moment, trying to be like Athena. Trying to be wise.

Is this really happening? Am I not just imagining these almost imperceptible movements? And why do I feel scared? Haven't I stood face-to-face with crazy addicts in the past, taken them down with a few quick moves? I rule an empire. What exactly am I afraid of?

But then his terror materialised. In some ways, it felt better. When a branch broke behind a tree, the noise overpowering the strengthening wind, he knew that they were there. Somehow, it was comforting. A confirmation. He couldn't see them, but he picked up the pace.

It was almost pitch black now and it felt as though he was running through an ancient forest. Branches were whipping at him. His thick gold chain was jingling and clinking like a cowbell.

Animals, he thought, hurling himself over the road. Not a car in sight. It was as though the world had ceased to exist. Just him and some beings he didn't understand.

More forest. Trees everywhere. The wind whistling through him. The icy wind. Shadows were shifting at the edge of his vision. Ancient beings, he thought, crossing a narrow road and running straight into a fine-meshed steel fence. He clambered up onto it and it swayed beneath him. He climbed and climbed. His fingers slipped. Not a sound other than the wind. Wait, there: the owl. Piercing. A distorted owl. A terrible sound, joining forces with the incessant wind.

An ancient cry.

The razor-sharp mesh ripped his fingertips to shreds. The presence was everywhere. Darker shadows dancing in the darkness.

He grabbed his pistol from his shoulder holster. He hung from the fence with one hand and shot with the other. Shooting in all directions. Indiscriminately. Silent shots out into the ancient forest. No return fire. The shifting continued unabated around him. Unchanged. Undaunted. Uncontrollable.

He managed to shove the pistol back into its holster, a couple of shots left, one last safety measure, and the closeness of the shadows gave him superhuman powers, at least that's what he thought as he heaved himself upwards and outwards and grabbed hold of the barbed wire at the top of the fence.

Superhuman powers, he thought with an ironic smile, working the metal barbs out of his hands and swinging over the top.

Now then, he thought as he hopped down into the greenery on the other side of the fence, get over that if you can.

And they could. He immediately felt their presence. He clambered up out of the shrubbery where he had landed and found himself staring straight into a pair of slanted, yellow eyes. He cried out. Pointed ears pricked up above the eyes and a row of razor-sharp teeth appeared beneath. An animal, he thought, throwing himself to one side. Straight into another similar animal. The same slanted, yellowish eyes seeing a completely different world to the one he was seeing. Ancient eyes. As he staggered on through the woodland, suddenly he was back before the ice age.

Wolves, it occurred to him. My God, weren't they wolves?

What kind of city is this? his mind was screaming. How the hell can this be a major European city?

He jingled. His path was a roaring motorway. He snatched at his thick gold chain and tore it off, hurling it away into the vegetation. Straight out into nature.

Then he reached a wall and he grabbed it with his bloody, throbbing fingertips, pain pulsing through his entire body; like a mountain climber he clambered straight up the vertical wall, heaving himself up and over it, over a fence on top, and beneath, nature itself seemed to be wrapped up in shifting shadows, the trees seemed to be moving, the forest drawing closer, the motionless wolves part of the movement with their entire collective, ancient indifference. He reached for his pistol and shot in the direction of the animals, towards the whole shadowy nature. Nothing changed. Other than his pistol clicking. He threw it towards the shadows. His entire field of vision was warped. He didn't know what it hit.

Suddenly, he found himself on a road. Asphalt. Finally asphalt. He hurled himself up a slope, and all around, animals were staring at him, dark and indifferent, and the stench and the noise filled the whining air and he tried to find a name for these shifting shadow beings which were following him and which never never never seemed to give up.

Names can be calming.

Furies, he thought as he ran. Gorgons, harpies. No, not quite. No, what were they called? Goddesses of vengeance?

Suddenly, he realised that that was exactly what they were. That they really were the goddesses of vengeance. Irrepressible primordial deities. Female revenge. Though what was their name? In the midst of the insanity, he searched for a name.

Names can be calming.

He ran and ran but it was as though he wasn't getting anywhere. He was running on a treadmill, on sticky asphalt. And they were there, they materialised, they kept shifting but became bodies. Bodies. He thought he could see them. He fell. Was felled.

He felt himself being hoisted up. It was pitch black all around him. Ancient darkness. The ice-cold wind was whistling. His body was spinning. Or was it? He didn't know. Suddenly, he didn't know a thing. Suddenly, everything was a nameless, structureless chaos. All he was doing was looking for a name. A name for these mystical beings. He wanted to know who was killing him.

Then he saw a face. Maybe it was a face. Maybe it was many. Female faces. Goddesses of revenge.

He was spinning. Everything was upside down. He could see the moon peeping through between his feet. He saw the stars burst out into blinding song. And he saw the darkness growing darker.

Then he saw a face. It was upside down. It was a woman who was all women he had ever hurt, raped, abused, degraded. It was a woman who was all women who became an animal who became a woman who became an animal. A cute little weaselly snout which cracked into an enormous, murderous grin. It bit down on his face and he could feel his bloody fingertips dancing on the soft ground and he felt a pain beyond all comprehension, one which made the animal's attack — the animal which had just made off with his cheek — feel more like a caress. He understood nothing, absolutely nothing.

9

Other than that he was dying.

Dying of pure pain.

And then, with a last burst of satisfaction, he remembered the name of the shadowy figures.

Earth seeping into his bloody fingertips was the last thing he felt.

It calmed him.

CHAPTER
TWO

The old fisherman had seen a lot. In actual fact, he thought he had seen it *all*. But that evening as he packed up the watermelon stall which had long since replaced his fishing nets, he was forced to admit that there were still some surprises left. Even that had surprised him. Life — and above all tourism — still had plenty of madness to offer. It felt . . . comforting. A sign that life wasn't quite over yet.

It had been years since the old fisherman had first realised that the money he could earn selling watermelons to tourists vastly exceeded the amount his nets could bring in. And that it required much less effort.

This particular fisherman wasn't especially keen on effort, which any fisherman worth his salt probably should be.

He looked out over the Ligurian Sea, rising and falling in the spring evening like it was enjoying it just as much as the casual observer. The old fisherman's gaze wandered up towards the wooded slopes surrounding the little town and then on towards the walls ringing the old town, which had once been an Etruscan harbour. Not that the old fisherman knew anything about that. But what he did know, as he let the pine-scented sea air fill his lungs, was that Castiglione della Pescaia was his home and that he was happy there.

He also knew that today he had been surprised for the first time in a long, long while.

It had all started relatively harmlessly. With his slightly darkened vision, he had spotted a blue-and-white parasol in the middle of the beach on which the majority of sun worshippers were lapping up the spring sunshine with as little protection as they could. But under the parasol, three children of different ages had been sitting, each of them chalk white, their bodies as pale as their hair. Another had appeared and sat down beneath it, followed by a woman holding another small child by the hand. Six utterly chalk-white people were cramped together beneath the parasol, sharing the little circle of shadow it was casting down onto the moderately sun-drenched beach.

Fascinated by the strange sight, the old fisherman had forgotten all about his business for a moment and heard, as though in the distance:

"*Cinque cocomeri, per favore.*"

His surprise at the strange family beneath the blue-and-white parasol was compounded by his surprise at this enormous order — and was given yet another boost at the sight of the customer's good-natured smile.

It belonged to a thin, utterly chalk-white man dressed in a loose linen suit and bizarre sun hat with a bright yellow Pikachu on it.

12

Despite the strange pronunciation, his order had been perfectly clear. If somewhat absurd.

"*Cinque?*" the old fisherman exclaimed.

"*Cinque,*" the chalk-white man nodded, taking the watermelons and staggering like a drunk tightrope-walker along the beach, clutching them in his arms. One by one, they dropped down into the sand by the parasol, like enormous seeds being planted by a giant. The chalk-white man practically threw himself into the shade, as though he had been wandering lost in a radioactive area and finally come across a protective safe zone.

The old fisherman wondered for a moment how five watermelons could be divided between seven people. Then he asked himself the inevitable question:

Why travel to Italy, to the Tuscan coast, to Maremma, to Castiglione della Pescaia, *if you couldn't bear the sun?*

Not even Arto Söderstedt knew quite what to say to that. "Beauty" wasn't really a satisfactory answer for taking five children out of school during an important few weeks in spring. "Peace" wasn't quite enough of a reason for two adults to take months off from their jobs in the public sector either, particularly when, as with his wife, Anja, you were a tax inspector and the self-assessments had just come flooding in.

So, of course, his conscience was there, picking holes in both the "beauty" and "peace" arguments. The only thing his conscience hadn't reached was his own situation. Arto Söderstedt didn't feel the slightest bit guilty at having temporarily left the police corps.

The A-Unit, or the National Criminal Investigation Department's Special Unit for Violent Crimes of an International Nature, had certainly been busy over the past year, but since the Sickla Slaughter case had reached its peculiar conclusion, the big, all-consuming cases had been noticeable in their absence. They had come extremely close to a disaster of huge international proportions during the Sickla case. But that was almost a year ago now, and time does have a tendency to heal old wounds.

And so when the money came pouring in like manna from heaven, Arto Söderstedt didn't hesitate for a second.

Besides, he also felt *burnt out*, without quite understanding what that meant. Everyone was *burnt out* nowadays, everyone but him — mainly because he had never quite understood the meaning of it. He had probably been burnt out for years without having been any the wiser.

It was his turn now, in any case. In the name of "beauty" and "peace", he allowed himself to tend to his burnout — regardless of whether it existed or not. And there was plenty of both in Tuscany, that much he knew after having been there only a few days.

The family had rented a house in the Tuscan countryside, nestled among the vineyards. It wasn't a villa — in Italy, a villa was something completely different to elsewhere — but a rustic little stone house on a pine-scented slope not far from the village of Montefioralle and the town of Greve. At the foot of the slope, the wine estates spread out like eternity's own

14

fields, as though the sky had split to make room for small pieces of paradise to fall down to earth and form an other-worldly patchwork quilt.

Arto Söderstedt was enjoying it to the full — all while feeling oddly *unworthy*. It felt as though St Peter had fallen asleep just as a chalky-white detective inspector had slipped his slender body in through the gates of paradise. Thoroughly undeserved. He often found himself sitting on the porch, waiting in the nights with a glass of Vin Santo or a majestic Brunello di Montalcino washing over his taste buds. He had deliberately and uncritically devoured the whole Tuscany myth and he was enjoying himself enormously. He would never forget a single moment from his trip to Siena, that magical town. Even though the kids had howled away in the heart of the cathedral. Organ pipes was all he could think, watching those five little creatures standing there, in order of both height and pitch, screeching at the top of their lungs. Until a guard had decided that enough was enough and thrown the whole rabble out, that was. When that happened, Söderstedt had denied his paternity without a single pang of conscience. The guard had glared suspiciously at his identical, albeit slightly larger frame. Lying about such a thing in the house of God . . . He had wandered around inside the cathedral for an utterly peaceful thirty minutes after that, drinking in Donatello, Michelangelo, Pinturicchio, Bernini, Pisano. When he came back out again, the children had been sitting calmly on the cathedral steps, slurping Italian gelati.

Not even Anja, slurping worse than the children, had seemed particularly annoyed.

He had even switched his mobile phone off.

But sitting there now beneath the blue-and-white parasol, trying to remember how he had been planning to divide five watermelons between seven people of varying sizes, his thoughts turned to his Uncle Pertti. Thoughts of gratitude. And also of guilt.

He had completely forgotten the man was still alive. And now he wasn't.

Strictly speaking, Uncle Pertti had been his mother's uncle, and during his childhood the legend of him had never been far away. The hero from the Winter War. The doctor who became one of the greats in Mannerheim's army.

Söderstedt himself had no siblings — that was presumably why he and his only-child wife had five children together — and his side of the family was microscopic. His parents, themselves both only children, were long since dead, and he had no other relatives. As a result, there had been no other heir.

Arto Söderstedt fumbled with his knife and thought: five divided by seven, hmm, that's 0.714 of a watermelon each, assuming everyone gets an equal amount, but if they went by bodyweight instead . . .

He paused, glancing at his big, shadow-drenched family which, in turn and increasingly grumblingly, was looking at his passive knife. Were they really worthy heirs to Pertti Lindrot, the great hero of the Winter War, victor at Suomussalmi; one of the architects of the famous motti tactic, used to crack the Red Army's

16

road-bound troops by splitting them into smaller units as they passed through forests, surrounding them and defeating them?

"Just cut it into pieces," his second oldest daughter Linda said impatiently.

Arto Söderstedt looked at her, offended. He would certainly never work so sloppily. No, no. Arto was sixty-five kilos, Anja roughly the same; Mikaela weighed forty and Linda thirty-five, Peter too; Stefan weighed twenty-five and little Lina twenty. Two hundred and eighty-five kilos in total. Of that, twenty-three per cent — sixty-five divided by two hundred and eighty-five — should go to each of the parents. And twenty-three percent of five watermelons was . . .

"Just cut it into pieces," little Lina echoed.

. . . was 1.5 watermelons. More than one whole melon for each of the parents. Was that really how he had envisaged it?

If that was the case, there would be only 0.35 of a watermelon for little Lina, and that didn't seem fair.

Fair.

Was it fair that he, a man who had just gone up to his eyeballs in debt to buy a big family car, suddenly found that the whole thing had been paid off and that he had so much left over that he could, immediately and without the family's knowledge, go online and rent a house in Tuscany for two months?

No, it wasn't especially fair.

But what was fair in life?

Certainly not 0.35 of a watermelon for the little one, he thought with sudden decisiveness, cutting the melon into pieces and dividing them fairly between the various members of his enormous family.

More than a million. Who could have known that old Uncle Pertti, whose very existence he had forgotten, was sitting on such riches? With the money came memories, though Arto Söderstedt could really only remember him as a stinking mouth and a handful of half-rotten teeth. A hero who had let himself go, but whose heroic halo always shone brightly. As though he had the *right* to let himself go, that was how he understood his parents' attitude. He had always had the impression that it had been his parents, Pertti's last living relatives, who provided for the old man. And then it transpired he had been sitting on just over a million.

Nothing was ever really as it seemed.

When he reconstructed Pertti's life, it must have gone something like this: young, enthusiastic, provincial doctor finds himself drawn into the Finnish Winter War after an abrupt attack by the Soviet Union. He turns out to have a knack for guerrilla warfare in the frozen winter forests and quickly climbs the ranks. He becomes a hero after several decisive offences, and after the Russian victory, disappears into the forests like a classic guerrilla fighter. He returns after the Second World War, more or less a broken man. He starts drinking more and more and has trouble keeping his job as a doctor in increasingly remote backwaters. He eventually returns to Vasa and becomes an eccentric, living that sad old life until he turns ninety. End of story.

Or so Arto Söderstedt thought.

18

Until his inheritance arrived.

The inheritance which was now being consumed, in the form of watermelon, beneath the growing shade of an umbrella. The Tuscan spring sun was now touching the curving horizon of the Ligurian Sea. Before long, it had sunk low enough for the chalk-white family to venture out into the water.

After everyone else — shivering — had already left the beach.

Arto Söderstedt saw the old fisherman pack up his stall of watermelons, cast a last astonished glance at the shadow-covered family, shake his head, and head off for a glass of wine in his local *osteria*. Once there, he would tell his friends about the sun-shy family and pay with money which had once belonged to a different eccentric from a completely different part of the world.

For a moment, Söderstedt was fascinated by the movement of money, its transfer, its origins.

Then he took off his crinkled suit and ran at the head of a line of children towards the edge of the water, testing it with his big toe. Its icy coolness reminded him of the Finnish lakes of his childhood.

On the beach, Uncle Pertti sat, necking Koskenkorva vodka and laughing hoarsely at his cowardice.

He ran in. The children wailed like organ pipes.

And in his rucksack, up under the blue-and-white parasol, his mobile phone was still switched off.

CHAPTER
THREE

The girl who had been fortunate in her misfortune was sitting on a hospital bed with a surprised look on her face. She probably hadn't stopped looking surprised since the previous evening. It was now a permanent look of surprise.

Paul Hjelm found her surprise entirely understandable. When you were ten years old and walking hand in hand with your dad one spring evening, you hardly expected to be shot.

But that was what had happened.

She had felt cold; the wind had suddenly picked up, blowing straight through her thin quilted jacket and chilling her practically bare legs. She had been holding her dad's hand and clutching a balloon shaped like a happy yellow face. She had been skipping slightly, mainly to keep warm but also because she was happy about the bag of sweets she had fished up out of the lucky dip. Aside from the cold, everything was just fine.

And then she had been shot.

A bullet had come flying from somewhere and buried itself in her upper right arm. That was where it came to rest. Fortunately.

She had been fortunate in her misfortune.

"You'll be fine, Lisa," Paul Hjelm said, placing his hand on hers. "It's just a flesh wound."

Lisa's father's eyes were puffy and red from crying and he was snoring loudly in the armchair. Paul Hjelm poked his shoulder gently. His head jerked upwards with a snort and he stared uncomprehendingly at the policeman standing by the edge of the bed. Then he saw his daughter with the bandage around her arm and the awful reality came crashing back down.

"Excuse me, Mr Altbratt," Hjelm said courteously. "I just need to be absolutely certain you didn't see any sign at all of a perpetrator. No movement in the trees? Nothing?"

Mr Altbratt shook his head and stared down into his hands.

"There wasn't a single person anywhere nearby," he said quietly. "Didn't hear a thing. Suddenly Lisa just screamed and the blood started pouring out. I didn't realise she'd been shot until the doctor told us. Shot! What kind of world do we live in?"

"So you were walking along Sirishovsvägen in the direction of Djurgårdsvägen? Where had you been?"

"Does it matter?"

Paul Hjelm's phone rang. The timing wasn't the best. He hoped no respirators or heart-lung machines would crash when he answered. He could just see the headlines: "TEDDY BEAR KILLER! EXTRA! EXTRA! FAMOUS POLICEMAN MURDERS FOUR CRITICALLY ILL PATIENTS WITH MOBILE PHONE."

"Hjelm," he answered laconically. Unless you're severely disturbed — or an answering machine, perhaps

— how exactly *did* you answer a phone using more words than that?

A moment of silence followed. The Altbratt man was looking at him like he was busy ripping the feathers from an endangered eagle. The Altbratt girl still just looked surprised.

"Skansen?" the eagle violator exclaimed. That was all he said. Then he got up from the bed, patted Lisa on the head and held his hand out to the father.

"I've got to go, I'm afraid. I'll be back."

Cold morning sunshine greeted him on the steps of the paediatric accident and emergency department. The Astrid Lindgren Children's Hospital. He searched his pockets as he wandered over to the car park. His keys were gone. Then again, this wasn't an unusual occurrence and so he went through his patting ritual once more, and hey presto, they appeared from one of the pockets of his much-too-thin jacket. Same procedure as last year.

It was a fresh spring morning of the newly woken kind, the type often seen during the first week of May. The kind of day which looks so inviting from indoors but turns out to be a slyly masquerading winter's day. Hjelm, always dressed too lightly, was now practically naked. His pitiful scraps of clothing offered absolutely no protection against the icy wind. He tried to pull them tighter around him but couldn't find anything to pull.

It was nine in the morning and the traffic around Haga Södra and Nortull was at a complete standstill. Car traffic had increased dramatically in Stockholm over the last year. For some reason, it had suddenly become extremely attractive to be stuck in traffic. Cheap psychotherapy, presumably; a line of metal boxes full of screaming Mr Hydes. The alternative was the newly privatised commuter train which never seemed to be running, or else the metro which seemed to be forever standing in dark tunnels for hours on end, or else you could cycle along one of the sadistic cycleways no one dared to use since they seemed to have been deliberately designed to cause particularly awful injuries.

OK, so he was a whiner.

He didn't really have anything to complain about. The red metro line was relatively free from stupidity. He continued to devote his long daily journey from Norsborg in to central Stockholm to intense, reality-fleeing jazz listening. After a jaunt into the world of opera, like some kind of slightly depraved Inspector Morse, he had gone back to jazz. He couldn't quite tear himself away from the bebop years around 1960. But at the moment, he was hooked on Miles Davis. *Kind of Blue*. It was, quite simply, a masterpiece. Every single track on it. Five classics: "So What", "Freddie Freeloader", "Blue In Green", "All Blues" and "Flamenco Sketches" — all more or less improvised in the studio during the golden year of 1959. The musicians went to the studio not having seen the music before, Miles turned up with a bundle of notes, and all five tracks were said to have been recorded on their very first attempt. Somehow, it felt like music that had been created as it was performed, music which

23

immediately and naturally took shape. A new kind of blues, infinitely down to earth, infinitely sophisticated. Every second of it a pleasure.

But during work hours, he had his service vehicle. He pushed the key which had miraculously appeared into the lock on the old beige Audi, looked out at the traffic and sighed deeply. It would probably be quicker to *swim* over to Djurgården.

That was where he was headed. His colleague and partner in crime Jorge Chavez had had that mysterious, expectant tone in his voice, the kind Paul Hjelm had been longing for for months. "I think you should head over here, Paul. To Skansen."

The fact that he had just come from another case with links to the area around the Skansen open-air museum and zoo made it even more interesting.

He got caught up in traffic *within* the gates of the hospital and made a conscious decision not to turn into Mr Hyde. It just wasn't worth the effort. Instead, he slipped the *Kind of Blue* CD into the car stereo and smiled as its opening notes spread their honey over his eardrums. As he meekly fought his way out of the enormous hospital area, he started ranking strange surnames. Wasn't Altbratt a candidate for strangest? He'd come across heavyweights like Kungskranz and Riddarsson before, Äppelblohm and Sarkander, but did they really stand a chance against Altbratt?

Anton Altbratt was the wealthy owner of a fur shop in Östermalm, living in Djurgårdsstaden and currently on his second marriage, of which ten-year-old Lisa was the fruit. He also had a couple of adult children from

24

his previous marriage, and they hadn't been able to get in touch with his new wife, Lisa's mother. She was on a business trip to some unknown location. To Hjelm, the whole thing stank of intricate erotic arrangements, but he decided not to enquire further.

Instead, he was trying to work out what could be behind the shooting of poor little Lisa. With any luck, her father Anton had been the intended victim. It was much easier to imagine a rational motive if that was the case — the young wife, the upper-class business activity, maybe even an attack by militant vegans. Though the lack of sound implied a silencer, which in turn implied some kind of professional criminality — in other words, it sounded more like the wife had wanted to get her husband out of the way for financial or sexual reasons, or else it was down to some kind of dodgy business links, or maybe even illegal fur dealings. Something like that. If any of those were true, it didn't seem half as dangerous. An unsuccessful one-off attack. But if Lisa had been the target, it was much, much worse. That would mean the majority of plausible motives disappeared, making some kind of madman more likely. A madman specialising in children.

Paul Hjelm didn't really want to follow that thought through to its logical conclusion.

But of course there was a third alternative: that neither father nor daughter had been the intended target, and the bullet had simply found its way into Lisa's arm by pure chance. If that was what had happened, the picture which emerged was of some kind of underworld dispute in among the trees of Djurgården.

There was, in other words, plenty to be done. They needed to check the wife's activities the previous evening, what her relationship with Lisa's father was really like; they had to check who knew about the children's party up in Rosendal, any possible irregularities in the business, any possible threats from militant vegans or similar, and search the wooded area from which the shot had, in all likelihood, been fired. Et cetera, et cetera.

And then they had to wait and see whether it was anything other than a coincidence that two crimes had been committed so close to one another — whatever it was Jorge had to offer up at Skansen.

Time, time, time. He was really stuck; as usual, the engine temperature of his Audi shot up drastically the moment it found itself in the slightest hint of a queue. The car lacked all patience. Since the driver refused to become Mr Hyde, the car would have to do it instead. As though every queuing car and its driver were, by definition, forced to explode. Paul Hjelm turned the heating up high and thanked his Maker that it was winter and not summer in Stockholm. With one eye on the engine temperature gauge, he allowed his thoughts to drift along with Miles Davis, John Coltrane, Bill Evans, Cannonball Adderley, Wynton Kelly, Paul Chambers and Jimmy Cobb's unrivalled improvisations.

A picture of his life, it struck him.

A stony, controlling eye on an engine about to explode. Trains of thought taking the form of reckless improvisations. All while the vehicle crept forward extremely slowly.

Yup, that was exactly how it was. Though the picture wasn't quite complete.

Just as "So What" faded out into "Freddie Freeloader" and a more familiar twelve-bar blues started streaming out into Hjelm's sauna masquerading as a car, a gap appeared in the right-hand lane at Roslagstull. He sped forwards, accelerating so violently that the tyres screeched, made it through on the newly introduced European-standard amber light, and suddenly found the whole of Birger Jarlsgatan empty ahead of him.

Well, he thought. That's it, now the picture's complete.

"Freddie Freeloader", he thought, putting his foot down.

It was remarkably smooth-going all the way to Stureplan, where he found himself in a slight, inevitable tussle with one of those reckless drivers, the type who worked in advertising, who thought they were in the right regardless of how wrong they were. Paul Hjelm didn't care. Let them have their way, he thought, mumbling along with the final notes of "Blue In Green". Even down in the confusion of traffic by Nybroplan, he held his tongue. Just as he was singing along like a fool to a favourite line from "All Blues", windows down, he saw Ingmar Bergman staggering up the steps into the National Theatre, cane in hand. The old man turned round, astonished, and met his eye for a brief moment. It seemed like more than a coincidence.

Strandvägen was worse. It seemed awfully big.

No, he thought. Now the picture was complete. A brief free stretch and then back to the slow, sluggish, grind. A plod.

The traffic eased slightly and he crossed Djurgården Bridge without problem. By that point, the picture had already gone up in smoke. As he parked, terribly, outside the entrance to Skansen, the last Spanish-tinged harmonies of "Flamenco Sketches" were playing. That was what you called precision. His route — from Astrid Lindgren to Skansen via Ingmar Bergman, practically a trip through the heart of Sweden — was the exact same length as Miles Davis's *Kind of Blue*. That was that.

It was quarter to ten when Paul Hjelm marched in through Skansen's gates, was handed a little map and sent in the direction of "the wild animals" in the north-east corner of the big open-air museum. As he stepped onto the long, covered escalator heading up the hill, Hjelm wondered which animals *weren't* wild. Was man a wild animal? He reached the top and stepped out into completely different weather from at the bottom. It was as though winter had been blown away. In its place, he found himself wandering through the museum's mock-nineteenth-century town in highest possible summer. April weather, he was on the verge of thinking, even though it was in fact May. Thursday the fourth of May, in the two thousandth year of Our Lord.

Twenty hundred. As the sun reflected on red-painted walls, his thoughts drifted to the way people spoke about the year. In general, they had naturally gravitated towards calling it "the year two thousand", a perfectly logical choice. But Paul couldn't help but wonder why it wasn't twenty hundred, like the beginning of the previous century. He found a certain pleasure in taking what he called the either/or approach, occasionally using both. It never failed to raise an eyebrow or two.

That was what was playing on Detective Inspector Paul Hjelm's mind in this, the two thousandth year of Our Lord — a year in which the kingdom of Sweden had been singled out by Amnesty International for a sharp rise in police violence; a year in which the police had regularly turned their batons around to strike out with the hard end; a year in which Kosovans and Albanians had been sent back to their war-torn homelands with five thousand noble Swedish kronor in their pockets.

For a short moment, it felt like *someone else* had taken over his thoughts.

He wondered where all the good old-fashioned sexual fantasies had gone, those fantasies the latest research said should grip us at least fifteen times a day.

One last thought flashed through his mind before he caught a whiff of the predatory animals: who the hell were these model people who had enough time for fifteen sexual fantasies a day? But then the stench took over and Paul Hjelm found himself feeling genuine expectation, like a child in the minutes before Father Christmas turns up, at that moment when fathers sneak off to the toilet with an utterly expressionless look plastered on their faces. In this case, Father Christmas's real name was Jorge Chavez and he was a detective inspector in Sweden's national CID.

Just like Paul Hjelm.

The smell disappeared as quickly as it had appeared. Paul Hjelm was lost. He would later deny all knowledge of the incident, but he really was lost inside Skansen. His children were nearing twenty and it had been years since the cheap trip-to-Skansen trick had last worked on them, the thing you resorted to when you ran out of other ideas. The section for wild animals had been completely rebuilt during that time, and he suddenly found himself talking to an utterly listless, cud-chewing male elk that looked more mechanical and stuffed than real. He had no one else to converse with. It was nearing ten, and Skansen was still closed. There wasn't a person in sight and the bloody elk didn't have much to say.

Above all, he seemed remarkably clueless about where the bestial predatory animals could possibly be living.

Eventually, Hjelm found his way to the bear mountain. This was unknown territory. Everything was heavily reinforced and he finally made it out of the labyrinthine construction with the feeling that he was following an unravelled ball of yarn. He passed horses and lynx, wild boar and wolves, and suddenly he was there.

At the wolverine enclosure.

There were considerably more people around him now. He immediately recognised the white-clad technicians who, like amateur mountain climbers, were moving up and down the little hills inside. He recognised the blue-and-white plastic tape stretched here and there in front of the safety fence, screaming "Police". He recognised the more or less weather-beaten, eighty-odd-year-old face belonging to the chief medical examiner, Sigvard Qvarfordt. He also recognised the stern Germanic-looking face of the chief forensic technician, Brynolf Svenhagen. And he recognised the particularly energetic face of his close colleague — who was also Chief Forensic Technician Svenhagen's son-in-law. His name was Jorge Chavez.

Chavez caught sight of Hjelm and his face lit up. He moved towards the deep moat separating the wolverine enclosure from the rest of the park, holding out his hands and shouting, as though he had rehearsed it (which he probably had): "Cast off your human shell, O crown of creation, and enter into our animalistic orgy."

Paul Hjelm sighed and said: "How the hell do I do that, then?"

Jorge Chavez raised an eyebrow in surprise and glanced around. Eventually, he turned to Brynolf Svenhagen, who didn't seem to be doing much other than wandering around looking stern. As though it was his life's mission.

"Was it you who nicked the gangplank, Brunte?"

Brynolf Svenhagen looked at his son-in-law with sincere distaste and helpfully replied: "My name isn't Brunte."

Whereby he continued his stern wandering.

Chavez scratched his head.

"Porn police probably took it," he said. "They'll be letting the wolverines in soon."

Paul Hjelm climbed up onto the shaky wooden fence, balancing for a moment before taking a reckless leap into nothingness. He floated like a butterfly over the deep, water-filled moat and landed safely on dry ground next to his colleague. It was highly surprising.

"Nice," Chavez said appreciatively.

"Thanks," Hjelm replied, still not quite believing that he wasn't covered in wolverine shit, having stumbled backwards into the moat and cracked a couple of vertebrae.

He glanced around. The wolverine enclosure was fairly extensive, a piece of hilly terrain which stretched up to a relatively high peak. There were holes dotted here and there, presumably dens, and large areas of the grass-covered ground seemed to be littered with tiny shreds of material, almost like feathers, all different colours and different materials. The forensic technicians were doing all they could to stop the light morning breeze from blowing them away.

Paul pointed at the fibres. Jorge nodded, grabbed hold of his arm and pulled him in the direction of the enclosure's bottom corner, where the moat was nothing more than a three-metre vertical concrete drop down to the earthy floor.

"Let's start from the beginning," Jorge said.

The two men stopped. Over in that corner, the fibres had slightly more coherent shapes, most notably the leg of a pair of light pink-coloured trousers.

A few inches of chewed-off bone were sticking up out of it.

Probably a tibia and a fibula.

"That's the biggest bit left," Chavez said calmly, squatting down. Hjelm did the same and waited for him to continue. He did.

"*Gulo gulo*, they're called. Latin for wolverine. Cute little things. Look like fluffy little bear cubs. Their closest relatives are the badger, pine marten, polecat, weasel, otter and mink. They're endangered, there are just a hundred or so left in Sweden. High up in the mountains. They can grow up to a metre in length and as a rule they live on voles and lemmings. Though sometimes they change their prey —"

Hjelm stood up and stretched his back.

"OK," he said. "Someone got drunk, climbed into Skansen and ended up among the predators. Can't be the first time."

"Would I have called you here if that were the case?" Chavez asked, meeting his eye. "These are specially evolved killing machines. Don't you know your Ellroy? They'll tear a man to pieces at the slightest provocation, especially if there's a pack of them. They've got jaws like bolt cutters. They can break bones and grind them up like they're nothing. It's pure luck we've got so much left here."

Using a pencil, Chavez carefully lifted the trouser leg up. There was still some flesh clinging to the bone a bit further up, holding it together. There was also a knot. On a piece of rope.

"Ah," Hjelm said, squatting down once more.

"Exactly," Chavez replied, adding: "M."

"U," said Hjelm.

"R," said Chavez.

"D," said Hjelm.

"E," said Chavez.

"R," said Hjelm.

"No doubt," said Chavez. "And it would be nice if we could find a head. At least it's a variation on a theme," he continued, stopping Qvarfordt as he was passing by. "Any news, my good man?" he asked gallantly.

"Negative," the eternally-working Sigvard Qvarfordt replied, pushing his loose dentures into place with a well-practised movement. "No head, no fingers. It'll be hard to get an ID. We'll be able to get some DNA, but as you know the system isn't especially well developed. It is a man though. An adult male. The coagulation level of the blood suggests the time of death was yesterday evening or last night. I'd be surprised if he'd been here longer than that. There would definitely have been some complaints from the parents if our friend here had been eaten in broad daylight. That's all I've got for you."

Just then, they heard a shout from the hill. One of the forensic technicians was waving something he had fished out of a hole in the air. It looked like a wolverine turd.

Paul Hjelm tried the phrase a few times. Wolverine turd. How many times had he said that in his life? Zero.

"Probably a wolverine dick," Chavez whispered loudly.

"Let's just hope the wolverine wasn't still in the hole," Hjelm half whispered back.

As the technician struggled down the hill, Hjelm thought for a moment about association paths and their meanings. The technician made it over to his boss, who still had a stern look on his face. Brynolf Svenhagen took the object, twisting and turning it in his hands for a while before wandering over in the direction of Hjelm, Chavez and Qvarfordt. He held it out to old Qvarfordt, who peeped at it through inch-thick glasses and nodded.

"Fantastic," was all he said.

The stern Svenhagen reluctantly turned to his son-in-law and his equally detestable colleague. He held the object up for them.

It was a finger.

"Fantastic," Chavez said, without showing any desire to get a closer look at it. "Fingerprints," he added unnecessarily.

Svenhagen turned on his heels. Chavez grabbed his flapping white arm and pulled it towards him. It looked like a foretaste of the football World Cup.

"For God's sake," Svenhagen said doggedly.

"Can we go over the letters, Brunte? If it's not too much to ask?"

Brynolf Svenhagen nodded gravely.

"We are policemen," Hjelm added helpfully.

Svenhagen made yet another non-verbal expression of his distaste and then overcame himself. He led the two inspectors towards the edge of the wolverine enclosure, right next to the three-metre drop beneath the viewing area. The ground here was dark earth, and it was where the concentration of multicoloured fibres was greatest. They could also make out the only trace of blood — a darker spot which had been almost entirely soaked up by the earthy ground.

"Tread carefully here," Svenhagen said.

"How many wolverines were there?" Hjelm asked.

"Four."

"Four bestial creatures devoured a person and there's hardly a trace of blood anywhere. Isn't that strange?"

Svenhagen paused and directed an icy-blue don't-you-know-anything look at Hjelm.

"It rained last night," he said, squatting down. "Fortunately, this is still here," he continued, pointing.

In the ground directly beneath Brynolf Svenhagen's index finger, Hjelm could make out some depressions. After some effort, he realised they were letters. Five of them. He worked his way through them.

"Epivu?" he said.

"That's what it looks like," Svenhagen confirmed. "Just don't ask me what it means."

"Did he write it?"

"We don't know. The size of the letters is consistent with a human finger, I can say that much. And the number of fibres around here suggests that it might be where the actual . . . ingestion took place. If that's the case, we might assume that our victim, with his hands and feet bound, wrote a last message. We've taken samples from the letters to see whether there's any

36

trace of blood or skin in the soil. Maybe that finger can help shed a little light on all of this."

"Have we got any idea at all about how he ended up here?"

"No," Svenhagen replied. "Plenty of fingerprints on the fence, of course, but otherwise nothing. We'll have to go through everything."

"If we assume he was the one who wrote 'Epivu', then he didn't end up here without a head. How can a head disappear?"

"There are several possibilities," Svenhagen replied, looking at Hjelm. Perhaps the man wasn't the utter idiot he had previously assumed him to be. But Brynolf Svenhagen wasn't someone who enjoyed having his preconceived notions overturned. If possible, that made him even harsher. He continued sternly: "The wolverines might simply have eaten it. It's really not so unlikely that they gobbled up the entire thing, cranium and teeth and cerebral cortex. Everything. Then of course it might be the case that he didn't write those letters at all. You'll have to check with the keepers, that's your job. One of the wolverines might be called Epivu, what do I know?"

Hjelm didn't let him go. He glanced around the rugged terrain.

"So the skull could just as easily be here somewhere? We'll have to keep looking. I assume you'll be having to sift through plenty of wolverine shit in the near future. It might not be just *one* person, maybe those naughty wolverines gobbled up two or three or an entire football team."

At the mention of wolverine droppings, Hjelm noticed the space between Svenhagen's eyes twitch. The hyper-organised chief forensic technician clearly hadn't thought that far ahead. It felt quite gratifying. These odd little power struggles which fill our social environment . . .

Why do we find it so difficult to spend time together without being transformed into children?

Svenhagen moved off. Hjelm looked at Chavez.

"What do we have here?" he asked.

"I don't know," Chavez answered, "but it's certainly not normal."

"No," said Paul Hjelm. "It's certainly not normal."

They went for a coffee in the cafe at the top of the museum's observation tower. They sat there munching dry cheese sandwiches and looking down at the sun-drenched museum and the crowds growing in size with each moment that passed. Stockholm's assembled pensioner corps seemed to be there, clutching lethal pieces of bread which would soon be transformed into monstrous, deadly lumps, responsible for the death of more seabirds than the country's poachers combined.

Though that wasn't exactly what Paul Hjelm and Jorge Chavez had on their minds. They were thinking about a murder.

If it was in fact a murder.

"Underworld," Chavez said, trying in vain to bite through the slice of cheese in his sandwich. He wished he had bolt cutters for teeth.

"Ellroy?" Hjelm asked, staring blindly out at the magnificent view of Stockholm. "Which Ellroy?"

"In one way or another, it's the underworld," Chavez explained.

"In one way or another, yes. But not in *any* way at all. This isn't a simple drugs deal, it's not a normal execution. If it was, we wouldn't have this. This is something special. There's a message here."

"Epivu?"

Hjelm shook his head but said nothing. Chavez continued to think aloud.

"He was probably tied up and then thrown to the wolverines. Then he had time to write 'Epivu'. But why did he do it? Why didn't he try to get away instead? I mean, even a mediocre sportsman like Paul Hjelm can make it over the ditch without any real bother."

"His right groin," Hjelm said, taking a sip of his remarkably viscous coffee. "Pain in the right groin. Radiating to the knee."

"Sounds like cancer," said Chavez. "Groin cancer, the most dangerous kind. Ninety-seven per cent death rate according to the latest research."

"In his defence, it's easier to jump in than out."

"If you get thrown in to a wolverine enclosure, you don't just sit down and write in the ground with your fingers. That's not the first thing you do. You try desperately to get out."

"But then even assassins aren't likely to throw someone in to the wolverines and run off immediately. They'd probably stay there to watch. They'd probably be pointing a gun at you. They'd probably stop you

39

from escaping. They'd probably stand there enjoying the show. Like some kind of gladiator games."

"Doesn't that sound a bit complicated?" asked Chavez. "You decide someone's going to be killed. You tie that person up, take them into Skansen after hours, carry them through the animal park where straggling keepers might turn up at any moment, and you do all that just so you can throw them to the wolverines? Doesn't sound like something you'd do unless you had a very specific reason for it."

"Which takes us right back to Ellroy," said Hjelm. "Who is this Ellroy?"

"Or," Chavez shouted, slamming his coffee cup down with such force that the saucer broke into two neat half-circles, "or maybe they were chasing him and ended up in Skansen by chance."

"And if that's what happened," Hjelm said, nodding, "it makes sense that he fired a couple of shots somewhere along the way, and that one of those bullets made its way into a ten-year-old girl's arm."

Chavez gave him a slightly surprised look. Hjelm paused for effect long enough that Chavez started squirming with anticipation.

Yes, he knew it was childish.

"At 22.14 yesterday, a 9mm bullet got lodged in the arm of ten-year-old Lisa Altbratt as she wandered down Sirishovsvägen."

"And where's Sirishovsvägen?" asked Chavez.

"It joins Djurgårdsvägen, coming down from Rosendal."

40

"Skansen map," said Chavez. Hjelm pulled the crumpled paper from his inner pocket and handed it to Chavez.

"Sirishovsvägen is here," Hjelm said, pointing.

"And where was Lisa Alstedt when she got shot?"

"Altbratt," Hjelm corrected him. "About here."

He pointed to a spot close to the point where Sirishovsvägen joined Djurgårdsvägen, not far from the Oakhill villa and the Italian embassy. The Skansen fence ran right alongside it.

"Hmm," Chavez said. He sounded like Sherlock Holmes when he was thinking. "Lisa Altbrunn here. Wolverine man here."

"Altbratt," Hjelm corrected him, following Chavez's pencil with his eyes. Chavez continued.

"The bullet?"

"Right arm, walking down towards Djurgårdsvägen."

"Meaning it came from somewhere inside Skansen. Here. Can you get over the fence here? Which part is that?"

"What does it say? Wolves?"

"Exactly: right there. Yeah, wolves. There."

Hjelm followed the pencil as it moved up from the map to the window of the observation tower. Chavez pointed it out at the real Skansen. Hjelm could make out the labyrinthine bear enclosure and his gaze swept further, past horses and lynx, wild boars and buffalo; past the wolverine enclosure where the blue-and-white tape was fluttering in the morning breeze, finally reaching the extensive pen which housed the wolves.

The fence was high but not impossible to scale, though there was barbed wire on top of it.

Paul Hjelm nodded. His face cracked into a malicious smile.

"I think Brunte's going to have to expand his search area slightly. Do you want to break it to him?"

"With the greatest pleasure," Jorge Chavez replied, grinning.

CHAPTER
FOUR

Professor emeritus. He wasn't quite used to the title, despite having had it for years. He was, by now, a very old man.

And yet, it was only during the past few days that he had started to feel old.

Since everything had started coming back to him.

It was difficult to put a finger on what had changed. Nothing had actually happened.

But still, he was convinced he was about to die.

He hadn't given much thought to death. It was just one more part of all that needed to be repressed. And he had succeeded. He had succeeded beyond all expectation. He had succeeded in drawing a line over the past and starting afresh. As though life was a piece of blank paper, waiting to be filled. He assumed that his own sheet was full now, he assumed that was why it had started spilling over onto the other side. Onto the back, where all that had been repressed was written, everything that half a century hadn't managed to erase. He no longer wrote — he read. And that was much, much worse.

It had started as a presence, nothing more than that. A faint, diffuse presence which had suddenly appeared in his peaceful, structured life. In a way, he was thankful: not everyone was given the chance to walk, for a while, with death at their side; not everyone had the opportunity to reflect over what life had had to offer before they reached their end. Though in a way, it would have been better simply to die without warning. To die without regret, without reflection, without remorse. To drop down dead on the street one day, and be swept away like a broken bottle.

The End, as American films had once proclaimed. Just so there could be no doubt it was over.

But no. For some unfathomable reason, he had been given this . . . respite. He couldn't understand why.

Or rather: the longer it went on, the better he understood it.

It had been a morning like any other. No great ailments, just the usual sciatica and his sluggish stomach. No outward changes at all.

Aside from the sudden arrival of this presence.

Yes. The tranquil presence of death.

Until then, life had gone on like always, the way it does for a formerly active man in his early eighties. Slowly, in other words. He saw the grandchildren as normal, went to their always-delightful Sunday dinners, observed the Sabbath and celebrated Passover, Sukkot, Hanukkah and Yom Kippur with them as he always had. This illusion of normality was what made it all so eerie. Because it was eerie, wasn't it? Wasn't dying eerie? He wasn't quite sure.

The most worrying thing was that the whole thing lacked a rational explanation.

He had devoted his life to the brain. The human brain. He had been a researcher in a field which had been practically non-existent before he ventured into it. Right after he arrived in Sweden, learned the language and became a member of Swedish society, he had started his medical research. What had struck him was how absurdly little we knew about our own brains. He had, essentially, launched brain science in Sweden. In the 1950s, he became a professor at the Karolinska Institut, and since then his name had figured in discussions about the Nobel Prize every single year. The prize never materialised, but he did gain an increasingly concrete belief that human beings were matter through and through. "The soul" was an antiquated construction used to cover over a void in human knowledge — in other words, it represented our lack of understanding of the brain. And so, as knowledge of the brain's functions increased, the need for the soul disappeared, in the very same way that gods and myths and fantasies have always given way the moment science gains ground. He married, had children and experienced all kinds of everyday miracles without ever losing his belief in materialism. Human beings were controlled by nerve impulses in the brain. That was that.

And then, aged almost ninety, this sudden presence for which there was no rational explanation, for which there seemed to be no place among these nerve impulses.

Perhaps he was simply lacking knowledge about what was happening to him.

He started travelling; it became an overwhelming need. No grand chartered trips over far-flung oceans; no epic train journeys across Russia; no scaling Mount Everest. It was simply a matter of being on the move. He used the metro system, as a rule — it seemed most logical. Pure movement. Being able to feel the journey, the movement, without necessarily being taken anywhere. Such was his need.

And so he had spent the past few days riding the metro. He simply travelled, without destination, without purpose. In some ways, it mirrored the internal journey he was making. Towards the repressed letters on the other side of the paper. The paper he had tried to turn to give an illusion of blankness.

Things came towards him. They came flying out of the tunnels, pouring towards him from the platforms, gushing towards him down the escalators. Scenes, that was all, short sequences, and he had no chance of putting them into any kind of order. It was all very strange. He was doomed to wandering, doomed to being in motion, as though he would die the moment he stopped. Like a shark.

Or like Ahasver, the wandering Jew, doomed to eternal life and eternal suffering.

But there was still so much left to understand, that much he understood.

He was sitting in the metro. He had no idea where he was. It didn't matter. The lights rushed by, sometimes a station, sometimes only sporadic flashes in the tunnels. There were arms on top of him, legs on top of him, thin, thin legs, thin, thin arms, and he saw an upside-down face, and he saw a thin wire being pushed into a temple, and he saw the upside-down face distorted by pain. And then he was writing in a book. He was reading the words which he himself was writing and the book was talking about pain, about pain, pain, pain.

He looked at his arm where the line of digits was tattooed, and the numbers passed through him, moving away from him.

He passed further, further through the heart of the city, and death was by his side, death wanted something and he couldn't understand what.

All he did was travel.

CHAPTER
FIVE

Since Sara Svenhagen was having trouble working out why she was in an unmarked police car, en route from Kungsholmen to a motel somewhere in Stockholm's southern suburbs, her thoughts drifted back to that morning. They floated in through an elegant doorway in Birkastan, up a genuine art nouveau staircase and in through a door marked with the area's only foreign name, through the stylish but messy kitchen of a little three-roomed flat and then into a loudly creaking marital bed. Just as she caught a first glimpse of her fiery latin lover's olive-coloured skin, the long panning shot of her thoughts was broken by an aggressive honking of a horn. Her attention was brought back to being in the passenger seat of an unmarked police car, en route from Kungsholmen to a motel somewhere in Stockholm's southern suburbs.

So it goes.

Kerstin Holm let out a particularly coarse string of abuse, turned round and said: "I am sorry."

Sara Svenhagen pulled a face and managed to focus on her older colleague behind the wheel.

"I don't know what I'm meant to be forgiving," she answered honestly.

48

Kerstin Holm looked at her and smiled wryly.

"Let me guess where you were," she said, giving the finger to a confused old man in a checked cap driving a silvery Volkswagen Jetta.

"What did he do?" Sara Svenhagen asked, still half asleep.

"He just proved that driving licences have a best before date. Don't try to change the subject. You were in the bedroom of a newly bought three-roomer in Birkastan. Right?"

Sara smiled weakly and felt like she had been caught red-handed. Kerstin nodded self-righteously, struggling with the lid of a stubborn pot of snus tobacco and eventually managing to push a portion of it up under her lip.

"You still haven't told me what it cost."

"It was pretty run-down . . ."

"That's a new one. Nice. Normally I hear: 'We exchanged for two rentals', 'the price per square metre was surprisingly low', and then the cryptic 'second mortgage rates are pretty good at the minute'. I want a hard figure."

"Two point two."

"Thanks," Kerstin Holm said, accelerating gratefully.

"Including two rentals. One of which was in Rågsved."

"Sounds pretty cheap."

"It was a good price. The price per square metre *was* surprisingly low. And it *was* pretty run-down."

"What did you get for your place on Surbrunnsgatan?"

"I didn't sell it illegally. We exchanged."

"Who said you sold it illegally? That came from the heart."

"Three hundred thousand. And I think they saw Jorge's bloody studio in Rågsved as more of a punishment. A cross to bear."

"So it was up around two and a half million?"

"Almost. We were thinking of having a house-warming party next weekend. What do you think?"

"Sounds good."

"Other halves are welcome too."

Kerstin Holm accelerated slightly less gratefully.

"Wow, what a subtle turn of events," she said gloomily. "What a smooth interview technique."

"Let's hear it now," Sara Svenhagen said, turning to face her. She couldn't quite escape the feeling that Kerstin Holm was the proudest person she had ever met. Even in profile — her dark, elegant, dishevelled hair; the well-defined lines on her face — everything suggested a kind of innate proudness which, she had to admit, she admired. It had been almost a year since Sara Svenhagen had joined the A-Unit and the two women had worked together a few times, but she had never felt that she was a real, proper equal. In her eyes, Kerstin Holm was the best interviewer the police corps had to offer, and she still had plenty to learn from her. That did mean it was tough sometimes, when you knew she had seen right through you. After a conversation with Kerstin, it was as though you had no secrets left. Everything always came out. But with Kerstin herself, the exact opposite was true: she was one big mystery. So that meant it felt good to have turned the conversation around. Even though Kerstin had clearly seen straight through it.

"I'll be coming alone," Kerstin said, guiding the old Volvo out onto the E4 motorway. "If that's OK with you."

And with that, the conversation was over.

They drove in silence for a while. Both were searching for something to talk about. It wasn't an easy task. Sometimes, it was just too awkward. Sara knew that back in the beginning, Kerstin had been with Paul Hjelm, a married man. Her own husband Jorge Chavez's partner and best friend.

It all felt a bit complicated.

"Is it true he's the only *darkie* in the neighbourhood?" Kerstin Holm eventually asked.

That broke the ice. The two of them laughed. It felt good.

"It's very, very true," Sara said, then, changing tack: "Where are we going, exactly?"

"No idea," Kerstin Holm said, still laughing. "No, we're going to the Norrboda Motell in Slagsta. The refugee centre is full, so the immigration authorities have been renting rooms in the motel. Apparently some of the refugees staying there have gone missing. There seems to be a whiff of international criminality to the whole place, so they've called us in to take the case. If it even turns out to be a case. Any other questions?"

"What kind of whiff?"

"The motel seems to have been a bit too self-sufficient. A whole load of smuggling has been linked to it, with the Russians and the Baltic states mostly, but there've also been suggestions of prostitution. And a few of the women who've gone missing now are suspected to have been involved in that."

"So in other words, a group of whores have disappeared?"

Kerstin Holm pulled a face as they drove through Skärholmen in the cool but bright May afternoon.

"It's looking that way," she reluctantly admitted.

"Who reported it?"

"The owner, apparently. He's been the subject of certain suspicions himself. Jörgen Nilsson's his name."

"What kind of suspicions?"

"Not seeing, saying or doing anything. But he's been cleared. Reporting this is probably just a way of showing us that he's on the right side."

Sara Svenhagen leaned back in the worn-out passenger seat. She was forced to admit that she didn't quite understand the priorities of Swedish immigration policy. From certain countries, primarily the EU member states, it was clearly possible to immigrate quite freely. Becoming a Swedish citizen was no problem. But from others, it seemed to be a completely impossible task. To even stand a chance, you had to seek asylum and claim to be a refugee. That meant you had to make sure not to stop off in any other countries along the way. If you managed that trick — which in itself meant increasing numbers of deaths, with people suffocating in containers or dying of dehydration in the boats transporting them — then you ended up in a refugee centre while your case was considered. The combination of growing numbers of asylum seekers, tougher regulations and more sweeping staff cuts meant that waiting times were becoming more and more absurd, the refugee centres brimming over and being outsourced to private businesses, usually second-rate motels and hostels. There, you would find people with terrible experiences behind them, rotting away in some kind of limbo for years on end. Sara couldn't quite understand how they were then expected to become integrated, functional citizens — nor how so many people actually managed it.

She had tried reading up on the subject. It was impossible to avoid it. On 1 July, the national immigration authority would change its name to Migrationsverket. The idea was to enable a general oversight of migration and the movement of people, as well as the country's immigration, integration and return policy. The latter was something new. *Provisional refugee* was a concept that had only recently emerged, above all in connection to the Yugoslav wars. Simply put, the Swedish government let people stay for a while, until it was safe for them to return home, and when they did eventually go back, it gave them a small contribution for not becoming the burden on the state they would otherwise have become if they'd stayed. In doing so, they gave the whole business an aura of voluntariness. An idea which was a pure fiction.

The essence of this new migration concept was — if Sara had understood correctly — that returning was viewed as an equally crucial moment as integration. You could infer a great deal about contemporary society's attitudes from that, she thought.

The old Volvo had reached Slagsta, which lay squashed up like an artificial idyll against the shore of Lake Mälaren before you came to places like Fittja, Alby, Norsborg and Hallunda — names synonymous with a high immigrant population. In any case, it was home to the ugly Norrboda Motell, a long, five-storey building of classic seventies architecture. Both detectives stood speechless for a moment, each of them longing for a glimpse into the mind of the architect. That was, in all likelihood, precisely what they got the moment they set foot in its uniform corridors, clad in urine-coloured carpets and matching, age-faded institutional material on the walls and ceilings. So this was the first image that Swedes-to-be were given of their future homeland.

It was probably a deliberate part of the national return policy.

Just past the deserted reception, they found the manager's office; it was nothing more than a motel room among others. Jörgen Nilsson met them with a nervous heartiness. Sara thought she recognised the type immediately. An idealist from '68, someone who had wanted to fundamentally change society but instead found himself transformed into something resembling a prison guard-cum-bureaucrat. The grimace of bitterness writ plain on his face.

Perhaps that was unfair. He was probably doing his best.

Jörgen Nilsson gestured for them to sit down in his utterly anonymous office. He perched on the edge of the desk and began speaking with the energy of a self-righteous man.

"Four rooms have been emptied. There were two women in each. Eight missing asylum seekers."

"What does 'missing' mean?" Sara Svenhagen asked innocently.

"That they should've reported to me this morning," Jörgen Nilsson replied, looking at her with a surprised expression, "but didn't. I went to their rooms — they're next to one another — and realised they were gone."

Kerstin Holm felt obliged to explain.

"We're from CID," she said. "We don't normally get involved in immigration cases."

"CID?" Jörgen Nilsson blurted out, his face turning noticeably pale. "It's just a few . . . women who've gone underground. It happens every day somewhere in Sweden."

"But it's happened a few too many times here, hasn't it?"

"I've been completely cleared of all those allegations. They were bitter, rejected refugees, those people who filed reports against me. Completely baseless. You know that full well."

Sara Svenhagen shifted in her seat and said: "What were you planning on saying just then, instead of 'women'?"

Jörgen Nilsson stared furiously at her.

"What? For God's sake, haven't you got anything better to do?"

"You were planning on saying something other than 'women'. You paused like you were swallowing some kind of ill-thought-out word. What was it?"

From the corner of her eye, she caught a glimpse of an appreciative look from Kerstin. It gave her encouragement.

"I don't know what you're talking about," Nilsson said, getting up from the edge of the desk and pacing around the tiny room. It seemed slightly laboured.

Kerstin Holm pushed another portion of snus tobacco under her lip. She took a piece of paper from her pocket and unfolded it with malicious slowness. Reading it, she eventually said:

"You moved here in September last year. In October, a Russo-Lithuanian cigarette smuggling group was uncovered. In December, it was the illegal movement of Coca-Cola from Turkey. In February, a couple of Gambians were stopped with large amounts of brown heroin. And in March, we had reports of prostitution. It was the word 'whores' you were trying to stop yourself from saying, wasn't it?"

Jörgen Nilsson continued his pacing. Despite his highly strung state, he seemed to be busy weighing up the pros and cons of talking. He came to a decision, paused, and returned to the edge of the desk.

"Yes," he said, his eyes fixed on Kerstin Holm. "You've got to understand how hard it is. These people seeking asylum are locked up for months. Years, sometimes. Obviously they've got to have sex lives of some kind during that time. The whole thing's a powder keg from the very start, and trying to control their sex lives would be like putting a match to it. I admit, the number of partners does get a bit much sometimes, if you see what I mean, but reporting them for it would be the same as sending them straight back home. I try to be tolerant. And yes: sometimes I might've looked away a bit too often. Let's call it my form of civil disobedience. I won't be a concentration camp guard, for God's sake."

"You're not the one we're after," Holm said, feeling sudden sympathy for the exasperated man in front of her. "But we're worried something might've happened to these women. Why else would they go underground if — with your blessing — they've been able to go about their business relatively undisturbed here? They didn't have any rent to pay, after all."

"Though it's entirely possible they were paying in *one way* or another," Sara Svenhagen said, looking at Holm, who pulled a disapproving face. It was plain it was the thought she disapproved of, not what Sara had said.

Jörgen Nilsson's diatribe was preceded by a brief shifting gaze. Then it came:

"Am I accused of anything here? Just come out and tell me exactly what it is you want. Are you seriously accusing me of sexually exploiting asylum seekers? Just spit it out! Do you think I've chopped eight women up into pieces and eaten them or something like that?"

Sara felt like she might — though only might — have gone a step too far. She had taken on the role of "bad cop" voluntarily, without thinking it through. It had just happened.

"Like we've said, you aren't the one we're after," she said courteously. "But it's important you aren't sloppy when you think it through — because that's what you've got to do now. Has anything unusual happened, anything at all, the past few days? What about yesterday evening, last night, this morning? Could any of the neighbours have seen anything? Who knows about the prostitution? Do you know any of the johns? Is there a pimp?"

Kerstin waited until Sara was finished. Then she stood up, pushed a pad of paper and a pen over to Jörgen Nilsson and said: "Keys to the rooms, please. We'll go and have a look round while you get your answers to those questions together. And provide us with the most comprehensive information on the missing women you can."

The keys were placed in her hand, and as they left the manager's office, they could clearly hear the scratching of pen on paper; frenetic, as though done by a man with a knife to his throat.

Both detectives walked down the corridor with stony faces — right until they turned the corner and reached the stairs. Then they started giggling like schoolgirls. The moment passed. As they climbed the stairs, Kerstin Holm said gruffly: "*It's important you aren't sloppy when you think it through.*"

"It just came to me," Sara said with a hint of smugness, running her hand through her cropped blonde hair. "What reason could he have for keeping quiet about prostitution in the refugee centre?"

"Just when I'd started to like him. I actually fell for his whole civil disobedience thing. Me, an old dear, I'm more naive than you. That feels weird."

"Don't say that. All the crap I saw when I was working with the paedophile unit . . . It's nothing to be jealous of. And you're not an old dear."

"Mmm," Kerstin Holm replied, gravely serious.

They came to the rooms, four doors next to one another in the middle of a seemingly endless corridor two floors up. Rooms 224, 225, 226 and 227. After fumbling with the keys, they made their way into number 224. Unmade beds against two of the walls; an empty desk; a couple of empty wardrobes, doors flung wide; ugly strip lighting on the ceiling and the same piss-coloured wall-to-wall carpet and institutional fabric as everywhere else. It was clear that the atmosphere wasn't part of what the brothel had to offer. People came here for raw sex, nothing more, nothing less. Even the reading lamps were bare strip lights.

They stood for a moment, taking in the scene.

"What's your intuition telling you?" Kerstin asked, a question aimed as much at herself as Sara. "Is it worth calling the technicians in? Do you think they've just done a runner? Or has something happened to them? Sara?"

"Fingerprints, semen . . ." Sara thought aloud. "Yeah, well . . . should we take a look at the other rooms first?"

The other rooms were remarkably similar. In fact, there was barely anything to distinguish them. It was like that classic nightmare: no matter which door you opened, the very same room was waiting on the other side.

Both women knew that it would take multiple, time-consuming interviews before they would even start to form an idea about what had happened here. And by then, it would be too late for the technicians. They would have to go on their intuition. Breathe the rooms in. Try to find some small clue as to what had happened.

They thought about the decree from above — from the CID department head, Waldemar Mörner — which obliged staff to minimise their use of the National Forensic Laboratory, since its services were, in his view, "criminally overpriced".

They stood for a moment, trying to get a sense of the atmosphere. Then they nodded, both at the same time.

"Yup," said Kerstin Holm. "Something's not right."

"No," said Sara Svenhagen. "Something's not right."

And so they called in the technicians. Not that it was easy; they were busy elsewhere.

"Skansen?" Kerstin Holm exclaimed into her mobile. "What the hell are they doing there? Wolverine shit?? OK, OK, someone's been reading their Ellroy . . ."

She hung up on her boss, Detective Superintendent Jan-Olov Hultin, and shook her head. Doing so still hurt slightly. Just over a year ago, she had been shot, leaving her left temple paper-thin. Her hair was still refusing to grow back over it. She poked at the little bald spot which her dishevelled black hair was managing, with some trouble, to cover.

"Don't ask," was all she said as they relocked the doors and headed back downstairs.

When they reached the manager's office, Jörgen Nilsson had already filled ten or so sheets of A4. They looked at one another and groaned.

It would be a long afternoon.

CHAPTER
SIX

Detective Superintendent Jan-Olov Hultin was sitting in a traffic jam, trying to work out how much of his life he had spent sitting in traffic jams. He gave up once the numbers started reaching astronomical heights. From what he could tell, he had spent more than a year in traffic jams. The thought was unbearable. He was sixty-three years old, and of those sixty-three years, more than one had been spent in traffic. That must be what people meant by progress.

He pulled out onto the E4 by Norrviken in Sollentuna, where he lived, on a highly sought-after plot of land on the shore of Lake Ravalen. Gravely criminal estate agents still stopped by every now and then, trying to buy the land for a song. He had chased the latest of them away with a needle-sharp rake. The estate agent had wet himself and screamed, tears in his throat: "Tool killer!" Jan-Olov Hultin had regretted it for the rest of the day. It had been less than a year since he had actually killed a man. In a hotel room in Skövde. In addition to that, he had jammed his service weapon into the mouth of an unarmed man and had come damn close to shooting him too. Only Arto Söderstedt had stopped him, a debt he would forever struggle to repay. Granting him a few months' leave without a word had been a matter of course — despite the fact that it went against all the usual rules and regulations.

It often happened — much too often — that Hultin found himself back in that hotel room in Skövde. Of course, it could just be called a dream — it probably was a dream. Only, it didn't feel like one. He was really there. It was so strange. The whole sequence of events, every little detail, repeated itself, and the odd thing was that throughout it all, he knew exactly what was going to happen. But despite that, he still couldn't do a thing about it. He was reliving the whole thing — fully aware of what would happen — night after night. Paul Hjelm shot a thug and was shot in the arm, Kerstin Holm was shot in the head. And Jan-Olov Hultin killed one man and jammed his pistol into the mouth of another.

Killing a man wasn't so easy.

The events in Skövde were just one part of the previous summer's strange, complicated, eye-catching series of crimes. The media had been able to summarise the A-Unit's earlier cases with relative ease, talking about "The Power Killer" and "The Kentucky Killer", but this third case had proved trickier, and thankfully the press hadn't managed to cling on to every single twist and turn. There had been a patchwork of unusual names instead — "The Kumla Explosion", "The Sickla Slaughter", "The Skövde Shooting" and the "Kvarnen Killing" — and not even the most eagle-eyed of readers had managed to link these diverse incidents to one another.

But there had been a link, and it hadn't been pretty.

It had been relatively tough for them all to get back to work again afterwards. Hultin had officially returned as operating chief of the A-Unit, having been involuntarily retired before the case began. That was something for which he would never forgive Waldemar Mörner, the group's official boss.

Usually, he hit the first traffic jam as soon as he turned off onto the E4 at Norrviken. Those were slow mornings. But this particular early May morning, however, it was plain sailing all the way to Ulriksdal. Now the rain was lashing down and he was sitting in a motionless traffic jam, feeling bitter.

Not least because he had wet himself.

It wasn't really a problem, because he was wearing a pad specially designed for the purpose. He had chronic incontinence and there was nothing to be done but swallow the bitter pill. Give up and retire on health grounds or say to hell with it and ignore it. He had chosen the latter.

But the more he thought about it, the clearer the link became between his condition and those bouts of rage which, just over a year ago, had resulted in a couple of headbutted eyebrows and escalated to a climax in Skövde. Though for the past year he had — the tool-killer incident aside — actually managed to stick to his mantra of "live and let live". Also in relation to the weeds in his garden, now thriving like never before.

Their last case might well have resulted in a number of his team giving up; it had been unbelievably

64

demanding. Thankfully, though, they had all stayed put. Thankfully, they were all still alive.

It struck him that as time went on, he saw them more and more as his children. He knew it was wrong. He, more than anyone else, had always managed to draw a line between his work and his private life; he thought perhaps he had gone sentimental in his old age. They had been through so much together and they had formed a bond like no other group he had worked with before.

The Devil had found religion in his old age.

In a brief moment of reckless honesty, he decided that Paul Hjelm and Kerstin Holm, Jorge Chavez and Arto Söderstedt, Viggo Norlander and Gunnar Nyberg — even Sara Svenhagen, the competent newcomer — were more like his children than his biological sons, both business-minded bachelors who visited him once a year at Christmas and then spent the time clock-watching and talking on their phones.

Jan-Olov Hultin could feel himself sinking into a muddled pool of mixed emotions. Then he decided enough was enough with the sentimental whining. He had arrived at the police station and no matter how good a detective he was, he would never be able to work out where the time had gone. Those gaps in time were one of life's great mysteries.

A car was parked. A detective superintendent wandered through a station. A detective superintendent reached an office. A briefcase was put down by a desk. A watch was checked. A toilet visited. An incontinence pad was changed. Sleep was rubbed from a left eye.

Corridors were walked down. Doors were opened. The Tactical Command Centre was empty. Stop.

The world took on a near-telegraphic style when everything went according to routine. But then suddenly it changed. Stop. Where was his team? Why was the sad little meeting room which — not without a slight sense of irony — went by the name "Tactical Command Centre" completely empty?

Detective Superintendent Jan-Olov Hultin checked his watch again. It was thirty-three minutes past eight. Their morning run-through was meant to have started three minutes earlier. Even if the A-Unit wasn't a marvel of temporal precision, at least one of them should have been there by now.

With resolute steps, Hultin headed for the desk where he usually sat waiting and watching like an old high-school teacher who was still refusing to retire. He picked up the phone and dialled the number for the talking clock. In its human — much too human — voice, it said: "eight, sixteen and ten seconds. Peep."

Not that the voice actually said "peep".

Hultin's mind drifted to black holes in the space-time continuum, to gravitational time dilation and other such things. Had he been transported to another, parallel universe while he was wallowing in that pool of mixed emotions? For forty years, his wristwatch — an expensive Patek Philippe — had never been more than a few seconds out. Suddenly it was fifteen minutes fast. And during a period of time which seemed like it had disappeared, at that. He shuddered and allowed his thoughts to drift on. It was common knowledge that time passed more slowly inside a gravitational field than outside of it. The weaker the gravitational force, the quicker the time. A clock on top of Mount Everest will always be quicker than a clock at the bottom of the Mariana Trench. Einstein had long since demonstrated what happened to time at high speeds with his theory of relativity — not that a traffic jam snaking through Stockholm really moved that fast. But just imagine if the opposite was true. Imagine if those traffic jams were so unnaturally slow that they reduced the gravitational force for a moment and made time pass more quickly. Imagine it was God's way of saying: "Now, my children, enough of the madness. You sit alone in your cars as they spew out the carbon dioxide that's devastating this world. In addition to that, you're barely budging an inch. I need to give you a sign, a sign that you should stop making fools of yourselves and carpool, at the very least. No fewer than three in a car, and you can use the bus lanes whenever you like." Thus spoke the Almighty to the Not-Quite-So Almighty, who now looked up and saw twelve more or less attentive eyes fixed on him. He looked at his watch. Thirty-three minutes past eight. The second hand was moving as normal.

Jan-Olov Hultin froze. He realised he was faced with a choice. It was a parallel to his incontinence — he could have sunk down into it; he could have devoted the rest of his life to searching for explanations as to why he in particular had been struck by such an evil, mocking, relentlessly embarrassing condition. But he had realised he would never find any answers. He had realised it would lead to nothing more than an endless state of hopeless brooding which, in all likelihood, would result in either drug abuse or suicide. And so he had accepted the unfair hand fate had dealt him, put his incontinence pad in place and got on with his life.

But now, though? Was that a real, mystical experience he had just had? A modern-day Meister Eckhart or Francis of Assisi? Or was it nothing more than his tired old watch going crazy?

What had happened to time?

He came to a decision. He would drop the watch off for repair. If it happened again, he would book himself in for a CT scan to check whether he was having a stroke.

Because God's voice had sounded remarkably like his own. At one point, years from now, he would experience the same sensation of complete disengagement with life. By then, he would have managed to retire no fewer than three times, but he would be back in charge of an investigation into an explosion on the Stockholm metro. Sitting in a room with both the A-Unit and the top brass from the Security Services, the same feeling of utter surreality would pass over him. As state secrets of the highest order were being discussed, he would once again experience that exact same sensation. But that was a long way off yet.

He looked out at the A-Unit, cleared his throat, leafed through the pile of papers on the desk in front of him and said, in his most ordinary voice: "Right then, my friends: today's business."

He stole a glance at them through his owl-like glasses, to see if anything had shown. They looked like they always did. Not a sign that any of them had noticed anything unusual. He breathed a sigh of relief and continued.

"Yesterday, as you know, we had a couple of unusual events for the first time in a long while. None of you hesitated to use the forensic technicians and I'm sure the bill will be enough to turn Mörner's stomach. But you did the right thing, of course. So this means we've got three ongoing cases, since Viggo and Gunnar are looking after the commuter train fight. Are we getting anywhere there, Gunnar?"

Before he fixed his gaze on Gunnar Nyberg, his eyes passed over his watch. It was twenty-five to nine. Time seemed to be back to normal again.

The sight of Gunnar Nyberg's face was nearly as much of a surprise as it often had been lately. Though only nearly. By now, Hultin had — against all odds — started to get used to the idea of Sweden's Biggest Policeman having abdicated the role. Nyberg's 146 kilograms were more like 100 these days. He had done the impossible: he had lost weight. And since the former Mr Sweden rarely did anything by halves, he had *really* lost weight. Forty kilograms, something he put down to the whole dieting package: healthy food, jogging, swimming, and even acupuncture and reflexology. It was deeply impressive.

Nyberg knew all too well that not a single member of the team had failed to see through his all-encompassing motive; they were even helping him along the way. So far, though, he hadn't really had much luck.

Gunnar Nyberg needed a woman.

Some of his A-Unit colleagues had "set him up" with "single women" from their groups of acquaintances. He had been on a few "dates" and was starting to get tired of all the Anglo-American expressions which seemed to go hand in hand with the opposite sex. Though he was far from tired of the opposite sex. On the contrary — a decades-long, self-imposed celibacy had come to an end; Gunnar Nyberg no longer felt the need to lash himself like a medieval monk. He had managed to repair his relationship with his children and even his ex-wife who, during the dark years of his bodybuilding period, he had mistreated in the worst way possible. These days, he regularly spent time with his grandson Benny, who was almost three now and would soon be getting a sibling — a sister, the ultrasound had mistakenly revealed.

Unfortunately, he was forced to admit that the woman who had been granted the dubious honour of freeing him from his celibacy had almost entirely slipped his mind. It wasn't enough that he couldn't remember her name, he couldn't even remember what she looked like. He had been so nervous that he had been climbing the walls of his old bachelor pad in Nacka. All he could remember was that Viggo Norlander had been behind it. She was a colleague of Norlander's partner Astrid, a woman in her forties. They had planned to meet at his flat and then go out for a drink in Nacka Centrum. That much he

70

remembered, but after that his memory failed him. He didn't think they had even gone for that drink. All he had was a vague recollection of surprisingly immediate sexual activity. Nothing more, nothing less. The two had never met again, and the only lasting impression was something Viggo Norlander had said a few days later, with an ambiguous smile on his lips:

"You sly dog."

He assumed Norlander had meant it as praise and not criticism, but Gunnar Nyberg had no idea. Just to be on the safe side, he never saw her again. He met other women instead, and as he became slimmer and slimmer, his confidence grew. By now, he felt nothing but excitement at the delights the opposite sex had to offer. He was ready for something more long-term.

He cleared his throat and said: "You all know the details of the so-called commuter train fight. Night train from Kungsängen. Three pro graffiti artists completely renovated the carriage where a group of alcoholics were sitting. Five full-blown alcoholics in their forties — apparently they were morally outraged at the damage and set on the vandals, who were fit young twenty-somethings. It turned into a real fight. Two of the alcoholics were left brain-damaged, one of the vandals died; everyone was hurt in one way or another. When the train arrived in Karlberg, a pensioner with a little lapdog boarded a real bloodbath. It really is as boring as it sounds, from an investigative point of view. I hope these new cases are a bit more stimulating. Viggo and I don't have anything else to add. Everyone involved has been taken into custody and charged. Aside from the pensioner, who had a heart attack. He's out of danger now though, finally."

Hultin cast another glance at his watch. Everything seemed fine. He nodded and thanked Nyberg.

"OK then," he said. "We can probably consider that one closed. Time for ferocious little animals."

Jorge Chavez looked up from a pile of papers and cast a glance at Hjelm, who gestured for him to take charge.

"OK," said Chavez. "Have any of you heard of the *Gulo gulo?*"

Clearly none of them had.

"It comes from the Latin for glutton. It's another name for the wolverine. As I'm sure you can guess, it's hinting at the animal's insatiable greediness. They eat small animals during the summer, but in the winter they'd happily eat a reindeer or two. The night before last, four of the wolverines in Skansen were clearly feeling quite wintery, because these little creatures — which don't weigh more than about thirty kilos each, by the way — guzzled down a man, virtually every last bit of him. We've got some fibres from a pale pink suit, a section of his leg, complete with a piece of eight-millimetre red-and-purple polypropylene rope, plus a right index finger and this."

He held up a dog-eared playing card.

The queen of spades.

"We found traces of the probable basis for their greediness. Cocaine. An analysis of the flesh and blood samples showed the same: that our victim had recently consumed a pretty large amount of cocaine. Since the drug was in his blood, it added to the wolverines' insatiability.

"Everyone knows that the worst things always happen — in war, for example — under the influence of drugs. Apparently the animal kingdom isn't much different from the human race in that respect. Put simply: the cocaine drove the wolverines crazy, and from what we can tell, they even managed to work their way through almost his entire skeleton, his head included. We haven't found it yet, at least. Despite that, my father-in-law's men from the lab have managed to produce both a DNA analysis and a usable fingerprint. Neither of them match anything in the Swedish databases, so we've sent them on to Interpol and Europol.

"We didn't find our man's fingerprints on the wooden fence around the enclosure either. None of the fingerprints from the fence match any entries in the database. His finger, which was pretty cut up, was full of earth that we've managed to link to the soil in the southern corner of the wolverine enclosure — the area right beneath the viewing platform. We also found both blood and skin fragments from the victim in that area — in five letters which, from what we can tell, he scratched in the ground with his finger. The word, if it even is one, is: 'Epivu'. Capital E, the rest lower case. Does that mean anything to anyone?"

It didn't.

"No," said Chavez. "It didn't mean a thing to us either. Or the Internet. Not one single hit."

"Moving on from the wolverine enclosure," Paul Hjelm continued. "Because of the rope around his leg, we automatically assumed he'd been carried there, either unconscious or already dead. I took too long to react, if I'm honest. I'd just come from the Astrid Lindgren Children's Hospital, where I'd been talking to a little girl who'd been shot just after 10p.m. the night before. In Djurgården, not far from the eastern edge of Skansen. If we look at the path of the bullet and follow it back, you end up at the Skansen fence — parallel to the wolf enclosure. The lucky technicians had to expand their search to that enclosure too.

"They eventually managed to find three things: firstly, our victim's blood, high up on the fence — including on the barbed wire at the top and then also on the concrete wall beneath the viewing area on the other side. Secondly, they found a thick, broken neck chain, eighteen-carat gold, and finally, a 9mm Luger with a silencer. The magazine was empty. They did some sample shots. The gun's a perfect match for the bullet taken from ten-year-old Lisa Altbratt's upper arm. She'll be absolutely fine, by the way."

"So in summary," Chavez took over. "Who is our man? He was wearing a pale pink suit and he had a thick gold chain around his neck; he snorts cocaine from the queen of spades and he's armed with a silenced Luger. The print from his one remaining finger — the right index finger to be precise — is on all three of them: the card, the chain and the gun. It's unambiguous. So who is he?"

"Hit man?" asked Nyberg.

"Drug dealer?" rejoined Norlander.

"Porn star?" Nyberg countered.

"Pimp?" Holm and Svenhagen blurted out in unison. The two women glanced at one another.

"We'll have to wait and see," Chavez said firmly. "At the very least, the whole thing screams underworld. He's not in our databases, which means he's probably foreign. If he was Swedish, the systems would've gone crazy with matches."

"So what happened to him?" Hjelm continued. "Someone chased him through the Djurgården woods. He shot at them, but there's no indication of him hitting anyone other than Lisa Altbratt. He made it to the fence and decided to climb up, even though there was a little path right alongside the fence. What does that tell us? Desperation, maybe? Blind panic? He ripped his fingers to shreds on the fence, didn't care about grabbing the barbed wire — it cut deep into his hands — and then threw himself into the wolf enclosure. Luckily for him, they seem to have been well fed and content."

"One thing," Kerstin Holm said pensively. "Was there even anyone following him? Maybe it was just some kind of drug-induced psychosis? The only thing suggesting a crime is surely the rope around his leg. But maybe we should assume he had that there for some other reason. I don't know, sexual maybe — some sort of bondage thing? He might have just been running from his own demons and fallen into the wolverines in blind panic?"

There was silence. Chavez leafed through his papers.

"The rope had been chewed off," he said quietly. "There's no evidence it was tied around both legs, so it might have just been around one of them. Some kind of decoration. But," he added more loudly, "is that really likely?"

"The key thing's got to be whether there's any sign of anyone else there," Holm continued. "It could be in a number of places, if I've followed everything you've been saying: outside Skansen, on the fence, in with the wolves, on the wall at the edge of the wolf enclosure, on the ground between the wolves and the wolverines, in with the wolverines. It doesn't seem too likely we'd find anything in with the wolverines, but what about the other places? If his blood is all over the fence then why don't we have anything from whoever was following him? Why didn't they leave a single trace behind?"

Chavez tore his papers.

"Apparently there aren't even any clear footprints from him. In the wolf enclosure, the ground's practically all rock between the fence and the wall. There's no trace of him on the asphalt — not on the fence around the wolverine enclosure, either."

"But in with the wolverines, surely his footprints have got to be there?" said Holm. "I mean, he was writing in the earth with his fingers. It must be porous. Is there no sign of him there, by the letters?"

Chavez nodded — the way a man who has missed something nods.

"I know, Kerstin, but there aren't any. There are wolverine prints, a general kind of chaos, traces of the actual ingestion . . . but no footprints. It rained that night, remember that."

"But not enough to get rid of the letters . . ."

"He might've been thrown down once he was already tied up," said Hjelm. "If he was thrown in, maybe he got injured. All he managed to do was write that word which, for some reason, was more important than getting up. And then the wolverines appeared."

"And there's no sign of anyone else having been there at all?" Kerstin Holm persisted. "Not even on the fence?"

"No," Chavez replied doggedly.

"So let's try to work out what happened with the wolves," said Hjelm. "Let's imagine he got rid of the gun because he'd emptied the magazine. Not a smart move, but understandable. Blind fury. Then why did he tear his expensive chain off, that ridiculous extension of his penis, and throw it to the wolves?"

"Maybe that's just another sign of drug psychosis," Holm said. Hjelm thought he knew her well enough to realise she was now doing it just to annoy Jorge, who had a dark look in his eyes. It didn't help that Hultin concluded:

"So in other words, we don't even know if a crime has been committed —"

"Yes," Chavez said irritatedly. "This is a murder. If it isn't, I'll throw myself to the wolverines. That's a promise."

The A-Unit stared at him. It was true that each of them had been hoping for a real case — for no more fights on commuter trains — but none more than Jorge Chavez. That much was obvious.

"That'll be a nice crowd-pleaser for the summer concerts in Skansen," Viggo Norlander said, blowing his nose. "Lasse Berghagen introducing the daring Wolverine Detective."

"Shut up," Chavez said.

"Isn't that my line?" retorted Norlander.

"Honestly," said Holm, "if we look at that incomprehensible writing and the fact that he wrote what he did instead of trying to get out . . . Doesn't it all just suggest he was mad?"

"Yeah," said Hjelm. "I think he was mad. Drugged up and mad with panic. But I also think his panic was justified."

"But whoever was following him *doesn't* seem to have climbed into the wolf enclosure after him," said Holm. "Is there any other way in?"

Hjelm and Chavez exchanged glances. It wasn't a pretty sight.

"We'll look into it," Hjelm said drily.

Hultin pulled himself together, glanced at his watch and continued.

"Well, that took a while. We've still got another event to go through. Kerstin?"

Kerstin Holm looked slightly out of it. Her fingers touched the bare patch on her temple and she imagined she could feel her thoughts breaking up on the other side of the thin bone.

"Could you start, Sara?" she asked.

78

Sara, who had been sitting quietly, looked up in surprise. She still thought of herself as Kerstin's inferior and had been expecting — at most — a word or two. She took a sip of her cold coffee, pulled a face and composed herself.

"Eight asylum seekers, all strongly suspected of having worked as prostitutes, disappeared from the annexe of a refugee centre the night before last. From the Norrboda Motell in Slagsta, to be precise. Where they were living and working.

"They're all from Eastern Europe: three of the women from Ukraine, two from Bulgaria, two from Russia and another from Belarus. The two Russians, Natalja Vaganova and Tatjana Skoblikova, were in room 224; two of the Ukrainians, Galina Stenina and Lina Kostenko, were in room 225; the other one, Valentina Dontsjenko, and the Belorussian, Svetlana Petruseva, were in room 226; the two Bulgarians, Stefka Dafovska and Mariya Bagrjana, were in room 227. I'm sure you'll remember all of that.

"We worked late into the evening yesterday, talking to their neighbours. It seems like it was a pretty open secret that they were prostitutes. We've got names for some of the johns and we've managed to get a pretty good idea of how they were able to run their business. Jörgen Nilsson, the manager, didn't just turn a blind eye to it; we've also got reports that he made use of their services. As a customer. I don't think he's got much of a future left in his job."

Kerstin Holm had managed to collect herself and took over.

"We had two key questions. When did the women disappear, and had their disappearance been preceded by anything unusual? We couldn't expect to know much more than that by this point. What we do know is the following: for the past week or so, the women had been more uneasy than usual; something had clearly happened to make them nervous. Their neighbours were pretty much in agreement on that.

"From what we can tell, the eight women were there all evening on Wednesday. One witness claims he heard them talking in a foreign language, probably Russian, as late as three on Thursday morning. They were meant to report to Nilsson at nine that morning, but they never showed up. None of their neighbours — and we've spoken to most of them by now — saw or heard them disappear. All that with a side note, most of the interviews were carried out using an interpreter."

"So we don't even know if a crime has been committed," Chavez pointed out vindictively.

Holm gave him an amused look. Svenhagen gave him an angry one. The look of a wife whose husband was acting like a child.

"No," Sara said, managing to sound restrained. "But we do have to ask whether it's really just a coincidence that an unidentified pimp-like man was chased to his death just a few hours before eight prostitutes from a refugee camp disappeared into thin air. We can speculate a bit here. Was he their pimp? If that's the case, then doesn't it seem fair to assume that the whole brothel's just been wiped out by the competition?

They're probably dead already, if that's true. And then we'd have a real sex war on our hands. Plus, battles between brothels usually mean drug wars, too. Or maybe he was just a competing pimp, put to death by the eight's pimp before he grabbed his women and went underground?"

"Hang on a second now," said Hultin. "What are you up to, Sara? Do we have anything at all suggesting a link between these two cases — which might not actually even be cases?"

"Nothing concrete, no," Sara replied, slightly browbeaten. "It's just a hunch."

"I'm starting to get very tired of all these vague hunches," their great leader emphasised clearly, stealing a glance at his watch.

"Slightly more concrete, then," said Kerstin Holm. "Unidentified men with that kind of brash, high-up-in-the-underworld appearance aren't exactly common; we normally know who they are, it's that simple. Which means this man is, in all likelihood, a new arrival. The women in Slagsta had been uneasy since a few weeks back. On that basis, it's not unreasonable for us to check for any possible sightings of a cocaine-snorting man in a light pink suit and with a thick gold chain around his neck in the area around the Norrboda Motell over the past few weeks, is it? We might even get a description of him if we do that."

"Sounds better," Hultin muttered.

"It could be Lasse Berghagen himself," said Viggo Norlander.

"If we turn that reasoning around," Gunnar Nyberg suddenly said, "did those ladies chase after the pimp and push him into the ghouls?"

"*Gulo gulo*," Chavez corrected him sourly.

"Hardly," said Holm. "They were in Slagsta until at least three in the morning. Several witnesses saw and heard them around ten, when our man was busy climbing over the fence into the wolves."

"Did they have any johns then?" asked Hjelm. "Was it business as usual?"

Kerstin Holm turned to him and gave him a look he struggled to interpret, but which almost made him recoil. The relationship between them had been slightly tense since the incident in Skövde, a year ago. Both of them had been shot — him in the arm and her in the head — and they were lying next to one another on the ground, their blood mixing together beneath a sky which had just opened, and she, utterly exhausted, utterly drenched, utterly bloody, had whispered: "Paul, I love you."

Her words had been difficult to take. Not least because he was a married man.

Eventually, she answered: "We haven't been able to get a clear picture of that. We need to check more closely. There might be indications that their entire prostitution business had been quiet lately."

"Right then," Hultin said, gathering a pile of papers together. "The day's activities are starting to become clear. Paul and Jorge, you can go back to Skansen and look for alternative routes around the wolves. We need to know if it's a murder we're looking at. Kerstin and

82

Sara, work with Viggo and Gunnar and talk to more people from the Slagsta brothel. We really need to know whether it's a crime we're looking at there, too. We might be completely wrong. Oh, this came too."

He held up a postcard covered with pictures of wine bottles.

"Ah, yeah," Chavez said, still sourly. "The heirs."

"From Arto Söderstedt in Chianti, yes," Hultin said, pulling his owl-like glasses down to the end of his nose and reading: "'You rascals. Here I am, toiling away trampling grapes while you laze about in glorious spring Stockholm. Fate apportions her favours unequally. By the way, do you know the best way to split five watermelons between seven people? All suggestions gratefully received. Pieces is just lazy. Greetings from a warm, pine-scented, Vin Santo-hazy Tuscan afternoon.'"

"That piece of shit," said Viggo Norlander.

CHAPTER
SEVEN

He travelled. Like a worm, he moved in distinctive patterns beneath the city. He had got it into his head that these underground shapes formed letters, a subterranean script identical to the text on the reverse of his page. The text that was growing increasingly legible. That was becoming clearer and clearer — and increasingly impenetrable.

Simultaneously.

He was nearing ninety, professor emeritus. As a former brain scientist, he had made a conscious decision not to go senile in his old age, not to let his brain cells wither away. He had deliberately devoted his time to mental gymnastics, keeping his cerebral cortex in shape. He enjoyed literature and read the news in four different languages, he solved the most difficult crosswords in *Dagens Nyheter*, forced himself through at least one differential equation a day, and viewed the world with a sober, analytic, penetrating gaze.

Until a few days ago. When a vague, shifting presence had found its way into his life.

It was death.

Death didn't normally make demands. Death didn't normally walk alongside you for days, waiting for something to happen.

He was starting to understand what was expected of him.

Once upon a time, more than fifty years ago, he had turned a new page in his life. The old page had been full. It told a story which couldn't go on. One which had reached its conclusion. He had realised that to keep on living, he had no choice but to turn to a new page and pretend it was blank. Doing so would mean he could keep writing. Could keep living.

And so he had turned the page. He had left the past behind him and consciously — with precise, deliberate mental gymnastics — eradicated it. The text on the reverse of the page disappeared and a completely new life began. A Swedish life.

But now that his Swedish life was also about to end, he understood what was required of him. *He had to turn the page once more and reread his old story.* The problem was that it wasn't something you could just do. His old story came towards him like a punch, like a blow from an axe, like a metal wire jammed into his temple.

He hadn't realised that such old people could experience such intense feelings. It went completely against the very latest brain research.

He looked at his arm. The numbers were peeping out from beneath the sleeve of his coat. The numbers on his arm. As soon as he looked at them, they began moving.

Just like he was. They were on their way away from him.

It was one of the things he didn't understand.

And then came the pictures, like a blow from an axe.

There were arms on top of him, legs on top of him, thin, thin legs, thin, thin arms. He was moving through a pile of people. Dead people. He saw an upside-down face and he saw a thin wire being pushed into a temple, he saw the upside-down face contort in pain. And he wrote in a book. He read the words which he himself had written and the book was talking about pain, about pain, pain, pain.

And then he saw another image. One which took his breath away. He opened a door. The outer door to his own house. Here. In Sweden. That picture didn't belong. He opened the outer door from within and found a man without a nose waiting on the step outside.

And then the man without a nose was dead on the floor in front of him.

He woke up. He was sweating more than a ninety-year-old should be able to sweat. The metro was speeding through the dark tunnels, on and on. He had no idea where he was. It didn't matter. The pattern was all that mattered.

He didn't understand. The pages were mixed up. The front and the back of the page were mixed together. Why?

Then he saw an extremely pale man dressed in uniform. The extremely pale man in uniform was holding a thin metal wire in his hand.

The image vanished.

His train was approaching a station. He was alone in the carriage.

He closed his eyes for a moment. Mental gymnastics. Come back. You don't have the right to close your eyes. You're not allowed to close your eyes to anything.

He returned to the pattern his journey beneath the city had been creating. He was increasingly convinced it was forming symbols, letters. The Stockholm metro system was hardly as complex as the network of streets in New York, but symbols could still be formed. And formed they had. He had travelled and he knew *how* he had travelled. Not where, but how.

The first day's journey appeared slowly before his eyes. First a vertical line.

The train stopped at the station. The doors opened. The station was almost completely deserted. He didn't know where he was.

First a vertical line and then three horizontal. A letter.

On the first day, he had travelled in the shape of a letter.

A lone woman was standing on the platform, talking on her mobile phone. A group of teenagers spilled out of the carriage behind his.

It was an E. An upper-case E.

The train doors closed. The teenagers were approaching the woman. As the train gathered speed, he saw the flash of a knife.

He couldn't do a thing.

Other than reconstruct the second day's letter.

Sometimes, the right conditions just came together entirely by chance.

Usually, though, it needed lots of planning: the right time, the right place, the right person. You had to bide your time — waiting, watching and sneaking glances. You had to spread out and make it seem like you weren't together. That was when you struck. Once you'd grabbed enough, you went straight online. Sometimes there was as little as an hour between theft and sale.

"Freshly nicked phone for sale." And then the time.

The responses always came quickly. As though there were people just sitting at their computers, waiting for their moment. The pigs didn't stand a chance.

But then, every once in a while, one of those chance occurrences appeared. They were the best. Unplanned openings. Some bird all by herself on a platform, for example.

Hamid saw her straight away. He exchanged a quick glance with Adib and stepped off the train. The small fry tagged along. There were five of them and they were dangerous. No one ever put up any resistance. They just handed over their phones. If anyone tried to be clever, they got a punch. If anyone put up a fight, they got a cut.

Sometimes people shat themselves. It was disgusting.

She was good-looking, the woman. He could see that even though she was standing with her back to him, talking on her phone. Long black hair, red leather jacket, tight black trousers, black trainers. She turned round and caught sight of them. She ended the call.

She really was good-looking. If they had been somewhere more secluded than the station, he would have given her a little extra treatment.

The adrenalin had started pumping through his body. Hamid pulled out the knife. Her lower lip should be starting to tremble right about now.

In the distance, he could hear a train coming from the other direction.

"Phone, you whore," he snarled.

Her lip wasn't trembling. It tightened. Her dark eyes narrowed.

The knife went flying. He didn't know what was happening. Suddenly, she kicked him in the face. He saw the bottom of her shoe. Reebok. He felt his teeth bend inwards. Upside down, and as though at high speed, he saw Adib being thrown onto a bench and then slumping to the floor. He heard the small fry running away.

He found the knife and struggled to his feet. Fucking hell, he thought, running his tongue along his front teeth. They were angled towards the roof of his mouth. He could feel a broken root poking through his upper lip.

All he could taste was blood.

"You slut," he lisped, grabbing the knife from the platform and holding it out.

She was standing opposite him, completely motionless. He threw himself forward and grabbed the phone. In return, she kicked him hard in the stomach. Unable to breathe, he felt himself being pushed away, across the platform. He heard the train. He saw the lights appear in the tunnel.

He was struggling like a madman. His arms were flailing, his chin grazing the platform. He was fighting for his life but there was nothing to fight against. His body was pushed out over the edge, slowly, inexorably slowly, and the increasingly loud noise from the metro became a deafening, maddening scream — the last sound Hamid would ever hear.

And just like that, he became a split personality.

CHAPTER
EIGHT

The little dears were drinking water. Like cute little bear cubs, they crouched awkwardly down and lapped at it, their tiny pink tongues like kittens'. They were the kind of animal children wanted to take home and cuddle.

Though that would have been an unwise move on the part of the parents.

The little dears were wolverines.

Paul Hjelm watched them wander off, slightly pudgy and happily swishing their squirrel-like tails. He really was struggling to picture these good-natured little things chewing on a human skull.

"Come on," Jorge Chavez said impatiently. "Don't let them hypnotise you. Think of Ellroy."

Hjelm leaned back against the wooden railing, took a deep breath and asked, loudly and clearly: "Who the hell is Ellroy?"

But by then Chavez had already left Skansen's wolverine enclosure and moved on to the wolves on the other side of the road. When Hjelm caught up with him, Chavez said: "The wolf pen is pretty big. It stretches all the way from the lynxes. Ends right here. So what happened?"

It had stopped raining but the ground was still dangerously sodden. They turned at the edge of the wolf enclosure and every step they took was treacherous; a slippery downhill slope stretching all the way to the outer fence. A gangly man dressed in overalls and protective goggles was squatting by something which looked like a gate. He was busy welding. Bluish flames curled up around him like a stray firework.

They waited for him to finish. The firework fizzled out. He pushed his goggles — more like a face mask with built-in glasses — up onto his head. They cleared their throats and he turned round.

"Hi," said Hjelm. "We're from the police."

The man in overalls nodded quickly and looked like he was about to get back to work. Chavez grabbed his shoulder.

"One minute," he said. "What happened here?"

The man took off his mask, stood up and stared down at Chavez.

"I think it costs a fortune to get into Skansen these days too," the man said. "And then the kids want to go into that bloody aquarium as well, to see that man with the beard from TV. That's five hundred gone, just like that. And then you've got to eat and ride those stupid cars and buy tickets to win all that Pokémon crap Nintendo makes millions and millions from, and then you're suddenly nearing a thousand. So then you wish you'd just gone to the theme park next door instead, but if you'd done that it would've been a few thousand

92

more gone up in smoke. Though at least you would've been able to go on that free-fall ride."

Both policemen turned round in confusion to check whether the man was talking to someone behind them. There was no one there.

"Sorry," Hjelm said. "I don't understand . . ."

"Someone cut the wire to get in," the man said, nodding towards the mesh fence. "And I can understand why."

"When did it happen?"

"They found it yesterday, apparently. I don't work here."

"It looks like you work —"

The tall man in overalls sighed deeply.

"I'm from the fence company. We're repairing it temporarily. It's Friday — we can't deliver the new fence before the start of next week."

"So this happened — when? Wednesday night?"

"Must've been. And two days later, we've got a couple of plain-clothes policemen on the scene to catch the trespassers. Nice to see such good priorities in these austere times. Don't you think they might've disappeared by now?"

"Yes," said Paul Hjelm. "Most definitely."

A policeman in uniform came running out of Odenplan metro station and threw up at Viggo Norlander's feet.

So, Norlander thought, examining his new Italian shoes and sighing inwardly. It's one of *those*.

Once he had checked that his shoes had made it through unscathed and accepted the guilty police assistant's apologies, he turned to Gunnar Nyberg, who met his gaze with a look that said: Yep, one of *those*.

One of *those* cases.

They had been interviewing asylum seekers in the Norrboda Motell in Slagsta when Hultin had called to say: "I think we've got something you should go and take a look at."

And so they had driven back into town.

As they ducked beneath the blue-and-white plastic tape and went below ground, closely followed by the sniffing, ashen-faced police assistant, Viggo Norlander was thinking about sick. The past year had practically been drenched in the stuff. Just think, he thought, of the difference between adult and child vomit. And how different they were from baby sick in particular — that thin, white, almost pleasant-smelling liquid which washes over new parents like nectar. But then suddenly, it changed. Suddenly it started smelling like . . . vomit.

It was a defining moment in any parent's life.

It had happened recently in the Norlander household. Viggo, the out-and-out bachelor who had unexpectedly become a father at the age of fifty, had suddenly noticed one day that little Charlotte's sick smelled awful. It had been a terrible discovery. She would start walking soon, too. And with that, he felt ancient. He was struck by the realisation that he could have been Charlotte's great-grandfather.

Her *great-grandfather*.

For the first time, he started to wonder what it would be like for Charlotte, having such old parents. The thought threw him into a crisis. One which lasted a few minutes. For Viggo Norlander, that was an unusually long time.

The platform was completely deserted, an eerie sight. The station area had been cleared, with replacement buses taking the passengers between Rådmansgatan and S:t Eriksplan. But within half an hour, the train system needed to be up and running again. That was when rush hour began in central Stockholm. And when that happened, no number of replacement buses would suffice.

Viggo Norlander and Gunnar Nyberg had, in other words, just thirty minutes to try to establish a chain of events.

Hultin had phoned them immediately.

"Why?" Nyberg had asked.

There had been a moment's silence. Nyberg had recalled what Hultin had said that morning, during their meeting: "I'm starting to get very tired of all these vague hunches." Hultin was well aware of that fact.

"I know," he had said quietly. "It's vague. But it's not exactly something common, so I think you should head over there right now."

"Can we drive fast?" Nyberg had asked hopefully. As part of his new way of life, he had swapped his battered old Renault for a brand-new model. He had first owned a Renault 4 during his teens, a lethal box made from paper-thin metal, and since then, he had never given up on the French car make. It was a lifelong love.

"Yes," Hultin had replied compliantly. "You *should* drive fast."

And so they had. Slagsta to Odenplan in fifteen minutes. On roads with a serious risk of aquaplaning.

They sped smoothly underground on the escalator. In contrast to most of the other metro stations in Stockholm, the platform at Odenplan was spacious and airy. The ceilings were high and the platform open, with no walls separating the tracks in one direction from those in the other. A young man was sitting in the middle of the platform with a bandage around his head. Two paramedics with a stretcher were standing close by, plus three uniform policemen. There was a plastic sheet next to the escalator on the left-hand platform. Another policeman was standing beside it. Down on the tracks to the left, there were a few more plastic sheets. A forensic technician was moving around, photographing the scene.

When they reached the bottom of the escalator, the police assistant whose vomit had only narrowly missed Norlander's new shoes said: "I hope you're ready for this."

His voice could hardly have been described as convincing.

"No," said Viggo Norlander, crouching down and lifting the plastic sheet. Nyberg was watching him from the other side of the sheet and couldn't see what was beneath it. Norlander was completely still. His face unchanged, he lowered the sheet, got slowly to his feet and vomited on his new Italian shoes.

One of *those* cases, Gunnar Nyberg thought, handing a tissue to his colleague.

He steeled himself, squatted down and lifted the plastic. Beneath it was the lower half of a body. Satisfied with that observation, he stood back up.

"Did you find anything in the pockets?" he asked the policeman who had been standing guard next to it.

The policeman nodded and held out a sealed plastic pouch. In it, Nyberg could see a key ring, a wallet and six mobile phones.

"Well then," he said, taking the bag.

"Hamid al-Jabiri," the new policeman said. "Twenty-four years old. From Fittja. Two years for assault and aggravated larceny."

"Imagine that," Nyberg said, moving along the platform. Norlander was sitting on a bench, wiping his shoes. He let him sit. Then he took a deep breath and said to the policeman who had been standing guard over the body: "Should we have a look at the rest, then? What's your name, by the way?"

"Andersson," he replied, before pointing down at the tracks. "There are three more bits."

Nyberg jumped down onto the tracks, closely followed by Andersson, who continued: "The one closest to you's the worst. It's one big mush. The upper body and head. The head's really not pretty."

Nyberg lifted the plastic sheet and saw that Andersson wasn't lying. There wasn't much they could do there and so they moved on to the next sheet.

"These last two are the arms," Andersson explained. "Both of them must've been ripped clean off. They're in slightly better shape."

Norlander turned up, his face deathly white. Nyberg found himself thinking of Söderstedt, and welcomed him down.

"Back in the saddle," Norlander said, heaving heroically.

The two remaining plastic sheets were right next to one another, ten or so metres from the body. The first hand, the right, was holding a knife.

"Well, what do you know," said Nyberg.

The other was clutching a mobile phone.

"One last grab," said Nyberg. "I hope it was worth it."

Andersson placed the plastic sheet back over the arms and leapt energetically up onto the platform. He seemed remarkably unfazed by the awful sight. Nyberg and Norlander dragged themselves up onto the platform like fifty-year-olds. Nyberg was annoyed he didn't find it easier. After all that damned healthy food.

"Should we talk to his pal now, then?" Nyberg panted.

"Adib Tamir," Andersson nodded. "Exact same story: assault and larceny. Twenty-three years old. He's got concussion."

They were on their way over to the other side of the platform when a phone started ringing. Both Nyberg and Norlander checked their phones. It wasn't them. Nyberg glanced down into the plastic bag containing the six mobiles. He held it to his ear. It wasn't any of them, either. He glanced at Andersson, who shrugged.

"For God's sake!" Gunnar Nyberg exclaimed, charging back towards the tracks. Norlander and Andersson followed him.

They jumped down onto the tracks. Nyberg tore the plastic sheet from the left arm.

The mobile phone in the hand was ringing.

Nyberg bent down and tried to loosen the fingers. They were gripping the phone like a vice. Eventually, he managed to prise it loose. He beckoned for Norlander and Andersson to come over. They leaned in, their heads grouped like a team ahead of a handball match.

Nyberg pressed the green button. The three men were silent.

From the phone, an incomprehensible tirade began. A woman, speaking a foreign language. There was a moment's silence, then something which sounded like it was probably a profanity, then silence again.

The three policemen exchanged a surprised look. Eventually, Nyberg piped up and said: "Remember what you just heard. We'll try to write it down, each of us."

"Why?" Andersson asked, confused.

"Because that was a message to the murderer," Gunnar Nyberg said quietly.

CHAPTER
NINE

They seemed like nothing more than arbitrary clusters of letters. Letters thrown together at random. And the three offerings he had weren't especially alike.

Epivu, Detective Superintendent Jan-Olov Hultin thought. Was that just another arbitrary cluster of letters?

He was sitting in his plain, anonymous office as the rain lashed down outside, peering at three pieces of paper in the uninspiring, flickering glow of a dying strip lamp. It was half past seven, it was Friday evening, and as far as he could tell, he was all alone in the A-Unit's corridor in the police station on Polhemsgatan.

It had to be a Slavic language. Despite the differences between the three versions hastily scribbled down and despite the peculiar spelling, Hultin thought that the words looked Russian. Nyberg and Norlander had thought so too. Which other Slavic languages were there, other than Russian? Czech, Bulgarian, Serbo-Croatian. Was Serbo-Croatian still a language? Or was there Serbian and Croatian now? He wasn't sure.

They would have to call in a language expert. Present them with the unenviable task of working it out.

Still, it had been unexpectedly quick thinking from Gunnar Nyberg. He had gone from strength to strength as a detective, ever since Hultin had first brought the A-Unit together to solve the case of the Power Killer God knows how many years ago. From sluggish grizzly bear on a manhunt in the underworld, to modern, clear-thinking, newly slender online policeman.

Hultin picked up another piece of paper. Notes from the interview with Adib Tamir. He skim-read. Lone, good-looking woman of medium height; long black hair; red leather jacket; tight black trousers; black trainers. There had been a few other minor characters with them. Nameless wannabes. They had run off. First, she took down the knife-wielding Hamid with a kick. A kick to the face. Then she threw Adib, also armed with a knife, headfirst into a bench. He went out like a light and when he woke up, there were people screaming all around him. He saw Hamid's legs and his guts spilling onto the platform a few metres away and passed out again. When he woke again, the platform had been empty, save for a group of pigs. That was all. He had no idea who the small fry were. Hangers-on. There were always some. Hamid and Adib were the pros. Sure, he could try to help out with a sketch, but he had hardly seen her. She'd had her back to him until she turned round and broke the unbreakable in just a few seconds.

Closing words: "She must've been a secret agent or something."

Well, Adib, Hultin thought. Who knows? She *had* managed to grab an armed Hamid by the legs, push him like a wheelbarrow across the platform and hold half his body out over the tracks, just as the train was approaching. Then she had disappeared without a trace. Red leather jacket and all.

Though her mobile phone had still been in Hamid's hand. A real KGB agent would never have made a mistake like that.

Weren't the events of the past few days starting to draw closer to one another? Wasn't some kind of link starting to emerge?

Adib Tamir had been made to look at photographs of the eight women who had disappeared from the refugee centre, just in case: Galina Stenina, Valentina Dontsjenko, Lina Kostenko, Stefka Dafovska, Mariya Bagrjana, Natalja Vaganova, Tatjana Skoblikova and Svetlana Petruseva. He had shaken his head.

"No," he had said. "No, not at all."

"Not at all"? What did that mean? Hultin spread out the eight passport photos on the desk in front of him and examined each of them in turn. Ah, he admitted. He understood exactly what Adib's "not at all" had meant. These women looked *browbeaten*. Their eyes were dull. There was no life in them. Not one of them was a day over twenty-five, but each of them looked much older. Life had been hard on them and it showed. Like all the other Eastern European working girls flooding into Sweden and elsewhere in Western Europe, they had probably been prostitutes since their teens. An awful tidal wave of debasement was washing over the Continent and the Western world was playing an active part in the business.

102

For a brief moment, Jan-Olov Hultin felt ill. Because of his fellow men. Because of where he had been born. Because of his sheltered, easy life.

He got back to work. According to the technicians, it would be possible to trace the mobile phone contract. They had the SIM card. It wasn't Swedish, but that shouldn't be any real hindrance. Moving forward, they should be able to get hold of a comprehensive list of all calls, both received and made.

He was looking forward to that.

Until then, he would just keep working on the puzzle. They had the pieces, but the question was whether they belonged together.

A lot had happened in just over twenty-four hours. But that said, many crimes were committed across the country in any period of just over twenty-four hours. It was by no means certain that the three incidents had even the slightest connection to one another.

Strictly speaking, they weren't even certain that a single crime had been committed. The women might simply have disappeared from their motel in Slagsta; he would probably have done the same if he was being held in custody there. The man from Skansen might just have been running from his own drug-fuelled demons; even the newly discovered hole in the fence might be entirely unrelated. And the metro incident might have been nothing more than self-defence.

And even if they were crimes, the incidents didn't necessarily have anything at all to do with one another.

But, as we know, belief can move mountains.

And so Jan-Olov Hultin kept working on the puzzle.

First and foremost: why did it fit together? The A-Unit's collective experience and wisdom said — as good as unanimously — that that was the case.

It was true that Kerstin was teasing Paul a little via Jorge, but that was part of some private game Hultin didn't want to know about. He lacked the necessary curiosity. He could feel wonder, a thirst for knowledge — but not curiosity. As long as their private lives didn't encroach onto their work, he would leave them be. After all, he had a newly married couple in the team now, and that worked much better than people generally made out. Hultin wasn't really one for implementing directives or strict regulations; Mörner could worry about that. None of them cared, in any case.

He started over: why did it fit together? Because the entire thing stank of international criminality — Hamid and Adib were the closest to something Swedish they had. Because it had all taken place in such quick succession — a day and a half. Because nothing about it was normal — wolverine murder, missing prostitutes, violent women.

On Wednesday 3 May, at quarter past ten in the evening, a man who, in all probability, was a relatively high-level international criminal, had been chased through the wolf enclosure in Skansen; the value of his gold chain had been estimated at around three hundred thousand kronor.

The fact that his pursuers had clipped the fence to give themselves a considerably shorter route alongside the wolf pen suggested meticulous planning: they had *driven* him into the wolves; they were counting on him climbing the fence and getting out on the other side of the enclosure. They had found a way to be waiting for him up there. So in other words, they were probably *aiming* for the wolverines. From what Hultin could tell, the whole thing had been carefully planned — and the victim had acted just as they had hoped. The question was whether they were also counting on the wolverines getting such a kick from his drug-addled blood. If that was the case, it was utterly sophisticated.

They seemed to know their Ellroy.

On Thursday 4 May, at sometime after half two in the morning, eight Eastern European prostitutes had disappeared from the annexe of a refugee centre. In other words, a few hours later the very same night. Was there any possible link there? Sara Svenhagen might have been closest after all — even though a certain detective superintendent had attacked her "vague hunch". *If* there was a connection — and this still felt like the weakest link — then it would probably be related to one of two things.

One: that the Skansen man was their protection, and with him gone they were kidnapped or, in worst case, murdered. Two: that the Skansen man was a threat, one which had been neutralised, meaning the women could finally have their freedom. Either way, it seemed likely he was their pimp, whether a good one or a bad one. Though good pimps weren't especially common . . .

Hultin leafed through the printouts from the interviews at Slagsta. Like any good post-industrial employer, he counted them. Two from Norlander, four from Nyberg, seven from Svenhagen — and twelve from Holm. OK, Norlander and Nyberg had left the place a few hours earlier than the others, but the difference between twelve and two was still striking. Plus, he also had a number of reports from the women from the previous day. In total, thirty or so stacks of paper.

Thankfully, Kerstin Holm had summed it all up in a separate report ahead of the weekend. If he ever — against all odds — finally retired, she was looking more and more like his natural successor. She should probably have been made Superintendent long ago. Though on the other hand, so should Hjelm, Söderstedt, Chavez and Nyberg. Well, everyone but Norlander, he thought slightly evilly.

Two measly interviews.

He summed up Kerstin's summary. Unfortunately, no one from Slagsta could remember having seen anyone wearing a thick gold chain around his neck, nor a pale pink suit. Despite that, it was becoming increasingly clear that something had happened just over a week ago. Several of the extremely reluctant johns had noticed a change in the eight women's moods. They had seemed deeply uneasy but hadn't wanted to answer any questions. "She fucked like a bloody machine," as a habitual sex-addict security guard from the neighbouring area had said of Mariya Bagrjana.

Nice turn of phrase.

A couple of neighbours had recalled hearing a loud engine in the early hours of Thursday morning.

106

"Sounded like the bin lorry," an old woman with the unusual name Elin Belin had said, "but why would the bin lorry come round at half three in the morning?" The other neighbour, an unemployed butcher who, by his own admission, "hadn't slept more than six hours the last six months", had been insistent that it was closer to four when he heard "something like a bus — but on the wrong route, because we don't have a single useful night bus up here, and you, you're from the authorities, maybe you can pass my complaint on to the management". That had come from Viggo Norlander's meagre share of the interviews, which was strange, because who could mistake Viggo Norlander for someone from the authorities?

The most important information had come from the manager, Jörgen Nilsson. After some pressure — Kerstin had clearly come down quite hard on him — he had admitted that he knew of a pimp. Back in November, Nilsson had been contacted by a man who wanted to make sure he wasn't getting involved in the business; he was told that if he kept his mouth shut, he could have free access to rooms 224–227. From what they could tell, it seemed like Nilsson had made use of that free access an indecent amount. "A regular", as an agitated Somalian dentist in room 220 had sat up from his prayer mat to say. Holm had eventually managed to drag Nilsson off to the police artist to produce a good old composite sketch. They would be running it through all the registers they could think of tomorrow. Judging by appearances, however, this ghost pimp *wasn't* a match for their wolverine man.

The noise of a phone not only startled him out of his wits, it reminded him that his reasoning was wrong. The information from Nilsson wasn't, despite everything, the most important.

"I thought you'd still be there," a gruff voice barked down the line.

"You too, I see, Brunte," Hultin said as his racing heart slowly calmed.

"My name isn't Brunte," Chief Forensic Technician Brynolf Svenhagen said with great emphasis. "My ill-bred son-in-law has been spreading that kind of dung around, I suppose?"

"It's normally horses that spread dung," Hultin said.

There was a moment's silence at the other end of the line. Svenhagen was clearly searching for a crushing reply. Since crushing replies weren't exactly the stern scientist's strong point, he remained silent instead.

A telling silence, Hultin thought.

Eventually, and hardly sounding ready for battle, the chief forensic technician said: "Do you want this information or not? I've been working like mad to get it ready for you. It is Friday evening, you know."

"I'd really like it," said Hultin, pouring oil on the troubled waters. He even added a thanks.

It was enough to placate Svenhagen. He shot from the hip. "I've got a full list of calls made to and from rooms 224, 225, 226 and 227 of the Norrboda Motell in Slagsta. Is that of any interest to you?"

Despite the fact that it was of great interest, Hultin was more angry than overjoyed. He had, quite simply, forgotten about the telephones in the four rooms. Was

108

he starting to lose the plot? Were those gaps in time more alarming than he had convinced himself they were? Was it a blood clot, inching relentlessly closer to a much-too-narrow vessel in his brain?

"Are you still there, Jan-Olov?" Brynolf Svenhagen asked uncertainly.

"Yes," Hultin said, cheering himself up. "Fantastic, Brynolf. Can you fax them over?"

"They're already in the machine," Svenhagen replied self-righteously.

While he waited for the fax machine to rumble into life, Hultin glanced at his watch. It was thirteen minutes past eight — soon it would be exactly twelve hours since the hole had loosened up the space-time continuum. "Eight, sixteen and ten seconds. Peep."

Maybe he was already in the middle of the gap in time . . .

The fax started rattling and brought the good superintendent back to reality. Though he wasn't quite happy with that term.

Reality . . .

Hultin sat there watching the growing pile of paper, wondering whether it really was reality he found himself in. He stayed there a while, staring at the sheets jolting forward out of the machine. Krrr-krrr-krrr-pritt. The pile was getting big. Time vanished in hypnotic monotony. Krrr-krrr-krrr-pritt. Krrr-krrr-krrr-pritt. Krrr-krrr-krrr-pritt. Krrr-krrr-krrr-pritt.

A pair of eyes were staring at him through the darkness. He gave an unusually violent start and glanced down at his wrist. It was thirty-three minutes past eight — just like that morning, when it was actually only sixteen minutes past. My God, he thought. It's really happening.

Paul Hjelm was standing there in his much-too-thin linen jacket, holding an umbrella adorned with the police logo and with headphones in his ears. His hand, raised in greeting, sank uncertainly down through space-time.

"Is everything OK?" he bellowed.

"Don't shout," Jan-Olov Hultin said, staring at his watch. The second hand was ticking away — but wasn't it going abnormally fast? What was Paul doing here? Was it suddenly morning? Was it time for the morning meeting in the Tactical Command Centre? Had he been transported forward half a day by a black hole in time?

"Sorry," Hjelm said, pulling the headphones from his ears. "*Kind of Blue*. Miles Davis."

"You can listen to music in your free time," Hultin said, still confused.

Paul Hjelm looked at him searchingly.

"You don't seem well, Jan-Olov," he eventually said.

"What are you doing here at this . . . time of day?"

"I was just going home. I've been through all the material and I'll be damned if it doesn't fit together. What are *you* doing?"

Hultin was completely still. He ran his hand along the edge of the desk. Yes, he thought, this is reality. This is something I can feel. Space isn't time. I'm here, in time, in a different way to the way that I'm here, in this room. I'm here and I am now. To hell with the rest. He turned towards the fax machine. One last krrr-krrr-krrr-prritt and the pile was complete. He grabbed it, straightened the sheets against the desk and said, firmly: "Gravitational time dilation. You should try it sometime. Gives you perspective on existence."

Hjelm's jaw dropped. It was all very entertaining.

"Where's the phone from the metro station case?" Hultin asked sharply.

"In my room," Hjelm answered quietly.

"What's it doing there? Why don't the technicians have it?"

"I borrowed it when they went home for the weekend. I wanted to have a closer look at it."

"Great," said Hultin. "Go and get it."

"No fingerprints other than Hamid al-Jabiri's, apparently. How can you not leave fingerprints on your own mobile phone?"

"Go and get it," Hultin repeated.

Once Hjelm had disappeared, he glanced quickly through the enormous pile of paper the fax machine had spurted out. He immediately found what he knew he would find.

Hjelm came back with the phone.

"Put it on the desk," Hultin said with his own phone in his hand. He dialled a number.

The mobile phone on the desk started ringing.

It didn't feel like a surprise.

"Now," said Detective Superintendent Jan-Olov Hultin, "this is a case."

CHAPTER
TEN

It was the weekend. The Special Unit for Violent Crimes of an International Nature was off work. The whole gang. Fortunately, the rain had moved away from the Stockholm area, meaning that all the usual weekend activities were possible.

Jan-Olov Hultin entered the woods outside his cabin on the shore of Lake Ravalen, walking straight through the garden's awful collection of weeds, more wood-like than the woods themselves, and peered up at the returning migratory birds through his binoculars. It was as though space-time had split into segments.

Gunnar Nyberg was up with his son Tommy in Östhammar. He had taken his running shoes with him and managed one jog, despite his grandson Benny relentlessly clinging on to his grandfather. He had hung from his neck for five kilometres, really adding to his workout.

Viggo Norlander was in bed with his partner Astrid almost all of Saturday. Their daughter, little Charlotte, was there too, unceasingly trying to walk by shuffling along the side of the bed. Not for a moment did she stop to think about her elderly parents' peculiar activities in bed above her.

Kerstin Holm was taking part in a big concert with an orchestra in Jakobs Kyrka, where she sang alto in the church choir. During the Kyrie's dense golden minutes in Mozart's *Requiem* she felt her paper-thin skull vibrating, putting her in direct contact with the cosmos. *Kyrie, eleison. Christe, eleison. Kyrie, eleison.* That was the whole text. *Lord, have mercy. Christ, have mercy. Lord, have mercy.*

The married couple, Jorge Chavez and Sara Svenhagen, took a long walk around the Vasastan area of town, ending up in Vasaparken where they sat down on a park bench and began, initially at least, to soberly discuss the pros and cons of starting a family. It ended with them screaming abuse at one another. When an old woman with a cock-eyed wig called the police right in front of them, they went home to their newly bought apartment in Birkastan and made love uninhibitedly and wordlessly.

Despite all that, it wasn't any old weekend. None of them, not even Viggo Norlander, managed to go an hour without thinking about an utterly peculiar case.

That applied not least to Paul Hjelm. He and his family were out at the summer house in Dalarö. It had been a few years since they first came across the ramshackle old house with a fantastic little beach and its own tumbledown jetty tucked away behind it. The owner was an extremely lively but wheelchair-bound lady who happened to have been Sweden's first female boxer. Hjelm had never quite been able to work out whether she deliberately ignored the all-embracing rules of the market or whether the market simply hadn't found its way out there yet. If that was the case, the cabin was the last blank spot on the map. Maja — that was the former boxer's name — could have easily asked for three or four million, just for the plot. Instead, she rented it to the Hjelm family for seven thousand a year, choosing to stay in her little two-room flat in the centre of Handen. Once a year, she came to visit, spending the night in her old bedroom. As a rule, she usually went out to Dalarö the first weekend in May, before it got — to quote Maja — "much too sweaty in the knickers".

Now she was sitting on the porch, taking deep breaths of the chilly sea air and saying: "It really wasn't easy being a lesbian back then."

Since every visit involved a new surprise, Paul and Cilla simply glanced at her and waited for her to continue. She did.

"Yep," she said, throwing her strong, crooked arms around the married couple. "This is a proper little hotbed of scandal you're renting here, my children. My, my, my, the orgies we had. Not a bloke as far as the eye could see. Just a horde of skinny-dipping nymphets. The neighbours' wives were hysterical, though the men didn't protest too strongly, I can tell you that."

"A few of the neighbours' wives are still alive, I think," Paul Hjelm said.

Maja gave a roar of laughter and punched him on the arm. He instinctively knew it would leave a bruise.

"I always forget you're a detective," she laughed. "You don't look like a detective, Paulus."

"I think he does," Cilla said in an icy tone.

114

"Now now," Maja barked, "you can save your marital bickering for later. You've got guests. I'd love another Dry Martini, by the way. A bit drier this time, if you can."

"We'll have to distil our own then," Paul Hjelm said, glaring furtively at Cilla.

He stood up and poured yet another neat Beefeater for Maja, who was roaring with laughter.

"You're right, of course," she said, slightly more composed now that the drink had been served. "Those women seduced the gentlefolk, settled down on their golden estates — and ended up with a group of water nymphs as neighbours. Slightly unexpected when you've married into society and have been expecting a traditional family life. As long as any of them are still living, I'm not going to sell. And don't worry, my children, those old dears are hardy."

Cilla stood up and started fiddling about with something which absolutely didn't need fiddling about with. Her back to the table, she said: "I'll tell you why he looks like a detective. It's because he's always thinking about a case. He's never really present."

"Sorry for existing," Paul said maturely.

"A case?" Maja exclaimed blissfully. "So exciting! Tell us more, Paulus."

"Paulus," squawked a faltering voice from inside the cottage.

"Are the kids here?" Maja asked in surprise. "I thought you said you'd left them in town."

"Left them in town," the half-stifled voice harped.

115

Paul Hjelm sighed. "I live with a parrot," he said, casting a glance at Cilla.

She was still standing with her back to him and mumbled: "It must just have woken up."

"A real parrot?" Maja said with distaste. "So disgusting."

"Isn't it?" Paul said weakly.

"I don't like animals," the old woman continued, slurping her gin like a real sea dog. "Something from my childhood. People who're afraid of animals do exist. Not afraid of snakes or spiders or cows, I mean a general fear of animals — people who panic at the slightest contact with the animal kingdom. It's quite hard work."

"You don't seem like someone who panics unnecessarily," Cilla said, still facing away from them.

"Panic might be a bit much," Maja admitted. "But it does exist. The genuine fear of animals. I've seen it close up. I brought a little city girl I was in love with out here, must've been the late fifties, and when I grabbed a frog from the stream she panicked and screamed and swallowed her tongue. I pulled it back out with the wobbler. A few years later when I saw her again, she said she could still taste raw fish in the back of her throat."

Paul chuckled, poured a big Beefeater for himself and said: "If I wasn't prevented from talking about the case, I could've told you something about a fear of animals."

"Fear of animals," the parrot croaked from inside the cottage. Paul and Maja laughed. Even Cilla couldn't stop herself. She laughed, sat down at the table with a thud, poured an enormous drink, took a gulp big enough to have been two large schnapps and said: "OK, for God's sake. I'm revoking your vow of professional secrecy. You might as well just get it out of your system."

And so Paul Hjelm talked. As darkness fell over Gränöfjärden, transforming the overcast day into a shimmering golden dusk, he told them about drug-addled wolverines and Eastern European whores, about the strange fate of a mobile phone thief and invisible pursuers in Skansen, about a macho woman in a red leather jacket and a particularly inappropriate manager of a refugee centre. Maja listened raptly, almost falling from her wheelchair on several occasions. Every now and then she added comments that were sometimes wanton, sometimes wise. The most stimulating thing was that even Cilla seemed to be listening, not just because she was slightly drunk and tired, not just because she had promised, but because she was genuinely interested in what he was saying.

When he finished, the sun was still hovering just above the surface of the water. Paul took Cilla's hand and Maja said: "Go down to the jetty a while, you two, drink in the atmosphere. I'm going to turn in."

"Can you manage it yourself?" Cilla asked.

Maja placed a hand on top of theirs.

"I'll lie on the floor and wait, if the worst comes to the worst. I've done it before."

They went down to the water. The jetty, which had suddenly gained a sinful past, stretched out into a glittering, orange-coloured glow, like the old black wreck of a ship in a romantic painting. Since there wasn't a breath of air in the bay, as far out as the horizon, and since a Dry Martini or two had lined their throats, the May evening didn't feel particularly cold.

When they reached the jetty, Cilla slowly took off her clothes, piece by piece, calmly and naturally, until she was standing naked in the deep orange light. Paul's thoughts started dancing. He looked at her slim, blonde body, surrounded by light; the body which had, by and large, shaped his entire sexuality. There stood the mother of his two children, each of whom was now old enough to have children of their own. And she looked young. Eternally young.

She slowly and sensually ran her hands through her messy blonde hair. It was a spring gift, that much he understood. He moved over to her and embraced her. She loosened his clothing, something she hadn't done for a long time. Eventually, he was as naked as she was and they stood there, entwined, on the ramshackle old jetty, the light gradually fading around them. He lifted her up and she wrapped her legs around him, allowing him to enter her. Darkness fell. She pulled back, hovering above him, and then took him in again, as deep as she could, and then he pulled out and lay down on his back on top of the clothes they had strewn on the jetty. She slowly lowered herself onto him, surrounding him, and something bigger than the two of them united them.

She rode him in time with the rhythmic noise of the small waves hitting the shore, waves caused only by the movement of the jetty on the mirror-calm water. The earth seemed to rise up, seemed desperate to move closer, seemed to push up towards them, and the dark sky sank down and down until it was perforated by bright spot after bright spot, and the light from another, underlying, better world drove wedges into the blackness, coming closer and closer and rising and falling, and with sound and movement and patterns spreading over the surface of the water, the moon casting a thin layer of light into the darkness, a jetty of light which carried them over to the better world; they entered into it and it smiled at them; all was light and glimmering and ultimately a powerful beam which spoke of something else, something better, existing here and now, and all sounds were just rhythms, streaming through the holes and openings in the heavens' dark blanket of light which spurted and came and emptied and exploded in sound which was light and light which was sound, and then it was all over.

After that it was very, very still on the little jetty.

A phone rang.

Their faces were joined. They didn't see one another, simply felt one another. He shook his head slowly and she nodded.

She was the one who nodded.

In her nodding was a deep, deep insight; he felt that as he rifled through the pile of clothes and answered his phone.

He didn't say a word. All she heard was the faint click when he ended the call.

119

"Your story wasn't quite over, was it?" she asked, stroking his cheek.

"No," he said. "It wasn't."

CHAPTER
ELEVEN

For five days now, he had been travelling. It felt like a lifetime. In a way, it was. But now he understood that his wandering was coming to an end. A transformation was about to take place.

The presence was stronger now. It had started to feel more physical, like an old friend he had been waiting for for a long time. More than fifty years. Two old, very old men, meeting one another halfway, each from their own side of a page covered with scribbles. It was as though he was about to arrive, to come home.

And someone was waiting for him there.

Waiting with unswerving loyalty.

It was all pictures now. They were rippling through him. It was the river of death; he needed to evoke them to be able to cross, to be given permission to die. All he needed now was a ferryman. That was who was waiting for him. That was who would guide him to the other side. He wouldn't stop until he reached the bottom of the funnel. Though anything was better than wandering, being forever unburied on the banks of a river which didn't exist. The wandering of Ahasver. But now the river was there. The eternal suffering could begin.

He was looking forward to it.

Every now and then, he managed to look up from the flood of images. To catch his breath. A chance to recall his route during those five days. Each day's travel formed a letter. The first had been "E", an upper-case "E". The second day's journey was a "P", that was what he had worked out.

The images were relentless. There wasn't much time to look up. The tidal wave washed over him but the story failed to emerge. The pictures didn't fit together. There was no order to it. As soon as any kind of order appeared, he would be ready. Then he would no longer need to travel.

There were arms on top of him, legs on top of him, thin, thin legs, thin, thin arms. He was moving through a pile of people. Dead people. One of the dead people is a man without a nose and he is lying on the floor of a living room in Tyresö; a hand clutching a kitchen knife pulls back and the blood flows from beneath the man without a nose, and on the wrist by the knife there are numbers in movement, on their way away from him.

He is upside down and a metal wire is being forced into his temple and he feels no pain, though he should be feeling pain beyond all comprehension. He isn't the one who is upside down, it's the man waiting with unswerving loyalty, on the banks created by the river of death. The book he is writing talks of pain, of pain, pain, pain, where does it go? Where does it come from? Is he the one writing his own book?

122

He opens the outer door of his house, and there stands a man without a nose, and then the man without a nose is lying dead in front of him. He sees an extremely pale man in uniform. The extremely pale man in uniform is holding a thin metal wire in his hand. Beside the pale man is another, darker man. He has a purple birthmark on his neck. In the shape of a rhombus. Behind both men, bathed in a strange, artificial light, he sees a third man, and the third man also has a thin metal wire in his hand, and he should see him, but he doesn't. On his wrist, the numbers are on their way away. The man without a nose says "Sheinkman", and he is standing completely still and watching him, and the man without a nose says "Sheinkman" once more, and this time he points to himself and cracks into an enormous smile which covers his entire face, and then he comes up out of the river and sees that the metro station is Sandsborg.

He was close now. The day's route is clear to him. A "U". Today, he travelled in the shape of a "U". The last letter. How did he travel yesterday? He would have to go in and travel through the previous day again. Slowly, it became a symbol. A letter.

As the train left the station, he realised that it was no longer moving through tunnels. It was out in the daylight. Though it was night now, so there wasn't much light. They were heading towards the night, he thought, feeling the presence with great clarity. Death was sitting beside him, travelling with him, and it was an entirely ordinary person.

But then it broke up — death's outline broke up. Why? Can't he die now either? Or wasn't it death pursuing him? Was it some other being?

Everything was impenetrable again.

A muddle. Arms, a man without a nose, three men with a light behind them, numbers on the move, a thin metal wire, an upside-down face, a book being written in, legs, thin, thin legs, a stench beyond all comprehension.

Yesterday's letter was a "V". As the train came to a halt at Skogskyrkogården station and he stepped onto the platform with shaking, unsteady legs, that much was utterly clear to him. It was obvious. He has been following an internal map.

Dusk fell slowly around him. Leaning on his stick for support, he crossed the street and tottered into the cemetery area. The street lights illuminated his path like beacons, and here and there, candles were burning on graves. There was less and less town here, more and more forest. Only the rows of gravestones separated the place from the woods. Beneath his feet, the dead were travelling. The trees, the bushes, the plants: all took their nourishment from the rotting bodies. For a moment, he imagined that the vegetation seemed different to elsewhere.

As though plants nourished on bodies took on a different shape.

He tottered on through the evening. The scent of newly bloomed spring mixed with the stench of the past. There was an air of putrefaction hanging over the

124

cemetery. Christian graves had always made him uneasy — finally, he was starting to understand why.

The strangely shaped trees were completely motionless. There wasn't a single breath of air. Still, he felt some kind of presence which was no longer the comforting presence of death. The safety of death had left him now. The presence was utterly tangible but still only vague, like a mirage. Things that seemed to be moving at the edge of his field of vision.

He wouldn't let terror take hold of him. He couldn't get bogged down in the mire of fear. He dragged himself up, above the surface. Mental gymnastics. For five days now, he had been travelling. His journey was still missing a letter. The middle letter. The journey from the day before yesterday. He recalled it as he shuffled on through the big cemetery. An animal made itself heard. An owl, hooting.

He remembered that he got off the metro and made a pointless little trip on the bus in the far north of the city. That it was in the shape of a ring — or a dot.

The dot above an i.

The third letter was an "i". That meant that all of the letters, aside from the opening "E", were small. Lower case.

Without realising it, he had left the Christian graves behind. He had reached Bet Hachajim, the Jewish congregation's area of the cemetery. Södra Begravningsplatsen. There were small stones on some of the graves. At the top of the headstones, two Hebrew letters: "Here lies". At the bottom, five Hebrew letters meaning: "May his/her soul be bound up in the bond of eternal life." It felt like home. And yet it didn't at all.

Then, out of the corner of his eye, he saw a shadow move behind a tree. Then another.

He stood still. The owl hooted again. It was the sound of death, completely logical. He stood there, putting his five days' journeys in order. Five letters, each taking its place behind the preceding one like playing cards. First "E" and then "p", then "i" and "v", and finally "u". "Epivu".

Utterly meaningless. How tragic, dying with yet another unsolvable riddle on his lips. He laughed silently. Gallows humour.

But then the incredible happened: the pictures started to arrange themselves in order, like playing cards, in perfectly clear order.

He started moving again. Not much movement. He tottered, half hanging from his cane. All around him, nature seemed to be enveloped in shifting shadows, the trees seemed to be moving, a forest drawing closer, and he grabbed the first playing card and glanced at it.

His entire life changed character.

Then, through the darkness, he saw that several of the gravestones were lying flat on the ground. One of them was completely broken. Of course it was that one. The one he has always been heading towards. He laughed. He heard his own laugh and it echoed emptily. Incredibly emptily.

It was entirely logical that only that particular gravestone should be the one which had been broken. He knelt down next to it and peered up. In the distance, he could make out a couple of figures. They were shouting, throwing bottles and breaking another one of the gravestones over there; their heads were shaven. He snorted, touching the broken gravestone. It was a disappointment. Was that really his fate? Skinhead neo-Nazis? So . . . banal.

He glanced through the internal images, so well ordered by this point. This was probably just the clarity that came right before death. Life reviewing itself.

So, he thought. It was utterly, utterly clear. Of course. That was it.

Naturally, it wasn't something with which you could live.

And just like that, he also understood the letters. "Epivu". Of course.

It was simply a matter of changing your perspective.

That wasn't a dot above the "i".

And the skinheads weren't his fate. It felt good. More just.

"You've been hunting a long time," he said aloud, though he didn't know which language he had used.

"Yes," a woman's voice replied. "Quite a while."

He felt himself being hoisted up. It was pitch black. Ancient darkness. The ice-cold wind was whistling. His body was spinning. Everything was upside down. He saw the moon peering through between his feet. He saw the stars burst out into blinding song. And he saw the darkness darkening.

Then he saw a face. It was upside down. The man who had been waiting with unswerving loyalty for more than fifty years was a woman, and she was now leading him onto the ferry which would take him over the river of death which has finally, finally poured from within him. He was the one who was upside down.

Then came the pain.

A half-century late.

And it was exactly as he imagined it would be.

CHAPTER
TWELVE

"For God's sake," said Jan-Olov Hultin. "Is that gin I can smell?"

"No, not at all," Paul Hjelm replied. "Dry Martini."

The moon floated silently from behind invisible clouds and the place was transformed. It was no longer a damp, dark, ancient forest, crawling with invisible life; it was the barren, cruel place where death dwelled. With the emergence of the moon, the gravestones came into vision, one by one, until the scene looked like more like something from a poem by Edward Young.

Grave poetry.

"Are the others here?" Hjelm asked.

"The only one I could get hold of was Gunnar, but he's in Östhammar. The others had their phones off — and I don't blame them. You — how the hell did you get here? I hope you didn't drive . . ."

"Taxi," Hjelm said curtly as they wandered along the narrow path where the Christian graves gave way to the Jewish. Södra Begravningsplatsen. The gravestones looked slightly different — but essentially, it was all the same thing.

A place for the dead.

"Let's hear it," Hjelm said as they turned a corner and a cluster of uniformed policemen came into view. They looked ghostly in the faint moonlight. Around them was the obligatory blue-and-white plastic tape, and both detectives ducked under it into the circle.

"I'll start without words," Hultin said, nodding to one of the police assistants. He reached into the darkness and a bright spotlight burst into life. Hjelm was blinded. Somewhere in the burning, corrosive sea of fire which had replaced his field of vision, he saw a person. When the blaze abated, he saw — still with eyes half closed — that the person was upside down. He finally managed to open his eyes.

Things grew clearer.

An extremely old man was hanging from an oak. A rope looped from his bound ankles up into the tree. His hands were dragging in the gravel and his wispy grey hair was almost touching the ground, where a walking stick and a broken gravestone were lying. From his temple, a thin metal wire was protruding. A strange smile was playing on the man's face.

It was an eerie sight in the bright glow of the spotlight. Like the final scene of a play. An ancient tragedy.

"Jesus," Paul Hjelm said.

Hultin plucked the rope a few times, as though playing a double bass. A dull tone rang out through the night.

"Feet bound with a reef knot, polypropylene rope, eight millimetres thick, red-and-purple stripes."

130

"Racial killing?" Hjelm asked, pointing to the broken gravestone.

"Seems that way," Hultin replied. "There are a few tipped or broken graves over there. Broken schnapps bottles, too."

"No footprints," Hjelm nodded.

"No. Not exactly."

"No footprints in the wolverine pen, I meant. He was hanging like this. And wrote words in the ground with his bloody fingers."

"From what we can tell. Do you know who this is?"

"No. Jewish?"

Hultin pushed the old man's jacket sleeve back. His cuffed white shirt moved with it.

Down his arm was a line of tattooed numbers.

Hjelm felt himself grimace and recoiled.

"Oh shit," he muttered.

"Professor Emeritus Leonard Sheinkman," Hultin said quietly. "World-renowned medical researcher. Born in Berlin in 1912, making him eighty-eight years old."

"Strung up like this? Christ."

"Exactly."

Hjelm crouched down to get a better look at Sheinkman's wrinkled old face. Carefully, he poked at the metal wire jutting out from his temple. He shuddered and thought back to an earlier case in which terrible metal instruments had been pushed into heads. It wasn't a case he particularly wanted to think about.

"Bad blood comes back around."

Though they would never say so again.

"I don't know what that is," Hultin said, squatting down next to him. "But it certainly reminds me of something."

"Torture?"

"Maybe."

They stood up.

"We'll have to send Brunte back to the wolverines," Hjelm said.

"Doesn't seem much better . . ."

Hultin gestured to the police assistant by the spotlight and the glare vanished. They were enveloped in darkness once more. Their ability to see in the dark had been destroyed and the moon had passed back behind the invisible clouds.

"Witnesses?" Hjelm asked.

"I just talked to a family who saw a gang of skinheads running flat out through the Christian part of the cemetery at about half eight."

"Skinheads?" Hjelm exclaimed.

"It's their style, isn't it?" Hultin said, shrugging slightly. "Kicking Jewish gravestones over. Wouldn't be the first time."

"But this," Hjelm said, pointing to the old man dangling from the branches in the darkness, "*this* would be a first."

"True, but we've still got to find those skinheads."

"Sure. Of course."

The words were so small and irrelevant. It all felt so awful. Their shudders said more than a thousand words ever could. An old Jewish concentration camp survivor strung up and tortured in a Jewish cemetery in Sweden. It was beyond all words.

Could Swedish skinheads really have done such a thing? And if so, what was their link to the anonymous wolverine man in Skansen? Had skinheads really chased that — by all appearances — foreign-looking man through Djurgården's wooded areas in the same way that they must, in that case, have followed the old Jewish professor through the cemetery's?

It seemed . . . unlikely. It was true that the A-Unit had, not so long ago, been faced with a terror group made up of right-wing extremists, with contacts anywhere that undemocratic and inhumane activities held sway; and sure, they had seen all those so-called patriotic web pages which named well-known Swedish Jews they considered to be involved in the great, global Jewish conspiracy — but this was something new.

It certainly wasn't normal.

With one final glance at the old man, Detective Superintendent Jan-Olov Hultin said, slightly unexpectedly: "Breathe on me."

Paul Hjelm stared at him.

"What?" he exclaimed into the face of his boss.

"Thanks," Hultin said. "I needed a pick-me-up."

CHAPTER
THIRTEEN

Kerstin Holm stared at the short-haired man and tried to look stern. It wasn't easy, considering it was eight o'clock on Sunday morning and she was suffering the after-effects of the previous night's blowout with some of the others from the choir and the orchestra — a night which had lived up to the Mozart family's party traditions. It had also been just five minutes since she was given a brief overview of the case. As she sat there, trying to look stern, she was also trying to bring together a lot of vague threads. It was a considerable balancing act, not least because she also felt awful.

"I know you're not really prepared," Hultin had said, having phoned and woken her to a splitting headache only forty-five minutes earlier; she wasn't sure she would make it through the day without being sick, much less whether she could carry out a proper cross-interrogation of a suspect who was, per definition, reluctant.

"But," Hultin had continued, "you're our best interrogator. And Paul will be there, too."

As though that was any consolation. Hjelm, sitting next to her, seemed to be in even worse shape than she was. Beyond all hope. She quickly read the papers in front of her and tried to look like she was ultra-competent.

She looked at the man sitting opposite her in the sterile interrogation room and tried to imagine him as a meticulous, sophisticated killer. It was hard work. He looked more like a petrified little brat. Though, she thought, hardening her heart, he was a skinhead.

"Right then, Andreas Rasmusson," she said, fixing her gaze on him. "According to our preliminary report, you were wandering about Central Station 'like a ghost' last night. And this morning, you've been identified by a family that was out laying flowers on their grandmother's grave in Skogskyrkogården at half past eight yesterday evening. You were seen running away from the Jewish cemetery, where ten or so gravestones had been damaged. We've lifted your fingerprints from a broken bottle of schnapps found at the scene. You're eighteen years old and you don't have any priors, so you should just tell us what you saw right now. If you do that, maybe you can keep it that way."

Paul Hjelm glanced at Kerstin Holm. He didn't feel well. She, on the other hand, seemed completely unaffected by the difficult circumstances and the ungodly hour and the previous day's activities. How could she be so unaffected?

Kerstin Holm felt like she was about to throw up. She stood up and said, with a harsh but somewhat stifled voice: "Think about what I just said for a few minutes."

And with that, she was gone.

Aha, Hjelm thought. New interrogation technique. Nice.

He glanced at Andreas Rasmusson. In a couple of years, he would probably have left the skinhead life behind him and become an ordinary member of society. He would distance himself from his earlier life but never quite leave the ideas behind. He would say one thing and think another. That was an explosive kind of existence. Sooner or later, it would all blow up in his face.

For a moment, Paul Hjelm thought about the State of Affairs. The Swedish State of Affairs. He wasn't quite sure he understood it. The market was king, that much was clear. Share worth had replaced human worth. And it wasn't so much a question of what that meant for the present day, since that was quite obvious: economic redistribution from the poor to the rich. It was money that earned money now, not work, and that money had to have originally come from somewhere.

Talk of ordinary people being free to buy shares was a weak alibi for being able to get on with the real business: in order for money to make money, it needed to be *big money*. But, of course, ordinary people didn't have big money. It was that simple. Ordinary people could earn thousands on the market, but it didn't mean a thing — except for in the public's view of the market. It was simply a matter of marketing. Playing the markets was just like playing Bingolotto. If you were lucky, you could earn a bit of money, and there was no problem at all with that. The marketing had succeeded. Virtually free of charge.

No, the question was what it meant in the long term. How would this unprecedented, general obsession with money change people?

Paul thought he knew. A fundamental change was under way. He had come across it so often at work. All forms of democracy and humanity were built on the ability to change places with the person you were talking to. That was all. Actually being able to see yourself in the other person's shoes, to take on their collective experiences. Only when that occurred did you have two human beings really facing one another. And what he had seen over the past few years was that this basic, simple ability was starting to vanish. A screen of some kind had appeared between people, and they had started regarding one another as objects. Investment objects. *What kind of return will my conversation with this person bring me?*

There was no world outside of economics. And without that free zone, the coast was clear to treat people however you wanted. The number of people without a conscience was growing and growing. That was what Hjelm thought he had noticed, anyway.

Though on the other hand, there were lots of things he thought he had noticed.

Kerstin Holm was staring at him from above.

"Knock knock," she said. "Anyone in?"

"Humans aren't the masters in their own house," Hjelm said, pulling himself together.

Her gaze lingered for a few seconds before she turned to the eighteen-year-old skinhead and said: "So, Andreas, what've you decided?"

"I don't know what you're talking about," Andreas Rasmusson said, his face pallid.

Pallid, Hjelm thought. Where did these strange words come from?

"OK," Kerstin said, straightening her papers. "We'll go to the prosecutor and have you put in remand, then. It'll be court after that, years in prison with all those ruthless immigrant gangs — you can look forward to life as an old jailbird."

She left the interrogation room, taking the papers with her.

Paul stared at the door for a moment. Then he got up and followed her out. He went into the room behind the two-way mirror and saw Andreas Rasmusson blinking confusedly where he sat. He had expected to find Kerstin there, but she was conspicuous in her absence. He stood there for a while, watching the skinhead. Like vague outlines in a sea of fire, the old man's upside-down figure came back to him. The grey strands of hair hanging down towards the broken gravestone.

He really didn't feel well.

Kerstin came in and stood next to him. She smelled . . . awful. He turned round in surprise.

"Christ," he said. "Have you been sick?"

"Why else do you think I've been running in and out like an idiot all morning?" she asked, her eyes on the mirror. "I had actually been planning on having the day off today. You don't smell so great either," she added, turning towards him.

"No," he said. "Probably not."

138

"Did he react?" she asked.

"He just looks terrified."

"New try?"

"I think so."

They returned. Andreas Rasmusson looked up at them without any noticeable reaction.

"Your retorts are normally more caustic," Kerstin Holm said. "According to your file, you've been called in for interrogation fourteen times and you've always put up some kind of a fight. Why are you so quiet today? Is it because it's Sunday? The Christian Sabbath?"

He looked at her without really seeing her.

Paul Hjelm said: "According to the police in Central Station, you were practically mad with fear when they brought you in. What did you see?"

"I want a lawyer," said Andreas Rasmusson.

Sunday 7 May was a peculiar day. Something that might have been called *passive chaos* was reigning in the corridors of the A-Unit. On the one hand, they had plenty of leads to be chasing up, from plenty of different directions; on the other hand, they had nothing concrete to grab hold of. It was Sunday, after all. The Christian Sabbath.

Waldemar Mörner, division head for the National Police Board and official boss of CID's Special Unit for Violent Crimes of an International Nature, had lost the plot. Since this was part of everyday life rather than some special weekend event, he had been running around the department without anyone taking the slightest bit of notice of him. He opened the door to Detective Superintendent Jan-Olov Hultin's office and pointed at the clock.

"Press conference in fifteen, J-O. Top banana."

And with that, he closed the door again.

Jorge Chavez and Sara Svenhagen, who had just been brought up to date on the case after having been unreachable all morning, paused at his expression. Top banana? What wisdom lay behind those particular words?

With a slight grimace, Hultin said: "He was actually a candidate for the Nobel Prize."

Two seconds later, the door flew open and Mörner's thick, blond hair — which everyone assumed to be a toupee — entered the room again. Thoroughly flustered, its owner snorted: "He was actually a candidate for the Nobel Prize."

Sara and Jorge stared at Hultin, who simply shrugged.

Waldemar Mörner continued on his way down the corridor. There wasn't much time now. He opened yet another door and peered in at two stout middle-aged men, throwing balls of crumpled paper into a waste-paper basket.

"What're you doing here?" he exclaimed in confusion.

"This is our room," Gunnar Nyberg replied.

"We've been called in on a Sunday," said Viggo Norlander.

And so they had. The entire A-Unit had been called in. Once there, however, there was little for them to do.

140

It wouldn't have been unjust to call the decision to bring them in — one which had been made by Waldemar Mörner — hasty.

"Where's Holm?" he bawled, the collective wonder of the universe behind him.

"Wouldn't be unheard of," said Nyberg, "for her to be in her room."

"And not in ours," Norlander finished.

Mörner rushed off down the corridor with his eyes on his brand-new, albeit very fake, Rolex. It was thirteen minutes to one. The world's press was waiting. Very soon, he would have to walk out in front of them and disclose information about the Nobel Prize candidate in six different languages.

No, there was something wrong there somewhere.

He tore open another door with excessive force. Still not the right room. It was the door to the women's toilets.

He was just about to plough his way through the rest of the police station when he suddenly realised Kerstin Holm was staring up at him from the sink where she had been splashing water onto her pale-looking face.

"What're you doing here?" he shouted.

"Shouldn't I be the one asking that?" she asked, gargling.

"You're actually just the person I've been looking for," he said in confusion.

"And ... ?" she said slowly, drying her face with a hand towel which looked like it had seen better days.

"I need you," Mörner said, sounding like an impassioned lover from beneath a balcony.

Kerstin Holm put the towel to one side, pulled a face and stared at him sceptically.

"The press conference," he explained, pointing at his fake Rolex. "We're in a bit of a hurry. Twelve minutes. No, eleven."

"You need a female hostage," she said in an icy tone.

"Exactly," said Mörner, not registering even the slightest shift in temperature.

"I'm ill," Kerstin Holm said, still drying her face. "Try Sara."

"But she's the baby."

"Even better."

Waldemar Mörner stood there in the women's toilets, thinking it over for a few seconds.

And so it came to pass that Sara Svenhagen, without having been brought fully up to date on the case and fresh from a session in the swimming pool, found herself standing behind a podium next to Waldemar Mörner and Jan-Olov Hultin, an enormous bouquet of saliva-drenched microphones in her face. She stared at the television cameras and felt her chlorine-soaked hair stand on end.

Paul Hjelm was in his office, making notes in the form of a system of coordinates, when she and her greenish hair appeared on the TV screen.

"Green?" he said.

"Chlorine," Kerstin Holm, sitting next to him, replied. "They swim a kilometre every Sunday. After a while, blonde hair goes green."

"A kilometre? Jorge?"

"Twenty lengths. Quiet."

142

Waldemar Mörner cleared his throat. That always boded well. Language lovers were in for a real treat.

"Distinguished members of the press corps and other honoured guests," Mörner began. "Since we realise that rather considerable demands will be made for official transparency in connection to the recent racial killing of a well-known Swedish scientist, active in the cerebral branch, we have decided to anticipate your utterly just demands and enter into a state of openness now, for we live in an open society and the resources of the police force are finite; with that said, we now await your finely honed questions regarding Professor Emeritus Leonard Sheinkman."

The members of the press looked expectantly at one another, hoping that someone else had understood. Eventually, a brave youngster said: "Who was he?"

Waldemar Mörner blinked forcefully and exclaimed: "He was actually a candidate for a Nobel Prize."

The picture vanished. Paul looked indignantly up at Kerstin.

"Now's not exactly the time to be revelling in Mörner's howlers," she said, putting the remote control down on the desk.

He would just have to agree with her. He saw a series of numbers looping around a wrist and felt a distinct sensation of unease.

"OK," he said, pointing to the piece of paper on which he had drawn a system of coordinates that looked like a big plus sign. "Four squares, four incidents. The horizontal line is a dividing one. 'Skansen' and 'Skogskyrkogården' above it, 'Slagsta' and 'Odenplan metro station' beneath. Do we have anything concrete linking the things above with the things below?"

"The rope links the two above," Kerstin said. "A reef knot on an eight-millimetre red-and-purple polypropylene rope. Anything else?"

"Not exactly," Paul said. "Maybe the fact there weren't any footprints in the wolverine enclosure. He could've been hanging upside down from the railing, I suppose, completely out of his mind on drugs and drawing in the earth with his fingers; Professor Sheinkman's hands weren't bound, after all. We need to check whether the technicians found anything like this when they went back to the wolverines."

He held up a long, rigid, millimetre-thick metal wire with a needle-sharp point. Kerstin took it from him and examined it.

"And this was . . . where? In his head?"

"Jammed into his right temple. We're waiting for more information from the brain surgeon helping Qvarfordt with the autopsy. I don't know if they're finished yet."

"Should we infer anything from the fact that this wire was found in the brain of a brain scientist?" Kerstin asked, putting the wire — not without a certain repulsion — down.

"Maybe," Paul said. "We'll need to speak to the relatives anyway. What about revenge for an old case of misconduct? Scalpel accidentally left behind in the cerebral cortex or something?"

144

The door flew open. Jorge Chavez came rushing in, grabbing the remote control and switching on the television. He sat down in the middle of Hjelm's system of coordinates, crumpling it.

"Look," he said breathlessly.

His wife's face filled the television screen. Her short, straggly hair had an undeniable greenish tinge to it.

"I understand what you mean," Sara Svenhagen said to the crowd, "but at present we have no reason whatsoever to suspect that the Kentucky Killer has struck again."

"What does she know about the Kentucky Killer?" Paul Hjelm asked darkly.

"Everything I know," Jorge said. "Quiet."

"We aren't even certain it's race-related," Sara continued. "It's too early to speculate."

"Though judging by appearances, it's a racial killing," Waldemar Mörner interrupted. "We've already arrested a suspect."

In the right-hand corner of the screen, half of Hultin's face came into view. It was twisted, as though he had just passed half a dozen kidney stones.

"For God's sake!" Paul Hjelm said, throwing his pen at the wall.

"You've arrested a suspect?" at least six members of the press clamoured. One of them, a fierce woman from *Rapport*, continued: "So have you been sitting there lying to us this whole time?"

There was a moment of violent crackling. Hultin had grabbed the entire cluster of microphones and hauled them towards him.

145

"An individual has been brought in for questioning," he said in a crystal-clear voice. "We will shortly be bringing in more people for questioning. At present, however, no one has been arrested. I repeat: no one has been arrested."

"Waldemar Mörner, why did you claim that a suspect had been arrested?" the fierce lady from *Rapport* continued.

Mörner blinked intensely. His mouth moved but no sound came out.

"Can we move the microphones back?" an irritated technician piped up.

Jorge Chavez switched the television off. The trio exchanged glances which veered between rage, irritation and hilarity.

"How long is it possible for someone like Mörner to cling on to his job?" Kerstin Holm eventually asked. "Where's the limit?"

"Far, far away," Jorge answered. "She was good, wasn't she?"

"Television makes colours look brighter," Paul said. "Twenty lengths?"

"*Say no more*," Jorge replied in English, pursing his lips. "What're you working on?"

"Could you get up?"

"If you tell me what you're working on."

"I can't until you get up."

They had, in other words, reached a deadlock. A clinch. An unprecedented power struggle playing out between the room's two males. Kerstin Holm sighed

146

deeply. Eventually Chavez shifted slightly so that Hjelm could pull the paper out from beneath him.

"Draw," Chavez said, jumping down from the table, grabbing the spare chair and sitting down.

"I suppose so," said Hjelm, smoothing the crumpled sheet of paper. He pointed at the big plus sign and continued: "A little system of coordinates for the past couple of days. We asked ourselves if there was anything concrete linking the top part with the bottom."

Chavez pored over the paper. At the top, "Skansen" and "Skogskyrkogården". At the bottom, "Slagsta" and "Odenplan metro station". Between "Skansen" and "Skogskyrkogården", the word "rope" had been written.

"So the rope was the same?" Chavez asked. "I've been looking into it. The combination of colours, red and purple, seems to be quite unusual. But otherwise it seems to be a perfectly normal polypropylene rope, the kind you can buy anywhere. I've been in touch with a couple of manufacturers in Sweden and abroad and they said they'd send some samples over. Those should be coming this week."

"Eastern Europe?" Hjelm asked.

"That too, yeah. Russia, Bulgaria, the Czech Republic and a couple of others."

"Good," said Kerstin Holm. "Then there's the link between the two squares below, 'Slagsta' and 'Odenplan metro station'. The fact that someone in one of the rooms in the motel in Slagsta made calls to and received them from the ninja feminist from the metro platform. The link goes both ways, in other words. It was room 225, where the Ukrainians Galina Stenina and Lina Kostenko were staying."

"Ninja feminist?" Hjelm asked.

"It was a popular term a few years back. Nothing you blokes would understand."

"Nina Björk," Chavez said nonchalantly. "About the construction of femininity. She objects to certain strands of feminism — to difference feminism, those people who think there's a kind of innate maternity in women or ninja feminists who take man's weapons and turn them against him."

Both Hjelm and Holm stared at him in surprise.

"Clearly it's not just swimming you've taken up," Hjelm noted.

"It's more of an all-round workout," Chavez said. "All the muscle groups."

"Can we try to concentrate now?" Kerstin Holm said, turning man's weapons against him. "Some rational thinking please, guys. This is interesting. The last conversation between them came from our ninja feminist, who called Galina Stenina and Lina Kostenko in Slagsta at 22.54 on Wednesday evening. As you might remember, the bullet hit ten-year-old Lisa Altbratt in the arm at 22.14 that same night. It might not be a coincidence."

"Or maybe it is," Paul Hjelm said reluctantly.

"Think about it," Kerstin continued. "Our eight women in the refugee centre had been uneasy for a few weeks. Something happened. Then the first call from the ninja feminist to room 225 — that's Galina Stenina and Lina Kostenko's room — was made on the twenty-ninth of April, just about a week before they disappeared. We know she speaks some kind of Slavic language, judging from what Gunnar and Viggo heard on the phone. They were in contact back and forth for five days after that, nine calls in total. The last call was made to Slagsta just before eleven on Wednesday night; it's the very last registered call. After that, they must've discussed it among themselves in rooms 224, 225, 226 and 227 until at least half two in the morning. Then the women disappeared. But a couple of neighbours heard some kind of loud engine sometime between half three and four in the morning. The bin lorry or a bus that'd lost its way, they thought."

Jorge nodded enthusiastically. "That's the link then," he exclaimed.

Paul nodded too. Then he said: "Can we work out where our ninja feminist was ringing from? Was it always from Sweden?"

Kerstin leafed through her papers.

"What I'm reading comes from the four contracts in Slagsta. The list from Telia which Brunte faxed to Jan-Olov on Friday night. You can't tell where the calls were coming from using this, no — not whether she dialled a country code or anything like that. They're working on getting a list of calls from the mobile phone. I think it's possible to get that from the SIM card."

"So what does that mean for the link?" Paul Hjelm asked. "That it was the ninja feminist who threw our man to the wolverines?"

"Could see it that way," Kerstin Holm replied.

"Fine, so there are links in different directions," Jorge Chavez said, "but the connection to an eighty-eight-year-old professor emeritus, and one who survived Buchenwald at that — it was there, right? — how the hell does that fit?"

"Buchenwald," Hjelm nodded. "Yeah, Kerstin, what's the link there?"

"It ruins the whole thing," Holm said, throwing her pen at the wall.

"Don't pick up bad habits like that," Chavez said sternly.

"Who is she then?" Hjelm asked abruptly. "If we're assuming what we've said is right — who is she, the ninja feminist? And what does she have to do with eight prostitutes? Is she busy setting up some kind of mega-brothel somewhere behind the former Iron Curtain?"

"Of course," Kerstin Holm said sourly. "An anti-Semitic mega-brothel with a sideline in wolverines, right in the centre of Moscow. It goes without saying."

"Don't get sarcastic on us now," Chavez said, feeling like a bachelor again. "Let's save that for later. Should we try linking everything up before we go to the Sheinkman children? Three of them, aren't there?"

"Three," Hjelm nodded.

"Seems like a coincidence, one Sheinkman for each of us. Let's look at each part of your square first. Quadrants, I think they're called. Everything that needs to be done and everything we're still waiting for. Quadrant one: 'Skansen'. Left to do: identification. We're waiting for a response from Interpol about the fingerprints. Should come soon. Our man's in a crime

150

database somewhere, I'd bet my neck on it. The serial number from the silenced Luger has been sent to Interpol as well. We're also waiting for a response on that. What else?"

"The metal wire," Hjelm said. "The technicians collected half a ton of rubbish from the wolverine enclosure. It's been sent to the national forensic lab. Whoever finishes with their Sheinkman kid first can head over there. Maybe they've already found a sharp, rigid metal wire and just haven't linked it to the wolverine man."

"Under way with the rope, like I said," Chavez added.

"And then there's this 'Epivu'," said Holm.

"Oh God, yeah," Hjelm said. "That word's been bothering me for a few nights now. I'm getting absolutely nowhere with it."

"Summary," said Kerstin Holm. "Fingerprints, pistol, metal wire, rope, 'Epivu'. We're waiting for answers on all of them apart from the last one. We'll have to find an answer to that ourselves. Write, Paul."

Paul wrote.

"Quadrant two," Chavez said. "The empty one. 'Skogskyrkogården'. Slightly inaccurate, since it should really be 'Södra Begravningsplatsen', but we'll let that slide. Conversations with his relatives are about to take place. What else?"

Hjelm took over. "I guess the broken gravestones will be solved just as soon as Andreas Rasmusson starts talking. They probably don't have a thing to do with the case. A gang of skinheads probably just *happened* to be up to their repulsive business when an even more repulsive event came their way. Rasmusson's fear is probably the result of him witnessing something more awful than even he could've *imagined*."

"Two things," said Kerstin Holm. "First: modus operandi. Why such an unusual method of execution? Hanging someone upside down by a rope and pushing a long nail into their head, it's not the usual."

"No," said Chavez. "It's not usual."

"It suggests something really specific, doesn't it? That there's some kind of history. We'll have to look everywhere we can think of and try to find similar cases. If we don't turn up any leads, you can hang me up by the scruff of my neck."

"We don't want to do that," said Hjelm. "But a bottle of whisky would do."

"I won't say no to that," Kerstin replied tersely. "What kind?"

"Cragganmore."

"OK. Second: the murder scene. Going by Andreas Rasmusson's reaction, Södra Begravningsplatsen was also the murder scene; I don't think there's any doubt he witnessed a murder, nothing less. Sheinkman probably made his way to the scene himself. What was he doing there? Did he have any reason for visiting the cemetery? Was he visiting a grave? Was it purely coincidence that he was strung up right there? Which graves are nearby? Et cetera et cetera."

"Good," said Hjelm, writing on his sheet of paper. "Relatives, modus operandi check, brain surgeon's verdict on the impact of the metal wire on the brain, skinhead witness, other witnesses, check of the murder scene. What else?"

"Nothing else," Chavez said firmly. "Quadrant three: 'Slagsta'. Go through the rest of the incoming and outgoing calls to the motel — that's a whole load. Read through the forensic report on rooms 224, 225, 226 and 227. So far, not much has come up. Throwing money away, calling the technicians out. Must be female logic behind it."

"The vehicle," Kerstin said, ignoring him completely. "If something like a bus passed through little Slagsta at half three in the morning, it shouldn't have gone unnoticed. I'll put some uniforms on it."

"Great," Paul said. "Then we've got our phantom pimp, right?"

"Sure, yeah," Kerstin replied. "The john, aka the manager Jörgen Nilsson, was in touch with a pimp back in November. You don't want to know what I had to do to get that out of him."

"Oh?" Jorge said, utterly ignored once again.

"There's an e-fit being put through the system. Are you writing, Paul?"

"Non-stop. Phone call check, forensic technicians' report, vehicle, phantom pimp."

"Do our eight runaways have their passports, by the way?" Jorge asked.

"No, they were in the manager's office," Kerstin replied.

"Last quadrant, then," said Jorge. "The incident in the metro station. Can we get any more out of — what's his name? — Tamir?"

"Adib Tamir," Paul replied. "Gunnar was looking into that and I think he's squeezed him enough. The main point under 'Odenplan metro station' has to be the mobile phone. Hopefully its owner can be identified and we can get a list of calls from it. It's probably our biggest hope. And I've got to admit, I've been messing about with that phone — it's a good old Siemens E10, by the way — wondering how you can handle a phone without leaving a single fingerprint on it."

"Then there's the language expert," said Kerstin, "who has the dubious honour of discussing phonetics and Slavic languages with Gunnar, Viggo and a police assistant called Andersson."

"Do we have anything else?" Paul asked, scribbling as though his life depended on it. "Phone, list of calls, language expert."

"I'm wondering what we can get out of our ninja feminist's behaviour on the platform," Jorge Chavez said. "It all seems so neat. Bish, bosh and the people attacking her are gone. But then she leaves the phone behind. What happened? True, she was attacked by Hamid — he was waving a knife and everything — but still. Did she really have to carry him like a wheelbarrow across the platform and hold him out in front of the train? Wouldn't it have been enough to give him another kick in the face? He must've been groggy already. What happened? Pure sadism?"

"I actually think," Kerstin said, "that she was busy calculating. She was counting on the phone being smashed to pieces. It's a miracle it wasn't. According to the autopsy report, both arms went right under the train and were ripped clean off, bouncing along beneath the carriages. The fingers were like a shield for the phone, they stopped it from breaking. There's not a scratch on it."

"Siemens quality," said Hjelm. "Just think of the ovens."

"What ovens?"

"The crematorium ovens in the Nazi concentration camps. They were Siemens."

There was a moment of silence. A ghost passed through the room. The ghost of Professor Emeritus Leonard Sheinkman. It was as though he wanted something.

They shuddered.

"There's one thing we've forgotten," Paul Hjelm said after a moment, glancing down at his extensive diagram.

"What's that then?" two hopeful voices asked simultaneously.

"Isn't this Hultin's job?"

CHAPTER
FOURTEEN

It was Sunday afternoon and three different cars were en route to three different addresses. They had drawn lots to decide which. "Channa Nordin-Sheinkman, Kungsholmen" was written on the scrap of paper Chavez had picked; Holm's read "David Sheinkman, Näsbypark", and "Harald Sheinkman, Tyresö" was printed on Hjelm's. The three names belonged to the late professor's three children. Given that he had been eighty-eight when he died, not arriving in Sweden before 1945 when he was thirty-three, that put the children around the fifty mark. As much as ten years older than Hjelm himself.

Only once he was on the way to Tyresö did he realise that the address to which he was heading — a street called Bofinksvägen in a place called Nytorp — was identical to the address listed for Leonard Sheinkman in the telephone directory.

The old man must have been living with his eldest son.

Paul Hjelm ploughed on through the Sunday traffic on Tyresövägen and felt a certain relief at not having to be the bearer of bad news; Sheinkman's son could hardly have missed hearing about his father's awful death by now — it had been all over the papers and television for the past twenty-four hours. Hjelm just hoped that someone from the local police had stopped by to break the news before that.

The sun was low in the sky, which was an unusually deep shade of blue. Not quite like when a sly thundercloud camouflages itself as clear blue sky and dumps its heavy artillery on astounded sun worshippers with a dark laugh; it was more like a blue film had been stretched over the firmament, to disguise the fact that the sky was no longer blue. There was a dead weight bearing down on the pretty spring landscape and the light seemed artificial; as though an opera set designer had tried to imitate nature.

Or maybe it was just because Paul Hjelm was filled with dread.

Dread about having to barge in to a house deep in mourning. Dread about having to put all the usual questions to a grieving son. Dread about being a blond, secularised Christian, raised in a sheltered environment. And — here came the real admission — dread about having to bring up the Holocaust and concentration camps and European anti-Semitism.

He was Swedish, after all, and Swedes did not like taboo subjects. Their armpits started sweating. Ideally, they avoided them, but if they absolutely *had to* broach them, they did so with a kind of remote reverence and a string of clichés about never allowing it to happen again. The Holocaust was an abstraction they liked to talk about from a pedestal, using big words. They didn't like to tackle it properly. They hadn't been a part of it, they could never understand it, they had nothing to do with it, everyone else could look after all that. Sweden's lack of a sense of history and its pseudo-neutrality in an unholy alliance. Because they *had been* involved, to the highest degree. They *did* have something to do with it, to the highest degree. They *could* understand it, to the highest degree. They *had to.*

World champions at brushing things under the carpet.

Yes, Paul Hjelm admitted. His agitation stemmed from the fact that it was about him. Him and his pitiful, pitiful knowledge. Fragmented images of dead, emaciated bodies. Dates. 1939. 1945. D-Day. The Desert War. Stalingrad as the turning point. Sterile and doctored, like the laminated crash-landing procedures in the back pockets of plane seats. Docile and happy, we pull on our oxygen masks, breathe slowly and calmly and make our way to the emergency exits. Then, with grins on our faces, we speed down inflatable slides into the blue waves lapping invitingly beneath a clear blue sky.

Soon, though, all the witnesses would be gone.

There really was a great weight bearing down on the countryside. The blue sky wasn't blue. The greenery wasn't green.

And he had arrived, on Bofinksvägen in Nytorp.

The house where Leonard Sheinkman had lived, where his son Harald was still living, could hardly be described as luxurious. Still, it was pretty. An original functional house. A stylish thirties building, set back from the road, with a pretty sea view. Presumably an architectural original from those days when houses like that weren't just reserved for the newly rich, insistent on designing everything themselves. In line with their IKEA-tinged style.

He clambered out of the old Audi which, in the absence of any traffic, had been well behaved on the way over. He hoped his sweaty armpits didn't smell. There were two types of armpit sweat, after all: the kind that smells and the kind that doesn't. The odourless kind was the sweat of exertion. The other kind, nervousness. Time would tell which variant was currently pouring from his armpits beneath his linen jacket and pale yellow T-shirt.

Maybe he should have worn something more respectable?

Too late, he thought, ringing the bell.

A girl, aged around sixteen, opened the door. The same age as his own daughter, Tova. She was dark-haired and soberly dressed, and she looked genuinely sad.

"Hi," he said, holding up his ID. "My name is Paul Hjelm, I'm from the police. Are your parents in?"

"Is it about Grandpa?"

"Yes."

She disappeared. In her place, a well-dressed man in his early fifties appeared.

"Yes?" he asked.

"Paul Hjelm, CID. Harald Sheinkman?"

The man nodded and gestured for him to come in.

Paul Hjelm stepped inside and was shown into a room which he assumed was the library. Its walls were clad with books, in any case, and the otherwise unassuming room was dim and cosy. Perfect for reading. He immediately felt at home. He wanted to go over to the bookshelves and pore over their spines, but sat down on the old sofa instead. Harald Sheinkman sat down next to him. The closeness didn't even feel uncomfortable.

"He was nearly ninety," he said quietly. "I mean, we knew he might go at any time, but the circumstances . . ."

He fell silent and stared down at the rough pine table.

"I'm sorry for your loss," Hjelm said, feeling awkward.

"What do you want to know, Detective Hjelm?"

"First of all, whether you have any idea what he was doing in Södra Begravningsplatsen. Do you have relatives there, Mr Sheinkman?"

"No. On Dad's side, there are no relatives — for obvious reasons — and my mother's family are all buried in Norra Begravningsplatsen in Solna."

"So you don't know what he was doing there?"

"We reported him missing to the police."

"Missing?" Hjelm exclaimed, perhaps a touch too gruffly.

Sheinkman looked up. "I take it you didn't know? Don't the various police authorities talk?"

Hjelm thought for a moment. "I'll check why that information wasn't passed on to me. I'm sorry. So your father had gone missing?"

"Five days ago."

"Was that unusual?"

"He had his own routine and he was a bit of a loner, really. Plus, he had his own annexe, so we didn't necessarily see each other every day, but as far as I know he's never been away overnight before. Not since Mum died. We reported it after the first night."

"Your father was nearly ninety. Was he in any way . . . confused? At that age, it's not so unusual."

"Not at all," Sheinkman said, looking up. "He was a brain scientist; he deliberately kept his mind active so he could avoid all kinds of senility. The day he disappeared, he'd left the big *Dagens Nyheter* crossword behind. Solved down to the very last letter."

"Did you look for him?"

"I tried. I went up to the Karolinska hospital — he used to work there; I went to KB, he often spent time there."

"The Kungliga bibliotek?"

Harald Sheinkman smiled faintly.

"Most people ask: *KB? The pub?* But no, he never went to the pub. The library, on the other hand . . . Yes. He spent whole days there, as far as I know. But when I started looking, it struck me how little I actually knew about his daily routine. I'd been working too much and neglected him, and then it was too late. That's what I realised. I didn't know where to look. No one I asked had seen him anyway."

"And there was no indication of anything having happened? Nothing unusual?"

"No. And I can't work out what he was doing in Södra Begravningsplatsen, either. He was an atheist and materialist, through and through — still respecting

161

our Jewish traditions, of course — so I have absolutely no idea why he would go there."

"Can I ask how it came about that he was living with you?"

"It was the other way round, actually. This is my childhood home. He bought the place in the fifties, straight from the architect. Anders Wilgotsson, if you've heard of him? I'm the eldest son, so Dad suggested I could take over the house and he could renovate the attic. It was a good arrangement. Family ties and complete independence at the same time. Maybe a bit too complete . . . I mean, he disappeared without me noticing. And then he went and got himself murdered. It's unbelievable."

"What do you do, Mr Sheinkman?"

"Can't we stop with this 'Mr Sheinkman' formality? It feels a bit forced. My name is Harald and yours is . . . Paul?"

"Yes. Yeah, sure."

"I'm afraid I follow in my father's footsteps. I'm a doctor. Though not in the . . . cerebral branch."

Hjelm managed to disguise a hoot of laughter as a cough, followed by a peaceful smile.

"I take it you saw our esteemed boss on TV."

A similar smile appeared on Sheinkman's face.

"Not an especially dignified appearance, if I may say so," he said with a neutrality to rival Hultin's.

"No," Hjelm said. "Not especially."

"But they say you're pretty good. The A-Unit — is that really its name?"

162

"It's a pet name. A nickname — whichever you like. Officially, we're the Special Unit for Violent Crimes of an International Nature."

"Sounds like you're well suited to something like this."

"We are, unfortunately. What your father was subjected to has to be called a violent crime of an international nature. Do you know the details?"

"Yes," Harald Sheinkman said, looking down at the table. "It sounds like some kind of torture."

"Possibly. It's not something you recognise? As a doctor? As the son of a ... concentration camp prisoner?"

Sheinkman peered up at Hjelm with a different look in his eyes. It was as though he had just decided to cut the crap, to stop the euphemisms. Perhaps something was telling him to trust this anaemic policeman with serious sweat patches and a red pimple on his cheek.

He said: "I know very little about his time in the camp, actually; my dad was very reticent, as though he'd deliberately suppressed it. Plus, my competence as a medical expert is limited. I was a doctor in what we call the problem areas for practically my entire working life. I looked after people who had fled from torture and starvation and hardship. It was a round-the-clock job a lot of the time, often verging on unbearable. It was completely impossible not to take it home with me. Plus, I joined Médicins Sans Frontières and started travelling the world.

"By the end, I was burnt out. Utterly passive for a few months; it's only now that it's starting to affect

163

journalists that people have started taking notice. Health workers have been burnt out for decades. My wife left me and took our daughter with her, I couldn't pay the mortgage on our flat in Södermalm and had to move in with Dad. Out here. That was twelve years ago. I just lay here on the sofa, completely out of it. I was thirty-nine and had suddenly lost everything.

"That was when Dad had the idea of signing the house over to me and building a flat for himself in the attic. I suppose you could say it saved me. I started over. Built everything up from scratch. Got access to my daughter. Started working again, started writing too. I'm back up to my old workload again now, though it's a bit different.

"I started by writing reports on the current situation within the Swedish health care system and in the refugee-dense suburbs. It was hard to get anything published. I started writing . . . well, literature after that. I've had a couple of short stories published in cultural magazines and I'm working on a novel. You might say that I went in the complete opposite direction to my dad."

He fell silent. Paul Hjelm observed him. It had been a warning: that was how easy it was to get the wrong impression of a person. That was how easy it was to decide, in advance, what kind of person someone was. He had seen Harald Sheinkman as nothing more than the professor's son, born with a silver spoon in his mouth, and in some ways that was true. But in others? Not at all. It was a life lesson: never come to hasty conclusions about other people. It always ended badly.

164

He would have liked to say something to Harald Sheinkman about his thoughts on the present day. That we really did need to keep a close eye on contemporary right-wing extremism — but that history probably wouldn't repeat itself in such a *straightforward* manner. He was quite convinced about the return of fascism, but suspected it would probably take place in a much more subtle, indirect way — it would sneak in by a back route while we kept watch over its more obvious, simplistic manifestations — and then we would suddenly find ourselves standing face-to-face with a person but see them as an object instead, an item, a potential return. He was convinced that economism was the first step towards the new fascism.

But he said nothing. Instead, he became a policeman once more.

"In what way did you go in the complete opposite direction to your father?"

"I'm the doctor who became an author. He was the author who became a doctor. Before the war, he was an author — I know that much about his past. He was from Berlin and he had a family, a wife and a young son who died in the camp; so in other words, I've got a long-dead half-brother.

"His entire family was wiped out; he was the only one left. He couldn't cope with that, so he started over. You could say he turned the page on that chapter of his life. He'd been an author before, a fairly dreamy and lyrical poet, judging from his diaries, but after the war he turned to the natural sciences and to medicine. I guess he needed something more concrete and permanent. His soul died in the camp, but the material survived. I suppose that's one way of looking at it."

"He kept a diary in Buchenwald? Does it still exist?"

Sheinkman nodded. "Up in his room."

"Speaking of which," Hjelm said. "I have to ask, could I take a look at his apartment?"

"Of course," said Harald Sheinkman, nodding and getting up. Hjelm followed him through the house and up a spiral staircase which seemed to have only quite recently been installed. They came to Leonard Sheinkman's neat little annexe. It was bright and warm. Here, too, the walls were covered with books, primarily medical texts but also a number of literary classics. Just as Harald Sheinkman had said, the solved *Dagens Nyheter* crossword was lying on the kitchen table — nothing else. The place was clinically clean.

"Did you tidy up?" Paul Hjelm asked.

"No," said Sheinkman. "He managed all that himself. He didn't like disorder, that's my main memory from childhood. Always clean and tidy. It was really hard work. For Mum too, if I recall. Though I don't remember her so well. The memories are slowly fading. Soon there'll be nothing left."

"Is it OK if I have a look around myself? We'll send some forensic technicians over later."

"Of course," Harald Sheinkman replied, disappearing without a sound.

Paul Hjelm watched him leave. Then, slightly awkwardly, he began wandering around the little flat; he counted two rooms and a kitchen. The light was pouring in through a line of sloping skylights and each of the walls was leaning inwards. It was some kind of slanted existence. And that slanted existence was, without a doubt, impeccably well kept. Not a speck of dust in sight.

First a Jewish poet in cosmopolitan Berlin during the 1920s and 30s. Then a wife and family. And then the concentration camp where his son, wife, mother, father and all other relatives had died under awful circumstances. The man emerged an undernourished and tortured surviver. All illusions, all beliefs, all hope was gone. He moved to a new country, away from it all. He started over, from scratch. Learned the language, began a new family, got an education and a respectable job, became an esteemed researcher, bought a functionalist house straight from the architect, saved a son spiralling out of control and lived in the house together with him after his wife's death.

It sounded as though Leonard Sheinkman had managed the impossible — like such a remarkable number of others. He had managed to create a good, new life for himself. But how he had felt, deep down, that was impossible to know. His obsession with order and cleanliness was entirely natural after years in the concentration camp; you couldn't draw any conclusions from that.

Paul Hjelm needed to read his diary.

It was essential.

He eventually found it on a shelf, resting on top of a row of books; it was the only thing in the entire flat which seemed slightly askew. The yellowed, dog-eared, handwritten pages had been intensively read, turned and thumbed. The little book was no more than ten or so pages thick.

And it was in German.

An unforeseen obstacle. But compared with Leonard Sheinkman's achievement, it was nothing. It was simply a matter of brushing up his long-forgotten high-school German.

The pages were meticulously dated and numbered, and none seemed to be missing. It was just a matter of getting started.

Just . . .

He grabbed the little book and whirled down the spiral staircase. Harald Sheinkman was sitting on the sofa, looking exhausted. He stood up when Hjelm came spinning downstairs, walking over to him.

"This must be the diary," Paul Hjelm said, fluttering the pages. "Is it OK if I take it with me? You'll get it back."

"Sure," Harald Sheinkman said. "So you read Yiddish?"

Hjelm blinked, staring in confusion down at the yellowed pages. The words changed shape before his eyes. Then he looked up at Sheinkman. A faint smile was playing on his lips.

"I was just joking," said Harald Sheinkman. "It's German."

Paul Hjelm looked at him and started chuckling. He liked this man.

"One more question," he eventually said. "What kind of man was your father?"

Sheinkman nodded, as though he had been expecting the question.

"I've spent a while thinking about that. It's hard to say, really. When we were kids, he demanded a lot of us. He was always fairly strict, a classic patriarch. We were to be doctors, all three of us, there was never any discussion. His campaign succeeded, to an extent. It went best with my little brother, David; he works as a brain surgeon and lecturer at the Karolinska hospital, he'll probably be made professor soon. Later than Dad was, though. He's forty-three now.

"Channa, the middle child, she's the one who rebelled. She was active in the left-wing movement in the seventies; she's teaching in a school of social studies now. And then me, the eldest son, I obediently went down the medicine route but then refused to specialise in anything other than general medicine. He took it hard to begin with; he'd seen me as the chosen one. And when I started working in the poorer suburbs, in Tensta and Rinkeby, he just shook his head. But eventually, I think he found a certain respect for what I was doing.

"He wasn't an impossible person. When I came up against the wall, he was a real rock. When the whole world seemed to be falling apart, he was my anchor point. Our relationship was really good back then. He'd just retired and was full of life, and he'd finally managed to pull himself back together after Mum's death. He was a man who'd had a completely different life once, and we never made it into that life — not even Mum."

Hjelm nodded and held out his hand.

"Thanks very much, Harald," he said. "We'll be in touch."

"I enjoyed our chat, Paul," Sheinkman said.

"I did too."

On his way out, Hjelm said goodbye to the daughter. He found himself sitting, for a while, in his old Audi. He leafed through the yellow pages. Text which had been written inside a concentration camp, in the terrible Buchenwald. Leonard Sheinkman, the poet from Berlin, had somehow got hold of paper and a pencil and managed to keep it all hidden from the guards. It was a remarkable achievement.

He turned the ignition, left Bofinksvägen and drove out onto Breviksvägen. The sky was still clear and blue, but it was as though the film had been pierced and wiped away — and the sky was actually blue behind it. The weight which had been pressing down on the landscape had been evened out. Nature was peaceful and beautifully springlike.

Summer would come once more this year, in spite of everything.

His mobile phone rang. Jorge Chavez said: "Yup."

He said no more, but Paul Hjelm immediately understood.

"They found it?" he asked.

"The technicians managed to gather an unbelievable amount of stuff from the wolverine enclosure, I have to say. Everything from pieces of bread — as though the things were ducks — to rat traps. They found two rat traps in there. One of them was still set."

170

"It's a new pastime. Tormenting animals. Horses are regularly abused in our open countryside."

"Plus eight beer cans. The long, sharp wire was inside one of the cans. A drug-addled wolverine must've gobbled down the skull, found the wire in its mouth like a fishbone and somehow spat it out into a beer can."

"The Lord works in mysterious ways," Paul Hjelm said, heading home.

Home to the police station.

CHAPTER
FIFTEEN

At half eight in the morning on Monday 8 May, a miracle occurred in the police station in Kungsholmen, Stockholm. For the first time in the history of the world, the sun was shining in the Tactical Command Centre.

One by one, the members of the A-Unit entered the gloomy lecture theatre; one by one, they paused at the sight of the little patch of sunlight just inside the doorway. They crept reverently past it and headed for their seats, further inside the room. When the last of them arrived and closed the door, the little patch of sun disappeared. Viggo Norlander opened the door and just like that, it came darting back.

The people gathered in the Tactical Command Centre were detectives, not mystics. A cause needed to be ascertained and a miracle shattered. Joint efforts deduced that the little pool of sunshine had been made possible by five factors. First, the fact that the sun was actually shining outside. Second, that it was shining in through the window of the ladies' toilet. Third, that the door of the ladies' toilet was slightly ajar, having caught on a crumpled cigarette packet on the floor. Fourth, that the sunlight from the window in the ladies' toilet was also falling on the glass of a third-rate painting which had been temporarily placed against the wall directly opposite the door to the Tactical Command Centre, waiting to be hung in Waldemar Mörner's office whenever the aforementioned dignitary arrived. Fifth, that the sunlight hitting this painting of a bawling child was being reflected in through the open door of the Tactical Command Centre.

The door was closed. The miracle shattered. Jan-Olov Hultin let his owl-like glasses slide down his enormous nose until they were practically level with his invariably well-shaven upper lip.

"Good news," he said neutrally, "but we'll save that for later. Firstly, I want to apologise to Sara for being dragged into yesterday's TV debacle. A person should be thoroughly prepared before they take their place next to Waldemar Mörner."

"And a person shouldn't move an entire bunch of microphones."

Who had said that? Who was this reckless person who had, so daringly, stuck their head into the lion's mouth? They glanced around the room, waiting for the headbutt to come.

This time, their combined efforts deduced that the words had, in fact, come from Jan-Olov Hultin himself. Self-criticism? A drastic change of personality was clearly under way.

Was it a stroke? wondered four people whose names shall, for all eternity, remain anonymous.

"It was a bit of a surprise," Sara Svenhagen said mildly.

"Let's move on," Hultin said as though nothing had happened. "The forensic technicians' preliminary survey of Södra Begravningsplatsen gave us nothing. Not a single usable footprint; not a single fingerprint on the rope or the body. They found Leonard Sheinkman's fingerprints on a few pieces of the broken headstone below him, though. Should we just interpret that as a sign of pain? Or is it an indication that the gravestone had some kind of significance to him? Had he been on his way to that particular grave?"

"The name on the grave," Jorge Chavez said, "has been reconstructed as 'Shtayf'. That's all. We'll have to find out more about that body."

"That can be your job, Jorge," Hultin said. "What else? What happened with our skinhead, Andreas Rasmusson?"

Kerstin Holm glanced at her papers.

"Apparently he had some kind of psychosis last night. He's been moved to hospital."

"Under guard?"

"If you're arrested as a suspect, you're treated as a suspect. Yes, there's an assistant watching over him day and night. From what they've said, he seems to be completely out of it."

"I think it's very important we find out what those skinheads saw," said Hultin. "There must be some way of finding out who he was with, who he met that day, et cetera, et cetera. Gunnar?"

"OK," said Gunnar Nyberg.

"After you've been to the university, though. You and Viggo and Police Assistant Andersson are meeting a

174

Slavicist called Ludmila Lundkvist in the Department for Slavic Languages at ten o'clock. Get hold of Andersson and get yourselves up there to Frescati."

"*Da*," Nyberg said like a good linguist.

"Now," Hultin said with brutal neutrality, holding up a piece of paper on which a large plus sign had been drawn, "this diagram was sent anonymously to me. There are four segments —"

"Quadrants," said Chavez.

Hultin gave him a very long, very neutral look.

". . . four segments labelled, in turn, 'Skansen', 'Skogskyrkogården', 'Slagsta' and 'Odenplan metro station'. Beneath Skansen, it says 'fingerprints, pistol, metal wire, rope, Epivu'. Beneath 'Skogskyrkogården' it says 'relatives, modus operandi check, brain surgeon's verdict on the impact of the metal wire on the brain, skinhead witness, other witnesses, check of the murder scene'. I've taken the liberty of adding 'Shtayf'. Is that acceptable to my superiors in the congregation?"

"Yup," said Chavez. "Good work, young man."

Yet another tremendously long look.

Then he said: "Moving on. Under 'Slagsta' it says: 'phone call check, forensics technician's report, vehicle phantom pimp'. And beneath 'Odenplan metro station', it says: 'phone, list of calls, language expert'."

Jan-Olov Hultin stood up and moved over to the whiteboard. With a dramatic gesture, he spun it round so that the back was facing forward. It revealed the same plus sign as the paper.

"So let's use this anonymous masterpiece as the hub of the investigation. Don't let me stand in your way. If we work backwards, we've got the 'language expert'. That detail will be settled today. The following points, 'mobile phone, call list', are with the technicians, who are working on the SIM card and things like that. With any luck, we'll have the contract details and a list of calls sometime today. So then the previous . . . quadrant: 'Slagsta'. We've got the 'phantom pimp', the face reconstructed by Jörgen Nilsson. Viggo, you'll work on identifying him when you get back from Frescati. OK?"

"OK," said Chavez.

Norlander looked at him sternly and said: "OK."

"Then what does 'vehicle' mean? An unidentified vehicle heard in Slagsta at half three or four on Thursday morning. Not so easy, but interesting nonetheless. More neighbours to talk to, bus companies and bus departures from Sweden via different tollbooths to be checked. Does that sound unbearable, Sara Svenhagen?"

"No, it'll be fine," said Sara, sighing inwardly.

"I can answer the 'forensics' findings' point myself, because I went through the material last night. In the four motel rooms, they found — listen carefully now — semen from eighteen different men. Such is life in a Swedish refugee centre. They found a large number of fingerprints as well, but so far none of them have been a match in the database. That means that these eighteen men seem to be normal, respectable Swedes."

"Plus a neighbour or two from the Norrboda Motell?" added Kerstin Holm.

176

"There were no bloodstains, at least, no signs of violence. Physical violence, that is. Basically nothing. The rooms had been emptied of all personal items. Finally, the point called 'phone call check'. Could that be something for Paul Hjelm? As thanks for this."

Hultin pointed to the plus sign on the whiteboard.

"If I'm given time."

"You can have time," Hultin said neutrally, continuing: "Quadrant two: 'Skogskyrkogården'. The new point, 'Shtayf', is Jorge's. Then there's 'check of the murder scene', which is done: no answers. After that, we've got 'skinhead witness' and 'other witnesses': Gunnar will be looking into the other skinheads. As far as we know, there weren't any other witnesses, but the media's been blowing it up for a whole day now; maybe someone else will come forward today. We'll see.

"The cumbersome point called 'brain surgeon's verdict on the impact of the metal wire on the brain' is now in the material world — if incomprehensible in places. Qvarfordt reports in his usual style that: 'The eighty-eight-year-old body is well maintained for its age. No sign of atherosclerosis of any kind. Absolutely no sign of age-typical encephalomalacia. Unusually large cerebrum. Digits tattooed above the left wrist. Evidence of cervical spondylosis. Circumcisio post-adolescent. Rheumatoid arthritis, early stage, presenting in the wrists and ankles.

"The assisting medical examiner, a brain surgeon called Ann-Christine Olsson, continues slightly more informatively: 'The metal wire in the brain cannot definitively be considered the immediate cause of

177

death. It has been inserted via the temple and subsequently moved forward and back through the cerebral cortex. The cerebral cortex is the brain's pain centre — the part of the brain that makes us aware of pain. The result of a direct trauma of this kind to the cerebral cortex would result in a maximum pain experience. It is possible (though research is divided on this) that the pain experienced may be so strong that it results in death. The fact that the victim was also hung with his head to the ground may have intensified the pain, as a result of increased blood flow to the cerebral cortex. The cause of death is, as such, unclear. The heart stopped. This could depend on either shock or pain.'"

Hultin paused.

"On Sunday afternoon, a similar metal wire was found among the material gathered from the wolverine enclosure in Skansen. That means both our men seem to have been put to death by being subjected to such enormous, overwhelming pain that it took their lives. The pain itself killed them, in other words."

"Unless the wolverines got there first," Chavez said.

"True," Hultin admitted. "But this is worth considering anyway. If it's true, there must be a great deal of hate involved. Coming up with such a refined, painful method of execution requires a certain kind of man."

"Or woman," said Holm.

"Or woman," Hultin admitted again. "So the following point, 'modus operandi', is therefore of greatest interest. Has a similar method of execution been used anywhere else in the past? When, where, how? Kerstin?"

"Sure," said Kerstin Holm. "I'll try."

"The previous point, 'relatives', has already been completed. Kerstin, Jorge and Paul visited each of the Sheinkman children yesterday afternoon. The reports from each of them have been left on our desks. Can we have a summary?"

"I went to the middle child," said Chavez. "His daughter, Channa Nordin-Sheinkman, living on Fridhemsgatan in Kungsholmen. A radical woman with strong views. Child of the '68 movement. Had reduced contact with her father after her mother's death in 1980. She didn't have much to say, other than that he'd been an extremely authoritarian man whom she'd wanted to get away from as soon as she could. She wanted me to note down that she wasn't grieving. I made a note of that. She also offered me an enormous hash pipe. I want *you* to make a note that I declined it. It looked filthy."

"I went to the youngest son," said Holm. "David Sheinkman in Näsbypark. He'd largely taken over his father's work as a brain surgeon and researcher at the Karolinska hospital. Married, four kids between eight and seventeen. Unlike his father, he's quite religious and active in the Jewish congregation. He's taken responsibility for the complicated funeral arrangements and I got the impression he was grieving deeply. It seems to have been some kind of love from a distance, mind you. They only met on special occasions, and in quite a formal way. You could probably describe David

179

as quite a formal person. Zealous and restrained. I also got the impression his father had been quite like him. David Sheinkman's probably as close to Leonard Sheinkman as we're going to get, but he had very little to say about his father as a person."

"I think it seems like our best link to the family is through Harald Sheinkman, the eldest son," said Hjelm. "Leonard was living in the attic of his house, which had originally been his own. Leonard's, that is. Harald hit the ropes sometime during the eighties, divorced and burnt out. He's a doctor, not a researcher; these days he's an author too. A really nice man with a dark sense of humour. That kind of thing's appreciated. I went through Leonard's flat, though maybe someone else should go through it again. I can do it if I have time. I also found out quite a bit about Leonard's life before the war: poet, family man. I've written a proper report for anyone interested and I have his diary from Buchenwald. I'm planning on reading it. Though it's in German."

"Great," said Hultin. "In your spare time, of course."

"Of course."

"You're starting to look tired, but we've got one so-called quadrant left. 'Skansen'. Let's see what our anonymous artist has written here. 'Epivu'. We're no further with that than we were before. I'm assuming the word is etched into your brains by now, preferably into the pain centre. So, 'rope'. Being looked into by Jorge, I understand?"

"Yep," said Chavez. "Samples should be arriving from the various factories today."

180

"Then there's 'metal wire'. Found. Part of Kerstin's modus operandi check. Point number two is 'pistol'. As yet, no news on the Luger's serial number. But — and I started by promising you a little good news — the anonymous author's very first point is 'fingerprints'."

Detective Superintendent Jan-Olov Hultin had the room's undivided attention. He continued: "Interpol sent two matches for the wolverine man's fingerprints. From two countries: Greece and Italy. Our man was Greek. His name was Nikos Voultsos, born in Athens in 1968. First conviction for assault in Greece in 1983, when he was fifteen. Then there's a whole string of more or less serious crimes, including procuring.

"He disappeared when he was suspected of the murder of three women in 1993. That was when he turned up in Italy. Not that he ever really turned up. Nikos Voultsos was clearly under constant suspicion by the Italian police, but they could never track him down. He went underground in Italy — in Milan to be more precise — where he committed at least twenty serious crimes: protection racket, drugs, assault, rapes, murder. And then procuring again. In other words, our man is actually a pimp."

Sara looked at Kerstin. Kerstin looked at Sara. The glance they exchanged was a satisfied one.

"The details from the Italian police are quite vague," Hultin continued, "but between the lines, it might indicate 'organised crime'. And what that means in Italy is pretty clear."

"The Mafia?" asked Chavez.

"If we're being really precise," said Hultin, "the Mafia's a Sicilian phenomenon. Naples has its Camorra, which is similar. And then there's a northern equivalent, which is just as powerful. It seems as though Nikos Voultsos ran brothels for the north Italian Mafia. If we can call it that."

"And then he came to little old Sweden," said Kerstin Holm. "To run brothels for the north Italian Mafia?"

"And got himself eaten by wolverines instead," said Chavez. "That's what you call an alternative career path."

"The Italian police were clearly keeping an eye on him. They lost track of him in the middle of April. He died in Skansen on the third of May. It's easy to imagine the bigwigs in Milan thinking the attention was getting too much and sending him away. Like in *The Godfather*. Michael Corleone. But he was probably on a mission. It doesn't seem too much of a leap to assume it had something to do with the procuring side of the business."

Kerstin Holm was thinking aloud. "A week or so before they disappeared, the women in rooms 224, 225, 226 and 227 of the motel in Slagsta started getting uneasy. That takes us back to around the twenty-fifth of April. Maybe we can assume that was when Nikos Voultsos arrived? The first call from the violent Odenplan woman was made to Slagsta on Saturday the twenty-ninth of April. They called one another right up to 22.54 on Wednesday evening, not long after Voultsos died in Skansen. A couple of hours later, they disappeared."

"They were freed," Sara Svenhagen said breathlessly.

"She really *is* a ninja feminist," Jorge Chavez said, receiving a surprised look from his wife.

"If that's the case," Kerstin continued, "then she murdered a Mafia man. Once you've done that, you probably have to disappear sharpish."

"It all fits," said Paul Hjelm. "It's all coherent. But where the hell does Leonard Sheinkman come into it? What does an eighty-eight-year-old professor emeritus like Leonard Sheinkman have to do with a man like Nikos Voultsos, with north Italian Mafia whorehouses and ninja feminists with violent tendencies? Why was *he* of all people murdered in the same way as a notorious rapist and killer? It makes no sense."

"I agree," said Hultin. "Is it just a coincidence? Maybe he got in the way? Hardly. Someone hated him intensely, but it's by no means certain it's the woman you're calling the ninja feminist, whatever that is. The link to her is too vague."

"Do we have any pictures of this Nikos Voultsos?" Kerstin Holm asked.

"Of course," Hultin replied, holding up a colour picture of a swarthy-looking man with cold eyes. A classic gangster. He was smiling wryly, dressed in a summery light pink suit, and wearing a thick gold chain around his neck.

"I hope he was good," said Sara Svenhagen. "At least in that sense."

"If you go to Slagsta, Sara," Hultin said, "take this photo with you and show it to everyone. Someone up there might've seen him, despite everything."

Sara nodded silently.

"We're going to need to work more closely with the Italian police," said Hjelm. "We're still missing a lot of information."

Jan-Olov Hultin stood up and leaned forward over the desk.

"That's just the beauty of it," he croaked. "We've got a man on the scene."

CHAPTER
SIXTEEN

Anja saw it long before he did. Five children saw it long before he did. The entire world saw it long before he did.

That he had, just maybe, had ever so slightly too much "beauty" and "peace".

Arto Söderstedt wandered around the little stone house in Chianti, telling himself he was still enjoying it as much as ever. As the spring evenings turned into night, he sat on the porch with a small glass of Vin Santo, dipping his cinnamon biscotti and thinking: *I'm enjoying this*. And of course he was still enjoying it. Of course the regenerative powers of the Renaissance had been making their way all the way up to his rustic Tuscan bedroom. Of course marital life was blossoming like never before; he half suspected Anja might be planning a sixth child — what had happened to the usual preventative precautions? And, of course, it was still utterly agreeable to be able to sleep as long as he liked in the mornings, before diving into the books he wanted to read, the music he wanted to listen to, the wine and coffee he wanted to drink, the bits and pieces he wanted to busy himself with. But somehow, somewhere, it still wasn't quite enough. Somehow, the fruits of Uncle Pertti's money weren't quite enough.

Anja, on the other hand, was enjoying herself to the full, but she didn't make such a big deal out of her enjoyment. Arto possessed the male species' tendency to display his well-being to all — displays which have a tendency to consume whatever is being displayed. In the end, the show becomes the main event. And so at that moment, he was living in a shell made from the enjoyment of life. If someone were to inadvertently bump the surface, it would crack and break into pieces and Arto Söderstedt would find himself staring down into the deepest, darkest infernal abyss.

Well, not quite. But occasionally, as he sat there on the porch looking out at Anja's increasingly magnificent plants, it struck him that he was an addict.

A work addict in detox.

Anja had one passion in life — other than Arto, whom she probably loved as intensely as he loved her. Her second passion was herbs. During their time living in Västerås, she had pursued that passion with a burning frenzy; in the pots lining the windows on Bondegatan, things had been slightly more hesitant. But here, in Tuscany, in the heart of Chianti, in the immediate vicinity of the wonderful little medieval town of Montefioralle, crowning the hillside outside the wine capital, Greve — here, her passion was blooming. She never wanted to leave. The garden was bathed in the most delightful of scents. Her fingers were greener than ever and, according to locals, no one in the whole of Chianti had ever managed to grow sixteen different

186

types of basil. The fact was, they hadn't even known there *were* so many different kinds. Still, they were impressed, the neighbours.

The neighbours, yes.

But there was one person enjoying herself even more than Anja. It was Mikaela, their eldest daughter. She was sixteen years old and the most beautiful thing in the whole world. But one morning, she had come down to breakfast in their roomy Tuscan kitchen and no longer been a virgin.

Arto would never be able to put his finger on exactly how he had known, but it was undeniable. She was glowing. Her entire being was shining. He wondered whether he should take on the role of disgraced father, heading out into the bushes with a shotgun and blasting to smithereens every single teenage salami hanging from every single teenage body in the neighbourhood. But things didn't turn out that way.

All he did was smile a smile that was probably as blissful as Mikaela's; her own vanished the moment she caught sight of its own depraved mirror image. She ran out among the vines, thoroughly ashamed of herself. He followed her, shouting that it was all OK so long as she made sure the boy used a condom. Four white heads, each a different height from the ground, stood there staring at him as he shouted P-words at the vines. Even little Lina knew about P-words and she knew that they weren't good, but she didn't know exactly what P-words were. Porn words, the second eldest daughter explained, a glimmer of the forbidden in her eyes. Oh, said Lina, not knowing what porn words were either.

Eventually, Mikaela crept out from the vines with flame-red cheeks, like a Colorado potato beetle.

When Anja crawled out of bed and came out onto the terrace, her husband and daughter were hugging one another in the mild morning sunshine, flanked by four white heads, each a different height from the ground. Her herbs were wrapping the scene in a heaven-scented blanket, and birdsong was echoing between the olive trees. It was an image she would never forget. Paradise really did exist.

But for Arto, it was still just a shell. Anja could see that and so she secretly turned on the mobile phone. They would ring sooner or later, that much she knew.

And just a few days later, they did.

The Söderstedt family was in Florence at the time. It was their second visit of their stay in Tuscany. The first time they went, Arto had lost the plot in Michelangelo's Medici Chapel in the San Lorenzo Church and simply refused to leave. After half an hour in its handful of square metres, the rest of the family had had enough and headed outside. They had gone for a hearty lunch in a popular restaurant down on Lungarno Acciaiuoli, over by the Arno River, and then wandered back to Piazza di Signoria and Il Duomo and returned, after three hours, to the Medici Chapel. Their father had still been standing in the tiny space, his eyes fixed on its green-and-white marble walls.

He was convinced that he had suddenly, as though in a vision, understood all the secrets of the Renaissance. The restrained excess always present just beneath the surface of Michelangelo's unfailingly precise handiwork was hypnotic. Everything was possible — and yet all was not done. There was a distance there which wasn't aesthetic, but rather showed that now, right now, in late-fifteenth-century Florence, everything, absolutely everything was possible. They had to drag him away with force.

And so the family had returned for a slightly more normal visit. Acting more like a proper tourist family from barbarian Scandinavia.

They were sitting, looking out over the city, at a round table in a restaurant on Piazzale Michelangelo, on the other side of the Arno. Viewed from above, they would have looked like a perfectly circular pearl necklace.

That was when the phone started ringing.

Arto Söderstedt, who had been excused from driving, had ordered a bottle of wine and didn't react. The phone kept on ringing, and he continued not reacting. His family was looking at him with growing scepticism.

"Is Daddy dead?" little Lina asked, worrying that she might have said a P-word.

"Maybe, maybe not," said Anja. "It doesn't make much of a difference."

Finally he spoke, his voice robotic. "That can't possibly be my phone. My phone is switched off. Switched-off phones don't ring."

They waited. Time stood still.

Later, with a high-calibre pistol jammed into his mouth, Arto Söderstedt would look back at that moment and think: Then, right then, anything had been possible. Then, just then, it would have been possible to resist, and not just aesthetically. Right then, you could've resisted answering the phone. Everything could have stayed as it was, in a state of paradise which you, you rogue, foolishly failed to set any worth on. You had the chance to resist and you turned it down. It had been a terrible decision.

He answered: "Arto by Arno."

And with that, he was silent for exactly fourteen minutes.

"What about now?" little Lina asked. "Is Daddy dead now?"

Those were the only words spoken. Anja tipped the bottle of wine slightly, trying to assess just how much her husband had drunk. Deciding that it couldn't have been much more than a glass, she drank the rest of the bottle herself. It took exactly fourteen minutes. When he hung up, she said, perhaps not all that clearly: "I'm afraid I can't drive home."

To which Arto replied, with crystal-clear logic: "We've got to find a fax machine."

The family trundled off to a nearby luxury hotel, where he explained that he was a policeman and that he would like to receive a fax. The porter would long regret his readiness to help.

Söderstedt phoned Hultin on his mobile and told him the number for the fax machine. Soon after, sixty-five sheets of paper came tumbling out. The porter thought about ink cartridges and engaged phone lines, but maintained the expression of friendly indulgence he had been taught to wear. Once all of the sheets were gathered together, he was handed, to his surprise, one hundred thousand lire.

"Could I have a receipt for that?" asked Arto Söderstedt.

Having written his first ever tip receipt, the porter said goodbye to the strangest family he had ever met. Quite how it had happened, he didn't know, but he was one hundred thousand lire richer.

Milan was a big city in a completely different way to Florence. Everything was noisy. Arto Söderstedt weaved around in his big family car, always managing to return to the exact same place: a stinking refuse-disposal plant with flickering flames that reached ten metres up into the sky. No matter which way he turned the map, he couldn't understand how this damned refuse plant ended up as the absolute centre of the city.

Milan was, after all, a city which really did have a centre. It had been built in concentric circles around the majestic, almost grotesque cathedral, which Söderstedt eventually drove past. He chugged around like an exhaust-fume terrorist and, after some shilly-shallying, managed to find a parking space less than five or so kilometres from the police station on Corso Monforte.

That was where he was headed.

After a walk which was better suited to the name "city orientation", he made his way in through the entrance — and, in doing so, entered the fifties. The place was a time machine. Somehow, he had stepped into a worm hole and been flung back four decades. (It was, without doubt, the 1950s he found himself in.) Austere-looking men in white shirts and narrow black ties; women in dresses and high-heeled shoes; rows of desks where the main tools were pens and paper. And rubber stamps, of course. Stamps, stamps, stamps. Not a single computer as far as the eye could see.

He went over to a woman sitting at one of the desks and asked: "Commissioner Italo Marconi?"

Without looking up, the woman pointed to a closed door thirty or so metres away. As he walked over to it, he counted the number of desks he passed. He was on the verge of falling asleep on his feet. It was like counting sheep.

Sure enough, on the door, in minimalist letters, a plaque read: "I. Marconi". Short and sweet.

He knocked, receiving a muttering in reply.

He opened the door.

It had been hot and humid out in the big fifties office, but it felt much cooler and more comfortable inside Marconi's room. There was an ultra-modern computer on the enormous antique oak desk. Söderstedt understood. He had passed through the twilight zone and found his way back to the present.

The man behind the desk was in his early fifties, roughly the same age as Arto Söderstedt, and had a mighty moustache. His slender body made it seem even bigger, like a great big propeller in the middle of his face. Söderstedt was worried he might lift off at any moment and chug off through the window. The man stared at him, like Söderstedt was some kind of albino assassin from a terrible gangster film. Then his face lit up like the sun.

"I see," he said in English, walking the considerable distance around his desk and holding out his hand. "Mister Sadestatt from Sweden."

"That's right," said Mister Sadestatt from Sweden. "And you must be Italo Marconi."

"Yes, yes," Marconi replied. "I hear your country has animals responsible for killing one of my nastiest pimps. Could I import them?"

Arto Söderstedt laughed politely and was immediately confronted by a tricky-to-translate word. He couldn't for the life of him remember the English word for wolverine. Was it wasp? No, that wasn't it. Or . . .?

To hell with it.

"Yes," he said. "It was you, wasn't it, who was in charge of the investigation into the Greek, Nikos Voultsos?"

Italo Marconi's smile faltered; all his preconceived notions about socially inept northern Europeans had been confirmed. He made a gesture towards a chair opposite the desk and Söderstedt sat down on it. Or rather *in* it. It was quite soft.

"That is correct," said Marconi. "Nikos Voultsos was a particularly unpleasant criminal. Completely lacking a conscience. We were happy when he disappeared and we're even happier now that he's dead."

Plain talking, Söderstedt thought, before asking: "Was it you, Commissioner, who was responsible for the case summary which was given to Interpol and sent on to Stockholm?"

"It was," Marconi nodded. "Would you like some coffee, Signor Sadestatt?"

"Yes, please," said Söderstedt.

"I'll go and ask for some," said the commissioner, disappearing out of the room. He came back after a few minutes. It looked as though he had been laughing.

"The coffee will be here soon," he said, repeating the walk around the desk, sitting down, leaning forward and continuing: "I know my report might have seemed sparse, but there just isn't room for all the information in such a report. But I'm completely at your disposal — I just checked with my superiors. What is it you would like to know?"

"Was Voultsos a mafioso?"

Marconi spluttered. How to explain the national state of affairs to the village idiot?

"There is no Mafia here," he said. "It sticks to Sicily. We do, however, have local criminal gangs. Our assessment is that Nikos Voultsos was tied to one of these gangs."

"How was he able to commit a whole string of serious crimes without you even arresting him?"

"You really are getting stuck straight in," Marconi replied, observing his chalk-white counterpart. "It's important you understand a few fundamental things about the Italian justice system. We have to move slowly and pay close attention to where we step. There are always plenty of things to be taken into consideration in a whole host of different directions. I can't go into any more detail than that. The important thing is that we had Nikos Voultsos under surveillance."

194

"Were you watching his brothel?"

Marconi snorted with laughter.

"There are brothels and then there are brothels," he said, fixing his gaze on Söderstedt. "I can see that you are impatient, Signor Sadestatt. You've been without anything to do for too long, poking your toe in the dry Tuscan earth in search of pastures new. And now you've been given an opportunity. You're charging ahead like an addict on the hunt for his first hit of the week."

Arto Söderstedt wasn't keen on Marconi's turn of phrase. Not keen at all. But he knew what he meant.

Without raising his voice, but with his moustache about to start spinning, Marconi continued: "Your boss described you as one of Sweden's most intelligent policemen. I have no reason to doubt Signor Oltin — he sounded like a level-headed man. But he also pointed out that you would probably act as you have until now: hot-headedly. In a minute or two, my secretary will bring the coffee and a tiny little grappa, to toast your presence in Tuscany — a place which, for us up here in the north, also seems like paradise, if a bit boring. So let's partake of these drinks and see if we can't find some other tone for the conversation."

Söderstedt, normally so good at taking the bearing of a situation and breathing in the atmosphere, immediately realised that Marconi was right.

He nodded weakly and said: "You're absolutely right. I apologise."

That wasn't something which happened so often.

As their conversation turned to familial structure and living conditions, Arto Söderstedt began to understand what the Italian way of working was like. He was recovering from an accident.

A culture clash.

The coffee arrived. The tiny little grappa turned out to be a glass filled to the brim. Marconi raised his glass slightly and Söderstedt mirrored the gesture. He sipped the grappa — a good one, it tasted of grapes rather than industrial waste. Grappa, the Italian schnapps, was, after all, a by-product of the wine industry.

"Very nice," said Söderstedt.

"It makes me happy to see you enjoy it," said Marconi. "It's from your area, the Castello di Verrazzano vineyards up among the rugged hills to the north of Greve. Aside from this superb grappa they make, in my opinion, one of Chianti's best white wines, which are hardly a Tuscan speciality otherwise."

Then they sipped the magnificent espresso, the firm foam on which suggested that the police station had its own espresso machine tucked away somewhere in its jungle of desks.

"So," said Marconi, putting the little cup to one side, "now I want to say a few words about Nikos Voultsos. The events in Stockholm are more or less clear, and plenty of it fits with what we know about Voultsos and his employers. What doesn't fit in the picture is, of course, your Nobel Prize winner."

Nominee, Söderstedt thought, though he didn't say it aloud. He liked to think he had learned to sit. Even though he was an old dog.

"Well, from our side, you can't count on any link between Nikos Voultsos and" — Marconi read from a piece of paper — "Leonard Sheinkman. I'd also struggle to give you anything about the murderer's identity. That said, I can give you suggestions as to a motive.

"There's a kind of war going on in Europe, Signor Sadestatt. East, west, north and south are meeting, and that means several different types of criminality coming together — it means an endless war for control over the main spheres. Drugs have long been the most important, and weapons are big, of course — alcohol and cigarettes too; but data smuggling and the smuggling of stolen goods to the East — above all cars and boats stolen from the West — are relatively new. But the *really* big new market is *women*, and to a large extent Eastern European women.

"The big crime syndicates have only just started to realise that, and so they've started making serious moves into the prostitution branch. Talking about brothels is not exactly right — they do have them, of course, but they're secondary — it's more about controlling prostitution as a whole, from the most elegant of escort services to the weariest of whores on street corners.

"Sex is the thing we men are willing to spend most money on, more than alcohol and drugs. Maybe there's a glimmer of hope buried somewhere in that monstrous fact. Though hope is hardly the right word when it comes to the business itself. Prostitution comes increasingly hand in hand with drugs these days. They keep the women in check with drugs until they're worn out and then they just throw them away and bring in replacements from their inexhaustible Eastern European pool. What we've been seeing lately is that the women are being cast aside much, much quicker than before. These days, you're done being a whore by thirty. By which age, as a rule, you're also dead. At least if you come from the East."

Marconi lit a cigarette and held the packet out to Söderstedt, who took one without thinking. Since he had smoked a total of three cigarettes in his entire life, the grappa alone made the next ten minutes bearable.

That and Marconi's sparse information.

"So there's your background," he continued. "The Italian criminal organisations, though they've been overshadowed slightly by the Russians, have started to catch on to these developments in the modern slave trade. They buy in experienced pimps and send them out across Europe to take over independent groups of prostitutes. Nikos Voultsos was that kind of pimp, probably sent there by a crime syndicate here in Milan.

"As far as we know, the syndicate brought him over to Italy as early as 1993, after he murdered three prostitutes who tried to get away from him in Piraeus, Athens' seaport. The organisation in Milan, they're called the Ghiottone, realised he was someone they could use. I've spent my entire working life on that organisation and I've seen just how deep into north Italian society it reaches. That's why I've had to move forward so carefully.

"Everything suggests that highly placed individuals of all kinds are involved in the Ghiottone. And that's why I must also ask you to proceed as carefully as I have. One careless step from your side, Signor Sadestatt, and decades of work will be ruined. It's important you understand that. You look so white."

"I *am* white," said Söderstedt, realising that he was more green at that particular moment. "It's my nature."

He stubbed out the cigarette after smoking only half of it; that had to be enough to count as social competence.

Marconi looked sceptically at the cigarette and the empty grappa glass, and carried on regardless. "After a lot of work, we found the spider in the web; we're fairly sure that the brains behind the Ghiottone syndicate here in Milan is a respected old banker. He was active in local politics and is now one of the driving forces behind Lega Nord, if you've heard of it."

"Separatist party in the north which wants to split the country into a rich north and a poor south," Söderstedt coughed.

"Roughly, yes. I don't want to reveal the name of this man here, but the reason we left Nikos Voultsos alone, despite the fact that he was suspected of at least five serious crimes, is that we're after bigger fish. If we can break Ghiottone from the top then everyone else in the organisation will be biting the dust. Though it seems it was in vain. Your otters took that part of our job away."

"I see," said Söderstedt, feeling as though a pigment or two was starting to return to his face. Since he still couldn't remember the word for wolverine in English, he didn't bother to correct the commissioner's zoological mistake. Instead, he went on: "And the motive for Voultsos's murder?"

"Competition," Marconi said nonchalantly. "As I said, there's a war going on in Europe. For control of the prostitution. From what we can tell, it was an Eastern European crime syndicate with ambitions in Sweden which killed him. Using badgers."

Söderstedt nodded. Marconi was clearly planning on going through every single member of the marten family — other than the wolverine itself. It made him feel slightly annoyed.

Marconi held up what looked like a fax.

"Your assignment has been officially sanctioned, Signor Sadestatt. It seems you've been granted a provisional position with the European police agency, Europol. Formally, that means you have full access to my investigation. How is your Italian?"

"Not quite conversational," said Söderstedt. "But I can read it fine."

"Great," said Marconi, handing a cubiform box to his new Europol colleague, who stared at it in confusion. "A collection of CDs containing the whole Ghiottone investigation. I'm assuming you have a computer."

Söderstedt nodded. He had mostly been using his little laptop to play hearts, the banal but relaxing card game which came pre-installed with Windows. He very rarely won.

"You'll find the names of all the suspects, including the key figure, the banker. Your contract means you're

200

bound by professional secrecy and that any indication of anyone but yourself having access to these disks will be treated as a criminal act. Is that understood?"

"Understood," said Söderstedt. "One thing, though. The strange method of execution. Have you ever come across anything like it?"

"You mean the weasels?" asked Italo Marconi, smiling.

"No, I mean the wire in the brain. I mean the hanging upside down."

The commissioner nodded. He had understood. The whole thing with the otters and badgers and weasels was just some kind of game that Söderstedt hadn't understood — yet. But he knew that he would understand it soon. He resisted.

"I've actually put a few men on to that," said Marconi. "We're currently going through murders in our country, looking for similar cases."

"I suspected you might be," said Söderstedt. He thought Marconi would catch the appreciation hidden in that line.

Marconi's smile suggested that he had.

He stood up and held out his hand. Söderstedt took it. His respect for the Italian police force had increased markedly.

"I've got a feeling we'll be hearing from one another again," Italo Marconi said, stroking his enormous moustache.

"Same," said Arto Söderstedt, shaking the hand which had been extended to him and turning to leave. As he reached the door, he heard Marconi's voice.

"By the way, do you know what *ghiottone* means in Italian?"

Söderstedt turned round.

"No," he said.

"*Ghiottone* means wolverine," said Italo Marconi.

Söderstedt laughed.

Of course it did.

CHAPTER
SEVENTEEN

Andersson's first name was Hubald.

Hubald Andersson.

Gunnar Nyberg didn't quite know how to handle the fact that a sporty, tough and quite recently qualified twenty-four-year-old policeman with a look that could kill was called Hubald.

Now wasn't the time for laughing, in any case.

The dark little woman in her fifties was sitting in her office, looking Russian. "I'm Ludmila *Lundkvist*, senior lecturer in Slavic languages here at Stockholm University. And you're Detective Inspectors Gunnar Nyberg and Viggo Norlander, and Police Assistant Hubald Andersson. Is that correct?"

"Viggo?" Hubald Andersson said spontaneously.

"Hubald?" Viggo Norlander replied spontaneously.

At which both started roaring with laughter.

After that, Ludmila Lundkvist talked exclusively to Gunnar Nyberg, who was clearly a big, level-headed, handsome man in the prime of his life.

"Are you Russian?" the big, level-headed, handsome man in the prime of his life asked.

"Yes," Ludmila Lundkvist answered with a smile. "I'm from Moscow. I fell in love with a Swede researching Old Russian, Hans Lundkvist. We met when he came to a conference in Moscow in the late seventies. I took a long, winding road out of the Soviet Union and followed him back to Sweden, and then we got married. He died of testicular cancer five years ago. We never had any children."

Gunnar Nyberg probably hadn't been expecting such a detailed account, and he was still a little too fresh on the dating scene to realise that he was being flirted with.

"I'm sorry," was all he said.

"And you, are you married?"

"No," Nyberg replied in surprise, before adding: "Divorced."

Ludmila Lundkvist nodded with another smile, and placed three sheets of paper on the table in front of her.

"I assume it was you who came up with the idea of writing down what you heard on the phone, Gunnar?" she said.

Nyberg couldn't deny it.

"I thought so," Ludmila Lundkvist said, giving him a look that the vast majority of the male population over forty would have seen as sexy. Gunnar Nyberg simply felt confused.

"I want you to listen to two voices," she continued. "They're speaking two different languages that can sound quite similar. Here's the first."

She pressed play on a cassette player on the desk. A male voice began reeling off smooth-sounding diphthongs. There was a pause.

In that pause, Ludmila Lundkvist said: "The second voice will start soon."

The second voice began. It sounded similar but different at the same time. The diphthongs were smooth here too, but not in quite the same way. When it was over, the professor of Slavic languages continued.

"Which of those two languages did you hear?"

Hubald Andersson pointed senselessly at the cassette player. Otherwise, the room was completely still.

"It's the same voice saying the same thing in two different languages," Ludmila Lundkvist explained. "Gunnar?"

Nyberg still couldn't understand why he had been singled out as teacher's pet, but he felt the pressure. He delved back as deep as he could in his memory and said: "The second. Something about the sound pattern of the first one wasn't quite right. The diphthongs," he chanced.

Ludmila Lundkvist's face lit up.

"What about you two?" she asked with a neutral tone.

"Maybe," said Hubald Andersson.

"Perhaps," said Viggo Norlander.

The professor touched her lip and said: "My assessment of your rather disparate combination of letters fits with yours, Gunnar. It's the second one. The first voice was speaking Russian, the second Ukrainian. Most people don't even realise that Ukrainian is a distinct language, but it's spoken by fifty million people. It used to be called 'Little Russian' and wasn't recognised as a language in its own right until the start of the twentieth century. There's an obvious influence from Polish, by the way, and some of the sounds are midway between Polish and Russian. The most tangible difference in the sound pattern, as you quite rightly called it, Gunnar, is that the unstressed 'o' remains where Russian reduces it, and the Russian 'g' is a softer 'h'."

She glanced at the bewildered policemen and set the tape playing again.

While it was still quiet, she said: "What you heard were the classic opening lines to Nikolai Gogol's 'The Overcoat'. Let's listen to something else — my attempt at a reconstruction of what you scribbled down. It's me reading it, since it was a woman you heard. Listen carefully and try to work out whether it fits."

There was more silence. The cassette player was producing nothing but noise. Like a frustrated television reporter, waiting for a segment which never comes, Ludmila Lundkvist said: "It's coming soon."

And so it did.

Gunnar Nyberg may have been slightly influenced, but he did think that Ludmila's sensual voice sounded quite like the one he had heard on the phone he had wrenched from Hamid al-Jabiri's hand down on the tracks in Odenplan metro station. He said so.

"It's quite similar. It could easily have been like that."

"Yeah," said Viggo Norlander.

"Why not?" said Hubald Andersson.

Ludmila Lundkvist said: "If that's true, then the voice is saying — in translation: 'Everyone through OK.

Three seven two to Lublin.' Then there's that pause. And then she says: 'Cunt' and hangs up."

"Cunt?" exclaimed Hubald Andersson.

"Like I said," Ludmila Lundkvist replied grimly.

Gunnar said: "No names?"

"Unfortunately not, no."

"But 'Lublin' should mean something to you, Ludmila . . ."

"You too, Gunnar. You must've heard of Isaac Bashevis Singer, the only Yiddish-speaking recipient of the Nobel Prize in Literature? In 1960, he wrote a wonderful little story called *The Magician of Lublin*. Lublin is a city in Poland, on European highway number 372, one hundred or so miles south of Warsaw. And not far from the Ukrainian border. The E372 goes straight into Ukraine."

" 'Everyone through OK,' " Gunnar Nyberg said thoughtfully. " 'Three seven two to Lublin.' So 'through' probably means 'through customs'."

"That seems likely," said Ludmila Lundkvist. "But all together, it supports my interpretation."

"It's very convincing, in any case," said Gunnar Nyberg, standing up and holding out his hand. She took it, clutching it a moment too long. He could feel himself staring foolishly at her.

The three men were standing out in the shabby university corridor. There was nothing to look at, nothing at all. The lift arrived, its doors opened. Suddenly, Viggo Norlander said: "You're not taking this lift, Gunnar."

"What?" said Gunnar Nyberg.

"You're going to go back to Professor Lundkvist's room and ask her out for dinner this evening."

"What are you talking about?"

Viggo Norlander held the lift doors open, leaned forward towards Gunnar Nyberg and whispered: "You're probably a much smarter man than I am, Gunnar, but I'm better at this than you. I've rarely seen such obvious female desire."

Gunnar Nyberg stared at the closed lift doors for a long while.

Then he turned, back down the corridor. The sound of his pounding heart filled the corridor like African drums.

CHAPTER
EIGHTEEN

Three men in overalls were wandering around among the broken gravestones, carting away the pieces in wheelbarrows. They handled the lumps of stone like critically injured living beings, on their way to intensive care.

Jorge Chavez was standing in the shadow of the oak where Leonard Sheinkman had hung; when he glanced up, he saw that the bark had been scraped away from a branch about four metres up. He tried to work out how they had climbed the trunk. It didn't exactly look easy. The branches were thin and brittle, all the way up. Whoever had hanged the old man from the tree must have been exceptionally light, agile and strong.

And unbelievably cruel.

The sun was shining on Södra Begravningsplatsen, wrapping the scene in its redeeming light, but it would probably never be possible to atone for such an unsavoury, cowardly, wretched crime. The perpetrator would probably be doomed to eternal damnation.

The ground in a Jewish cemetery was, after all, eternal — Jorge Chavez knew that much. The cemetery, Bet Hachajim, is permanent and cannot ever be moved. It was a holy place, holy ground, eternity's courtyard, and it was bound up by a number of unwritten rules which marked its holiness: you couldn't eat, drink or smoke in the cemetery, you couldn't take short cuts over the graves, and your head should be covered, as a mark of respect.

He leaned down and touched the remains of the gravestone which had once read "Shtayf". He compared it with the other graves. They were all roughly similar. At the top, two Hebrew letters he knew meant "Here lies", followed by the name, date of birth, date of death, and a symbol, often the Star of David or the menorah. Right at the bottom of all the graves he could see were five Hebrew letters which meant something like: "May his (or her) soul be bound up in the bond of eternal life."

There was enough of Shtayf's headstone left to reveal that neither a forename nor a date of birth had been inscribed on it, only "Shtayf" and a date of death: 7 September 1981. The question was therefore whether this mysterious "Shtayf", above whose broken grave Leonard Sheinkman had met his death, was in any way linked to him. It was all a touch vague.

A long shot, like they say in American films.

But even those worked out from time to time.

Chavez stepped into the sunshine and hopped gracefully over the blue-and-white plastic tape marked "Police". The three men in overalls turned to look at him.

He had walked over a grave.

"I'm sorry," he shouted, holding his police ID up for them to see. "I'm afraid I cut across a grave."

210

The eldest of the three men came over to him. He looked Eastern European, Chavez thought with a certain bias — like one of the men you saw playing chess in the Kulturhus.

"You shouldn't walk over graves," the man said sternly, "and you should cover your head."

It clearly wasn't the first time he had uttered those words because, as if by magic, a small hat appeared from his pocket — a skullcap. Chavez took it and thanked him.

"You wouldn't happen to be Yitzak Lemstein, would you?" he asked, placing the skullcap high on the crown of his head.

The old man looked sorrowfully at him.

"Yes," he said.

"I'm Jorge Chavez, from CID. You're in charge of the cemetery?"

"Yes," said Yitzak Lemstein. "My sons and I take care of it."

"I'm very sorry about the night's events. Things like that shouldn't happen in Sweden."

"They'll always happen. At all times and in all places on earth."

Chavez paused, slightly surprised. Then he said: "I understand there's been a lot of damage over the past few years?"

"Yes," Lemstein replied laconically.

"I was planning on asking you a few questions, if you have time. You heard what happened to Professor Leonard Sheinkman here last night. Did you know him?"

"No."

"And you have no idea what he might have been doing here?"

"No."

"I've been wondering about the grave he was killed next to."

"When can we take care of it?"

"What do you mean?"

"When can we take care of the gravestone inside the plastic tape there? It's not well."

Chavez observed him for a moment. Then he said: "I don't really know. It's probably OK now. I can ring and check with our technicians as soon as you've answered a couple of questions about it. Who was 'Shtayf'? And why is there no forename or date of birth on the stone?"

At that, the old man turned his back. He wandered slowly back to his wheelbarrow and began pushing it away.

Chavez stood where he was for a few seconds, slightly bewildered. Then he jogged after him.

"Why don't you want to answer that?"

"It has nothing to do with you. It's Jewish."

"Oh, for goodness' sake. We think Leonard Sheinkman may have been on the way to that grave. This is important."

Yitzak Lemstein paused, set the wheelbarrow down with a clank and fixed his gaze on Chavez.

"Are you familiar with Jewish humour?" he asked solemnly.

"Not really," Chavez admitted. "Woody Allen?"

Lemstein sighed and grabbed the wheelbarrow handles again. Chavez placed a gentle hand on his shoulder and said: "I'm sorry. You'll have to explain what you mean."

The old man stood for a moment, his hands still gripping the handles. He sighed once more, let go and turned to the stubborn Latino policeman.

"Humour is how we've survived," said Yitzak Lemstein. "Jewish humour is a special kind of gallows humour, often using wordplay. There were a whole lot of jokes in the Nazi camps. It was just one part of our survival strategy. Believe me, I know."

He held out his wrist for Chavez to see. The black digits were almost completely covered with thick grey hair. But sure enough, they shone with an utterly dark light.

Chavez nodded and said: "So 'Shtayf' is what — a joke?"

"It's Yiddish," the old man said. "'Shtayf' means 'stiff'. Corpse. We can make jokes in the cemetery, too."

"But why is it on the gravestone? What does it mean?"

"It means it's an unidentified body. The grave of the unknown soldier, as they say. Unknown dead Jew."

"Died in 1981 and still unidentified?"

"Yes."

"Were you there when they buried him? If it was a man?"

"It was a man. And yes, I was there when they buried him. I'm part of Chevra Kadisha. It's my duty in looking after the cemetery."

"Chevra Kadisha?"

"The burial organisation."

"If he was unidentified, how did you know he was of Jewish origin?"

"He was circumcised. And he had one of these."

He showed his tattoo again.

Chavez nodded.

"How did he die?"

"Murdered. A stab wound, I think. I seem to recall he was found naked out in the woods. I don't remember exactly where. No one could identify him. But you're a policeman, you can find out more."

"Yes, I'm going to. Do you remember anything else? How old was he?"

"Must've been in his forties. Oh yes, there was one other thing."

"What?" asked Chavez.

"He didn't have a nose."

Jorge Chavez felt utterly confused.

"Didn't have a nose?"

"It was gone."

"Whoever killed him had cut it off?"

"No," said Yitzak Lemstein. "It had been gone a long time. There was a big scar where it should have been."

"I understand," said Chavez, not understanding much. "Do you have anything else to add?"

"No," said Lemstein. "But you do."

Chavez stood for a moment, still feeling confused. Then he raised a finger to the sky, exclaimed "Ah!" and phoned the National Forensic Laboratory.

214

"Brunte," he snorted. "My dear old father-in-law. Our rock. How's it going with Södra Begravningsplatsen? Is everything wrapped up?"

He listened for a few seconds. Then he hung up and turned back to Yitzak Lemstein with a nod.

"You can take care of the headstone now," he said. "This 'Shtayf' has suffered enough."

Yitzak Lemstein stared at him, turned round, took hold of the wheelbarrow and moved off. Chavez stood there for a moment, watching him as, bow-legged, he pushed the sorry old gravestone away.

Chavez headed back to his car.

On the way, he phoned his wife.

"Hi, Sara," he said. "Where are you?"

"In my office," Sara Svenhagen replied. "I just got back from Slagsta."

"Did anyone recognise our Greek?"

"His name was Nikos Voultsos, you know. Do you want me to call you 'my Chilean'?"

"During intimate moments, why not, Mrs I-don't-want-to-be-called-Chavez-I'd-rather-stay-Svenhagen-like-Daddy-Brunte. Oh, I just spoke to your dad, actually. Lovable as ever."

"No," Sara replied calmly. "No one recognised our Greek. But it doesn't really matter. Arto just got in touch from Italy. From what he said, it seems like Nikos Voultsos was in Sweden for some big crime syndicate in Milan. He was meant to take over the eight women in Slagsta and bring them in to some kind of enormous prostitution ring. We've got a probable translation of the message to your ninja feminist as

215

well. 'Everyone through OK. Three seven two to Lublin.' I'm busy checking all the ferries I can think of now."

"Lublin?" said Jorge. "Poland?"

"Yeah. Seems like it's our eight women who came 'through OK'. It's probably something to do with a rival syndicate in Ukraine. I mean, their contacts in Slagsta were Ukrainian, and the message was in Ukrainian. In other words, the ninja feminist seems to be Ukrainian and part of some kind of sex syndicate."

"I don't know whether that sounds good or bad," said Jorge, just as Sara was replaced by a strange metallic voice. "From a purely professional point of view, it's good. Though it sounds a bit worrying. Are you there? Sara?"

Sara's voice had now been replaced by some kind of industrial process. Robocop, Jorge thought.

Then suddenly, her normal voice was back: ". . . how's it going for you?"

"I'm worried you're in the process of changing into something hard and cold," said Jorge Chavez.

"What's up with you?" an awful metallic voice said.

"Your voice sounds weird. It's disappearing again now. Anyway, if you have a few minutes, I just wanted to ask if you could go through all the unidentified bodies from September 1981. Jewish man in his forties. Had a concentration camp tattoo but no nose. I repeat: no nose."

But she was already gone. He cursed the invention of the mobile phone and hung up.

As he climbed into the car, a tiny little hat was still clinging to his head.

Sara stared down at the silent phone.

Something hard and cold?

She was in the office she shared with Kerstin Holm. Holm was, at that moment, absent. Sara didn't know where she had gone.

She cast a quick glance at the computer screen in front of her. It was displaying a schematised timeline. She was working with a period of time which stretched from four in the morning on Thursday 4 May, when the women had left Slagsta, to three in the afternoon on Friday the 5th, when the call from Lublin had come through to the disembodied arm in Odenplan metro station. That meant that in thirty-five hours, they had made it from Stockholm to Lublin.

If she stuck to the assumption that they had travelled in some kind of bus — and not in the bin lorry — then the ferries were key. Between Sweden and Poland, ferries went from Nynäshamn–Gdańsk, Karlskrona–Gdynia and Ystad–Świnoujście. But then there was also the Copenhagen–Świnoujście line. When Jorge phoned, she had been busy working out possible options. The Öresund Bridge was still two months away from opening, but that wouldn't have stopped a route via Denmark: Gothenburg–Frederikshavn, Helsingborg–Helsingør or Malmö–Copenhagen.

It was also possible to take the ferry to Germany from somewhere like Ystad or Trelleborg, heading for Sassnitz or Rostock. But then what about Gothenburg

–Kiel? The nightmare scenario was surely a route via Helsingborg–Helsingør and then Rödby–Puttgarten. If the women had taken that route, there wouldn't have been any checks anywhere; for all the other routes, locating a bus with at least eight women on board should be possible.

Most of the options were perfectly doable within thirty-five hours. At worst, they all were. That meant it was simply a case of going through all of the timetables. The task facing her seemed fairly hopeless.

And so she had nothing against taking on Jorge's peculiar request. During the challenging time she had spent with CID's child pornography unit, still headed up by an unaffected party policeman called Ragnar Hellberg, she had become unusually good at finding all kinds of data. She had no problem finding that particular case from almost twenty years earlier in the crime database.

An unidentified male in his early forties, a John Doe, had been found naked in the woods by a little lake called Strålsjön to the south-west of Stockholm on the morning of Wednesday 9 September 1981. Death, caused by two deep knife wounds to the back, was found to have occurred sometime on Monday 7 September. The spot where the body was found hadn't been the murder scene, that much was clear. The body had, in other words, been dumped there, in all likelihood from a car. The man was dark-haired and, according to Medical Examiner Sigvard Qvarfordt's notes, "moderately hirsute". The most remarkable feature was the absence of a nose. Qvarfordt had continued: "Even the nasal bone is missing; all that remains is a rather disfiguring scar. The relative smoothness of the scar suggests that the nose was removed surgically, possibly sawn off."

Besides that, the man was circumcised and had, on his arm, a tattoo "resembling a concentration camp tattoo, but with illegible digits, as though he had attempted to remove them, using a knife or similar". That was why Stockholm's Jewish congregation had taken it on themselves to bury the unknown man. The case, undersigned by Erik Bruun, was still open.

Sara saved the information and decided that it was, without a doubt, Jorge's "Shtayf". Then she returned to her ferry traffic.

If I wanted to take the bus from Stockholm to Ukraine, would I really go via Denmark or even Germany? Wouldn't I just go direct from Sweden to Poland? It was a likely first choice, anyway. And if I did that, then it would preferably be to Gdynia or Gdańsk rather than Świnoujście, slightly out of the way on the Bay of Pomerania, right by the German border. From the twin cities of Gdynia and Gdańsk, the E77 went straight to Warsaw, from which the E372 continued on to Ukraine via Lublin. Logic dictated that Nynäshamn should have been their first choice, since the shipping company Polska Żegluga Baltycka, now known as the snappier Polferries, had boats running to Gdańsk. Otherwise, they would probably have chosen the Stena Lines ferry from Karlskrona to Gdynia.

And so she started in Nynäshamn. One of the Polferries boats, either the M/S *Rogalin* or the M/S

Nieborow, had departed at 17.00 on Thursday 4 May, arriving in Gdańsk at 11.30 the next day. The question was whether it would have been possible to make it from Gdańsk to Lublin by 14.55, when the call had come in to the phone at Odenplan metro station. That was something she needed to work out. Stena Lines had a ferry, the M/S *Stena Europe*, departing Karlskrona at 21.00, arriving in Gdynia at 07.00. Both of these needed to be followed up.

Sara felt like she needed assistance, and for a moment thought Kerstin's absence slightly irresponsible. It was a purely egotistical opinion, of course; it was also a fleeting one. Instead, she phoned up her old friend from the paedophile unit, the rock she could always count on.

"Yeah?" Gunnar Nyberg answered.

"Are you in the building?" asked Sara. "I need your help with something."

"No, Sara," Nyberg answered, unusually bluntly. "I'm a bit busy right now, I'm afraid. I'll call you back in a few minutes."

And with that, he was gone. She cursed the invention of the mobile phone and hung up.

Gunnar Nyberg flipped his phone shut with a click and shoved it back into the pocket of his beige lumber jacket. He hoped it wouldn't get broken. He didn't want to go to his meeting that evening — it wasn't a "date", he refused to call it a "date" — covered in cuts and bruises, either. That would hardly make a good impression on a professor of Slavic languages.

220

He sighed deeply and glanced around the filthy, beer-drenched cellar bar just outside of Åkersberga. A Swedish flag was hanging on one of the concrete walls; on another, a Nazi flag. Standing in the right angle created by the two flags were four enormous skinheads, baseball bats raised.

Behind him, the door was in pieces.

"Fucking pig, you broke the door!" one of the skinheads shouted.

"Sorry," Gunnar Nyberg replied courteously. "But you should've opened up when I knocked, kiddies. I could hear you in here, even though you were trying to hide like Girl Guides."

A growl emerged from their ranks.

He continued: "I'm looking for Reine Sandberg. Is he here? I just want to talk to him."

The skinhead closest to him swung the baseball bat violently. Gunnar Nyberg didn't appreciate that. He had promised himself to never again use violence at work, but now he had no choice.

With a well-aimed sucker punch, he sent the skinhead flying into one of the concrete walls. The others drew back slightly. Winded, the man he had punched curled up into the foetal position and groaned faintly.

"I don't want to hurt you," he said to the muscular, adrenalin-fuelled skinheads. Coming from most people, such a statement would have sounded overambitious.

Not so coming from Gunnar Nyberg.

He took a step forward.

"Come on, help an old man out. I'm Swedish fourteen generations back. My forefathers ate raw eel together with Erik XI. Are any of you Reine Sandberg?"

The three skinheads still standing glanced at one another. They put down their baseball bats and the biggest of them said: "I am. What d'you want?"

"Were you kicking over Jewish gravestones in Södra Begravningsplatsen yesterday evening?"

Reine Sandberg grabbed his baseball bat and aimed a fierce blow at Gunnar Nyberg. With a sigh, Nyberg grabbed him. He moved round behind Sandberg and twisted the piece of wood from his hand. Then he pushed him down to the ground so that he was sitting with the baseball bat between his legs, and shoved him over to the concrete wall. He lifted the bat like a lever. Reine Sandberg bellowed.

"Give us a minute, will you?" Nyberg said to the two remaining skinheads.

They did. Quickly.

"I've tried being nice," Gunnar Nyberg said, lifting the bat slightly higher. "Let's try again. Andreas Rasmusson is your friend, correct?"

"Yeah," said Reine Sandberg.

"Great. The two of you were out drinking and breaking gravestones in the Jewish cemetery last night, correct?"

"Yeah."

"Good. What exactly did you see that put Andreas Rasmusson — eighteen years old — in critical care in the psych ward, while you, Reine Sandberg —

222

twenty-six years old — are swinging a baseball bat at a policeman as though nothing had happened?"

"Fuck all," Sandberg groaned. "It was dark."

"Are you sure you want to do it like this? I don't."

And with that, Gunnar Nyberg raised the baseball bat slightly higher once more. He could feel it crunching strangely against one of Sandberg's testicles.

"OK, OK, OK, take that off and I'll tell you. Take it away!"

Given that his voice had gone up an octave or so, it was probably time. Nyberg pulled the bat away from the skinhead's genitals. Sandberg sank down with his hands to his crotch.

"So," said Nyberg. "Let's hear it."

"It was fucking horrible. They came gliding out of the shadows, these thin, dark figures. Like they were coming right out of the trees or something. All in black with, like, tights covering their bodies and black hoods on, like executioners. They hung that guy up in the tree. Upside down. That's when we ran off. We fucking ran. We lost Andreas somewhere. He must've been running around the cemetery, totally lost. After seeing that, 'course he flipped."

"How many of them were there?"

"Dunno. It felt like they were everywhere. Just gliding. A . . . presence."

"A presence?"

"I don't know how to describe it. Yeah, for fuck's sake, a presence. At least five of them anyway, I think."

"What do you mean by thin?"

"The opposite of you, you pig."

Gunnar Nyberg looked down at his newly slimmed body with slight surprise. Could he really still be described as fat?

"So they were little? Little people?"

"No, not really. I don't know. Thin. Light. Like they'd just detached from the trees. Strips of bark."

"Strips of bark?"

"Don't just repeat what I've just said. For fuck's sake, we ran off as fast as we could. We thought they'd come after us, like mythological beings or whatever."

"Mythological beings?"

"You're doing it again," Reine Sandberg said, annoyed.

Gunner Nyberg was thinking. Mythological beings? Wasn't there someone he should contact about this — in the absence of Arto? Yes, there was.

"I've got to make a call," said Nyberg. "Then I'm going to arrest you and take you down to the station for vandalising Jewish gravestones. You're not going to get away with that. Your testimony might just count as an extenuating circumstance, what do I know?"

And so Gunnar Nyberg made a call.

"Paul Hjelm" came the answer at the other end.

"Paul, it's Gunnar."

"Hey, Gunnar. You busy bothering skinheads?"

"You could say that. I've just been talking to one who said they saw some kind of 'gliding presence' among the gravestones. At least five thin figures dressed in black, he called them 'mythological beings'. Thought it might be something for you, my old bookworm."

"Don't say anything like that to your 'date' tonight."

"It's not a 'date'. And how do you know about it, anyway?"

"The whole station knows. We'll be sitting at the table next to you with tape recorders."

Gunnar Nyberg cursed the invention of the mobile phone and hung up. Then he phoned Sara Svenhagen back. She had been waiting long enough.

"*One* call, you said," Reine Sandberg shouted from behind him.

Paul Hjelm was in his office at the police station, increasingly convinced that he had haemorrhoids. It seemed like all he did was sit these days.

The tones of Miles Davis were streaming uninterruptedly across the room. It had become more a fixation than a pleasure by this point. A need.

He spent a moment looking down at his mobile phone, as though it had been producing entirely unfamiliar sound waves. Something was starting to come together. The edges of a wound slowly growing closer.

He had spent the day going through the list of calls to and from the four rooms in the Norrboda Motell. After several hours' fruitless work, it had clicked. A phone number appeared, demanding his attention.

From Monday 24 April onwards, calls had been made to all four phones from a room in Stockholm's Grand Hôtel, room 305. The calls had been made at three-minute intervals around half four in the afternoon; in other words, this had taken place a week or so before Nikos Voultsos had died and the women had disappeared. A few days later, on Saturday 29 April, the women had also been contacted by the ninja feminist from Odenplan.

Grand Hôtel. If you were going to do something, you might as well do it properly. He phoned the hotel and spoke to a receptionist.

"Can you tell me who was staying in room 305 from the twenty-fourth of April?"

The porter was silent. Then he said: "Aha."

"Aha?"

"Apparently he disappeared. I don't actually remember him myself, but he signed in as Marcel Dumas, French citizen."

"Disappeared? What does that mean?"

"Sometimes guests leave the hotel without informing us. That's why we always take their credit card number, as a precaution."

"Instead of their passport?"

"Exactly."

"So you don't have his passport?"

"No, but we've got his Visa card number."

"So guests can disappear without any report being made to the police, because you can just take the payment from their card number?"

"That's right. The police are overburdened enough as it is."

"True," said Paul Hjelm. "But that means you're taking the law into your own hands. What if something had happened to him? Imagine he'd been, I don't know, eaten by wolverines?"

The porter was silent. Hjelm continued.

226

"When did this happen?"

"The fifth of May. He arrived on Sunday the twenty-third of April. We got suspicious on the evening of Thursday the fourth — we hadn't seen him for twenty-four hours. So when he didn't show up for a second night in a row, we emptied the room and charged the bill to his account. Twelve nights. The bill came to sixty-three thousand kronor."

"Sixty-three thousand?"

"Yes."

"Now I can understand why you didn't report it."
More silence.

"Anyway, please can I have the Visa card number?"

"I can't just give that out."

"I'm a policeman, for God's sake."

"How do I know that? Honestly: careless handling of card numbers will be the downfall of civilisation. We're told to be extremely careful with them."

"OK," said Paul Hjelm, thinking about that particular kind of Armageddon; maybe it wasn't so crazy. There was already a huge volume of account numbers from Visa and American Express floating around on the Internet, available for general use. He came up with a quick solution.

"I'll give you a fax number. You can check with the directory listing, make sure that it's a police number. Will that do?"

The porter thought for a moment. Then he said: "That'll do."

Paul Hjelm gave him the fax number and continued: "What happened to the guest's things?"

"We packed them up in his bag and put them into storage."

"Storage where?"

"We've got a storeroom for stuff people leave behind. If no one gets in touch within a few months, we give it away to charity."

"What did he leave?"

"I don't know, I wasn't the one dealing with it."

"And this storeroom is in the hotel?"

"In the basement, yeah."

"Someone will be over to pick up his bag today."

"Great."

"Though not for charity," said Paul Hjelm. "I'm going to send you a JPEG of a face. I want you to show it to all the staff you can think of, right away, to see whether it's a picture of the guest who disappeared from room 305. What's your name?"

"Anders Graaf."

"Fitting," said Paul Hjelm. "Email address?"

He was given the address and ended the call with the words:

"If you send that fax right away, I'll send the picture right away too."

Anders Graaf was clearly good at his job, because the fax whirred into life only a minute or two later. During those two minutes, Paul Hjelm had time to send Nikos Voultsos's photo and to think about the increasing risks of the modern digital society. Ultimately, Graaf had been right, but he had also been inconsistent. Paul Hjelm hadn't really needed to be a policeman. Plenty of information had been handed out with no qualms, practically everything but the card number. That was because it related to the most important thing in the world: money. They had neglected to report a missing person to the police in order to be able to charge the sixty-three thousand kronor to the man's account, but they hadn't wanted to give his account number to the police.

There were some interesting conclusions to consider there.

The fax came in; the card number was in Paul Hjelm's hand. He phoned the Swedish arm of Visa and was told someone would get back to him with information about the account holder.

He returned to his long list of telephone numbers. After an eventless thirty minutes, the phone rang. He answered.

"Hello, is that Detective Inspector Hjelm?" a woman's voice asked.

"*The one and only*," Hjelm replied modestly.

"This is Mia Bengtsson. I work at the Grand Hôtel."

"Hi," Hjelm said expectantly.

"Hi. Anders showed me the picture of that man. It's him."

Paul Hjelm felt a great inner peace. He waited for her to continue.

"He groped me a couple of times when I was delivering room service. He was at it down in the bar, too. And in the French Dining Room as well."

"The guest from room 305, between the twenty-third of April and the fifth of May?"

"Exactly. Rich drug addict. Had cocaine around his nostrils like some kind of rock star."

"Don't hold back. He's dead, after all."

"Oh! I shouldn't speak ill of the dead —"

"That's when you can really let rip," Paul Hjelm replied to loosen her vocal cords.

"Yeah, OK. I'd say he was an unusually nasty type, simple as that. We do sometimes see them at the Grand. Drug people have a lot of money, and always get room service; it's the worst — you're alone with them in their rooms. I tried speaking French but he didn't understand a word, he just poked my breasts and smiled horribly. He wasn't even French."

"No," said Paul Hjelm, "he was no Frenchman."

"Plenty of money though. Was throwing it around. I saw him rip a thousand-krona note to shreds. Just to show he was cool. There were a few women up in his room, too. I'm pretty sure they were prostitutes."

"Were you the one who realised he was missing?"

"I was the one who sent a message to management saying that the room hadn't been touched, anyway. I don't know what happened after that. Only that he was gone when I got there on the seventh. His room had been cleaned and emptied."

"Anything you want to add?"

"Not really. But I can't claim I'm really sad about him being dead."

"Thanks a lot for your help, Mia. Bye."

"Bye."

Paul Hjelm sat still. The link between Nikos Voultsos and Slagsta had been established. It was now a fact. As though the Ghiottone hadn't been enough. Paul Hjelm laughed. He had done the same when Arto Söderstedt phoned from Tuscany to tell him about wolverines and *ghiottoni*.

A picture of Nikos Voultsos's murderer was starting to emerge and it was multifaceted.

Hunting down a man with links to a crime syndicate like the Ghiottone and then throwing him to the wolverines in Skansen was tremendously subtle. A clear, direct message to Milan. Perhaps they hadn't expected his body to supply the wolverines with such a high level of drugs that they essentially obliterated him. The police had been very close to not being able to identify him at all. That was the first aspect of it: the message to Milan.

The second was the wire, which seemed to be more at home in the scientist Leonard Sheinkman's cerebral cortex. That said, Sheinkman's link to the whole thing was still unclear. There were German diaries waiting to be read. Aspect two, then: the metal wire in the brain. Was that a message too? Did the two belong together? Was that another message for Milan?

A third aspect was that which had been immediately apparent in the Odenplan metro station, and certainly in both Skansen and Södra Begravningsplatsen: enormous cruelty and a great deal of skill in the noble art of neutralising someone. They had a female suspect, which was in itself extremely unusual. Professionalism or . . . hate? Or both? Wasn't it a case of passionate feelings whichever way you looked at it? That was the impression he had, anyway. It wasn't just a message that was being sent, it was something more, something deeper.

Then there was the journey to Ukraine. "Everyone through OK."

It was, of course, nothing more than a Slavicist's interpretation of fairly shaky foundations, but still. If they were to believe the latest information, direct from the mouth of a skinhead, then there was a league involved, not a lone killer. That league had transported at least eight prostitutes across Europe. Would that have been possible if they had kidnapped them and forced them to move using violence? "Everyone through OK." Didn't that sound more ... considerate? A crime syndicate would have treated the women like objects. Would they have expressed it like that? "Everyone through OK." It was vague, but it was a hunch he had. They couldn't afford to let things like that slide. Besides, it was a case of a call being made from woman to woman. "Not a bloke as far as the eye could see," as old Maja had put it at the cottage in Dalarö. "Everyone through OK." Aspect four: the female.

And then there was the fifth. That which had already been hinted at by Nikos Voultsos's mad flight across Djurgården. The blind panic. He had shot wildly, ripped his hands to shreds, thrown his gun away and torn off his gold chain — the very symbol of his dominance. The same panic had sent a group of skinheads running across Skogskyrkogården at breakneck speed. All but one, who had been left behind in his own private inferno, and ended up in the psych ward. A dark, gliding presence among the gravestones, one which made a seasoned skinhead talk about "mythological beings".

Paul Hjelm sat still. Something was calling to him. Something was starting to come together. The edges of a wound slowly growing closer. All the different languages which had turned up during this case . . . It was like the Tower of Babel. A God, saying: "Go to, let us go down, and there confound their language, that they may not understand one another's speech." The richness of European languages. "Everyone through OK" in Ukrainian. "Shtayf" in Yiddish.

"Ghiottone" in Italian. "Wolverine" in English. And then "Epivu" in . . .

For God's sake. It didn't say "Epivu" at all.

Hjelm searched wildly on the computer. The folder of photographs from the case. The wolverine enclosure. There: the letters in the earth. "Epivu". He enlarged the image so that it filled the screen. Then he enlarged it further. He stared at the last letter: "u". He enlarged it further. Didn't it look like there were a couple of commas above and below the "u"? Of course.

It wasn't a "u" at all. It was a "upsilon". Broadly speaking, a "y".

On closer inspection, he saw that the middle letter had no dot above the "i".

Of course, it was Greek.

Nikos Voultsos was thoroughly Greek.

That meant that the "p" wasn't a "p" after all, but "ro". In other words, an "r". The "v" was no "v" but "ny", or "n".

It wasn't "Epivu", it was "Ερινυ", pronounced something like "Erini", with the emphasis on the last vowel. And which, in all likelihood, was a word.

Paul Hjelm even thought he recognised it.

He went online and found a Greek dictionary. No hits. Damn it. Then it struck him that there were several different types of Greek. Modern Greek had surprisingly little in common with Old Greek. This had to be Old Greek. Ancient Greek. After some effort, he managed to find an old Greek dictionary on an American website called "Perseus". He searched for "Ερινυ". He found a result.

Erinyes.

He realised why he had recognised it. It was something he had come across during the A-Unit's very first case. A young man called Gusten Bergström had been convinced that his sister, who had committed suicide following an attempted rape, was being avenged from beyond the grave by ancient goddesses of revenge. By Erinyes.

The Erinyes were antiquity's most terrifying figures. Known as the Furies, they came from the kingdom of the dead and demanded revenge for past injustices. To restore the balance. And they never gave up.

The Erinyes were female goddesses of revenge.

Nikos Voultsos's last act in this life had been to write down precisely who was killing him. He wrote it in Old Greek, the language of mythology. The man who had murdered three prostitutes in Piraeus and who had been about to take over a group of prostitutes in Stockholm was convinced that he was being hunted by female goddesses of revenge. Was it simply his conscience finally catching up with him?

Paul Hjelm shuddered. At least five thin, dark figures; a gliding presence among the gravestones in Södra Begravningsplatsen, like mythological beings . . .

No, he thought. No, this wasn't just some crime syndicate among others. This was no Eastern European mafia group, selling women like pieces of meat. No, sir.

He phoned Kerstin. It was a reflex.

"Kerstin Holm," she said.

"Are you in the building?"

"I'm in my room. Viggo's here."

"Well, what do you know," said Paul Hjelm. "This 'Epivu', it's the Erinyes, the ancient goddesses of revenge. "Εϱινυ". It's Old Greek."

"Jesus," said Kerstin Holm. "How did you work that out?"

"Long story. But it's not some Mafia syndicate."

"I never thought it was. You said it yourself: the ninja feminist."

"I think you were the one who said that. We just clarified it."

"Viggo's found our phantom pimp. The man who did the deal with the manager of the Norrboda Motell. His name was Finn Johansen, he was Norwegian."

"Was?"

"He committed suicide on the twenty-fourth of April. Shot himself in the head. With a silenced Luger that wasn't his. The serial number is pretty similar to Nikos Voultsos's gun. They're sister guns. From the same line."

"What time?"

"Time?"

"What time of day on the twenty-fourth of April?"

There was a moment's silence. Then Viggo Norlander's not-quite-so-pleasant voice came down the line.

"What're you playing at, Freddie Freeloader?"

"When did he shoot himself?"

"Never, I'd guess."

"Me too."

"About one, half past one in the afternoon, apparently. His prostitute girlfriend came home from the day's shift at about quarter to two and found him lying in a pool of his own blood."

"Nikos Voultsos came to Stockholm on the twenty-third of April. At half four on the twenty-fourth, he phoned each of the four rooms in the motel. 224, 225, 226 and 227. They'd lost their pimp, Finn Johansen, only a couple of hours earlier, and to a weapon almost identical to Voultsos's."

There was a scratching sound on the line.

"I hear you," said Kerstin Holm. "It's Sunday. Sunday the twenty-third. That's when the unease starts spreading through the four rooms. The girls know they've been taken over by another, bigger, and presumably worse gang than Finn Johansen's. The wolverines. *Ghiottoni*. A couple of days later, your ninja feminist rings —"

"She's not mine. And she's not a ninja feminist. She's a goddess of revenge; she's an Erinye."

"*Whatever*. Somehow, she offers the girls an alternative to the situation they've found themselves in; exactly what, we've got no idea. A week goes by, Nikos Voultsos cements his position as their new pimp; maybe he gives them a display of his power, probably in combination with some kind of drugged-up, hardcore sex. Maybe he's also taken over other groups in the same way, we'll have to check that. Maybe that bus to Lublin really is a bus, maybe it's full."

"Full of — what? Saved whores?"

"I don't like that word," said Kerstin, "but OK. Maybe. While he's busy carrying out his orders from the Ghiottone, someone is planning his downfall. And carrying it out. They creep up on him somewhere in Djurgården. They probably know that he liked to sit and snort cocaine out there. Then, with precision, they drive him towards the Skansen fence, right by the wolves. They'd probably already clipped a hole in the fence next to it, alongside the wolf enclosure. That's how they get in while he's struggling up the fence, over the barbed wire and into the wolves.

"Then they stand and wait for him at the top of the hill. They see him go crazy, throwing his pistol away and tearing his gold chain off, and they follow him. Then they catch him, bind his legs with a red-and-purple rope, push the metal wire into his brain and lower him to the wolverines. The animals take a first bite, maybe a bit cautiously, but there's enough cocaine in that bite to drive those greedy little creatures to a massacre. He'd probably already died by that point; he probably died in the same incomprehensible way as Leonard Sheinkman. Of pure pain.

"Once it's all over, they pull the rope back up. There's nothing left. The wolverines have managed to jump high enough to bite off the knot. It doesn't really matter, so they take the rope and clear off. Then, virtually right away, they phone Slagsta. One of the Ukrainians in room 225, either Galina Stenina or Lina Kostenko, answers. They find out that their tormentor, Nikos Voultsos, is out of the game and that their transport will depart as planned, at four in the morning. When no one is watching. They blissfully talk the night away. They're free. They're finally free. No more pimps. No more bad drugs. Never again. New lives. Time to turn over a new leaf."

Yes, thought Paul Hjelm. Of course, Kerstin, that's it.

He said: "But the league stays behind. To murder an old man."

"Yeah, that's the blow. You know what I mean — when everything seems to be making sense and then along comes the disappointment, flooding in and muddying everything else."

"I know all too well," said Paul Hjelm.

"Do you know what I'm doing?" asked Kerstin.

"You're wondering about the fate of the girls. Lublin onwards."

"Aside from that? Practically?"

"I haven't got the faintest idea. Washing your underwear? Pulling burrs from your hair? Cutting your toenails with hedge clippers?"

238

"Looking at a growing list."

Kerstin Holm was in her office, looking at a growing list. Viggo Norlander was sitting right next to her, looking at her as she looked at the growing list. She was a glorious woman. He wondered why he had never realised that before. Him, an expert after several years' intense interaction with the opposite sex in all of Stockholm's imaginable and unimaginable singles bars — before suddenly finding himself, at the age of fifty, with a live-in partner and a small baby. And all that had happened as a direct result of being crucified by the Russian-Estonian mafia, on a floor in Tallinn.

It was complicated.

It was probably because little Charlotte was learning to walk that he had regained his eye for the opposite sex. He didn't quite understand the link, but it was a fact. Fortunately, Astrid kept him busy, meaning that this eye remained theoretical.

The growing list on the screen was simply Kerstin Holm's inbox. It was growing bigger and bigger until eventually she had received emails from eight different police authorities.

"Eight," she said to the astonished mobile phone.

"Explain right now," the astonished mobile phone exhorted.

"The big inquiry through Europol and Interpol is starting to bring in results. General appeal for information to all the bigger police authorities in Europe. Something like the three hundred biggest cities on the Continent. I don't know if the answers are affirmative yet, but eight of these three hundred cities have something to say about our modus operandi."

The eight emails were sitting there, their titles in bold. Once she clicked on them, the font normalised after a few seconds. Once they had emptied their bowels.

Message one: Information from Dublin. Detective Superintendent Radcliffe. "I'm wondering whether I didn't hear about something similar in the former DDR. Get in touch with Benziger in Weimar. No idea what his title is, but he's friendly. As you also seem to be, Ms Holm."

Message two: A telling-off from Paris. Chief Superintendent Mérimée. "Misuse of Europol resources. Should be used exclusively for combating the following points: unlawful drug trafficking, crimes involving illicit immigration networks, illicit vehicle trafficking, the trafficking of human beings (including child pornography), the forgery of money and other means of payment, the illicit trafficking of nuclear or other radioactive material, terrorism and the illicit laundering of money in relation to any of the above crimes."

Message three: Confirmation from Budapest. Detective Superintendent Mészöly. "Very interesting. We had a similar case in October '99. Twenty-nine-year-old man, active in the prostitution branch, hung upside down and with a kind of metal wire inserted into his temple. We would gladly familiarise ourselves with your investigation, and you can, of course, have access to ours."

Message four: Another confirmation, this time from Maribor, Slovenia. Police Chief Sremac. "Same thing here in March. Serious criminal strung up, skull penetrated. Awaiting further information."

Messages five, six and *seven:* Yet more confirmations, from Wiesbaden in Germany, Antwerp in Belgium, and Venice, Italy. Chief Inspector Roelants in Antwerp added: "Don't be surprised, Ms Holm, if more confirmations turn up. Those of us who have experienced this crime have been in internal, official contact for several months. My judgement, however, is that, so far, none of us have managed to establish any direct links between the cases."

Message eight: Inquiry from Stockholm. Division Chief Waldemar Mörner. "Who in high heavens authorised this inquiry? Whose budget will this come out of? WM."

Kerstin Holm called Paul Hjelm.

"They've been at it just over a year," she said.

"In Europe?" he asked.

"In Budapest, Maribor, Wiesbaden, Antwerp and Venice so far. If we include our victims, that means seven people have been strung up and had their cerebral cortex pierced. Add to that Hamid al-Jabiri from Odenplan metro station and it's eight dead. There don't seem to have been any wolverines anywhere else."

"What kind of victims?"

"They seem to have been serious criminals, the lot of them. Everyone but Leonard Sheinkman."

"Do any of your contacts suspect a link to Ghiottone?"

241

"No. But it's all rudimentary so far. We'll exchange investigations."

"Online? Is that really secure?"

"What is secure nowadays?" asked Kerstin Holm.

And with that, she was gone. Paul Hjelm cursed the invention of the mobile phone and hung up.

CHAPTER
NINETEEN

12 February 1945

At long last, I have managed to get hold of some paper and a pencil. I shan't waste time and energy explaining how; I have much too little of either of those to spare. My time is running out, my strength ebbing away. I can feel it, I know it. It will soon be my turn. I have seen the list. I have seen my name on the list. Leonard Sheinkman, it said. Me. It seems only fair to be clear about that from the beginning. To avoid any misunderstandings.

This may be the very last thing I write in this life and I don't want to waste it on petty details. I have done more than enough of that.

I truly wish it were possible to describe love. I am an author, describing is what I do, and yet I cannot do it. Well then, who can? Perhaps it is only possible afterwards, once it is all too late.

If that is true, it should be possible now.

My son . . .

No. Not today. Today won't do.

Today I will simply have to make do with the pleasure of once more feeling the weight of a pencil in my hand, once more being able to caress the smooth paper beneath it.

Once upon a time, writing was what made me live. Will it simply be the memory of this I experience when pencil meets paper, or will I live again? One last flourish?

13 February 1945

It is so strange to see time. It is outside the window. My friends here, they are distant. They aren't friends, they are fellows in misfortune — the type of man best avoided, since they simply reflect yourself. Do I look the way they look? I am thirty-three years old and I probably look like an old corpse. There are men much younger than me here and they look older than the image I have of myself. I hope to be able to retain that image until I die.

That should be possible; it won't be far off.

I see time. One might think it is nothing but a black clock tower, something physical, a timepiece with a complex mechanical motion, a tower constructed to keep the ravages of time in check. Each second is the tower's triumph; each second of the ageing which has gone on century after century, marked by the mechanical precision of the clock. But that isn't what I see. What I see is time.

I cannot explain it, and yet I must try. Why else would this pencil be resting in my hand, why else would all this effort have gone towards placing time here, right here, at the point of pencil meeting paper?

What I can see is time. That is where I must begin. My time, and how time changed when I met Magda and walked hand in hand with her, at home in Berlin. Our Tiergarten . . . So calm and tranquil. Prior to that, I had been a suffering author. I had suffered from loneliness. But suddenly, I became a productive author. A productive man. I believe I produced something of a real life, too. A home. A life shared. A little bit of happiness. She read the words I wrote; she was my best reader. Then along came the baby. Our son. Miracles impossible to describe. Each movement was a miracle. The soft movements of those chubby little arms. The turn of a head. Those dark eyes, pupils shrinking and expanding. Everything was a miracle.

And that was time.

I can see it again now. Is it still a miracle? Can it still, ticking away so mechanically up there on the hexagonal black tower, send me the peace the miracle deserves? It can, for a moment — a short, short moment when pencil meets paper. But I can also feel the iciness descending the moment I lift the pencil. The spaces between words are blocks of ice. The words are freezing fast in them.

With their wounded heads, the men pace the corridors like corpses and I think: Do you see time too, people? Are you also able to see time for a brief, brief moment? How do you do it?

I myself have no method.

The text is fading now. The ice is spreading over the letters, freezing pencil to paper like a tongue to metal, and I wonder: Why did you die away from me? Why wasn't I the one to die away from you? My brain will be frozen solid. That is my only comfort and my sole, minuscule trace of resistance.

Dying.

14 February 1945

New day. I have seen the list again. The icy wind swept in through the window from the square, making the sheet flutter in through the barred door and come to rest by my bare feet.

Yet another toe will have to go, I think. The middle toe on my left foot is as black as the hexagonal tower which taunts me out there with its indifferent ticking. I don't hear it, but I see it. I see it constantly, unceasingly.

The list was lying there by my blackened toe, and I saw that my name had climbed higher. I welcomed it as a gift. A gift from the icy wind. Soon you will wrap the clock tower in your ice and your time, and then even the time moving through its mechanisms and the time being cast out in its ironic, rejoicing bells, even that time will be swept up in your ice, ice wind, and all time will cease. Each of us will move through a frozen existence, a moment frozen to emptiness, and all other people will be utterly still and utterly frozen in front of all others, and there will be as many worlds as people and all people will be living in their own world where all other people are frozen solid.

I know I should record facts. Leave behind my testimony. Produce detailed accounts. Something posterity can verify and from which it can learn. Some time, long, long after my death, everything that happens here will be judged, and I should already be planning the means by which to ensure that my papers will outlive me, finding a route for them, a means of escape; whatever the price, finding a benefit and use for this stump of pencil and these few sheets of paper which, even now, practically while I write — such moves time — have managed to yellow. But I cannot. I cannot record facts. My soul does not work that way.

It doesn't work at all.

It is nothing but a brain, a mechanism. Like the clock. And the body, it is the clock tower, built for one purpose and one purpose only: to hold.

Not to fall apart as the mechanism is dissected.

Perhaps they are watchmakers, those three officers.

But then I see time once more, and once more it is a miracle. He manages to sit up, my son. My wife clasps her hands, not that they touch his thin little back, but almost; it is like there is a field between her hand and his back, a magnetic field of life, and whatever exists between them, it also exists between myself and them, and I know that once I am no longer here, that magic which exists as a field of life between us, when it no longer exists they will no longer exist. They don't exist. They are dead. I am dead. Then why do I move? The twitching of a fish with a broken neck. The march of the hen after her head is cut off.

I am becoming too eager.

Where is my restraint?

I will stop for today.

Enough.

Die.

Live.

For a while longer. A few breaths longer.

Those crashes out on the streets, the clouds of stone dust blowing in through the window, they should wake hope. But I don't dare hope. There is no hope left for me. My family is dead and my name is too high up on the list.

Our Tiergarten . . . How we wandered. The zoo on the other side of the canal. Franz had laughed and pointed at a pelican. He had been sitting on my shoulders.

No, this won't do.

Or?

My son was on my shoulders. His little heels bumped against my jacket, leaving indelible marks. They are still there, though the jacket has been burnt and his shoes have been burnt and his tiny little feet have been burnt. They are still there, right in front of my eyes, and when my eyes burn those tiny little heel marks on my jacket, marks which made me so angry, they will still exist somewhere. They are chronicles. They are facts. They are testimonies and accounts.

They are life.

He pointed at the pelican and the pelican made an inimitable sound but Franz imitated it anyway; he sat on my shoulders and sounded exactly like the pelican on the other side of the water and how we laughed. I laughed, Magda laughed, and Franz laughed though he didn't know why, and that laugh, that short, baseless laugh, has kept me alive here in the land of death. I am inching towards the top of the list.

One day very soon, I will make it, and then it will be like it is for Erwin. Erwin is not Jewish. I believe he belongs to the category they call "substandard humans", with a slight disability which was essentially more social than genetic. He can't be more than twenty. I could have been his father.

The treatment has made him confused. In the beginning, we had intelligent conversation; he knew nothing about contemporary society but plenty about the more eternal questions in life. He had considered it all. Had plenty of time to think. He has not rushed through life the way I have. Now, though, there isn't much left. When I speak to him, there is no one there. He is nothing but an empty shell. Over the spot where it has been running out of his head, an innocent little gauze dressing.

It is worse than him being dead. He walks around like a constant reminder of what will soon happen to us all.

Not that there are many of us left.

But I am still many. I am Leo, I am Magda, I am Franz. And I am Erwin.

I am also Erwin.

16 February 1945

My son walked alongside me. He held my hand and we walked through the Tiergarten. It was dull and rainy, one of those bleak, wet autumn days Berlin so often enjoys

— bleak, wet, remarkably beautiful. The leaves had started to fall from the trees. They mixed with the mud in the puddles to form a brownish-yellow sludge. Franz suddenly paused right next to one of these pools. He let go of my hand, turned round and hugged me.

He came just up to my navel.

We stood there for a moment in the cool, fine rain. I held him. I had nothing to say.

And then he let go.

He headed straight for the muddy pool. And as he walked, he sank down into it, inch by inch. He said not a word, he simply walked and walked and sank and sank until there was nothing left. His little black head disappeared with a gurgle. The surface was oddly calm.

And I, I just stood there watching him sink. Not a finger did I lift to save him. Not a finger.

We could have fled. Magda had been nagging me: "Your friends are leaving, your colleagues are leaving, everyone we know is leaving. But us, we're staying. Why? Why do you want to stay and wait for death? Think of Franz, at the very least." And I said: "It can't be that bad. This is the twentieth century. We have cars, aeroplanes, the microscope. We have democracy and contraceptives and psychoanalysis and liberal arts. All we need to do is to survive the winter, hibernate as the storm passes by."

And I had been right: the storm did pass. But once it was gone, there was nothing left. We had been sucked into it. All of us.

Behind it, a desolate landscape.

I killed my son and I killed my wife. My stubbornness killed them.

Let everything be silent.

Let me die.

CHAPTER
TWENTY

He sat quietly in bed. Something swept by in the darkness, taking him with it.

Perhaps it was an icy wind.

Perhaps it was the Erinyes.

His fingers touched the yellowed paper. He could feel the distance between the barely legible pencil letters. Ice was growing between them. Between the letters. It would never melt.

Paul Hjelm took off his new reading glasses and placed them on the bedside table, switched off the lamp and stared out into the darkness.

So, he thought, groping for Cilla's warm body. His hand snaked beneath the blanket, coming to rest between her shoulder blades. She murmured. A sign of life.

So, that was how things could have been. Things could have turned out that way for him, too. If he had been born at the wrong time, to the wrong parents. His own thoughts could have been exactly like Leonard Sheinkman's during those bleak February days in 1945. Disjointed, loose, but still with great and terrible repressed emotion.

Leonard Sheinkman had been convinced he was going to die back then, but he hadn't. A few months later, the war had ended. He came out on the other side. He had been utterly, utterly empty, and now faced a choice: stay put and go under or move and make a new life for himself. Become someone else. He had chosen the latter, it had been a possibility for him. But what kind of end had he met? Being hung from a tree in the Jewish cemetery fifty-five years later? How was that possible? What had happened?

At that moment, Paul Hjelm was powerless to go through what he had read and draw any rational conclusions. He was much too moved. That was roughly what he had been expecting — and yet it was completely different. A different tone. Sorrow beyond all sorrow. As though it had been written from beyond the grave.

A weighty German-Swedish dictionary was resting on his stomach. In his left hand, he was holding the pages he had read; in his right, those he hadn't. The piles were roughly equal in size, meaning he still had half left to read. He was looking forward to it — but he was also dreading it.

Paul Hjelm felt completely destroyed. As though he had been ransacked. In a way, that was what had happened.

Buchenwald, Nazi Germany's largest concentration camp, was seven kilometres outside Weimar in the former DDR. The city had been the European Capital of Culture just one year ago; the place in which Goethe had changed the face of world literature. In 1919, the

253

first German democracy, the Weimar Republic, had been founded there. In 1926, the Hitler Youth had been formed there. That same year, the Nationalsozialistische Deutsche Arbeiterpartei, the NSDAP, had held its first party meeting in Weimar's national theatre. Then, between 1937 and 1945, two hundred and thirty-eight thousand people had been held prisoner in Buchenwald; there had been no gas chambers, but there had been a centre for "medical research". In total, fifty-six thousand people had lost their lives in Buchenwald, practically within sight of Goethe's Weimar. Between 1945 and 1950, it had also served as a Soviet detention camp for Germans. A further seventeen thousand people had died.

It was the cradle of the European paradox.

Paul Hjelm turned over to turn off the light.

Only then did he realise it was already out.

He fell asleep late that night.

CHAPTER
TWENTY-ONE

Hearts was but a memory. In the little stone house just outside the medieval village of Montefioralle deep within the hills of Chianti, there was no longer time for computer games.

There was Italian to be read.

It was hard work, going through Commissioner Italo Marconi's investigation into the Milanese crime syndicate, Ghiottone. New information was also constantly arriving from Stockholm via email, fax and telephone.

Still, if you were a Europol officer, you were a Europol officer.

The aim of The Hague-based European law-enforcement organisation was to increase the effectiveness and cooperation of the competent member state authorities, particularly when it came to preventing and combating terrorism and the illegal trade of drugs, as well as other serious forms of international crime. Europol had been founded in order to make a significant contribution to the European Union's efforts against organised crime.

"OK," Söderstedt said to his computer as he sat on the porch with yet another glass of Vin Santo in his hand. "OK, that was a quote. I confess, computer. I didn't even know I was a Europol officer when I went to Milan. So, yes: I'm sitting here, on holiday, citing police statutes with myself as the only witness. And you of course, computer."

"Who are you talking to?" Anja shouted from inside the house. She had managed to nurture a rather decent-sized purple ruffles basil plant in the garden and seemed to be quite frisky in honour of the occasion. Now wasn't the right moment to be unfaithful with a computer.

"The computer," Arto shouted back.

"Right," Anja shouted. "Come and see the little ones before they go to sleep."

"Where's Mikaela?" Arto shouted.

"Where do you think?" Anja shouted.

A lot of shouting went on in the Söderstedt family.

Arto immediately forgot her request to say goodnight to the little ones and went back to the computer. Technically speaking, it was the youngest member of the family. Though it was true, he never said goodnight to it.

Instead, without warning, it gave him the name of the old banker suspected of being the absolute ruler of the Ghiottone. His name was Marco di Spinelli.

There were plenty of pictures of this Marco di Spinelli. Di Spinelli was an old, thin, tough-looking man, not at all what you would expect of a Mafia boss. But then, he was also a northern Italian. Active in the separatist movement. Lega Nord and things like that.

There was even a picture of Marco di Spinelli and Nikos Voultsos together. They were certainly an ill-matched pair. The old, aristocratic silver fox dressed in a black polo neck and the coarse Greek in his pale pink suit, unbuttoned shirt, thick chest hair and fat gold chain around his neck. They were greeting one another outside a luxurious-looking restaurant in central Milan. Marco di Spinelli had his hand on Nikos Voultsos's shoulder, and Voultsos's smile seemed particularly subservient.

Paul Hjelm had called to tell him about the Erinyes. He had also told him that Voultsos had left a suitcase full of his belongings at the hotel, along with a Visa card number. There had been nothing but clothes in the suitcase; if there had been drugs of any kind in the room, they had long since disappeared into the pockets of unknown employees of the Grand Hôtel. The card number, on the other hand, was interesting. The Swedish arm of Visa had been in touch with the name of the account holder. It was a private limited company called S.A. Contra. Arto Söderstedt phoned Italo Marconi right away to tell him the news.

Marconi said: "Sounds about right. S.A. Contra is a money-laundering business at the edge of the Ghiottone organisation. Their accounts are often used for payments here and there. Not that we've been able to link any of it to the Ghiottone or di Spinelli, of course."

Söderstedt thanked him and hung up.

On the whole, he felt like he was starting to get a pretty good understanding of the structure of the organisation. Everything suggested that di Spinelli was the spider in the middle of the web, that all roads led to him.

As though to Rome.

But no matter how much of an authorised Europol officer he now was, Arto Söderstedt was powerless to do the slightest thing about either the Ghiottone organisation or Marco di Spinelli. That much was clear. Milan had countless competent, native policemen and women who had devoted years of their lives to getting at the syndicate. That wasn't his job; it would be taking on more than he could chew. No, his job was to help them get to whoever had killed Nikos Voultsos, Hamid al-Jabiri and Leonard Sheinkman. Nothing more.

Though going via the Ghiottone was clearly one way of doing it.

The question was whether it was doable. He thought about how best to carry out his job. He didn't need to think for long. As far as he was concerned, it was utterly obvious.

If anyone knew who had put his henchman to death, it would be the old banker himself.

Seven people, of whom six were serious criminals — all pimps, going by Kerstin's latest email — had been murdered by the same method across Europe. According to Marconi, there was nothing to suggest that any of these seven were linked to Ghiottone, but it still had to be in Marco di Spinelli's interests that whoever had killed his hand-picked Greek murderer-cum-pimp disappeared.

Di Spinelli was probably a man who took things into his own hands. He was probably already hunting for the Erinyes with a blowtorch. And it would probably be verging on impossible for a Swedish policeman to be given an opportunity to talk to him. However much authorisation his Europol status gave him.

Arto Söderstedt decided to ask Marconi anyway.

"Well, it might be a bit of a surprise," Marconi unexpectedly said. "Blunt, chalk-white Swedish police officer on a personal visit. It could catch his attention. He likes playing games with the police."

"Have you talked to him? Personally, I mean?"

"Many times. I'm practically a regular at his house. He's not at all shy in that Sicilian no-one-knows-who-the-godfather-is kind of way. On the contrary, for such an old man, he's really quite hungry for publicity. He's a politician. Or rather, he's a kind of politician . . ."

"Marco di Spinelli must be what . . .? Ninety-two?"

"And swims two hundred metres a day and takes part in sailing races and sometimes drives rallies. They say he likes the Värmland forests, whatever they are. Swedish?"

"Swedish. I might be able to fake an interest in rallying. I am Finnish, after all. A bit, anyway."

"I'll pass on your request," said Commissioner Marconi, and Söderstedt could almost feel — through the telephone itself — that big moustache start spinning.

Arto Söderstedt allowed his gaze to wander over the shade-bathed garden. The trees and bushes had been deliberately planted so that they formed a shadowy canopy. It was a Mediterranean method he was familiar with. As the days passed, the May sunshine seemed to be increasingly convinced that it was a bright summer sun rather than a lousy little spring one. Its self-confidence was growing relentlessly — and, with it, the need to take siestas. Arto had lost count of the number of times he had arrived at this or that shop only to find its shutters closed. What surprised him most was that he never learned from his mistake; like a psychiatric patient on the run, he made the daily journey into Greve only to find the entire town was deserted. Between one and four, Greve shut down — and between one and four, the chalk-white Finn would arrive in his big family car, try a locked door, and produce a series of undefinable noises. You could have set your watch by him.

He needed a siesta, that much was clear.

But now he was sitting in the shade on the terrace, sipping a *very small* glass of Vin Santo and looking at his watch. Two o'clock. Mid-siesta. He had been pleased that Marconi had answered immediately, but now, with hindsight, it struck him that he must have phoned at the worst possible time. Not that it was a problem — Marconi had clearly skipped his afternoon's rest, just like he had.

He refused to take a siesta.

One way or another, he would probably regret it. But right now, he was distracted. His thoughts were practically running away from him. This from the man who was normally so good at damming the flow and digging channels to allow his thoughts to pour in the right direction. Now, though, they were more like the Danube delta.

If he was given access to Marco di Spinelli, he would need to be prepared. Well read, like a real nerd. But he would also need to repress all that knowledge as best he could from his working mind, so that it didn't hinder the thought process and his ability to react. Arto Söderstedt sometimes managed to trick suspects into giving themselves away. He often did it by playing dumb — he had that kind of appearance. It was hard to deny that he could look quite vacant.

"Is Daddy dead?"

He chuckled slightly and gently dipped the tip of his tongue into the *tiny little* glass.

How should he go about grabbing di Spinelli's attention? How could he get him to loosen his tongue? He had ten or so pictures of the man open on his computer screen and was trying to get a purely visual understanding of him. So far, di Spinelli was still nothing more than a picture. Or rather, a collection of pictures.

He tried to imagine the entire situation, how he would be met, how di Spinelli would act, what they might talk about and — above all — how he would even begin to go about asking the important questions as though they didn't mean a thing. That was the great, decisive trick.

The thing he had learned from Uncle Pertti.

Arto Söderstedt was an unusually well-educated policeman, there was no denying that, with a past that he would much rather avoid talking about. A career lawyer in Finland by the age of twenty-five, keeping the scum of the earth away from lawful society. Specialising in the richest, most cunning and unconscionable of criminals. And then he had simply turned his back on that mad, dishonest life, fled the country and ended up in Sweden where, after a couple of years of hard work, he became a policeman; he proved much too obstinate for his superiors in Stockholm and was sent to Västerås, where he lived a peaceful, comfortable and utterly intolerable suburban life. Until a detective superintendent with owl-like glasses perched on his enormous nose came stomping into the police station and changed the direction of Söderstedt's life once more.

In the A-Unit, he had become the joker in the pack. The card a seasoned player would throw down to win the entire pot.

Or something like that.

But despite his varied life, despite the abundance of educational opportunities and pathways which had been available to him, it was Uncle Pertti who had taught him the great, decisive trick.

Pertti Lindrot — hero from the Finnish Winter War, victor at Suomussalmi, the man who had posthumously sent the Söderstedt family on a trip to Tuscany they would never forget — wasn't a positive figure from the past. He wasn't one of those relatives who leave fond memories behind in the minds of the children, thus prolonging their lives by a couple of decades.

He was a downtrodden, downright nasty so-and-so. Nothing more than a stinking great toothless, sneering mouth.

Memories . . .

But there was one thing he had taught little Arto. He had pulled him onto his lap one day and tried to talk some sense into him. Little Arto had done nothing less than try to get away as quickly as he could, of course. Even now, he could clearly remember the stench coming from Pertti's toothless mouth. But in the middle of it all, amid all his general slurring, the key questions came through. They sounded exactly the same as the slurring but had been accompanied by a look that wasn't usual for Uncle Pertti. That was when little Arto saw the real hero from the Winter War, the guerrilla fighter who had spent years hidden away in the frozen landscape. He had seen pictures of Uncle Pertti from that time and they really were something else. One image in particular had stuck in his mind. The pride beaming from Pertti Lindrot's fair-skinned face, standing in the middle of a snowdrift with his hand on the butt of a sabre was not only impressive, it was familiar.

Oddly familiar.

As familiar as a mirror image. It was as though Arto Söderstedt himself was the one standing in the snowdrift, his hand on the sabre, trying not to laugh. The likeness was uncanny.

And so he had adopted the slurring tactic. If not the stinking mouth.

OK, so his thoughts were drifting aimlessly. He tried to halt the rivulets and direct them back into the main stream.

It didn't quite work.

The pictures of the seemingly sophisticated and iron-fisted Marco di Spinelli weren't coming together to form one harmonious portrait. It remained superficial. It remained a series of inconsequential computerised projections. It remained elusive.

He would have to come back to it later, once he had renewed his strength.

Arto Söderstedt emptied the *very little* glass of Vin Santo in one gulp, switched off the computer and stood up.

He was going for a siesta.

CHAPTER
TWENTY-TWO

Kerstin Holm was busy. Normally, she enjoyed being busy — she liked her job. Sometimes, when she found herself alone in the police station at nine in the evening, she would tell herself to *get a life*, but then it always struck her that she already had one and that her job was an important part of it. Her life consisted of working, singing and a little bit of jogging.

Until one day it was no longer quite enough.

Suddenly, she found it bloody hard work being busy.

Her life was about to quietly undergo a metamorphosis. *Another* one. And no one had the slightest suspicion.

She was no longer in the habit of mixing her work and her private life. Her escapades with Paul Hjelm a few years earlier had been the final straw. Until then, her relationships had all been with other policemen. She was originally from Gothenburg and had been married to a colleague whose relationship to sex was utterly uncomplicated: whenever he wanted it, she wanted it. That was the starting point. It had resulted in several utterly unexpected rapes taking place in their marital bed. For a long time, she had thought that was just how things were meant to be. That was the extent to which her sexuality had been affected. By a male relative. With a fondness for special occasions and wardrobes.

That relative had long since died and her ex-husband had recently been suspended for alcoholism. Kicking someone while they were down wasn't really her thing.

Still, she thought she knew what a genuine, wild thirst for revenge was like. And that was precisely what she found herself faced with as she received reports and material from Budapest, Maribor, Antwerp, Venice and Manchester. The last had arrived that very day; so far, Chief Inspector Roelants in Antwerp had been right — it wasn't over yet.

A well-known pimp had, as far back as March last year, been put to death in the exact same way as Leonard Sheinkman in a park not far from Old Trafford. The case was stretching out further and further through time. The Erinyes had been busy for more than a year.

The goddesses of revenge.

Not a single witness in any of the other cases. That made their skinhead Reine Sandberg and his gang unique. They were the only people to have seen the Erinyes and survived. His associates had confirmed every last detail of his story. There had been four of them and, in blind panic, they had fled across Skogskyrkogården. When they reached the metro station, there were only three of them left. Andreas Rasmusson, who was now slowly starting to recover in the psych ward, had been wandering around among the graves for three hours. He had finally managed to find the train station and then continued his wandering in

Stockholm's Central Station, where the police had picked him up.

In a way, she wished she could feel sorry for him.

Kerstin felt like she understood. She felt like she really understood what this entire case was about: a pure, genuine, wild thirst for revenge.

The thin, dark figures dressed all in black were, without a doubt, women. What kind of women? Who had cause to murder pimps? Prostitutes, of course. It seemed likely that their so-called ninja feminist belonged to a gang of highly trained, detoxed prostitutes. According to Adib Tamir, she had been wearing: "red leather jacket, tight black trousers, black trainers". Had she been wearing the other get-up beneath the red jacket? Had she been dressed for battle when she was attacked? Was that why the whole thing had been so unnecessarily violent?

On the whole, though, it wasn't unnecessarily violent. They hadn't been taking down any old drug-addled, small-time pimps; they had been exclusively murdering pimps who also happened to be violent criminals. All had been murderers. And all had a rape or two under their belts.

In other words, they were scum.

But imagine if what happened in Odenplan metro station was a result of controlled acts of violence. Imagine if it was a first sign that violence can never take place without leaving a trace, without sooner or later exploding and running amok. Practically all the Vietnam veterans were serious addicts, the men who dropped the atomic bombs on Japan had virtually lost their minds, and they were only just starting to see the far-reaching consequences of the violence in Yugoslavia. Violent men — and presumably women too, for that matter — were always consumed by their violent acts in the end. Executioners had always gone mad, throughout history. Their job ate them up from the inside.

But Hamid al-Jabiri wasn't a murderous pimp. He was far from an angel, but had he deserved such a terrible end? Was he really one of those doomed to death? No, that was where the whole thing had gone off the rails. After a year. Perhaps that had been a reasonable amount of time to endure it all, before it became impossible.

Before the violence had gained a life of its own. It was no longer under control; it had started to do the controlling.

That was one interpretation, anyway.

The Erinyes had been at it for a year now. Their acts of violence were strictly controlled and didn't affect innocent bystanders — providing, of course, you excluded Leonard Sheinkman. They quite simply targeted men they considered worthy of death. And a terrible death was exactly what they gave them. But perhaps that wasn't all they did. What would be interesting was if their strength kept increasing. Were they recruiting at the same time as they were exacting revenge? Had eight seemingly worn-out women from the Norrboda Motell been initiated into some kind of army? Would they too start wearing tight black clothing and murdering pimps across Europe once they had finished their training? Was this a way of countering the aggressive growth of the prostitution industry?

Was it a sign that the women of Eastern Europe were fighting back?

If that was the case, Kerstin Holm hoped they wouldn't be caught.

Yes, she was a police officer. Yes, it was her job to prevent crime and to bring criminals to justice. And yes, she hoped that they wouldn't be caught.

That didn't mean she wouldn't be doing her job. She just didn't feel especially happy about doing it.

And not just because her life was undergoing a metamorphosis.

After divorcing her policeman husband in Gothenburg, Kerstin Holm had ended up in Stockholm. The A-Unit had been formed. During a brief, intense relationship with Paul Hjelm, she had lowered her defences and told him everything. It was the first time she had ever done so, and it meant that her relationship with him was special, even once it was over. She still loved him, just not in that way. She didn't want to spend the rest of her life with him. But he was, with his peculiar combination of awkwardness and precision, warmness and coolness, frenzy and passivity, intellect and feeling, a man who seemed particularly full of life. It was that simple. Everything was constantly in motion inside him. He would never stagnate.

It was just that the two of them were surprisingly similar. She had fallen in love with her own mirror image. That had been the mistake. During the past few days, she had realised that that had been the mistake.

She needed something completely different.

After Paul Hjelm, she had dived straight into a strange, intense relationship with a sixty-year-old priest, a man who also happened to be dying of cancer. It had been an overwhelming experience and one which forced her to reassess the very basis of her life. That was what she had been doing for the past few years.

And then this metamorphosis. The thing she suddenly found herself in the middle of.

On her computer, she was busy checking whether the reports from Hungary, Slovenia, Germany, Belgium, Italy and England in any way suggested that prostitutes had disappeared in parallel with the murders. She had no problem with the reports from Germany, Italy and England, and with the help of a little dictionary she had compiled herself, using all the buzzwords she could think of, she was making some headway with the Hungarian, Serbo-Croatian and Dutch reports too. But quick work it was not. Each country had sent a summary of their reports in English, all more or less distorted, but if she was going to do this properly then she was going to have to delve into the chaos of the original languages used to write the reports.

She started thinking about the eleventh chapter of the Book of Genesis. The Tower of Babel. Why had God really decided to split that unified human language into so many? Why had He decided to make us incomprehensible to one another? Did religion really have any sensible explanation for that?

She went online to look at the Bible. The only thing she found was an old translation. It would have to do.

The whole story of the Tower of Babel was told in nine cryptic verses beginning with: "And the whole earth was of one language, and of one speech." What happened next? Mankind worked out how to make bricks, eventually building a city and a tower which was to be so tall it would stretch right up into heaven. That didn't sound so bad. But their purpose was clearly to prevent themselves from being "scattered abroad upon the face of the whole earth". They wanted to speak one single language and live in one single place. That was when God turned up, thinking something like: it seems as though nothing is impossible for these people. And so He decided to "go down, and there confound their language, that they may not understand one another's speech". After that, He scattered them across the globe.

There was no real explanation for God's actions, but from what she could tell, He was using the confusion of tongues to spread mankind across the earth and prevent them getting up to any mischief in one single place. Because everything would have been possible for them if they had been able to stay as one. Even building a tower up into heaven, God's domain.

Kerstin Holm wondered whether mankind really would have been stronger had they been able to live together in one place, speaking one single language. Would anything have been possible for them if that had been the case? She thought it sounded stifling. The oft-slandered God of the Old Testament, the Jewish God, seemed rather to have saved mankind from near-fascist uniformity, and made possible a continuous exchange between people of different languages, experiences, climates and world views. He hadn't been afraid that the Tower of Babel would encroach into His heavenly domain at all — he had been afraid that the Tower would have been the downfall of mankind as a result of inbreeding.

If there was a God then He had, by creating the different languages, saved us from suffocating beneath our own self-sufficiency.

This reasoning in mind, she jumped straight into the strange Hungarian language and felt the challenging power of the unfamiliar mounting.

Detective Superintendent Mészöly's report was still waiting for her. The victim in Budapest had been a twenty-nine-year-old pimp strung up in his own home on 12 October 1999. She feverishly searched for missing prostitutes from the same point in time. Mészöly hadn't written a single word about anything similar.

Six countries, Kerstin thought, of which four were EU member states. Hungary, Slovenia, Germany, Belgium, Italy and the United Kingdom — none seemed to have a particularly good oversight on the women involved in the sex industry. The fact that she and her Swedish counterparts did was more a coincidence; the fact that they had discovered the women's disappearance was entirely dependent on their believing it was a case of asylum seekers going underground. *That* was when they reacted. *That* was when it was decided that the country was at risk of becoming impure. If eight prostitutes had simply disappeared from the streets of Stockholm, no one would have batted an eyelid. Eight fewer people to deal with at the social welfare office. Many would have breathed a sigh of relief. Little else would have happened.

The fact that no trace of missing prostitutes appeared in the foreign reports didn't mean that there hadn't been any. Time for another group message to the nations involved.

She went through the old messages; she couldn't get enough of number eight: "Who in high heavens authorised this inquiry? Whose budget will this come out of? WM." The more she read it, the more incredible it seemed. It was a brilliant summary of Waldemar Mörner's work.

Number two was also good. The scolding from the Parisian policeman, Chief Superintendent Mérimée: "You, Madame Holm, seem to be using Europol resources for Swedish petty crimes." Considering what was currently going on around Europe, it was almost worth saving that message just so she could shove it up the good superintendent's arse at the first opportunity.

Yes, it was true, that might have sounded a bit vengeful.

Message number one, on the other hand, was still waiting for her. The online flirt, Detective Superintendent Radcliffe from Dublin: "No idea what his title is, but he's friendly. As you also seem to be, Ms Holm." And this friendly man he alluded to happened to be called Benziger. "I'm wondering whether I didn't hear about something similar in the former DDR. Get in touch with Benziger in Weimar."

It was true, she had completely forgotten. She found an email address for the Weimar police department and wrote a brief inquiry to the complete stranger, Benziger.

Then she sent the group inquiry off to the six countries with pimps who had been strung upside down and had a metal wire driven into their temples.

The temple, yes. Right *there*. Kerstin Holm touched her own thin left temple, the spot where her hair refused to grow. Wasn't it an awful coincidence that these wires had been forced into the very spot where she herself had been shot less than a year ago, missing death by millimetres?

She didn't like coincidences. They rarely stayed that way.

She had a vague memory of lying on a mud-soaked lawn, her blood mixing with Paul Hjelm's beneath a heavy sky and whispering, completely exhausted, completely soaked, completely bloody, "Paul, I love you."

She was afraid he had misunderstood. Of course she loved him, she did, but she didn't quite know *how*.

In other words, she was undergoing a metamorphosis.

It just wasn't something she could touch upon yet.

CHAPTER
TWENTY-THREE

The beauty of the abstract. A case which was becoming increasingly complex, increasingly far-reaching, reduced by an anonymous artist to an extremely simple, extremely distinct plus shape.

Perhaps it should have been a minus sign.

Jan-Olov Hultin secretly wished he had been the artist. His diagrams were normally big, sprawling things, with lines and arrows in all directions, the whiteboard ending up so full that he often had to continue on the back. By the time the lines and arrows reached so far he had no choice but to spin the board to clarify each thought, his audience had usually given up.

And so he preferred the beauty of the abstract.

The polar opposite of which was piled up on the desk in front of him. For the first time since it all began, he had taken the time to read through the press reaction to the case. They had managed to keep most of it quiet so far — that was a first.

The "Skansen" quadrant, to begin with. The wolverine case wasn't really a case at all. During the first few days, there had been plenty of eye-catching headlines and close-ups of the chewed leg, and plenty said in the tabloids about just how dangerous Skansen really was for our innocent children. Pictures of children dangerously close to bears had been published. The Skansen management had been forced to stand to account in a number of television debates, with demands for their immediate resignation being made and talk of a general ban on wolverines being bandied about. The relevant government minister would be looking into the regulatory system.

Then the "Slagsta" quadrant. Hultin hadn't managed to find a single line about the eight missing women. It was, quite simply, not news.

Next, the "Odenplan metro station" quadrant. Hamid al-Jabiri's death had, fortunately, been reported as an accident. One paper had managed to take a photograph of his lower body on the tracks. They had printed it without hesitation. A television debate about safety on the metro system had so few viewers that several advertisers had clubbed together to write a discussion piece in *Dagens Nyheter*. It had inspired several follow-ups. One of those involved, the information officer for a brewery with a strong media presence, was estimated to have earned twenty-three thousand kronor for his articles. That in itself had started a new debate.

Lastly, the "Skogskyrkogården" quadrant. The all-important question of Leonard Sheinkman's tragic end had been treated like a racial killing of the worst kind, not least after Waldemar Mörner's blunder during Sunday's live press conference. Otherwise, it was Sara Svenhagen's chlorine-green hair that was being discussed, the result of which was that she had been sent three invites to film premieres and one to Café Opera's twentieth-anniversary celebrations.

A number of media representatives had desperately tried to bribe hospital staff into letting them talk to "the arrested suspect", Andreas Rasmusson. According to one paper, he had "not only violated Jewish graves on this occasion, but also brutally murdered an old Jewish professor of nuclear physics". The same piece had continued: "Obstinate police interviews with the suspect resulted in his admission to the psychiatric ward. One source claimed misuse of batons."

Sheinkman's hanging was being discussed, but the long metal wire had been kept from the press. One television channel had managed to get hold of the old cemetery caretaker, Yitzak Lemstein, who had shown them his tattooed arm. The studio audience had read signs telling them to be loudly horrified, and so they were. During the interview which followed, Lemstein had unfortunately brought up the visit from Chavez and the grave marked "Shtayf". Happily, it hadn't led to any further questions. The presenter had had some trouble comprehending the word "Yiddish".

Jan-Olov Hultin spent a moment thinking about what caused strokes before pushing the pile of papers away from him and saying, without further ado: "We'll have to wait for answers regarding the phone. It turns out the contract is Ukrainian after all, but apparently the Ukrainian company is unable to produce a list of calls. Their technology is about a decade behind ours, and it's impossible, from a technical point of view. Our technicians are slowly helping them onto the right tracks. Otherwise, you know about the other new development. Arto is now formally involved in the investigation, as a Europol officer. I just heard that he's been granted access to the suspected head of the Ghiottone organisation, the name of which means not only 'wolverine' but also 'glutton'. This man is a ninety-two-year-old banker called Marco di Spinelli. Arto will be visiting him this evening. Should we try to put this into some kind of order? Jorge?"

Chavez sighed gently and glanced at his papers.

"Bits of rope have started turning up," he said. "I guess we've just got to hope we find the exact one, that there aren't too many resellers, and that someone remembers whoever bought it. I know it's a bit of a long shot, so it should hardly be our top priority. None of the ropes have matched ours yet anyway.

"My second point is more interesting — the question is whether it was a pure coincidence that Leonard Sheinkman was strung up right next to the anonymous 'Shtayf' grave. There's a twenty-year-old murder case behind 'Shtayf'. The victim was in his forties, died of knife wounds and was a concentration camp survivor. It should've been possible to identify him from the numbers tattooed on his forearm, but he'd evidently tried to scratch them off with a knife, meaning they were illegible. His most distinguishing feature was that he had no nose. In my opinion, it's really odd that the Huddinge police investigation from 1981 was such a complete failure. *Someone* should've remembered seeing a man without a nose, his appearance should've

278

caught *someone's* attention, wherever he came from. The Interpol of the time also failed back then. I've re-sent them his face and fingerprints. Europe has grown and it's more accessible now."

Jan-Olov Hultin didn't look like normal. Since each minute shift in his stony face immediately caught their attention, the A-Unit held its collective breath. Was this the stroke they had been dreading?

"It was my case," he said, sinking into a hole in time. There was a jolt in the space-time continuum, the clocks rushing madly backwards. Jan-Olov was suddenly in his forties and found himself in a tiny, newly decorated office in the police station, leaning back with satisfaction and thinking "finally". The image was as clear as day.

A moment of silence prevailed. Then Chavez said: "No."

"What?" said Hultin, rapidly transported back through the ages. Clusters of stars raced by at a speed faster than light.

"That's not what it said," said Chavez. "Bruun. Superintendent Erik Bruun from Huddinge Police. Haven't I heard that name somewhere?"

Paul Hjelm laughed. They looked at him with a tangible scepticism.

"Erik Bruun's my old boss," he explained. "He's the one who coaxed me into the A-Unit."

"Right," said Chavez. "We went there once. But that was when he'd just retired."

"Heart attack," Hjelm nodded. "Too many cigars."

Hultin was becoming more like his old self again. They collectively breathed out. The blood clot was clearly keeping its distance this time, too.

He said: "It was then, in September 1981, that Bruun coaxed me into CID. Clearly he's done a lot of coaxing in his time. I was given the case on the ninth of September and started half-heartedly looking into it. I knew I'd be getting a response to my application to CID at any time; I didn't behave very professionally those last few days. It's the greatest blot on my career right up to the Kentucky Killer. I got the reply on the eleventh and moved here right away. Bruun more or less took over the wrecked investigation himself."

"I'll be damned," said Hjelm. "I started there as a newly qualified officer in 1984. I have no memory of him ever mentioning a case involving a man without a nose."

"It was never a proper case," said Hultin. "Just another John Doe among others. Not even the press showed much interest. You couldn't print images of bodies back then. Things are different now."

"What do you remember?" asked Chavez.

"He was found lying in a ditch by a little lake in Älta, right next to a highway. No tyre tracks to speak of. He was naked, two big knife wounds to the back — either of them could've been the cause of death. The numbers on his arm were almost illegible beneath a criss-cross of scars, as though he'd tried to scratch them off. And then that nose . . ."

"I've got a picture here," said Chavez, passing an old colour photo around the Tactical Command Centre.

280

"I didn't really manage to find anything. No witnesses, no clues. It didn't seem like anyone in all of Sweden had seen that noseless man. But like I said, I didn't look very hard."

"One thing," said Kerstin Holm, looking down at the photograph. "Why wasn't more done, considering how badly disfiguring his facial damage was? One single look would've been enough to make any plastic surgeon leap at the challenge."

"Good question," Hultin admitted. "Poverty? Lack of medical care? Outcast?"

"And a foreigner, too," Kerstin added, nodding slightly.

"Would it be worth talking to Bruun?" Hjelm asked hopefully. He hadn't seen his old boss since the heart attack had brought in a nightmare replacement by the name of Sten Lagnmyr.

"I think so," said Hultin. "You and Jorge."

"OK," Hjelm and Chavez said in unison.

"How's it going with the boats, Sara?" Hultin continued, looking more neutral than he had in a long while. Clearly it was time to compensate for his earlier emotional outburst.

"Great," said Sara Svenhagen. "There are plenty of options if you want to get from Stockholm to Lublin by bus, especially if you have thirty-five hours to do it. That's the amount of time between their possible departure from Slagsta and the phone call from Lublin.

"The most logical thing would be to get on the closest ferry, from Nynäshamn, and head to Gdañsk. It's a straight line from there, if you want to get to the

Ukraine via Lublin. It's a night ferry, leaving at 5p.m. and not arriving in Gdañsk until half eleven the next morning. It's roughly six hundred kilometres between Gdañsk and Lublin, and the phone call to Odenplan was made at three. So if we say it took maybe half an hour to get off the ferry, then you would have to drive at 150, 160 kilometres an hour to get to Lublin in time. It's just not possible. It's wrong.

"The other plausible option if you're going direct from Sweden would be via Karlskrona. The M/S *Stena Europe* left Karlskrona at nine in the evening and arrived in Gdynia at seven on Friday morning. That would mean they had eight hours to drive those six hundred kilometres. Sounds much better. So I got in touch with Stena Line to check how many buses they had on board on that date. Turns out there were eight buses on that particular ferry from Karlskrona, leaving on the fourth of May. Four of the buses were organised trips and then there was one Polish, one German and two Swedish; one of the Swedish buses was full of single men on their way east to find partners or venereal diseases or something like that. One bus was on the way to scrap in a Polish scrapyard, and the others were private hires. But here's the interesting part. What gets smuggled from Sweden to Poland rather than the other way round?"

"IKEA furniture?" suggested Viggo.

"Moose antlers?" suggested Jorge.

"Almost," said Sara. "Sea eagles."

"Poached?" asked Kerstin.

"Get to the point," said Hultin.

282

"The privately owned Polish buses were full to the brim with poached sea eagles. Swedish and Polish customs were evidently working alongside our environmental protection agency. It filmed the crackdown. There were a few minutes about it on *Aktuellt* on Friday evening. They've got quite a lot of extra film that they're going to send over a bit later today. If we're lucky, we'll be able to spot the other buses in the background. I was also planning on taking a trip down to Karlskrona to talk to the crew on the ship. The same crew is going to Gydnia again tonight. Will the budget cover a flight down to Karlskrona?"

"Purpose?" asked Hultin.

"To show them pictures of Galina Stenina, Valentina Dontsjenko, Lina Kostenko, Stefka Dafovska, Mariya Bagrjana, Natalja Vaganova, Tatjana Skoblikova and Svetlana Petruseva. To see what the crew remembers. If the women were on board, they must've stuck out in one way or another."

"Have you learned their names by heart?" Jorge asked in surprise.

"It's the least you can do, working on a case like this," Sara said cuttingly.

"Trip approved," Hultin said curtly. "Viggo?"

As though it was the most natural thing in the world, Viggo Norlander said: "We're having another baby."

"For God's sake, Viggo!" exclaimed Gunnar Nyberg. "Astrid's forty-eight."

"Forty-seven," Norlander corrected him. "And how old's Professor Ludmila?"

"Congratulations, Viggo," said Kerstin Holm. "Don't listen to those fossils. They're just jealous."

"Why the plural?" said Paul Hjelm. "Where did that come from?"

"The women congratulate and the men commiserate," said Sara Svenhagen. "Just as it should be. Congratulations, Viggo."

"Yeah, yeah, congratulations, you damn rabbit," said Hjelm.

A few more congratulations were uttered before Norlander, entirely unaffected, continued: "The circumstances of the other pimp's death are, as you know, murky. The pistol which killed him was apparently made three minutes after Nikos Voultsos's. The silencers were identical, too. *I rest my case.*"

"Who was he?" asked Kerstin Holm. "How did he get in touch with the girls in Slagsta? Was he the one who brought them here?"

"His name was Finn Johansen, but he doesn't seem the kind to have 'brought' any whores here," said Viggo Norlander. "Though he did seem to have a certain talent for sniffing out new free agents. His speciality was finding girls who didn't have any protection. So that's probably what happened. I looked into the Norrboda Motell a little. Why was it that eight whores were given rooms right next to one another? Jörgen Nilsson clearly wasn't the one who made that decision. He was brought in later, by none other than Finn Johansen.

"I think it went like this: Botkyrka's refugee centre was overflowing. When they were being moved, any single asylum seekers could put in a request if there was someone they wanted to share a room with. In the old centre, only a couple of our eight were living together. I think that they found one another somehow and decided to work together. It's entirely possible that some of them weren't working as whores before they came here. Though their pictures were really typical whore pictures. Johansen found out about the place and went down there to provide them with protection and drugs. I'd bet that was what happened. I've talked to a few whores who —"

"Could you stop saying 'whores'?" asked Kerstin Holm.

"Why? They are whores."

"There's something so violent about that word. It's like a rape, every time someone says it."

Paul Hjelm glanced cautiously at her.

"I'll try," said Norlander. "But old dogs are old dogs."

"Very true," said Kerstin.

"So, I've talked to a few girls," (without even a pause, Viggo thought happily, just as he continued), "who were part of Johansen's group. He could be tough, apparently, but if you behaved then he was one of the better pimps on the street. That probably just means they had to go to A&E slightly less often than the others. Otherwise, there's not much to say."

"Good," Hultin said honestly. "Paul?"

"You've all heard about Voultsos's stay at the Grand by now. Sixty-three thousand kronor, paid posthumously. Or rather, paid by his employer; according to Arto, the account belongs to the Ghiottone. I didn't find anything of interest among the other phone numbers to and from Slagsta. The incoming calls were mostly from johns, the outgoing calls mostly from Finn Johansen, but under an alias of course. Girlfriend's phone. Then there's this thing with the Erinyes. "Ερινυ". From a literary point of view, it's pretty damn exciting. Have you heard of Aeschylus?"

"I'm assuming you'll be looking into the literary side of it in your own time?" Jan-Olov Hultin said brutally.

"Of course," Hjelm replied, continuing without further ado. "In ancient Greece, in the fourth century BC, people used to compete in the field of tragedies. The authors of these tragedies each wrote three dramas: they took themes from older myths, and the three tragedies belonged together, like a kind of suite. Only one complete suite, a trilogy, I suppose, survived. It was written by the eldest of the three great tragic authors, Aeschylus, and it's called *Oresteia*. The first of its dramas is called *Agamemnon* and it's all about a Greek commander from the Trojan War coming home. He brings a lover with him as a war trophy, an enchantress called Cassandra. His wife Clytemnestra has also found herself a new lover while he's been away and she murders both her husband and his innocent lover. That's the end. It sounds pretty banal, but I'll be damned if it's not one of the most venomous things ever to have been written. OK, part two of the suite is called *The Libation Bearers*. In this one, Agamemnon and Clytemnestra's son Orestes is on the hunt for his mother and her lover. Honour demands that he avenges his father. A blood feud. Are you following?"

"Mmm," said Hultin tentatively.

"And just as he should, he takes his revenge and murders his mother. *End of part two*. The third part is called *The Eumenides*. Since he's guilty of murder, Orestes is now being hunted by the most terrible beings that mythology has to offer. They come from the most ancient parts of the kingdom of the dead. They're the goddesses of revenge, the Erinyes. 'We are the children of eternal Night, And Furies in the underworld are called.'

"They manage to catch up with Orestes, but just as the hour of vengeance is about to strike, Athena — the wise goddess of Athens — appears. In court, she replaces the ancient laws of bloodlust — the driving force behind the Erinyes — with a modern rule of law worthy of Athens' new-won democracy. Barbarism is subdued, civilisation is triumphant. And the Erinyes are tamed; they become part of society by being offered 'a calm and peaceful haven'. The era of primordial rage is over. The young, reasonable gods take over from the old, blind, hateful ones. And the Erinyes become Eumenides. Powerless, but with a new-found peace. For the first time ever."

Hjelm glanced around the Tactical Command Centre. It actually looked as though they were listening.

"Is that how we want this to end?" he asked.

There was a moment of silence. He looked at Kerstin; she looked back. With the same look he had given her. And it was very, very difficult to interpret.

Eventually, Hultin said: "Don't you read anything else?"

"Yeah," said Hjelm. "Leonard Sheinkman's diary. But it's too hard right now. I'd like to come back to it."

"Too hard?"

"Too hard."

"Right then," said Hultin, slightly paralysed. "Well, Gunnar?"

"One new thing," said Gunnar Nyberg. "The other skinheads confirmed Reine Sandberg's version of events. They went out there to get drunk, break gravestones and sing Nazi battle songs in the Jewish cemetery. Then they caught sight of the old man. He didn't have a little hat on, but they knew right away he was Jewish. They'd been planning on going over to harass him, maybe even beat him up a bit. And in that excited state of mind, they saw the black figures gliding over. That's when they got scared like only those with exaggerated, false courage can be. They ran like mad."

"And the new thing?" Hultin said neutrally.

"He'd stopped at the gravestone. Leonard Sheinkman was standing by the gravestone with 'Shtayf' on it."

"Yes!" blurted Chavez. "I knew it."

Nyberg continued, unperturbed: "When Sheinkman saw that the grave was broken, it looked like he started laughing. He bent down and touched the broken pieces. That was when the figures appeared. They peeled away from the trees like 'strips of bark', according to this Reine guy. The skinhead who stayed the longest says they were talking. Sheinkman exchanged a few words with the dark figures.

288

Completely calm. Then it all happened really quickly, as though the whole process had been practised."

"It had been," said Kerstin Holm. "It was the eighth time. At least. If I've managed to get on top of things, then it started in March last year. In Manchester. It was Antwerp in July, Budapest in October, Wiesbaden in December, Venice in February, Maribor in March — and Stockholm in May. You can see how the pace has been picking up. They're getting better and better. It took them two months to plan the Stockholm attack. They had a lot to coordinate here, after all.

"Stockholm was a renewal on many levels. A development. On the one hand, they were sending a sophisticated message to the Ghiottone organisation in Milan. On the other, they were going to murder another man, someone from a completely new category: an old professor. Both of these are a bit mysterious. Why send a greeting to Milan? Why murder a man who can't plausibly have had the slightest thing to do with prostitution or pimps? Does the message to the syndicate in Milan mean something like *we know who you are, you haven't heard the last of us?*"

"Doesn't sound so implausible," said Paul Hjelm. "Maybe they've finally managed to find one of the big crime syndicates behind the growth in prostitution across Europe? And now they're going after it, and they want them to know. They're doing their bit for their fellow man."

"Isn't it funny that we automatically say 'man'? I do it too. But the fact is, if that's true then they're doing it

289

for their fellow *women*. Our language always conditions us to put the emphasis on men. Just like society."

"And biology," said Jorge.

"What are you saying?" exclaimed Sara.

"I read a comment piece in the newspaper this morning, by a scientist in forensic psychology. According to him, male violence is a purely biological phenomenon and has nothing to do with man's role in society. There was even a diagram, with one line showing the concentration of testosterone in the blood and another the number of violent crimes which led to prosecution. The two lines followed each other point for point. Testosterone causes violence. Men who've been castrated have a decreased tendency for aggression. Evolution put this tendency for aggression in the male species so that they would compete with other men for the chance to reproduce and provide food. In all known cultures at all known times, men have been more prone to violence than women. All men are violent, but since we primarily focus on what's in our own interests, we realise that using violence in the type of society we live in doesn't have a positive effect. And so we divert our tendency to violence towards other, more productive activities, like sport."

"Just wait until you get home and we'll see if that's true," Sara Svenhagen said violently.

"I'm just quoting the article," Jorge Chavez replied, castrated. "It's interesting that this kind of thinking is actually in circulation among prominent scientists. He even had examples from the animal kingdom. I thought stuff like this had been disproved. Not least by huge female spiders killing their tiny males right after mating."

Kerstin Holm said: "Biologism is all about the idea of people being completely controlled by the laws of biology. Economism means that all human activity can be linked to some kind of profit. Two words we should learn."

"This is all a bit close to measuring skulls for my liking," said Hjelm. "State Institute for Racial Biology in Uppsala."

"The Erinyes," said Holm. "It's interesting that the ancient Greeks made their most violent beings women."

"Meaning our violently inclined Erinyes can't be women," Hultin said neutrally. "Rethink."

They looked at him. He didn't bat an eyelid.

"Should we try to move on now?" he said eventually. "So that at least *some* work gets done?"

Kerstin tried to go back to her earlier train of thought. Finally, it led to something:

"Maybe their Stockholm attack also involved a renewal of a third kind. We've got no proof that any prostitutes have been recruited before — but it seems like that's what happened here, that the Slagsta girls are being transported to their base in Ukraine. It might be the first time it's happened, and in that case, it's a matter of starting to liberate prostitutes. Though it might well have happened earlier — the various European authorities' knowledge of fallen women isn't always exemplary."

"What kind of girls are these Erinyes, really?" asked Viggo Norlander. "I mean, it doesn't just seem to be the woman from Odenplan who's highly trained; there seem to be at least five of them?"

"I still get the impression she's the leader," said Kerstin Holm. "She's the one who was in contact with Slagsta, the one they called from the bus in Lublin. But yes, they all seem well trained . . ."

"So at least five in Södra Begravningsplatsen," said Sara Svenhagen. "Plus at least one more on the bus, whoever it was who rang. The tour guide or something. Sounds like a pretty big organisation."

"And I think it's getting bigger and bigger," said Kerstin Holm. "But, Viggo, what kind of girls? It's pretty serious violence. There must be hate and revenge involved. I think it's a group of former prostitutes from Eastern Europe finally hitting back."

"With the maximum amount of pain possible," said Paul Hjelm.

"Yeah. First they practically scare the life out of their victims with their ghostly creeping about. Then they use a near-scientific method to cause as much pain as they possibly can. It's specialised, for sure."

"It's certainly not normal," said Chavez.

"No," said Kerstin Holm. "It's certainly not normal."

CHAPTER
TWENTY-FOUR

Palace. Palace was the word.

You couldn't call it anything else.

It was in the same area of the city as the cathedral, at the very centre of Milan's concentric rings. Arto Söderstedt looked up at its sixteenth-century facade with the same fascination he always felt when faced with works of the Renaissance. That feeling of anything being possible, that man had just crawled up out of the dark ages; the feeling that the winds of change had been blowing in our direction, that we would simply get better and better and never have anything to fear.

Things had been roughly the same with the IT revolution. Though now it was in a parallel world that anything was possible. This reality had been exhausted, but cyber-reality was entirely unexplored. An enormous map of nothing but blank space. Columbus, Vespucci, Cortés, Vasco da Gama, Fernão de Magalhães; each of them had been resurrected to colonise a new world for the wealthy holders of power. With any luck, genocide in cyberspace would prove to be slightly less bloody.

But its art would hardly reach such heights.

The palace was even featured in his guidebook. It had been built between 1538 and 1564 by an architect called Chincagliera, on behalf of the aristocratic Perduto family. The fact it was called Palazzo Riguardo seemed slightly ironic to Söderstedt. "Riguardo" meant "respect".

The garden, a glimpse of which could be seen through the wrought-iron gates, was magnificent if cramped, as all private inner-city gardens tend to be. Söderstedt closed the guidebook and put it back in his briefcase before pressing a button on the wall. There was nothing to be heard, nothing to be seen. The only exception was a lone cat stalking through the greenery, miaowing furiously.

He waited. The sun had been high in the sky all day. The first week of May was over, and summer had been inching its way up the Appenine peninsula, finally reaching Milan. He continued to wait, watching as the reddening sun peeped through between a couple of roughcast stone buildings which looked completely black against the bright disc in the sky. It was evening in the big city. The traffic was still intense, but the air felt cleaner. It was lucky that the drive from the hills of Chianti to the smog of Milan took so long; his lungs had plenty of time to get used to the pollution.

He waited. He wasn't going to give up.

Eventually, an abrupt voice said: "*Nome?*"

"Arto Söderstedt, Europol."

His debut. It felt absolutely fine.

"*Carta d'identità?*"

He held up his Swedish police ID and his provisional Europol card. He didn't quite know where to hold them — he couldn't see a camera anywhere.

294

"*Avanti.*"

The heavy iron gates swung silently open. He walked into the garden and up the stairs to the palazzo. Three sturdy-looking men in suits. Nothing new under the sun.

He was frisked twice by two of the men. The third emptied his briefcase and scrutinised the Pikachu figure dangling from his car keys. He squeezed it. It popped.

"Pokémon," Artö Söderstedt said as one of the men squeezed his genitals. Thankfully, they didn't pop.

The men said nothing. Söderstedt was utterly convinced he had ended up in some kind of low-budget film. The gates swinging back were the opening scenes, and he stepped right from reality into fiction. The film was under way.

During the rest of his time in Marco di Spinelli's palazzo, he acted as though he was playing detective. He could hear his cool, drawling Philip Marlowe voice making comments about a variety of events. "It was one of those days when I would've rather chopped off my right arm than get out of bed."

The three men — he avoided thinking of them as wise — took him down corridors awash with beauty. The distance between the men on the floor and the stucco ceilings above them seemed infinite — and not just in terms of time and space.

Eventually, they came to a majestic anteroom. It was higher than it was wide, but it was a miracle of well-restored wood carving. Behind a desk which, in all likelihood, was part of the original Perduto family furniture, a thin man in a dark drainpipe suit and fifties glasses was sitting. He was the spitting image of Mastroianni in *La Dolce Vita*. Clearly, he was di Spinelli's private secretary. The man who knew everything that went on. He looked like a member of the increasingly endangered species which rendered computers obsolete.

"Signor Sadestatt," he said, adjusting his glasses and holding out his hand.

That was clearly how his name was going to be pronounced. If nothing else, it was at least consistent.

Signor Sadestatt held out his hand and nodded mutely; he had already been introduced, after all. The other man obviously had no intention of introducing himself. He probably thought of himself as a function rather than a person.

"Signor di Spinelli will see you in a few minutes," the man said. "You will have a quarter of an hour. After that, I'm afraid Signor di Spinelli must leave for New York. He is already taking a later flight in order to entertain you at such short notice."

"Thank you very much," said Signor Sadestatt, suddenly feeling like he was in deep water. Literally. He was treading water and couldn't see land no matter which way he looked.

Time seemed to be taking a siesta. It was moving as slowly as treacle. He was treading water, trying to keep afloat. His movements were slow. After an indescribable amount of time, a boat suddenly appeared, plucking him up out of the water. Everything was back to normal.

With the exception that he was now talking to an Italian Mafia boss.

The pictures hadn't lied. Marco di Spinelli was wearing a sporty black polo neck beneath a thoroughly modern black suit. Söderstedt guessed it was Armani. His face was furrowed, but his eyes didn't look like a ninety-two-year-old's. They were clear, pale and brown, a perfect match for the grey-haired man. Silver fox was an adequate description after all.

Could this man really still have all his own hair at the age of ninety-two? Was that physiologically possible?

His office was unrivalled. Söderstedt had never seen anything like it. Three of the walls were clad in colourful sixteenth-century tapestries depicting a broad paradise landscape of shepherds, shepherdesses, sheep and fountains. Above a huge open fireplace on the fourth and final wall, Söderstedt could see two paintings. The style of both was immediately familiar. The first of them, a beautiful woman sitting on a wall, must have been a genuine da Vinci. The other, a perfect double portrait, looked like a Piero della Francesca. Above these figures, over six hundred years old and seemingly alive, the ceiling, lined with what was, in all probability, genuine gold leaf, arched up and away. An enormous chandelier covered with thousands of crystals looping across one another to create an exquisite glittering net hung in the centre. The whole thing seemed to be moving upwards, towards the ceiling. And beneath this golden net, right beneath the moving, dazzling chandelier, the first Perduto must have sat, gazing out at sixteenth-century Milan, his quill hovering above the inkwell. Then he must have continued, his hand light and his handwriting elegant, writing his polished sonnets.

The pictures belonged to di Spinelli.

He was standing next to one of the tapestry-clad walls, his hand somewhere behind the cloth. A gap appeared between tapestries, and in that gap Söderstedt caught sight of the bare stone wall. On it, an ugly red button. Marco di Spinelli was pressing it. The crystal chandelier's movement up towards the ceiling was nearing its end. The old man let go of the button and held his hand out to Söderstedt in silent greeting. Instead of any introduction or welcoming phrase, Marco di Spinelli's first words to Söderstedt were:

"Are you aware, Signor Sadestatt, that it was at this very desk that the Marquis of Perduto sat writing his famous sonnets to little Amelia, whom he met aged eight and never forgot?"

His voice was dry and his English flawless. An upper-class British accent.

"The concept seems familiar," Söderstedt replied, sitting down in an armchair next to the fireplace.

Marco di Spinelli chuckled gently, poured two glasses of Calvados and placed them on the little table between the armchairs. He sat down.

"It was that kind of time," he said. "Petrarchism was all the rage across Europe. Everyone was writing love poetry to a young girl they believed they had met in their childhood, someone they could never forget. A time of mass psychosis. Rather like now. Don't you agree?"

298

"In a way," Söderstedt replied, taking the glass of Calvados being held out to him. He sniffed it with the air of a connoisseur and said: "Grand Solage Boulard, if I'm not mistaken."

Marco di Spinelli raised an eyebrow and said: "Are you a connoisseur, Signor Sadestatt?"

"I saw the bottle," said Signor Sadestatt.

"I know," said di Spinelli.

"I realised that," said Söderstedt.

"I realised that you realised," said di Spinelli.

Their exchange could have gone on for a long time.

The ice had, at least, been broken, and Söderstedt had managed to work out roughly where he had di Spinelli. He was exactly where he had expected him to be.

"I must admit," the old silver fox said, "it was something of a shock when you walked into the room, Signor Sadestatt."

"It didn't show," said Söderstedt.

"You truly do remind me of someone I knew an eternity ago, back in the beginning of time."

"During the war? Did you have much contact with blond men during the war?"

Marco di Spinelli smiled grimly and said: "Let's return to the present, since I do unfortunately have other pressing matters to attend to. It's funny, isn't it, that we never do learn to wind down."

"I'll be concise, then," said Söderstedt. "A Greek by the name of Nikos Voultsos somehow managed to get himself eaten by the wolverines in a zoo in Stockholm. Were you aware of this?"

"I heard about it," di Spinelli nodded. "A peculiar fate."

"I have a photograph of the two of you together. The two of you are shaking hands and you, Signor di Spinelli, have your other hand on Voultsos's shoulder. It all looks very friendly. But Nikos Voultsos was far from a friendly individual."

Marco di Spinelli threw his hands out in a resigned gesture.

"Did you come here to repeat things the Italian police have said to me hundreds of times before? I had hoped you would be slightly more . . . original."

"I just want to hear you explain away the fact that you — an honourable banker and politician — knew that multiple murderer and violent criminal."

"It was deeply unpleasant when I found out he was a criminal. We happened to meet in a cafe one morning and simply started talking. My relationship with that man went no further than that. What was his name? Valtors?"

"Exactly," Söderstedt replied.

The old man looked at him, one eyebrow raised. Söderstedt continued.

"How would you interpret the fact that Nikos Voultsos was driven straight towards the wolverines — the *ghiottoni*, if you will — by unknown criminals, and that, once there, he was executed in a very particular way?"

"Oh," di Spinelli said, looking surprised. "The Swedish press said it was an accident. You surely didn't come here to let that slip, did you? This wouldn't happen to involve confidential matters, would it?"

"It's nice to hear you're so well read on the Swedish press's coverage of your brief acquaintance's death. You can read Swedish, can you? Perhaps we can speak Swedish, then?"

"Marconi told me. You must know the good commissioner and his disproportionate moustache? He is a good friend of mine. A very good friend."

"But don't the people who did this seem awful? We have to ask just who might have put that nasty Nikos Voultsos to death. *Nema problema.* Snip, snap, and he was broken up into very small pieces. And of the prostitutes, not even one stayed behind. They simply disappeared. Poof."

"You're starting to become vulgar, Signor Sadestatt. And time is getting on."

"What did you do during the war?"

"You've already read that in my folder. Don't act dumb."

"I'd just like to hear it from you."

"There isn't much to tell. I went into exile, away from the Fascists. To Switzerland. Why are you interested in my sorry war tale?"

"I'm afraid I'm prevented from answering that," Söderstedt replied indifferently before continuing: "Why isn't there a single trace of you in Switzerland?"

"Why are you repeating the same things the police have been asking for years? I had a number of aliases because the Fascists were after me."

"The Fascists were after you but now you're active in Lega Nord? A separatist party with a very close working relationship to the neo-Fascists?"

"A necessary evil. A political tactic. We aren't Fascists. We simply want to legally establish a border which is already there in practice."

"A North Italy and a South Italy?"

"All the money earned up here in the north simply runs down south. We want to keep it up here and become a country with normal European living standards."

Arto Söderstedt suddenly held up a photograph. He studied di Spinelli's expression closely.

"Do you recognise this man?"

"No."

"What about this one?" he asked, holding up another photo.

"No."

"The first was Leonard Sheinkman as an eighty-five-year-old, the second was Leonard Sheinkman as a thirty-five-year-old."

"Leonard Shinkman? I don't know any Leonard Shinkman."

"Sinkman," said Söderstedt.

Marco di Spinelli looked at him suspiciously.

"Thanks then," Söderstedt said, downing the last of his Calvados and getting up.

"Are you finished?" di Spinelli exclaimed in surprise.

"You said you were in a hurry. I certainly don't want to get in the way of your important New York trip. I've

302

got everything I wanted. Thank you. I hope to see you again."

He left the room before Marco di Spinelli even had time to get up. The man with the glasses was sitting at the desk, leafing through some papers. He glanced up at Söderstedt, perplexed. Söderstedt kept walking, out into the corridor. Three bodyguards were sitting there, eating apples. They immediately threw their half-eaten fruit into a nearby bin and began to reach for the bulges in their jackets. It was like synchronised swimming. Three men in perfect coordination, performing the exact same movements at the exact same moment.

Dunk, dunk, dunk, and the apples dropped into the bin.

"Teamwork," said Arto Söderstedt, rushing off down the beautiful corridor. One of the bodyguards pushed past him, the others still behind. Unless you followed procedure, you were probably dismissed. Rather than receiving dismissal pay, you were more likely to end up with a lump of cement around your feet. That was nice too.

Yes, Arto Söderstedt was behaving oddly. He stopped on the pavement and glanced up at the blood-red sun which was just sinking behind the Milanese rooftops. He was behaving oddly because he thought — though it was vague, no more than a suspicion, a tiny little first suspicion — that he had found out exactly what he wanted to know.

Uncle Pertti's slurring technique had served him well.

Marco di Spinelli had recognised Leonard Sheinkman. Not as an eighty-five-year-old, perhaps, but definitely as a thirty-five-year-old.

From 1947.

CHAPTER
TWENTY-FIVE

The two women Viggo Norlander would be watching videos with were really something. Alone with them in the small, sweaty room, he felt almost horny as he pressed play on the VHS machine.

It was true, he was having a hard time ignoring the short greenish hair, but given that it was crowning a face that was a triumph of youthful beauty, it was utterly irrelevant. The messy chestnut hair, on the other hand, was incredibly appealing. And the woman it belonged to, beyond description. He could see straight through her clothes. It was fantastic.

"Lay off, Viggo," said Sara Svenhagen. "They're practically popping out."

"What're you talking about?" Norlander asked with well-masked shame.

"It's like they say," said Kerstin Holm. "Whenever a man finds out he's fathered a baby, he suddenly gets hornier than ever."

"What is it with you two?" asked Viggo, blushing for the first time in thirty years. "What have I done?"

"Just press play, will you?" said Sara.

"I have," Viggo said confusedly.

It felt so strange to be blushing. Memories he had no desire to be reminded of were pushing forth. But at the same time, it felt good that they were returning. They had been gone for so long.

"It's coming in a second," said Sara Svenhagen. Norlander couldn't help but interpret her words in all manner of ways.

"The Environmental Protection Agency had four hours' worth of film," she continued. "They'd been following the poacher from the St Anna Archipelago in Östergötland, where someone had reported seeing a bus full of feathers. They were filming while the poacher was having a coffee on the ferry. They shot this sequence just as he was about to disembark and be busted by the Polish customs police."

The picture crackled into view, gradually coming into focus. The bow of a huge ferry. The bow visor rose slowly upwards; buses came driving out. A couple of tourist buses first, one German and one Swedish. Then a smaller one, an utterly clapped-out-looking thing. It was driving straight towards the camera, which followed its movements. The customs officers moved in. Tough-looking Polish officers in uniform, yanking the door open, rushing into the bus and hauling the driver out. The poacher was thrown to the ground. The camera was filming him as it passed by. The bus doors were open. The camera panned up the steps and then swung to the left, inside the bus. It moved over the passenger seats. Ten or so sea eagles were laid out on them. The picture swept down the left-hand side of the bus and then froze.

"There," said Sara, pointing at the television screen. Above the eagles, the bus window was visible. Through it, the front of another, smaller bus had appeared from the left.

She let the film play, as slowly as she could, until the front window of the other bus became visible. A face could be seen through it. She froze the image again.

"This," said Sara, "is Svetlana Petruseva, the Belorussian from room 226 of the Norrboda Motell."

Viggo Norlander and Kerstin Holm both glanced at Svetlana Petruseva's passport photo, comparing it with the slightly blurry figure from the screen.

"Yeah," said Viggo. "That's her."

"Seems that way," said Kerstin. "But the question is whether it holds up as evidence."

"There's more," said Sara.

The bus continued its slow-motion journey past the poacher's bus. Just as it passed by, the camera shifted slightly and the back of the other bus, the one in which they had seen Svetlana Petruseva, came into view. The picture froze again.

They had a clear view of the rear window of the other bus. Two faces were peering out at the customs raid. They immediately recognised one of them. It belonged to Lina Kostenko, the Ukrainian from room 225, the room the ninja feminist had been calling. The face next to her was unfamiliar, but belonged to a young, dark-haired woman, and in her hand a mobile phone was visible.

"There you have it," said Kerstin Holm. "A few hours later, that phone would be ringing a disembodied arm in Odenplan metro station."

"This is our first and last picture of a member of the league," said Sara Svenhagen. "The technicians are working flat out on it. They're working with this, too."

Her finger moved down the screen to a blurred, half-obscured registration plate.

"It's Swedish," she said. "But we can't see much else for the moment."

"Swedish vehicle . . ." said Viggo.

"Driving through Sweden, from Stockholm to Karlskrona, in a Ukrainian bus, would probably have been tricky," Sara replied. "It would've drawn too much attention. They probably rented it."

"Should we assume," said Viggo, "that the ladies also had Swedish passports? That they did the whole thing as Swedes? And their real passports stayed behind?"

"Yeah," said Kerstin, standing up and stretching. "It seems pretty likely they were given fake Swedish passports. Or Western European ones, at least. So there wouldn't be any problems with customs. We'll send the picture of that girl out, plus the registration plate, as soon as the technicians are done. Sara, are you still going to Karlskrona?"

"It's too late now," said Sara, glancing at her watch. "Apparently it's the same crew coming back from Gdynia tomorrow. I'll catch them then."

"Take Viggo with you," said Kerstin. "He doesn't seem to have much to do. Plus I think a bit of sea air will cool him down."

Viggo Norlander nodded eagerly.

It would be another thirty years before he blushed again.

CHAPTER
TWENTY-SIX

The time had come. Chavez couldn't quite understand why Hjelm was making such a big deal of it. They were in a drab old bachelor pad in Eriksberg, to the south of Stockholm. Their host, serving them coffee, looked like any other old man.

But for Paul Hjelm, it was a momentous occasion. He would probably have felt exactly the same if he were given access to Jan-Olov Hultin's legendary house down by the waters of Ravalen. Though he had worked under Erik Bruun for considerably longer.

The fact was, he had learned everything he knew from Bruun; nothing to make a fuss about.

But he didn't recognise him.

It wasn't exactly a tragic experience, like seeing an old sports star strutting about in a body that looked like it might fall apart at any moment. It was more complicated than that.

Detective Superintendent Erik Bruun had always been a fairly solid-looking man with a greyish-red beard that covered his multiple chins. His most distinguishing feature had been an omnipresent, foul-smelling, black Russian cigar resting between his lips. The health authorities had condemned his office in Huddinge, known as the Bruun

Room, on a regular basis. And it was that very fact, that he had incessantly gone against all conceivable rules and regulations, which had prevented such a brilliant policeman from advancing further through the ranks. If Erik Bruun had been National Police Chief during the past few decades, a lot of things would have been a lot better. Paul Hjelm was convinced of that.

But now, he was a shrunken old man with only one chin, no greyish-red beard, no black cigar. He looked much healthier — but also more boring.

And his legendary bachelor pad in Eriksberg looked like any other pensioner's flat. And this particular pensioner was serving — cinnamon buns.

"You know, I know exactly what you're thinking," he said, sitting down.

"Probably," said Paul Hjelm.

"I had to," said Erik Bruun. "I would've died otherwise. The legend would've lived on and I would've died. I'd rather the legend died and I lived."

"I can understand that," said Paul Hjelm.

"Of course," said Bruun, leaning forward. "Of course you *understand* it. But you don't accept it. You can't accept the fact that I've become a plain old pensioner who shuffles around in slippers and serves thawed cinnamon buns with a high mould content. It would've been better to keep living on the legend. And the fact is that at this very moment, you're thinking it's a shame the heart attack didn't finish me off."

"You're hardly a plain old pensioner," Hjelm argued, taking a bite of a bun. "Though the mould content's high all right."

"What is an ordinary pensioner anyway?" asked Chavez in an attempt to join in on what seemed to be some kind of mutual appreciation society. "Is it something like an ordinary immigrant?"

"Something like that," said Erik Bruun with a neutrality that immediately made Chavez understand. Understand Hultin's roots, understand Hjelm's roots. It was an enlightening moment. "Boys, boys, your boss is a former pensioner. It's not everyone can say that. When Jan-Olov was a pensioner, we used to play chess in the Kulturhus once a week. Those were the high points of my life. But we never do it any more. I'm lonely in the way that only an old policeman can be. Utterly lonely."

Hjelm and Chavez glanced at one another and realised that this might well turn out to be hard work.

"Just don't forget that I know exactly what you're thinking," Bruun continued with a smirk. "Both of you."

"You don't know me," Chavez said irritatedly. "How can you claim to know what I'm thinking?"

"Because I know what kind of policemen you both are."

"Come off it," said Chavez.

"You thought you were hearing the start of some kind of pensioner's lament just then, but that's not the case. I *am* utterly lonely — but I *want to be*. It suits me to a tee. I hope I'll get the opportunity to die utterly alone as well. I *want* them to find my body after it's started to stink. I *want* them to have to fish me out from a sea of maggots."

The combination of Bruun's imagery and the amount of mould in the cinnamon buns was worrying.

"What do you mean?" asked Hjelm.

"You know full well. You're the same, despite the wife and kids and cat and dog."

"Parrot," said Hjelm.

Chavez laughed, short and abrupt. Like a parrot. He still felt annoyed at the old man. He was a know-it-all, that much was clear.

"Jorge Chavez," said Bruun, glancing wryly at him, "you think I'm a know-it-all, don't you?"

"True," said Chavez, attempting to seem unperturbed.

"I just think that happiness has become a bit predictable. We know in advance what the concept of 'happiness' is meant to involve, and loneliness is right down at the bottom of the list. Behind mental illness and drug addiction. We can understand the mentally ill and the addicted, we're socially educated humans after all, but we'll never understand the lonely. Loneliness is an unpleasantness we try to overcome whatever the price. We'll go through any suffering necessary if it means we can avoid being lonely."

"So you want to rehabilitate loneliness?" Chavez asked sceptically.

"That's neither here nor there. Quite simply, we live in a society which is afraid of loneliness and silence. I want to be alone and I want to have silence around me. I know you two in the exact same way I want to know people in general: in detail, but from a distance."

"What do you mean? How do you know us?"

"How do you think we passed the time during those chess games? The way pensioners always do: we recounted old stories."

"So you sat there in public, discussing individual police officers' personalities?"

"You had code names. You, Jorge, were Soli. And you, Paul, you were Keve."

"Keve Hjelm," said Paul Hjelm. "What an uncrackable code."

"Keve Hjelm was the first person to play Martin Beck on film," said Erik Bruun, looking up at his former trainee.

"I'm hardly Martin Beck," Hjelm said self-consciously.

"Not exactly, no," Bruun replied cryptically.

"What about Soli, then?" asked Chavez. "What's that?"

"The Mexican composer Carlos Chavez's most characteristic work."

"You seem to have had a right royal time," Chavez said sourly. "What did you say about me, then? About . . . Soli?"

"That's confidential," said Erik Bruun with his head held high. "But we mulled over the pair of you so much that I think I can claim to know roughly how you think."

Without thinking, Paul Hjelm took another bite of his cinnamon bun. He regretted it long afterwards.

"What do you know about this case, then?" he asked, feeling the lump of mouldy bun stick to the roof of his mouth. Each attempt to poke it loose with his tongue was in vain.

314

"Much too little," Bruun said apologetically. "Jan-Olov hasn't really been himself. Do you think he's getting sick?"

"Hardly," said Hjelm. "But he's brooding about something. And he doesn't normally brood."

"No," Erik Bruun agreed, "he doesn't."

Jorge Chavez had grown tired of their empty chatter. He said: "You know about our interest in a man without a nose, at the very least."

"Of course," said Bruun.

"Have you searched your memory?"

"Wasn't necessary. I remember it all."

"How unexpected," Chavez said frostily.

Erik Bruun laughed. "Soli, Soli," he said, as though he was talking to a disobedient but dear grandchild.

"What do you remember, then?" Chavez persisted.

"There was really just one lead worthy of the name," Bruun said calmly. "It was 1981. The phenomenon of unregistered taxis had only just started to appear. An illegal driver called Olli Peltonen was sitting in a pub, reading the articles on the murder in *Aftonbladet* and shouting all about how he'd driven that body without a nose. A woman heard him and called the police. By the time we got there, he was gone, but the people from the neighbouring table told us who he was. It turned out that Peltonen had already gone underground as the head of Stockholm's first illegal taxi ring. We showed his photo everywhere, but he stayed hidden."

"Why wasn't there a word about this in your report?"

"I put in a reference to the illegal taxi investigation," said Bruun. "I suppose it got lost when they transferred

315

it all over to the new computer system. Unfortunately, the small print usually goes up in smoke. Especially with cases no one cares about."

Erik Bruun paused and stared up at the ceiling. Finally a gesture which Hjelm recognised. Then he continued, his face still raised to the ceiling.

"It was nearly twenty years ago. It's strange what a memory for faces you develop as a detective. I saw Peltonen in the paper a while back. There was a taxi driver strike up at Arlanda, if you remember it. Quite an interesting event, societally speaking. A group of petty capitalists tied to the syndicalists launching a wildcat strike because the taxi ranks closest to the airport had been reserved for three big companies. Petty syndico-capitalists protesting against big capitalists. Might well be the tune of the future."

"And?" Chavez said, sounding increasingly impatient.

"One of them was Olli Peltonen. There was a picture of him kicking one of Taxi Stockholm's cars. There was a name beneath the picture, but it wasn't Olli Peltonen. Apparently he's calling himself Henry Blom these days. He runs a little taxi firm with the confidence-inspiring name Hit Cab."

"And why didn't you tell the police?" asked Chavez.

Erik Bruun leaned forward and fixed his gaze on him.

"I keep my distance these days," he said.

Hjelm could see that Chavez was reaching boiling point. Small smoke signals were rising from his ears. It would have been interesting to be able to interpret them.

"He's got one thing left, at least," said Hjelm.

"What's that?" Chavez muttered.

"The ability to rub people up the wrong way."

Chavez mumbled something which, fortunately, was inaudible.

They were driving towards the Globe Arena. The enormous sphere was already towering up in the distance like a threatening ping-pong ball. "The Glob". The great big lump of snot.

Hjelm was driving. Chavez was sulking next to him.

Soli, Soli, Hjelm thought, trying not to laugh.

They had managed to track down Hit Cab fairly quickly. It was run out of an office right next to the Globe. Hjelm called and Henry Blom had answered in shaky Swedish. Hjelm told him his name was Harrysson and that he was the chief accountant of ClamInvest AB, an organisation which made investments in the shellfish business. Harrysson claimed to be interested in using Hit Cab's services on a regular basis. He asked whether Henry Blom would be in the office that day. He wouldn't, but considering the potential size of the agreement, he would be willing to rearrange his schedule. Harrysson thought that sounded like a fantastic idea. He and his assistant (cue a grumpy look from Chavez) would stop by Hit Cab within the hour. Henry Blom gave Harrysson detailed directions and ended the call expectantly.

"You're a terrible human being," said Chavez.

"Sometimes," said Hjelm.

And so Harrysson, chief accountant of ClamInvest, arrived along with his assistant at the Hit Cab office, right next to the World-Famous Glob.

Henry Blom was a bald man in his fifties who spoke terrible Swedish with a strong Finnish accent. He humbly greeted the two dignitaries, who sat down and were handed coffee by a girl who could hardly have been much out of high school. Henry Blom had already given the two dignitaries a couple of poorly assembled brochures when they suddenly held up their police IDs and said:

"Olli Peltonen, I believe, the godfather of illegal taxis."

He stared, fascinated, at the two men, who changed shape before his eyes.

"I'm afraid we've got to destroy Hit Cab's future," said Harrysson Hjelm. "Not just because you've been wanted for some time now in regard to illegal taxi rings, and not just because you started a business using a false name, but because you're also employing girls who seem much too young to be employed."

"Child labour, that's what they call it," said Assistant Chavez. "Really harsh sentences for that."

"But," Harrysson-also-known-as-Hjelm said, "there's an alternative."

Henry Blom or Olli Peltonen could sense that everything was about to come crashing down around him. It was clear that he had no escape plan.

"What alternative?" he stuttered.

"You tell us about a man without a nose."

With that, his mask finally came off. The man blinking profusely at them now was called Olli Peltonen and nothing else. Eventually he nodded, as though he had been gripped by an insight of some kind.

"OK," he said. "And if I talk?"

"We'll think about that when it happens," Chavez answered tryingly. "Hopefully things will be looking much better by that point."

"What?" said Peltonen.

"You tell us, we look the other way."

"OK, OK. He was the one who got murdered, right?"

"Exactly."

"Nineteen eighty . . . what was it . . . two?"

"One," said Hjelm. "September 1981."

"I picked him up, that really is true. I remember him pretty well. It was horrible. He looked bloody awful. Weird injury."

"Where did you pick him up?"

"Frihamnen. He must've arrived by boat."

"How did he get hold of you? You had no taxi sign?"

"No. Unregistered taxis are taxis without signs."

"That's what they call a euphemism. How did he get hold of you?"

"I think I must've just been driving round down there. That's how it still works, I think. I don't know, I don't have anything to do with that any more. You just ask people who look like they need a ride whether they need a ride."

"And when was this?"

"I don't remember the date."

"He was found on Sunday the sixth of September. It was a headline in the evening papers that Sunday so that must've been when you were sitting in the pub, shouting about how you'd driven him somewhere."

"Must've been the Friday then. Friday the fourth. In the evening. I mostly drove in the evenings, after seven."

"What else do you remember about him? How was he dressed? What impression did you have of him? What language was he speaking?"

"He sat in the back. The only impression I had was that he didn't have a nose — that pretty much takes the sting out of anything else. All he said was the address I should drive him to. Strong accent, I'm thinking. He was less Swedish than I am."

"And where did you drive him?"

"I don't remember."

"Come on, Ollipolli. Think."

"It's not child labour anyway," Peltonen said suddenly. "She's my granddaughter. She skives off school sometimes, and when she does, she comes to help out here. Rather that than her hanging out with all those drug addicts down in Högdalen."

"So it's some kind of charity work then?"

"She's my granddaughter. I love her. You can't send me down for child labour."

"We're not planning to. Come on. Where did you drive the man without a nose? Where did he tell you he wanted to go?"

"I need to know you're not going to send me down. Can't you write it down or something?"

"Of course not. Are you guilty of any crimes under the name Henry Blom? Answer honestly and we'll check later."

"No, no. Hit Cab was my way of returning to life. I was hiding for so long it got me down. It was unbearable. And then I realised I could find a new identity. It took time and it was hard work, but it was worth it. I'm honest now. I don't earn much money and the big companies take most of the work. I protested against it at Arlanda."

"When did you change your identity?"

"Three years ago."

"And you didn't think that the period for prosecution would've expired by then?"

Olli Peltonen stared at them furiously.

"It's a bit ironic," said Chavez. "To get away from a crime that was no longer a crime, you committed a more serious one, and it's the only crime we can send you down for. The fact that you call yourself Henry Blom."

"Please . . . is that true?"

"Yeah," said Hjelm. "You were hidden for so long that the law stopped caring about you. But the law doesn't turn a blind eye to murder. For that, the validity period is very, very long. So help us out now. Then you can be called Henry Blom for the rest of your life and no one will say a thing. You've got my word."

Olli Peltonen was quiet, thinking about the irony of fate. Then he said: "South somewhere."

That was all.

"Come on," said Chavez. "You're a taxi driver. You know every single street in the entire Stockholm area like the back of your hand. Where did you drive the man without a nose?"

Peltonen thought. He was forced to cross an enormous, terrible gap in time. He was balancing on the narrow plank, crossing the abyss. Step by step, swaying, he made his way across.

He made it to the other side.

"Nytorp," he said, a strange tone in his voice.

"What the hell's Nytorp?" said Chavez, who *didn't* know every little street in the entire Stockholm area like the back of his hand.

"Nytorp is in Tyresö," Peltonen said proudly.

Tyresö, thought Hjelm.

"Do you remember the address?" he asked. "The street?"

Peltonen racked his memory. It took its sweet time.

"It was the name of a bird," he said.

Silence.

"A common bird," he said. "A really ordinary Swedish bird."

More silence.

"Not the house sparrow," he said. "Not the great tit."

He stood up and exclaimed: "Bofinksvägen!"

Chaffinch Street.

Paul Hjelm leaned back in his chair.

He had been there recently.

To the house of a son who had just lost his father.

Leonard Sheinkman had lived on Bofinksvägen in Tyresö.

CHAPTER
TWENTY-SEVEN

17 February 1945

The noise has grown so loud now. It is almost starting to seem real.

Yet more real is my name, crowning the top of the list.

I thought the ceiling was going to come crashing down today. Pieces of it rained down onto us. They looked like ice floes. A shudder ran through the building. I do not know what is happening out there but I wonder whether we will survive.

Of course I know what is happening: they are, of course, bombs. The liberators' bombs, killing the interned.

Dare we speak of irony?

Yes, we dare. We must. How else would we be able to breathe? Our last breaths must be taken through a filter of humour. I have been running through all the old Yiddish jokes I know. Not that there are many. I have never been particularly successful in my faith. I had too much respect for the soul.

They walk the corridors; I see them from my cell window, walking like lost souls through an environment which is already gone. They wonder why they have been left on the banks of the river of death. Like drunk ships bobbing on its waters. Their bandages shine like lanterns on their empty skulls.

Yes. I cannot touch upon the fate which awaits me. It simply isn't possible. It is beyond all else.

I should not feel terror; it is a sign of life. I have no right to show signs of life.

I have no right.

The rain. Afternoons bathed in grey. They are taken away to be shot.

No. Elsewhere. Let me talk about time . . .

No. Not this time.

Speak clearly. You are on the verge of death, man. Speak clearly.

Your wife and your son were taken away to be shot. You saw them being led round the corner. They were being taken to their deaths at the execution spot. They were to be killed. Magda had stolen food from the barracks to give to Franz. He had been starving to death. For that, they killed my wife. And our son, as an example.

And I ended up here.

Though I was already in Hell.

18 February 1945

You think you will never manage to lift the pencil again. You think you have written the worst words imaginable. After that, what is the point of carrying on? And yet, you do. A new day always dawns.

The bombs are raining down more and more heavily now. I saw time itself shudder.

I am going to describe time. I think I have already done it. Time consists of two things: a clock and a tower. The tower exists so the clock can function. The clock exists to honour the tower.

The clock is our soul, the tower our body.

Though we are here to prove that the clock is substance. That the clock is simply the mechanism driving the hands forward. The same movement for all eternity.

Or until the tower falls.

I have seen it shudder. A bomb was about to fell it. A bomb was about to fell time.

Let me describe time.

Time has a white base. That base may well be quadrangular. Then comes the black. The black is made up of three parts. The lowest of these is hexagonal. On three of these six surfaces, every other one, there are two windows set one above the other. The lower window is slightly larger than the upper. And immediately above the upper window, the next section begins; the middle. It is just as black and shaped like a small, domed cap. This is where the clock sits. Finally, the spire. The spire is black and looks to be needle-sharp.

I am Jewish. I have never understood why churches must look so sharp. Our synagogues do not. I have always thought they look like breasts. Mothers' breasts.

Why am I describing time in such detail? Because soon it will no longer exist. Because the next bomb will fell it. Because it is already trembling in the breeze.

Because time is about to die.

Erwin is dead. He was a kind soul. One of the three officers told me. The kindest of them. He is less German than I, and very blond. He looks so sorrowful.

He kills with sorrow in his eyes.

Not the other two. One kills out of curiosity. He is not cruel, simply cold. He watches, observes, writes. But the man with the purple birthmark on his neck, a mark in the shape of a rhombus, he is cruel. He wants to kill. I have seen that look before. He wants you to suffer. Then you can die. Only then is he happy.

I do not know their names. They give no names. They are three anonymous murderers. They are not alike. Not even murderers are alike.

Erwin died of pain.

He is no longer living inside me. I felt him die, and with that I also felt myself die.

Tomorrow, if time still exists, I will write about when I died.

20 February 1945

Her voice speaks to me each night. Always the same words: "Why do you want to wait for death? Think of Franz, at the very least."

I thought I had been thinking of Franz. That is my only defence. He came up to my navel. We could talk. I asked him: "Do you want us to run, Franz? We'll have to leave everything behind." And he replied: "No." I listened.

Of course, I am lying. It is pathetic, lying when I have one foot in the grave. I know not why I wrote that. Why did I write that, God?

No. You won't answer.

Franz replied the way I wanted him to reply. I asked him simply so that he could say "No". How could he have said anything else?

I was the one who wanted to stay. I couldn't leave Berlin. It was my city, my country, my life.

And so I denied them.

That was when I died.

I promised I would explain today. I promised myself.

They took Magda and Franz away to shoot them. Magda was caught stealing bread from the soldiers' barracks. They shot them.

And I did not lift a finger. They would have shot me too, had I done so.

I don't know what kind of peculiar survival instinct that was. I already knew that I was dead. Why did I choose a long, drawn-out, painful death instead of choosing to die reconciled with my family?

Time is falling now. Here, before my eyes. As I write. The black tower and its old timepiece, the brickwork which has stood for hundreds of years — this very moment, it is falling. The church windows clink delicately with the clamour of the bombs, and framed by the ash-grey smoke of this doomed city's judgement day, a colourful cloud of glass fragments rises.

It could have been beautiful.

My name has reached the top of the list. Time has fallen. I saw it fall.

The kindest of the three officers came in to tell me. I would have an hour to prepare myself.

Soon, the little bandage will be pressed to my temple. Someone will watch me through their cell window and think that it is glowing like a lantern.

I do not know what I should say. Soon, the pain will hit me at a level I never thought possible.

That is the price of my betrayal.

CHAPTER
TWENTY-EIGHT

He had to admit it. He loved this case already. A couple of days had passed, information was flooding in from both Milan and Stockholm, and he was starting to realise that this was no ordinary case.

It certainly wasn't ordinary. And nor was Commissioner Italo Marconi. There was something about him.

"*A very good friend?*" he asked, fixing his gaze on the man on the other side of the table.

The man on the other side of the table said: "That was how he put it. He was very careful to emphasise it."

Marconi shook his head. His moustache bristled like reeds in a sea breeze.

"Signor Sadestatt," he said eventually, "you think I am Marco di Spinelli's very good friend?"

"Not at all," said Söderstedt. "But he wanted me to think you were. Why?"

"Because he once managed to get me to gang up on another policeman," Marconi said with sorrow in his voice. "I reported him for being corrupt. I was wrong, but I only found evidence of that once he'd committed suicide."

"He likes playing with the police," Söderstedt nodded, trying to imagine himself in a similar situation.

Arto Söderstedt accusing Paul Hjelm of being corrupt. Paul Hjelm committing suicide. Arto Söderstedt finding out that Paul Hjelm was innocent.

It was impossible.

The situation was so terribly different.

He hoped that would be the case.

"I'm sorry," he said, thinking that it sounded pitiful.

"Me too," said Marconi, pulling himself together.

"So he doesn't want to play with me any more?" Söderstedt asked.

"Doesn't seem to. He's refusing to meet you. What is it you think you'll achieve with a new meeting?"

"I want to press him a bit more."

"You don't *press* Marco di Spinelli."

"No, you can," said Söderstedt, "you just can't let him realise you're doing it."

"I'm not even sure I've understood what you think you found out last time? He knew your old Jewish man, Leonard Sheinkman?"

"I'm fairly sure he came across him sometime during the war. Do we have no idea at all what he was up to back then?"

"You've read his file. His life is well documented — aside from during the war. He was never a member of the Fascist Party, oddly enough. He's a self-made man from Milan's poor quarter. He stood out in the convent school he went to and was taken under the wing of a priest who helped him continue his studies. He became a banker early on, and just after the war he took over one of the leading banks in the city. Exactly how and when that previously respectable bank started to be used for criminal activities is still unclear. We're always looking for evidence, but we never find any. We're annoyed we can't find any evidence."

Arto Söderstedt nodded slowly. Then he said: "Was he going to New York?"

"No," said Marconi. "He never leaves his palace these days. It's over a year since he last left."

"I thought so," said Söderstedt.

He paused for a moment before continuing.

"I'd like a sketch of Palazzo Riguardo."

Italo Marconi glanced suspiciously at him.

"You want a sketch of Palazzo Riguardo?"

"Yes. Please."

"Maybe you can press di Spinelli without him noticing," said Marconi, "but you can't deceive me. Are you planning some mischief that might jeopardise my entire investigation?"

"Absolutely not," Söderstedt replied, feeling like a suspect. It was something he was quite used to.

"So what on earth do you need a drawing of Marco di Spinelli's palace for?" the normally so controlled commissioner blurted out. His moustache started to spin like a helicopter's rotor blade. He got up from his desk and went over to the window. He seemed to calm down. With his back to his Europol colleague, he continued sullenly: "I don't know what you're up to, Sadestatt, and that annoys me. I'm extremely worried about seeing years of work being ruined as a result of one stupid mistake from you. What were you thinking, going in and revealing confidential information to di Spinelli?"

"I've already tried to explain that," Söderstedt said patiently. "He already knows it all. What I told him wasn't news. We know that he knows and we're *telling him* that we know that he knows. That unknown killers threw the wolverines' henchman to the wolverines. That his man was about to set up an organised prostitution ring on behalf of the Ghiottone in Stockholm. That those prostitutes then went missing. He knows all that perfectly well. And he's already hunting for them. It's better if he knows that we know that too."

"And you don't think he'll see straight through all this?" Marconi asked, turning round, immediately more interested.

"Of course," said Söderstedt. "And that means he'll feel pleased. I think he'll just have realised that he felt pleased during our conversation. *That's* why he doesn't want to talk to me any more. I made him feel pleased and now he's mortified about it. He'll be wandering around wondering what he revealed while he felt pleased. That uncertainty is good."

"Seems like you're playing his game," said Marconi, sitting down with a thud.

"It's good if it seems that way," Söderstedt replied with a crazy look in his eye. Marconi looked at his facial expression, finding it fundamentally flawed. He nodded and smiled.

"And that's why you need a sketch of his palace? Utterly logical."

Arto Söderstedt smiled too.

"Exactly," he said. "Logical is an understatement."

Marconi was still nodding.

"So you think . . .?"

"Yes. That he's in danger."

"Marco di Spinelli is in danger? Do you know what kind of fantastical security systems that palace has? How many guards he has? Breaking in there would be like breaking into Fort Knox."

"You know you agree, Commissioner," said Arto Söderstedt. "They're coming for him."

"Who are?" Italo Marconi asked, without really asking.

Arto Söderstedt's answer wasn't quite an answer.

"The Erinyes."

CHAPTER
TWENTY-NINE

It was Friday 12 May. Time had started moving more sluggishly. It would probably be possible to relax a little at the weekend.

But time was also being difficult. It wasn't acting like normal.

It was probably out of sync.

Paul Hjelm suspected it was because there was a spanner in the works. Whenever the prelude to a chain of events was clear, time would trundle on like normal. Whenever the past was in order, with conflicts and injustices being discovered and revealed, and wounds were being healed, a certain degree of reconciliation was possible; time could move in a nice, linear fashion. But whenever the past was in some way false, deliberately falsified, then history would start to rot, a fly would appear in time's ointment, a spanner in its works, and time itself would start to act strangely. That was one theory, anyway.

Time was out of sync and who was Paul Hjelm to put it right again?

It would be a painful process.

Times of misfortune, that was what people used to call it. Back when people hoarded, built barricades, and refused to let any damn person cross their bridges. All while they hoped that their children would be born with one head rather than two.

They never understood that their behaviour was the very reason their children were occasionally born with two heads rather than one. Precisely because they always refused to let any damn person cross their bridges.

"Wake up."

"*Time is falling now. Here, before my eyes. As I write.*"

Leonard Sheinkman's words had sunk their claws deep into Paul Hjelm. He had deliberately avoided going back to the diary. He knew he wouldn't be able to read it with a clear, sober and analytical approach, though that was precisely what it needed.

Not that his decision had stopped it coming back to him. In actual fact, Sheinkman's words were constantly coming back to him. But only diverse phrases. The text in its entirety was still too difficult.

"Hello, wake up."

Leo Sheinkman's fate . . .

First he convinced his family to stay in Germany rather than fleeing. Then he watched as they were taken away to be shot — he didn't say a word. After that, he ended up in some kind of unit where he was forced to await his own painful death, something he could literally see coming closer. That was the state of mind in which he had been writing. That was the state of mind in which he had been released. That was the state of mind in which he had come to Sweden. It was hardly strange that he had needed to turn a new page in the book of his life, as his son Harald had put it when they spoke on Bofinksvägen. The newly arrived Leonard Sheinkman had needed to obliterate the past. He had needed to banish it. And so he became a scientist. He came to understand just how the brain worked. He consciously spent his time doing mental gymnastics. And he managed to turn the page. The side on which he wrote his new life was completely blank.

Maybe, every now and then, he had caught sight of a faint, blurred, back-to-front text through the, paper.

"Wake up, for God's sake!"

"Wha'?" said Paul Hjelm.

The whole of the Tactical Command Centre was staring at him. Lots of eyes. He counted twelve of them before he properly woke up.

"Whoops," he said. "I think I got lost in a time hole."

"Those seem to be pretty rife at the minute," Jan-Olov Hultin said neutrally.

Hjelm stared at a pile on Hultin's desk. Chavez was standing next to it. It was messy, but the dominant colours were red and purple.

"Samples from Europe so far," said Jorge Chavez. "Forty per cent of them aren't even red-and-purple stripes. Some manufacturers sent entire boxes of samples. We got a ten-centimetre-thick sample of rope for mooring oil tankers from a Czech company. It was white, made from hemp, and the postage was eight hundred kronor."

"Specially designed for the Czech coast," said Norlander.

They looked at him.

"There isn't one," he explained.

Chavez cleared his throat, slightly confused.

"Three of the samples could be a fit. The technicians are looking at their chemical make-up to see whether they match our rope."

He gathered up the samples, shoved them into a sports bag and returned to his seat.

"A model of conciseness," Jan-Olov Hultin said, brushing his desk with his hand.

Hjelm glanced at his watch. His feet were still dangling into the time hole. It was three o'clock. Three on a Friday afternoon. Almost the weekend. Almost time to go back to the diary.

"Do you think you could continue, Paul?" Hultin asked with ominous gentleness.

Hjelm tried to pull himself together.

"You've all heard about Henry Blom, aka Olli Peltonen. As you know, Gunnar and I have been working with Frihamnen for a while now. That was where Peltonen's illegal taxi picked up our noseless friend sometime after seven in the evening on the fourth of September 1981. It hasn't been easy, finding the old port archives, but I think we've finally managed. Seems like quite a lot of ferries arrived there that day. If we assume that Peltonen is right, and he drove him just after seven that evening, it narrows our scope a bit. That's also assuming our man without a nose — Shtayf from Södra Begravningsplatsen from now on — didn't just wait around, enjoying the sun down by the dock all day; it seems more likely that he headed straight for his final destination. In that case, three ferries seem interesting. Gunnar?"

Gunnar Nyberg had been keeping a relatively low profile since his confrontation with the skinheads in Åkersberga. That had very little to do with the skinheads themselves, however, and more to do with a certain professor of Slavic languages. He had, quite simply, been wondering what these strange sensations rushing through his enormous body were. Was he really in love? It had been such a long time, and if he was really honest, he wasn't even sure he had *ever* been properly in love before. He had, of course, felt love for his children, but before that? Had he ever been in love with poor Gunilla? He'd been horny, yes. But in love? No. Maybe, just *maybe*, he was now in love with Professor Ludmila Lundkvist.

They had gone to a little Russian pub down on Drottninggatan. For the first time in his life, Gunnar had eaten borscht and bear meat. A drop or two of vodka might also have passed his lips. Then they had gone back to her flat on Luntmakargatan; it had been so utterly obvious that they would. The night had been wonderful. Looking back, he couldn't remember whether they had even "had sex", as people so nicely put it nowadays. It was all just a feeling, sweeping sensations coursing through him. Then they had met again, at his house in Nacka. They had definitely "had sex" that second time, and it had been magnificent. She had also gone with him to his church to listen to the choir practice. The session had ended with the choir master saying that Gunnar's bass had sounded

338

unusually pure and clear that day. After that, they had gone home and made love. Unusually purely and clearly.

So no, they hadn't actually "had sex". They had made love.

Now, though, Gunnar Nyberg said, with uncharacteristic distinctness: "The three relevant ferries in Frihamnen that evening were: the French M/S *Marie Curie*, which arrived from Le Havre with a mixed cargo at 16.15; the Soviet M/S *Cosmopolit*, which arrived from Odessa with a mixed cargo at 18.25; and the German M/S *Mercedes*, which arrived from Kiel carrying a load of cars at 19.35. What we're doing now, trying to track these ferries down after twenty years and a redrawn map of Europe, it doesn't seem like it's going to be an easy task. Maybe we can say that, at this point, both time and space are pointing to *Cosmopolit*."

"From Odessa in the Soviet Union," said Paul Hjelm.

"Now Ukraine," added Nyberg.

They were silent for a moment. A system of coordinates very similar to a plus sign loomed large in a number of minds. A quadrant which had been standing alone for so long was slowly finding its way in towards the other three.

"Time for a hypothesis," said Paul Hjelm. "If the noseless Shtayf came from Ukraine and went to Leonard Sheinkman's house, then that's the link we've been looking for. Obviously it's still very vague, but if it's true then we've got a possible connection between our Ukrainian Erinyes and our professor emeritus. It's no less interesting given that Shtayf was killed on the same day he visited Sheinkman, and then found by the little lake to the immediate north-west of Tyresö. Nor that Sheinkman went on a pilgrimage to Shtayf's grave and met his death right above it nineteen years later."

"No, it's not," Hultin said. "What the hell is all of this? What's the missing link?"

"We might be going wrong somewhere," said Hjelm. "I've got a vague feeling there's something wrong somewhere."

"But vague feelings aren't what we do our job with."

"Don't say that."

"Do you have anything else?"

"No," said Hjelm. "Gunnar and I are still working on the ferries. Hunting down the old Soviet cargo ship, the *Cosmopolit*, is our next job. I'm going to be looking at Leonard Sheinkman's diary more closely, too."

"Haven't you done that already? Is it still 'too hard'?"

"Yes," said Hjelm.

Hultin sighed deeply and turned to Kerstin Holm: "Kerstin?"

She glanced down into her confusion of papers and replied: "Like I said, I'm still working on these murders around Europe. I'm carefully reading the investigations in each of the different languages. We haven't been sent any more, so that's one thing at least. But pestering Robbins in Manchester, Mészöly in Budapest, Sremac in Maribor, Roelants in Antwerp, von Weizsäcker in Wiesbaden and Gronchi in Venice has led to certain results.

"Maribor's the smallest of these towns. It was also the hanging immediately before Stockholm, in March. The Slovenian police have been making the greatest effort to be helpful European colleagues, and like I said, Maribor is a pretty small town. It seems as though a number of prostitutes did actually disappear from Maribor in March. There are certain hints from Commissioner Gronchi in Venice too, but they're more vague. Venice was the one before Maribor, in February.

"Wiesbaden isn't huge either, and Detective Inspector von Weizsäcker is quite certain: no prostitutes went missing there. That was in December. Maybe we can interpret this as a sign that our Erinyes started growing their ranks just this year? They've reached the point now where their strength can spread. And if that's the case, then we've just seen the beginning of it. Plus, I've finally managed to get a reply from Detective Superintendent Benziger in Weimar, in Germany. Detective Superintendent —"

"Do they really have titles like that?" asked Viggo Norlander. "The same plain old titles that we have here?"

"Of course not," said Kerstin Holm. "They're just rough translations. You've got to have really detailed knowledge to be able to understand the titles and promotion systems and hierarchies of these national police forces. It's hard enough here, with us. I barely know which title I have myself — and I'd have no idea how to translate it. Can I go on?"

"Let me think," Norlander replied jokingly. "Yes, yeah, that's fine."

341

"Thank you. Detective Superintendent Radcliffe in Dublin suggested I get in touch with this Benziger. He replied a couple of hours ago. He said: 'Dear Fräulein Holm. I sincerely apologise for not having been able to reply sooner. I've been on an assignment off grid. Jimmy was absolutely right to send you my way. James Radcliffe, that is. At an international conference recently, I told him that we had come across a modus operandi which reminds me of your case. I know very little about it, however, since it wasn't linked to any police operation. I refer you in this matter to Professor Ernst Herschel from the history department at the University of Jena. With kind regards, Detective Superintendent Josef Benziger, Weimar.'"

"So have you been in touch with this Herschel?" Hultin asked.

"No," said Holm. "I phoned but there was no answer. I've sent an email."

"Thanks. Anything else?"

"Not at the moment."

"In that case, we can finish off with a little film, can't we?"

"Yup," Viggo Norlander said cheerfully. "Your wife and I, Jorge, have been on the move. A kind of honeymoon. We even shared a room in Karlskrona."

"No we didn't," Sara Svenhagen retorted tranquilly.

"No, maybe not," Norlander continued without letting it affect him. "But I've been filming her in all manner of positions."

342

"If you don't stop, you can't come to the party," said Chavez, still relatively unperturbed, digging among the pieces of rope.

"What party?"

"Whoops," said Jorge, putting his hand to his mouth. "Maybe we forgot to invite you."

"Our house-warming," said Sara. "I take it you're all coming. Tomorrow evening at seven. Don't eat beforehand. Birkagatan. Though you've all got to make a solemn promise: not to say a single word about this case."

"Why didn't anyone say anything to me?" Viggo complained. "And after all the travelling we've done, Sara."

"You're not invited, Viggo," said Jorge. "Simple as that. We invited everyone but you."

"Stop it," said Sara. "You know full well you're invited, Viggo. Astrid already said yes. Charlotte's coming too. And we've had replies from everyone else, I think. Jan-Olov, what about you? Will your wife be coming too?"

"Yes," said Jan-Olov Hultin, suddenly revealing that he had a private life. "Her name is Stina," he added.

"And then Gunnar, I wasn't sure about how many . . ."

"Two," he replied, his voice clear and pure.

"So everyone's coming?" said Jorge. "I'll be damned. I'll have to go and buy some more Duca."

"What kind of South American crap is that?" Viggo persisted.

"It's a full-bodied Italian red. Duca d'Aragona, 1993. And it's not crap. But they've almost always run out. I'll probably have to go down to Nacka Forum to get some more. But I'll gladly do that for all of you."

Jorge Chavez was, in other words, a marvel of patience. Hjelm glanced sceptically at him. It was a front, it had to be a front. It couldn't be possible for a person to change so dramatically.

"Not everyone is coming," he said tryingly. "Arto's not."

"Don't be so sure of that," Jorge answered cryptically.

"Should we make sure our friend gets hold of his wine in time, then?" asked Hultin. "Press play, Viggo."

The remote control in Viggo Norlander's hand zapped life into the VCR machine over by the whiteboard. As the camera panned slowly over a drab-looking harbour, Sara said: "While you're watching the whole of the Karlskrona harbour area go past, I might as well start by saying that Viggo and I have sat through the whole of the Environmental Protection Agency's epic about the Polish poacher, Wojciech Bienek. His customers turned out to be German, Japanese and American. We paid particular attention to the film shot inside the ship. None of our Slagsta girls appeared there."

Once the camera had finished its panning shot across the harbour, there was a long, shaky sequence of paving stones rushing by. Every now and then, they caught sight of a brand-new Italian shoe, a right foot, which

344

had obvious specks of dirt on it. In the background, a mumbling could be heard:

"For God's sake, where'd the vegetable go?"

Viggo Norlander cleared his throat loudly.

"That should've been cut, Sara," he said severely.

"I thought it was worth keeping," she replied peacefully.

"I think so too," Hultin said neutrally.

Just then, the vegetable appeared on-screen. Sara Svenhagen's chlorine-green hair appeared opposite a weather-beaten man in a uniform, sitting in a tiny little cabin with greasy sea charts on the walls. He looked down at a piece of paper and said: "Nope, I've got nothing on that bus or its passengers other than that they booked three cabins."

"Sounds like there's some information after all," the vegetable said encouragingly. "How many people was the booking for?"

The weather-beaten man read from the paper, not without some effort.

"Eleven adults," he said eventually.

"Adults?" asked Sara Svenhagen.

"Not children," he explained.

Then he froze, a strange grimace on his face.

"Thanks, Viggo," Sara said, turning to the Tactical Command Centre. "Eleven adults means three more than our eight from Slagsta. We'd already accounted for two more: the driver plus the woman with the mobile phone, who we'll come back to. Now it seems like there was one more. The Erinyes seem to be growing relentlessly. Keep going, Viggo. You're all going to have to pay attention now, it's just a short clip. Very MTV."

Norlander pressed a button on the remote. The weather-beaten man disappeared along with his grimace. The picture cut to one of a young Slavic-looking woman dressed in white, standing in front of a variety of kitchen implements hanging from a wall.

"Just women, yes," she said in near-perfect Swedish. "Three cabins. Three in one, four in the other two. Four-bed cabins. Talk to Wislawa, I think she's the one who had those cabins."

The picture changed again to another dark-haired girl, this time younger and clad in a bikini, sitting in the sun on the deck. The camera shook slightly, but the notorious cameraman managed to resist the temptation to pan down her body.

"Where are you from, Wislawa?" Sara's voice asked, out of shot.

"I'm Polish," the girl in the bikini replied in good Swedish.

"Did you hear whether they were talking among themselves?"

"Yeah. Different languages. A bit of Russian, a bit of Bulgarian."

"Ukrainian?"

"I can't tell the difference between Russian and Ukrainian. Bulgarian sounds different, but I can't understand it. I know a bit of Russian."

"Did you hear what they were saying to one another?"

"No, they never spoke when I was nearby. I just heard their voices from out in the corridor. Never any distinct words. I was just cleaning though, Jadwiga was the one who actually served them."

New clip: another young girl, blonde, dressed in a T-shirt and jeans. She was just about to disembark with a man in sunglasses when she was stopped on the gangway. The picture shook violently and the sound of heavy breathing could be heard over the entire conversation which followed.

"Are you Jadwiga?"

"Yes," the girl said, flinching. "Stop filming me. What're you doing, you filthy old perv?"

"We're with the Swedish police," Sara said, holding up her ID.

"Him too?" asked Jadwiga, gesturing with her head.

"Amazing, isn't it?" Sara Svenhagen said neutrally.

"Do you have to pant like that?" Jadwiga said in a complaining tone.

"I'm an old man," said the panting voice.

"Do you recognise these women?" Sara asked.

Jadwiga looked at the photographs.

"Yeah, sure," she said. "Most of them were here, maybe all of them. Stayed in three cabins. I think they stayed in them the whole journey. Never left. I served them dinner in the evening and breakfast in the morning."

"She's the most important," said Sara, pointing to one of the pictures. "Can you tell us anything about her?"

Jadwiga scratched her head and said: "She was Russian, I think. Some kind of Russian dialect. My Russian's not so good."

"So you didn't hear what they were saying?"

"A bit, maybe. When I was little, we had to study Russian in school. But then just when I'd done a few years and was starting to understand the basics, we switched to English."

"Your Swedish is really good," said Sara.

"Thanks."

"Bastards!" came a cry, followed by a bang. The picture swung upwards to show the sky, as seen through the ship's railings.

New clip. Jadwiga again, a mug in front of her and people sitting drinking coffee behind her.

"Let's try again," said Sara's voice. "Are you sure it didn't break, Viggo?"

"Viggo?" Jadwiga said with amusement in her voice.

"Yup," said Norlander's no-longer-panting voice. "I slipped."

"Right then, Jadwiga. Where were we?"

"Her," she said, pointing to the sheet of photographs. "She was talking to the two others in her cabin in some weird Russian dialect. I heard a bit while I was serving them breakfast. When I served dinner the night before, they'd been completely silent."

"So she was in the cabin of three passengers?"

"Yeah," said Jadwiga.

"Would you be able to describe the other two?"

"I think so. In their thirties, maybe. South Slavic appearance, I guess. If we say I've got a northern one."

348

"And those two, they weren't any of these women in the photographs?"

"No, they were in the other cabins. Four in each. They were much more rowdy. Addicts, I think."

"And the three in the third cabin, you wouldn't say they were addicts?"

"No, I thought they were social workers or something. Taking a group of old addicts somewhere. A detox trip."

"Would you be able to recognise the two women from the third cabin? Or help us with a sketch of them?"

"Maybe."

"What did they say then?"

"What?"

"What did you hear while you were serving them breakfast?"

"Let me see if I can remember. Something about the weather first, that it was good it had been such a calm night. Then something about the girls having done really well. One of them said she was proud of them. Then there was something about having to contact someone once they were through. Then they asked me if we had any rye bread. And then someone asked when they'd been checked last. One of them said she'd done it ten minutes ago. And then they asked me if I'd been into the cabins next door. I said yes. They asked if they'd been nice to me. I said yes. One of them asked for another cup of coffee. I gave it to her. Then I left."

"Jesus," said Sara's voice. "You've got a good memory."

"Thanks."

"So they had to contact someone once they were through? Was that right?"

"You've got a good memory too."

"Who? Did they say a name?"

"Yeah, they said a name. But I can't remember it."

New clip. Jadwiga sitting at a computer. A fat man in a police uniform was next to her, jabbing at the keys and clicking away with the mouse. Half of Sara was visible next to them.

"Mm, I don't know," said Jadwiga, pointing at the screen. "Something like that. Eyes more slanted, maybe."

"Viggo," Sara said, a certain weariness in her voice. "There's no reason to be filming this."

"Oh yeah," an unmistakable male voice replied as the camera panned over the desk and focused on Jadwiga, who made an irritated, obscene gesture to it.

"Leave her alone," Sara said, even more wearily.

"Looks like Magdalena Forsberg," the policeman in uniform said, looking with disappointment at the computer screen.

Jadwiga, on the other hand, suddenly looked jittery.

"It's nothing to worry about," the unmistakable male voice said.

"No one thinks you've drawn the world's best female biathlete."

Jadwiga got to her feet. The camera followed her.

"That's it!" she exclaimed.

Sara Svenhagen appeared next to her and said: "What do you mean, Jadwiga?"

350

"The name," the young Polish woman said. "The one they had to contact."

"Magdalena Forsberg?" the unmistakable man's voice said.

"Magda," said Jadwiga.

That was followed by a clip in which they could see something like the edge of a car-repair garage. A man with a moustache and a Shell cap was standing in front of a number of more or less broken-down buses, wiping his oily hands. He was looking suspiciously straight into the camera.

"What's this then?" he asked in a broad Småland accent. "Are you German? *Sie können hier nicht fotografieren.*"

"Sorry," Sara's voice said. Her hand, clutching her police ID, entered the picture from one side. "Is this Anderstorp Car & Bus?"

"Yeah. Turn that camera off. Don't you need permission for that kind of thing?"

"He's got a point there," Jan-Olov Hultin said loudly.

"Shh," Sara urged him, as her voice double on-screen asked: "Are you Anders Torp?"

"Yes," the man with the moustache said, still suspicious but now with an obvious pride in his voice. "Anders Torp of Anderstorp."

"You rent out buses?"

"Yes," said Anders Torp in Anderstorp. "From time to time."

"Did you rent a bus with this registration number?"

A notepad moved into shot. Anders Torp looked at it and then nodded.

"An old Volvo, one of the smaller models," he said. "They hired it for a month. Must've been a few weeks ago."

"Brilliant," an unmistakable man's voice said.

"Is he with the police too?" Anders Torp asked, pointing straight down the camera. "I'm really wondering whether you can film like this without permission. Maybe I shouldn't answer any more questions."

"If you've got anything to hide then I suggest you do it," said Sara.

"Model behaviour," said Hultin.

"Shh," Sara retorted.

"I've got nothing to hide," Anders Torp said, offended.

"*Dåfortsätter vi resan*," said Sara. "As they say in 'Yellow Submarine'."

"You heard the Swedish part too?" Anders Torp said, beaming. "In the middle somewhere, where it goes a bit chaotic for a while? The Eagles had their backwards message, the Beatles threw in a line in Swedish. It's great."

"Who hired the bus?" Sara asked bluntly.

Anders Torp looked appreciatively at her. She had clearly broken through his mistrust.

"A girl," he said. "Not Swedish."

"Where was she from? Eastern Europe?"

"No, I wouldn't have rented it to her if she was. You know you won't be getting the bus back."

"She must've shown you her driving licence."

"And passport," said Anders Torp. "You have to, if you're a foreigner. I think she was German. I can check."

He disappeared for a moment. The camera turned to Sara. The unmistakable man's voice said: "Yellow Submarine?"

Sara pointed to the wall of the garage. The camera zoomed in on a tattered old poster covered in psychedelic patterns. The words "Beatles" and "Yellow Submarine" came into view. Then the camera moved back to Sara.

"Clever," the unmistakable male voice said.

"Yup," Sara replied, looking pleased.

Anders Torp of Anderstorp returned. He was carrying a piece of paper. It was fluttering in the late-spring breeze.

"Here," he said, pointing to the messy sheet of paper. "Driving licence and passport numbers."

Sara nodded and said: "We'll make a copy of it later. Was she one of these?"

She held up the sheet of photographs. Anders Torp slowly worked his way through the nine photographs. He shook his head.

"No," he said.

Sara held out two more photographs, slightly larger.

Anders Torp glanced at the first of them. Then he moved on to the second and his face lit up just like it had when she mentioned "Yellow Submarine".

"This one's very like her," he said, nodding.

Sara Svenhagen held a thumb up to the camera. The camera lurched and fell to the floor. They watched the sun slip in behind a cloud before the picture vanished into static.

There was a moment of silence before Jan-Olov Hultin said: "I'm not sure that video is a particularly good instrument when it comes to police investigations . . ."

Sara Svenhagen made a thumbs-up gesture to Viggo Norlander. He happily returned the gesture. This time, though, there was no camera to drop.

It was utterly clear he thought he had made an invaluable contribution.

Then Sara said: "So in other words, we might have a name for our so-called ninja feminist. Magda."

"Plus," said Norlander, "we've got these."

He held up three photographs like a fan. One was a proper photograph — the picture from the environmental protection agency film, cleaned up by the technicians, showing the woman with the mobile phone. It was followed by two obvious composite photographs, computer reconstructions.

"These two," Viggo said, "were made by a stout Karlskrona policeman, working with Jadwiga, the Polish waitress from the M/S *Stena Europe*." He put one of them down, holding the other up in the air.

"Anders Torp from Anderstorp rented a bus to this woman. We should probably assume she's the Erinyes' driver."

"Her passport and driving licence were German," said Sara. "But there's absolutely no doubt they were fake. Can you guess the name she was using?"

"No," came the chorus.

"Eva Braun," said Sara Svenhagen.

"Unfortunately the camera had broken by the time Anders Torp said that," Viggo Norlander said in his unmistakable man's voice.

"Poor quality," Jan-Olov Hultin said neutrally.

The phone suddenly rang. Hultin answered.

"Yes," he said. "Yeah . . . yes . . . What do you mean, hard? . . . Ah . . . OK . . . Good. Thanks."

He hung up and said: "That was Brynolf Svenhagen. He was agitated."

"Uff," Jorge Chavez said, staring at his watch. Being able to go and buy his wine was looking increasingly unlikely.

Hultin said: "We've got some information about our man without a nose."

"What's wrong with Brunte?" Paul Hjelm asked, receiving a sour glance from Sara Svenhagen in return.

"It's because the information we've got is fairly diffuse. They're claiming they don't have a cooperation agreement with Europol and they're refusing to release the name. They're demanding we send someone down there."

"Send someone down there?" said Chavez. "Haven't they heard of the Internet?"

"Barely, I should think," Hultin replied, picking up the phone.

"You're not thinking of sending someone, are you?"

"Yes," Hultin said, dialling an extremely long number. "We've already got someone on the ground in Europe. Arto can go after the weekend."

"But where's *there?*" asked Hjelm. "Where's our nose-man from?"

"That's why I'm going along with it without complaining," said Jan-Olov Hultin. "Shtayf was from Odessa. Ukraine."

CHAPTER
THIRTY

It was Saturday evening in Tuscany. The Söderstedt family were on their veranda, the sun slowly sinking in the distance. Its blushing rays fell among the rows of vines, painting the hills with stripes of golden light. The scent of seventeen different varieties of basil was drifting in from the garden, and the lingering warmth of the day was making the pine-scented evening air quiver slightly in the dusk. The remaining morsels of Anja's fantastic special pesto, made from her latest green-fingered triumph, a dark opal basil, were being eaten. It was perfect in combination with a full-bodied Brunello.

Everything — absolutely everything — was just great.

Arto Söderstedt glanced around the table. There was a dark-haired addition to the chalk-white family. The dark hair belonged to Giorgio, the seventeen-year-old son of a winemaker who had taken his eldest daughter's virginity. Mikaela had brought him home one day and introduced him to the family. Arto Söderstedt had thought that was something momentous; it felt like he was being thanked for managing to convince her that she had nothing to be ashamed of. Hopefully, that insight would follow her through life.

In his opinion, people should feel shame only when they did something bad to another person.

Then and only then.

Giorgio was a shy young man, living in the belief that his lover's father was, by definition, furious. That it was his duty to be furious. But not even Giorgio's own father seemed particularly angry. They had invited the winemaker and his wife over one evening. Both had seemed nervous, as though standing trial. These were the people whose daughter their good-for-nothing son had penetrated. And so the Söderstedts had mobilised their combined good natures to convince them that everything was fine, and slowly, slowly, the boy's parents had relaxed. The evening had ended with each of them attempting to surpass the others in their extolment of love and wine and life.

Someone at this table is pregnant.

Thud — the thought suddenly struck Söderstedt.

There was something in the air. That particularly female, utterly silent telepathy sending thoughts right over the table. He had experienced it before. Five times, to be exact. That made him an expert.

His eyes came to rest on Linda first, his second eldest daughter. She was fourteen. There didn't seem to be any danger there. She was busy wolfing down pasta and glancing wryly around, just like normal. Incredibly interested in Giorgio, above all else. With a smile, he wondered to himself what she was thinking. Where her thoughts were taking her.

Then came the critical moment. He gathered his courage and turned to Mikaela. She was shining. But it

358

was the light of love, nothing else, he was quite convinced of that.

OK, he thought, taking a breather. So I was wrong. I thought I would never be picking children up from day care again, but that isn't to be. Within a couple of years, I'll be picking up yet another baby from day care.

He turned to Anja, sitting there proudly tasting her dark opal pesto. She was glowing.

There was, after all, a difference between shining and glowing. A huge difference.

"So you're pregnant, are you?" he asked, taking another sip of wine.

Anja choked on her pesto. He had to get up, rush round the table and put the good old Heimlich manoeuvre into practice. He grabbed her beneath her breasts and squeezed. A huge lump of pesto flew across the table. Giorgio pulled a face. Mikaela was flame-red with embarrassment. She wasn't done learning yet.

Anja dried her tears with a napkin, which she then used to wipe the pesto from the table. Her face was completely expressionless. She sat down and stared out at the dusky landscape. Arto sat down too. He watched her, waiting for the telepathic waves to return.

Giorgio was looking sceptically at his half-eaten portion of pesto.

"You don't have to eat it," Anja said, without moving her eyes.

The telepathic waves were absent when Mikaela and Giorgio snuck away from the table to slander the adult world in intimate tones; they were absent when Linda and Peter ran off to creep around in the deepening darkness, frightening the daylights out of one another; they were absent when Stefan took little Lina's hand and dragged her away to watch Italian kids' TV.

But once husband and wife were left alone on the veranda, once darkness had fallen, once the fireflies had appeared, flashing like sparks in the night, the telepathic waves returned. Anja's distant gaze finally vanished and she met his stubbornly penetrating eyes. She sat there for a few seconds, watching her strange husband. Then she shook her head quickly, smiled and disappeared indoors.

Yes, there would be a new baby; there would always be a baby.

He moved over to his particular corner of the veranda and turned on the computer. It rattled and whirred. He lived in constant fear that it would be struck by an information overload and just die completely. All these CD-ROMs being fed into it, all the information spread across its hard drive — where was the limit of what it could withstand?

Arto Söderstedt opened the sketch of Palazzo Riguardo which Commissioner Marconi had, slightly reluctantly, given to him. In addition to that, the good commissioner had, even more reluctantly, pointed out the critical spots of the thirty-four-room building. After that, he had stood with his hands on his hips and said: "I should probably know why you want this, Signor Sadestatt."

Signor Sadestatt had replied: "What's the best way in?"

Naturally, Signor Marconi's jaw had dropped. Anything else would have been unthinkable.

Söderstedt had explained: "Not for me, for the Erinyes."

Marconi had looked at him. His jaw moved back to its usual position — and with it, his gaze.

"They can't get at him anywhere other than at home," Söderstedt had continued. "He hasn't left his palazzo in . . . what did you say? A year?"

Marconi had nodded, mute but not indifferent.

"And that means they've got to get into Palazzo Riguardo if they want to get to him."

"And you're quite sure that these . . . Erinyes are out for him?"

"I'm feeling increasingly certain of that, yes."

"Why?"

"Because the whole thing with the wolverines was so wonderfully clear. Because there's some sort of direct link between Leonard Sheinkman in Stockholm and Marco di Spinelli in Milan. Because the combination of wolverine and old man points straight to Palazzo Riguardo. Because di Spinelli is the spider in the middle of the web. All points lead to him, and all points lead from him. He's weaved the web that's going to end up snaring him. He's created the figures who are going to eat him up."

"That sounds quite convincing," Marconi had said encouragingly before throwing a spanner into Söderstedt's neatly oiled machine. "But is there really a single tenable link between Sheinkman and di Spinelli?"

"He recognised him."

"According to you, yes. But all that's based on a hunch. And if that's the case, shouldn't Sheinkman be the victim and di Spinelli the hangman? Why murder both the victim and the executioner?"

"Nothing is pointing to di Spinelli as the hangman. They might just be brothers in misfortune."

"Marco di Spinelli, a prisoner in Buchenwald? You're kidding."

"Your words, Signor Marconi, suggest that you're of the opposite impression, despite all your earlier neutrality."

"Look at Marco di Spinelli, Signor Sadestatt. Does he look like a man plagued by his past in a concentration camp, degraded by the Nazis as they murdered people on an industrial scale? Does he look like a man who now, after fifty years, still needs pills to be able to sleep just an hour a night? Does he look like a man who has been subjected to the most awful of medical experiments?"

Arto Söderstedt had actually been forced to pause for thought there. For an instant, the distinguished commissioner, usually such a marvel of self-restraint, had revealed the basis of his obstinacy.

It was personal.

In one way or another, it was personal.

"Your father?" Söderstedt had asked rashly.

"My entire upbringing," Marconi had replied, fixing him with his gaze. "My entire childhood in a nutshell. They can't sleep. They can never sleep."

Söderstedt had been silent. He had waited for Marconi, who continued with a composed but trembling voice.

362

"Buchenwald was Nazi Germany's biggest concentration camp. Towards the end of the war, there were practically only non-German prisoners there. The German Jews, those who hadn't been subjected to medical experiments, had already been shipped off to the extermination camps in Poland, and Buchenwald was becoming more and more a camp for foreign prisoners. My father was an Italian Communist. The Nazis, they were studying the movement of blood through muscle mass by watching it . . . live. Dissection of living right arms. Without anaesthetic, of course. He lived with that dissected, rotting arm hanging at his side for almost a year before units from the 3rd US Army reached Buchenwald on the eleventh of April 1945 and opened the gates."

Arto Söderstedt had observed him. It was hard to digest.

"I'm sorry," he had said meaninglessly.

"Me too," Marconi had replied, fiddling with various papers on his desk. "And so my experience tells me Marco di Spinelli was never held prisoner in a concentration camp. I'd bet my life on it."

"You're right, of course," Söderstedt had said. "It was just an idea."

"Complete your line of reasoning anyway," Marconi had replied; he was back to his old self once again.

"Someone who kills an eighty-eight-year-old concentration camp survivor by hanging him upside down and poking about in his brain with a metal wire is, by definition, a fascist. I think my colleagues in Stockholm assumed a bit too hastily that the Furies were out on some kind of mission. That they're liberating women who've been subjected to violence. I think they actually seem quite fascistic. Even if they are women."

Marconi had nodded. Then he had said: "There's a way in."

Arto Söderstedt had watched him as he leaned forward over the drawing of the palazzo they had unrolled on the desk. Only then did Söderstedt start to see just how intricately mapped each of the rooms in the palace were.

"We really do know every single nook and cranny of Palazzo Riguardo," Marconi had continued. "It's from here that the activities which destroy our country and our continent are organised. Marco di Spinelli's business is, quite simply, market economics in its purest form. An unregulated market economy holed up in a palace where the greatest artists in the West have, over the years, adorned the corridors of power. It's great, consummate beauty; it's education; it's a sense of history — and it's pure, brutal power."

Arto Söderstedt was starting to understand why the palace was so well documented. Marconi and his men understood the entire mechanics of the operation — they just couldn't stop it.

"The palace was built a bit like an onion," Marconi had made a sweeping gesture over the sketch. "With the difference that the palace has a heart. The heart is Marco di Spinelli's office. You have to go through layer after layer to get to it. When the Perduto family built the palace during the sixteenth century, they were facing threats from all directions. The palace was constructed like a series of surrounding walls. It's not something you notice as you tread its corridors, but the fact is you're crossing drawbridge after drawbridge, and they can be raised so quickly that you'd fall right down into the moat, if you'll forgive the metaphor. Despite the fact that the palace seems so open and roomy, there is just one way out of each of the layers, and by each of those doors is a closely watched and quickly raised drawbridge. Trying to make your way through the layers by these doors is pointless. But there's an alternative route. We call it 'the strait gate'."

Söderstedt had given a short laugh. " 'Enter ye in at the strait gate: for wide is the gate, and broad is the way, that leadeth to destruction, and many there be which go in thereat: Because strait is the gate, and narrow is the way, which leadeth unto life, and few there be that find it.' "

Marconi had given him a quick glance. A fleeting smile had passed over his face, and he had nodded. "Matthew, 7:13. It really is narrow, and few have ever found it. It's the ace up our sleeve. If ever we need to get in there quickly."

Now, on the veranda, Söderstedt watched Marconi's digital line snake its way through the palace on the map on his computer screen. It stretched out into the dark Tuscan landscape like the light trails left behind by fireflies. He imagined it was forming some kind of illegible text.

Once Marconi had finished drawing his line, Söderstedt had asked: "What do you think Marco di Spinelli did during the war?"

Marconi had put down his pen and stared at his Nordic colleague.

"It's obvious," he had replied. "He was a Nazi."

As though conjured up by the simile, a cloud of fireflies swarmed into the garden, performing a dance that remained visible long, long after they had disappeared. A magpie's nest of light which he couldn't blink away, making it impossible to distinguish Marconi's narrow gate.

Arto Söderstedt sat there for a good while, staring out into the nothingness and trying to read the fireflies' writing. He studied it for so long that the text slowly faded before his eyes. Until eventually, only Italo Marconi's pale line was left. It snaked right across the drawing, like a child's shaky pencil line through a comic-book labyrinth.

He could imagine how the Erinyes, perhaps even at that very moment, were sat hunched over the exact same drawing, pointing at the exact same line. They were coming, he could feel it. Suddenly, it felt as though the garden began to quiver. From the corner of his eye, he saw a shadow slip behind a tree. Then another. Until all of nature seemed to be awash with shifting shadows, the trees themselves in movement, the forest approaching.

Arto Söderstedt shuddered and tried to shake off his unease.

Who were they, these unrelenting figures from the forgotten depths of mythology?

Civilisation thought it had tamed them a few thousand years earlier.

366

They crept up on their victims. With great precision, they drove their increasingly petrified prey towards the designated murder scene. When they got there, their victims would be meek, shaken to the very core of their beings. They caused the forgotten, repressed depths to tremble, and then they hung their victims upside down and drove a terrible nail into their brains.

By that point, they had already scared their victims senseless.

All other than Leonard Sheinkman. He had spoken to them. Calmly and quietly.

It was as though he had been waiting for them.

As though he had been waiting for them for a very long time.

As though he had known that, sooner or later, they would be coming.

What had he been waiting for? Was it something he had seen in the concentration camp? Was it his own betrayal, which Paul Hjelm had described after having read his diary? His double betrayal?

Was he waiting for the spirits of his wife and son to seek their vengeance?

No, his betrayal wasn't of that kind. He could have taken his family and moved to America, of course — not having done so was, in itself, a betrayal of sorts. And of course, he could have protested loudly when his wife and son were slaughtered, but that wouldn't have made any real difference.

No, this was something else, something worse. On that point, Söderstedt was in complete agreement with

Paul. "I've got a vague feeling there's something wrong somewhere," as he had said on the phone.

And then the second conversation had come.

From Hultin.

"What do you say about the spookily beautiful Odessa?"

He would be leaving tomorrow. He would be leaving his neglected paradise and entering the wolf's lair, having to avoid being robbed and shot by aggressive beggars, and having to coax reluctant Eastern European policemen and women without computers into working with him.

It was the choice he had made.

And he didn't regret it for a second.

He glanced at his watch. It was time. He closed the document containing the drawing of Palazzo Riguardo and changed the CD for another, a newly bought one. He started the installation Wizard and opened a box on the table next to the computer. In the background, the cicadas were singing.

He took out a device that looked like a little flashlight, plugged it into his laptop and attached it to the top of his computer screen.

The installation was complete. He accepted all of its mysterious licence agreements and caught sight of himself on-screen. His face was dark.

He moved the floor lamp from behind him and pointed its beam of light at his face. As he did so, the face on the screen also lit up. For a moment, he thought it was Uncle Pertti he could see, the young Pertti, his hand gripping his sabre. So ludicrously similar to Arto Söderstedt. What was he doing there? A shudder ran through him.

Arto stuck out his tongue. On the computer screen, Uncle Pertti did the same.

The spell was broken.

He returned to his technology. It should all work now.

He got rid of his picture on-screen. It was his and his alone.

As he set up the Internet connection, the insects began to gather around the lone source of light. He could feel that his face was covered with unknown winged insects when a completely different but equally well-known face finally appeared on-screen, and he said:

"Hello, wage labourers."

CHAPTER
THIRTY-ONE

Cilla looked expectant as the hardened couple made their way in through an elegant doorway in Birkastan. The expression remained as they climbed the stairs — genuine art nouveau — and when it was still there as they reached a door marked with the neighbourhood's only foreign name, even Paul Hjelm allowed himself to feel expectant.

Though it was almost half past seven.

She took hold of his arm in a way he remembered from their youth. It had been so long since she had done it that he almost felt moved.

"Just think, finally getting to meet everyone," she said as he ceremoniously folded back the paper on the bunch of flowers he had just bought from the 7-Eleven on the corner.

"You've met them before, haven't you?" he said, surprised.

"No," she said, squeezing his arm.

He rang the bell.

Sara answered. She was wearing barely any make-up below her greenish crop, which seemed more straggly than usual in honour of the party; the simple, dark blue dress she was wearing made no attempt to hide her figure. She hugged them both and welcomed them in. The half-wilted bouquet from 7-Eleven was thankfully accompanied by a bottle of malt whisky.

She glanced at it, nodded, and whispered to Paul: "You haven't forgotten the golden rule, have you?"

Paul chuckled and shook his head.

To say not a single word about the ongoing case.

He would do everything in his power to keep that promise. But it wouldn't be easy.

Jorge came to greet them from somewhere in the bowels of the flat. He was wearing a blue shirt and a brand-new beige linen suit. It looked exactly like his old one.

"The food's ruined now," he said, forcing two glasses of Martini Rosso into their hands.

"Oh," said Cilla as she hung up her coat. "Are we late?"

"Ah," said Jorge. "You're glowing, Cilla."

"Glowing?" she said, hugging him.

He glanced at the bottle of whisky Sara handed him.

"Cragganmore?" he said.

"Perfect for when you're tired of the excesses," said Paul.

"Well, come in and have a look round, then," Jorge said with a confident, welcoming gesture to the late-arriving couple. "To think that not even you've been here, Paul. That's what I call social misery."

They moved on from the narrow hallway through a curtain of knotted Indian beads.

"Chilean," said Jorge.

The scent of garlic-saturated food beckoned them into the living room. On the way, Paul glanced into the kitchen. It was big and old and looked cosy. Though a wooden floor in a kitchen seemed a bit unusual. On the gas hob, a couple of stews were bubbling away.

"Gas," he said, pointing.

"Unrivalled," said Jorge. "But don't peep yet."

The women had already reached the living room. They were leaning over a group of people sitting around a small Indian-looking glass table. Each of them seemed to be holding a glass of reddish liquid.

Apart from one, who was holding a baby bottle. She was sitting on Viggo Norlander's lap.

Paul gave them a general wave and cast a quick glance around the room. It was quite big, with a relatively large amount of mixed furniture. There wasn't much space — probably because of the abnormally big circular table in the middle of the room taking it all up. A surprising number of books, and a couple of genuine-looking paintings on the walls. The overall impression was one of good, albeit chaotic, taste.

Something which probably matched Jorge and Sara fairly well.

Slightly distracted, he ruffled little Charlotte's thin, dark blonde hair. Then he held his hand out to the woman by Viggo's side. She had the same colour hair as her daughter and was wearing a sober floral dress; she looked as though she was rapidly approaching the fifty-year mark.

"Paul," he said.

"Astrid," she replied. "So you're the famous Paul Hjelm. The master detective."

Paul cast a surprised glance at Viggo, who shrugged ambiguously and threw a giggling Charlotte up in the air.

"Congratulations," Paul said.

"What for?" asked Astrid.

Paul cast yet another glance at Viggo, more uneasily this time, but Viggo simply continued throwing his daughter up in the air.

"For the new addition to the family."

"Ah," Astrid replied, surprised but not angry. "Right, yes. Thanks."

He turned to Viggo, pointed at little Charlotte, and said: "You must've been videotaping her too?"

"She's the one I've been practising on," Viggo replied, deadly serious.

Paul moved further along the sofa. He could see Cilla talking to Kerstin Holm out of the corner of his eye; it felt slightly odd.

A small, dark woman dressed in black held out her hand to him and exclaimed: "Ludmila."

He couldn't quite make the connection. He felt sluggish and ungainly. A fish on dry land.

"Paul," he said, his gills flapping. "Hi."

A bookcase swung to one side and an enormous body squeezed out from behind it.

"Christ, that loo's small," Gunnar Nyberg said, coming over to them. He headed straight for Cilla and greeted her politely, like a retired officer from the old guard.

"Yeah," Jorge said loudly. "That's the problem with this place. There's no room for a washing machine."

Only when Paul caught sight of Gunnar did he make the connection. Still holding the small, dark woman's hand, he blurted out: "Right! Ludmila. The professor."

"Titles are important, Detective Inspector," Ludmila said with gentle irony. He smiled to himself. It went quite well.

Gunnar Nyberg laughed a loud, rumbling laugh. Paul Hjelm wondered what Cilla had said to evoke such a bellow. He managed to elicit very few of them himself.

He had reached the inner corner of the sofa. An elderly lady with greying hair and pronounced lines around her eyes held out her hand with a neutral expression. That was enough for him to make the connection. It was getting better and better. He was starting to find his feet again.

"Mrs Hultin, I presume," he said archaically.

"Stina," the lady said neutrally.

"Paul," he said, unnecessarily adding: "Hjelm."

It was that whole thing with first and last names. He still found it ridiculously difficult calling Hultin anything other than Hultin and so his wife was automatically none other than "Mrs Hultin". Anything else would require far too much willpower. Deep down, he wished he knew why. It was probably some kind of hierarchical imprint he had never quite managed to escape.

The hour of the trial had arrived. Hultin was squashed into the corner, his glass so dry it seemed almost to have been licked clean. They greeted one another.

"Jan-Olov," Paul said with a display of sheer willpower. "Your glass is empty, I see."

"We got here forty-five minutes ago," said Hultin. "I've never trusted that saying 'Better late than never'."

"Me neither," said Paul. "And I'm still always last."

Just then, Sara appeared in the kitchen doorway, clapping her hands together like an old-fashioned hostess.

"Ladies and gentlemen," she said in a firm, resolute voice, "come to the table. Jorge — help carrying."

"Help and help," said Jorge, reluctantly peeling away from the others. "I cooked the food."

"And I'm the prime minister," Sara said, disappearing back into the kitchen.

The guests got hesitantly to their feet; there are very few people who want to be first to an empty table. Especially if there are no designated places set out, which turned out to be the case.

On their way over, Paul bumped into Cilla and Kerstin. He gave Kerstin a hug. Cilla stood alongside, watching them. It still felt slightly odd. Despite the fact that years had passed, spreading a comforting blanket of reconciliation over everything that had happened. If we want to wallow in clichés.

"Everything OK, Kerstin?" he asked.

"Yup," she replied.

With that, nothing more was said. Gunnar climbed up onto a chair. It strained as best it could to prove it could withstand all possible laws of physics. And it succeeded: it held his weight.

The great man on the chair counted out loud.

"One, two, three, four, five, six women. Seven including Charlotte. One, two, three, four, five men. Clearly uneven."

"We can sit next to one another," Kerstin and Cilla said.

Paul looked at them with suspicion.

"Let's do it like this," said Gunnar who, in his new-found euphoric condition seemed also to have been struck by a fondness for leadership. "Astrid next to me, then Jan-Olov, Sara, Paul, Stina, Viggo, Ludmila, Jorge, Cilla, Kerstin. And Charlotte can sit with . . .?"

"Astrid," said Viggo, just as Astrid said: "Viggo."

"Perfect," said Gunnar, hopping down from the chair with the freedom of movement of a newly-svelte man. And with that, it was settled.

Sure enough, Charlotte ended up sitting on Viggo's lap. They were served a Chilean meat stew containing a surprising amount of garlic. The wine, Duca d'Aragona 1993, was perfectly suited to it, and was subsequently consumed in near-bacchanal quantities.

"Wine consumption is a sign of Europeanisation," Ludmila said towards the end of the meal. She said it in a tone that didn't leave any room for objection.

"What do you mean?" Hultin asked, surprising the group by being responsible for the majority of it. The wine consumption, that was.

"When I first came to Sweden," Ludmila said, "you were as much a part of the vodka-drinking nations as us

376

Russians — just not quite to the same extent. But you've slowly switched to wine. You've moved from spirits like *brännvin* to wine."

"Hmm," said Viggo, stroking his sleeping daughter's head.

Ludmila ignored him without comment.

"But in Russia, or actually across the whole of Eastern Europe, vodka is getting even more of a hold. We're on the way to becoming a lost cause."

"And not just for that reason, right?" said Paul, drawing dangerously close to breaking the golden rule. A few of the others looked at him askance.

The women in particular.

"I'm utterly convinced," Ludmila continued, "that the condition of a nation can be measured by the proportion of wine in its total alcohol consumption. The greater the proportion of wine, the greater the spiritual prosperity."

"But there are hidden statistics too," said Gunnar, seemingly unaffected by the wine. "I should think Sweden has the highest in the world."

"You mean home-distilled?" asked Paul.

"And black-market spirits. But above all, home-distilled schnapps."

"Why's it called *brännvin*?" asked Viggo, still incessantly stroking his daughter's head. "It's not wine, is it?"

Ludmila searched her linguistic memory banks and came up with an answer.

"The word came to Swedish in the Middle Ages. It was called '*brännevin*' back then, from the Low

German *'bernewin'*, which means 'burnt, or distilled, wine'. In Dutch, it's called *'brandewijn'*, which eventually became 'brandy'."

Paul noticed how admiringly Gunnar was looking at her. After all these years, it transpired that *this* was what his taste in women was like.

"But that's no answer," Viggo obstinately pointed out. "We're still in the same old spot. Why did they call it a wine when it was a spirit?"

"Because the word 'spirit' didn't exist," said Ludmila. "It didn't appear in Swedish until the end of the eighteenth century, and it was a French import, not a German one. It comes directly from the French *'esprit'*."

"So wine meant spirit and spirit didn't mean shit?" Viggo half rhymed, unexpectedly aggressively.

"Language is constantly changing, Viggo," Ludmila said calmly.

"And don't you shout at my lady," Gunnar said, equally calmly.

It wasn't the fact that the bells of the Gustav Vasa Church had just struck nine in the distance that interrupted the slightly soured discussion, but the fact that Jorge had just placed a laptop computer in the middle of the dining table.

The nine peals reverberated through Paul's conscience. With each one, a realisation grew. It was as abrupt as it was absurd. Eventually it was so complete and so overbearing that he had to gulp down an entire glass of Duca d'Aragona to stop himself from breaking the golden rule.

Jorge had attached a little device to the top of the laptop screen. Then he spun the computer around so that it was facing his seat at the table, sat down and called out to the group.

"Gather round, people!"

They got reluctantly and sluggishly to their feet. Hultin took a couple of elegant sidesteps and smiled awry. His wife Stina propped him up and said, neutrally: 'They say wine counteracts strokes, but somehow I doubt that's true."

Gunnar squeezed his former giant's body in behind Ludmila's chair and touched her lightly on the neck. Kerstin launched herself sidelong over Cilla, who laughed loudly and, Paul thought, entirely without cause. Astrid moved over to Viggo and knocked fondly on his head; Viggo simply kept stroking his sleeping daughter's thin hair. Paul shuffled over and stood at the back. Sara came over and put an arm around him. He barely noticed.

The screen crackled and a strange figure appeared.

"Hello, wage labourers," the strange figure said.

"I'll be damned," Viggo exclaimed. "Everyone's favourite Finn."

"Arto," said Jorge, who had seemingly sobered up, "how're things? We're having a house-warming."

"So I see," said Arto Söderstedt's slightly jumpy image. "I've just given up my daily Vin Santo, myself. From today. Came to that drastic decision after three glasses."

A general murmur broke out in the flat on Birkagatan. Jorge hushed them with great authority.

"How are things?" he asked.

"Great, thanks," said Arto. "If it weren't for an upcoming trip. Don't people get robbed all the time in Ukraine?"

"You've just broken the golden rule, haven't you?"

"Right, yes. Sorry. No, but like I said, things are great. Aside from the fact my daughter lost her virginity, that I'll be having another baby, and that ancient goddesses of revenge are creeping among the basil plants."

Kerstin and Sara cleared their throats loudly. The Söderstedt-like figure put his hand to his mouth and made the sign of the cross.

"Apologies," he said. "Slip of the tongue."

"Baby?" Viggo shouted. "For God's sake, you old buck. We're having another one, too."

"Speaking of bucks?" Arto replied. "That's great, congratulations. Good for the babysitting, too."

"The family OK?" asked Jorge.

"Yes, yes," said Söderstedt. "We had a little Heimlich incident a couple of hours ago, but otherwise fine. Show me the flat."

Jorge detached the little camera from the top of the screen and slowly turned it round, round, round.

"Wow," said Arto. "Such green hair."

"Twenty laps every Sunday," Sara said laconically.

"Though we'll see tomorrow," said Jorge.

"No, listen, it looks really nice. Is the nursery ready?"

"What is this, kids' club?" said Jorge.

Sara said: "Soon."

They quickly moved on from that topic without further ado. Arto said goodbye to each of them in order. Anja appeared on-screen for a moment and said, sceptically: "The wonders of technology."

At that very moment, the picture vanished into a cluster of peculiar multicoloured squares. The screen looked more like a church window.

That was what Paul Hjelm thought, at least. The church bells were still echoing through him.

He was about to shatter.

The bacchanal group moved slightly unsteadily back to the sofas and armchairs after that.

Paul paused at the bookcase on his way over. For a brief moment, the ringing of the church bells disappeared, only to be replaced by something else. He pulled a book from the shelf. It was called *The Big Nowhere*. The author was James Ellroy.

Jorge was puffing on a cigarette with the inexperience of a schoolgirl. He laughed and pointed.

"There are your wolverines. James Ellroy."

"Though there aren't actually any wolverines," Kerstin said, smoking just as inexpertly and with a portion of snus tobacco shoved beneath her lip.

" 'Wolverine Blues'," said Jorge, giving Sara a wet, smoky kiss.

The bottle of Cragganmore was opened and asymmetric waves of discussion poured through the little flat until salsa music started streaming from hidden speakers and their unrhythmic feet began pounding the neighbours' ceilings. Hultin and Stina were dancing a waltz. They looked like a couple of wounded lemmings on their way towards a cliff edge. Jorge smoothly asked Cilla to dance, and they glided around the room with professional dance steps. In just a few minutes, she was transformed from blonde dishcloth to dark, mysterious Latino dance queen. The lights were probably just too low. Gunnar and Ludmila were dancing cheek to cheek. It looked lethal: a cat in the arms of a grizzly bear. A sucker fish on a shark. Viggo and Astrid reluctantly handed Charlotte to Sara, who sat there stroking her with long, lingering movements, and headed out onto the dance floor like a couple of mediocre folk dancers.

Only Paul and Kerstin remained standing where they were, watching the spectacle from a distance.

He was suddenly struck by a vision of a dying civilisation's staggering dance steps over an abyss. He saw figures like empty, storyless shells which, like marionettes, carried out their capers over depths they would never come close to unless their puppeteer let go of the strings and they tumbled loose-limbed down into the abyss. And by that point, it was already too late.

It lasted just a moment, and ultimately wasn't particularly rewarding. Distance is simply cowardice, he thought in confusion, finding Kerstin's hand and leading her to the dance floor. She let herself be led. In reality, it was more like she was leading and he was simply imagining that he was the one doing it. As he buried his cheek in her unruly dark hair, smelling scents he hadn't smelled for years, the internal church bells disappeared, and when he put his ear to the thin, thin patch above her left temple, he imagined he was making direct contact with her thoughts. And that wasn't the worst.

He had no idea how they ended up in the taxi, but there he was, with Cilla's blonde hair flowing over his shoulder, hearing her say: "I know the two of you had an affair."

He should probably have been indignant, but he wasn't. He slowly stroked her hair, staying silent.

"It's OK," said Cilla. "It was a long time ago, I know."

"Did she say that?"

"She said plenty of things. I really like Kerstin."

"You already knew?"

"I suspected. But I also knew it had been over a long time."

"Did you ask her?"

"No. She told me herself. It seems like she's putting the past behind her. Fixing the holes in time, she said."

Paul actually smiled. He really had been in direct contact with her thoughts earlier. Maybe they were Kerstin's thoughts he had been thinking. Maybe that was the real reason her cranium had been thinned out. So that her thoughts could reach him more easily.

Cilla continued: "It's OK, Paul. I had an affair too. Back then."

What about now? he thought. Shouldn't I be feeling indignant now?

"When we were separated?" was all he asked.

To restore a little order.

"Yeah, that spring, whenever it was. It was just a short thing. But oddly enough, I wouldn't undo it."

"Nor would I," said Paul.

"Haven't you noticed that something is happening to her?"

"To Kerstin? No, not really."

"She said she went through a crisis. A metamorphosis, she called it. She hadn't really even dared admit it to herself, she said."

"Did she say what it was?"

"Not exactly. But I think she's finding religion."

They fell silent. That was that with the direct contact, then, Paul thought, feeling the everyday come rushing back into the taxi.

Religion?

When they finally crawled into bed and were much too tired and preoccupied to carry out all they had been thinking about in the taxi, the church bells returned. Just before he fell asleep, he realised he had been released from his vow of silence. The golden rule no longer applied.

He told Cilla. The fact that she was sleeping deeply, snoring away peacefully next to him, didn't make a difference.

The main thing was that he didn't burst.

He might already have been half asleep himself when he said: "Surely there wasn't a church in Buchenwald."

CHAPTER
THIRTY-TWO

On compassionate grounds, we should skip over Sunday without comment, leaping forward in time to Monday instead.

Monday 15 May.

Monday mornings can vary greatly. For some, they represent nothing more than the pure joy of being able to get back to work again after a long, boring weekend of loneliness or matrimonial misery. For others, they represent the endless suffering of having to drag themselves up out of bed and face the meaningless, creativity-crushing week ahead of them. For others still, they are a torment, a reminder that everyone else is off to work, all those joyful souls who actually have a job to go to.

And then there is one final category. One which belongs to the happy few who, despite having had an extraordinarily pleasant weekend, look forward to getting back to work with the enthusiasm of a child.

Paul Hjelm belonged to this group.

It was time for him to return to Leonard Sheinkman's diary from those awful days in February 1945. The diary was still at the police station — had he had it at home, Sunday wouldn't have passed by in silence.

He managed to piece together rather a lot of things.

Though it had started slowly. Not that "slowly" was really the right word. It started with self-contempt.

He felt like a rapist.

The ten or so yellowed pages of the diary were spread across his desk. Wherever the pencil had touched the paper, it had formed letters. Those letters weren't simply a bank of information about an objectively reconstructable event from the past. They were words from the brink of death, and those words had reverberated through him and hurled him into the abyss. He had cried at those words, tears which had come from the very core of his being. The words had evoked a time and an experience that had started to pale away. They were almost holy, somehow.

He had the text in front of him now, splayed out like a victim, and he was planning on getting to work on it with the entire arsenal of rational structures which formed the basis of Western society: logic, analytical focus and stringent penetration.

He would, quite simply, be raping the text.

Like any good middle-aged, heterosexual, white, European man should.

To leave it untouched in its cocoon would be to shy away from the truth; it would be tantamount to renouncing knowledge, accepting a mystical and unchanging condition of fear, stepping back into a dark period of time and preparing the way for vague, inhuman forces.

386

Wasn't there any way of analysing it soberly and critically and *still* — perhaps precisely *by doing so* — managing to keep the striking mystery alive?

That felt like the deciding question. And not just for Leonard Sheinkman's diary, not just for this case in its entirety, not even just for Paul Hjelm's entire working life, but for society as a whole.

What had Kerstin discovered?

Had she realised that without mystery we are all just empty shells?

At that moment, Paul Hjelm got the better of himself, as is often said when things return to the same old rut, and immersed himself in the text. Using logic, an analytical focus and stringent penetration, he took on Leonard Sheinkman's diary from a week of decisive importance in 1945, not long before the end of the war.

Leonard Sheinkman *hadn't* been in Buchenwald, Germany's largest concentration camp, built on a desolate little hill named Ettersberg in 1937, just seven kilometres outside the cultured city of Weimar. A place where there definitely wasn't a church just outside the window.

There were two possible explanations: either the church was just an image — something in which to "see time", as Sheinkman had constantly written — or else it actually did exist, while *simultaneously* being an image used to "see time". What spoke so clearly in favour of the latter was that the church had been described in such detail, and in combination with the Allied bombings, which had intensified in Germany during February 1945.

Everything pointed towards Sheinkman having been in a town, not on a desolate little hillside.

So why had he gone through life claiming to have been in Buchenwald? Why had he told his children that he had been held in Buchenwald of all places?

Once again, there were two possible explanations here: either whatever he had been subjected to in that town was so awful that even the nightmare of Buchenwald appeared a kinder and more manageable alternative, or else he had something to hide.

Paul Hjelm decided that could wait. The town could wait too — it was, at present, still seemingly unidentifiable. He took on the place itself instead.

It was clearly an institution. The prisoners were being kept in cells of some kind. There was a list, and when you reached the top of that list, you were subjected to something terrible. The result of whatever you were subjected to was that your personality was, in some way, erased. That was what had happened to his comrade Erwin. *"When I speak to him, there is no one there. He is nothing but an empty shell. Over the spot where it has been running out of his head, an innocent little gauze dressing."* That dressing appeared again. *"Their bandages shine like lanterns on their empty skulls."* And: *"Soon, the little bandage will be pressed to my temple."*

Temple, Paul Hjelm thought, closing his eyes.

Of course.

A thin wall was separating Paul Hjelm from Kerstin Holm. On the other side of that wall, a conversation

388

with Europe was currently under way. Or rather, a conversation with Professor Ernst Herschel from the history department at the University of Jena.

He was rather reluctant. A so-called challenge.

"It was a mistake mentioning it to Josef," he said in academic-sounding English. Broken but grammatically sound.

"Josef?" asked Holm.

"Josef Benziger in Weimar. He was a student here. A very promising student. I don't understand how he could become a policeman."

"What was the context of you mentioning it to Josef?"

"We met for a beer and I scolded him for not continuing his postgraduate studies. I was careless enough to mention my new research project. Mostly to show him what a titbit he was missing."

"So it's your new research project?"

Silence from Jena. Kerstin continued.

"What's preventing you from talking about this new project?"

"Several things, Frau Holm."

"Fräulein," Kerstin Holm said youthfully.

"It's an extremely sensitive project, Fräulein Holm. Within a few years, I hope that my research group will be ready to publish our results. But at this stage, the entire project is in quite an unsatisfying position, from a scientific point of view."

The academic preserve, Kerstin Holm thought. It was obviously important to pick each word she said carefully here. Some well-paid American professor was probably hovering in the background somewhere, and Professor Herschel wasn't ready to sacrifice him.

Not even to support an international murder investigation.

She could force him. She could take a hard line with him and get hold of a court order which would force him to talk. But there were two problems with that: firstly, it would take much too long, and secondly, most of the important information — the kind of thing people only told others in confidence — would be lost. She had no choice but to coax him.

"We won't reveal any of your research," she said.

Professor Ernst Herschel laughed.

"Fräulein Holm," he said, "we are both employed by the state. We know how little we earn in comparison to every little errand boy in the private sphere. The world is, at present, incredibly unfair, and I wouldn't hold it against you if you sold the information to *Bild-Zeitung* for a couple of million. We both know that public institutions leak like sieves. The police don't know a thing that the press doesn't also know within a few hours."

"You're completely right," said Kerstin Holm. "So what are we going to do now then? Do you have any suggestions?"

Yet more silence from Jena, though it felt different this time. A contemplative silence.

"One more thing," said Herschel. "I know you think that this is just a case of academic preserve. I can hear it in your voice. But there is a more important aspect. Have you ever been to Hitler's bunker in Berlin?"

"No," said Holm.

"Very few have. And that is the point. On no condition can it be allowed to become a place of pilgrimage for the emerging neo-Nazi groups. History and scientific truth must be weighed against experience. It is a pragmatic question. Which is of most benefit to democracy? The truth or silence?"

"So we're talking about a potential new shrine for neo-Nazis?"

"Yes," said Ernst Herschel.

"I understand," said Kerstin Holm.

Another moment's silence. Herschel was thinking about the rapid rise of neo-Nazism in the undemocratically schooled former GDR. Holm was thinking about the Erinyes. She wondered whether her image of them was changing.

Eventually, she said: "I really do understand your concerns, Professor Herschel. It's an entirely justified worry for the future. But surely the future also has to be weighed up against the present. And your professional secrecy against mine. What I'm about to tell you is highly classified."

Again, silence from Jena. Yet another kind. A listening silence.

Kerstin Holm continued.

"I'm currently working alongside a few other European countries within the framework of a joint investigation. So far, in just over a year, seven people have been murdered in Sweden, Hungary, Slovenia, England, Italy and Germany. Each was killed by being hung upside down from a rope, and having a very particular kind of sharp wire driven into their temples and wiggled around in the pain centre of their cerebral cortex."

Silence from Jena. Gradually accepting, gradually becoming more willing.

"I see," Ernst Herschel said finally. "The future is already here."

"You could put it that way, yes."

"Who is behind it?"

"We don't know, but we've been calling them the Erinyes."

More silence from Jena. The silence of preparation. Then the floodgates opened.

"Weimar was a dilapidated GDR city when the Wall came down," the professor began. "Ten years later it was — with sixty thousand inhabitants — the European capital of culture. It was where Cranach, Bach, Goethe, Schiller, Herder, Wieland, Liszt, Nietzsche, Strauss, Böcklin and the Bauhaus architects lived and worked. It was the cradle of the first German democracy. It was where the Nazis held their very first meeting. It was where the Hitler Youth was born. It was where Buchenwald was built — initially Nazi Germany's biggest concentration camp, and then the Soviet Union's. The best and the worst of European culture has taken place here."

The professor paused.

"A few years after the Wall fell, some people entered a dilapidated and bombed-out building not far from the heart of Weimar, in Weimarhallen Park. It had been boarded up since the war. In the basement, they found the remains of a medical research institution. It was obvious that it had been abandoned in a hurry but that they had tried their utmost to remove all traces of themselves. The remaining archives had been torn up and some of them had been burnt. There were cells with extremely thick windowpanes and a couple of soundproofed research rooms. I was called in immediately and made sure that not a word got out to the press. I gathered together a small group of researchers. We went through every single inch of that place in minute detail; it took several years. What we are now working on is processing the results. The building was completely renovated a few years ago."

"What kind of institution was it?" Kerstin Holm asked breathlessly.

"It was called the Pain Centre," said Ernst Herschel.

On the other side of the thin wall, Paul Hjelm was reading on in Leonard Sheinkman's diary.

It was all becoming much clearer.

The people in the building were in a queue, waiting to be subjected to an experiment which robbed them of their souls through a tiny hole in their temples, small enough for a dressing to cover the wound.

"Erwin died of pain."

At the same time, the Allies' bombs were falling just round the corner. Leonard Sheinkman was coming closer and closer to the top of the list. Eventually, he reached it. The diary ended just as he was about to be taken away. Instead, he was liberated. He was saved by the bell. He emigrated to Sweden and obliterated his terrible past.

Two things of note were mentioned, Paul Hjelm thought with razor-sharp Western logic. Firstly, the church. Secondly, the tormentors.

There seemed to have been three of them. Sheinkman wrote about them on 19 February. They seemed to have had different characters. "*I do not know their names. They give no names. They are three anonymous murderers. They are not alike. Not even murderers are alike.*"

Sheinkman had had a kind of connection with one of them. "*The kindest of them. He is less German than I, and very blond. He looks so sorrowful. He kills with sorrow in his eyes.*" That was the first one.

"*Not the other two. One kills out of curiosity. He is not cruel, simply cold. He watches, observes, writes.*" That was the second of them.

And then the third. "*But the man with the purple birthmark on his neck, a mark in the shape of a rhombus, he is cruel. He wants to kill. I have seen that look before. He wants you to suffer. Then you can die. Only then is he happy.*"

Paul Hjelm made notes, systematising it all.

Tormentor 1: Very blond, not German, sorrowful.
Tormentor 2: Ice cold, dedicated scientist.
Tormentor 3: Cruel, sadistic, purple rhombus
-shaped birthmark on throat.

He couldn't get anything else from it.

On to the church, then. Where had Leonard Sheinkman's wife and son been killed? It was a camp. *"They were being taken to their deaths at the execution spot."* In all likelihood, that really was Buchenwald. And following that, he had been moved. *"And I ended up here."*

Sheinkman had told his children it was in Buchenwald he was kept prisoner. If he wasn't moved particularly far, then it could reasonably be assumed that he still considered himself to be in Buchenwald. An annexe of Buchenwald.

In other words, in Weimar.

The church. 18 February. That peculiar description of the physical appearance of time. *"Time has a white base. That base may well be quadrangular. Then comes the black. The black is made up of three parts. The lowest of these is hexagonal. On three of these six surfaces, every other one, there are two windows set one above the other. The lower window is slightly larger than the upper. And immediately above the upper window, the next section begins; the middle. It is just as black and shaped like a small, domed cap. This is where the clock sits. Finally, the spire. The spire is black and looks to be needle-sharp."*

Paul Hjelm went online and searched for Weimar. Sure enough, Allied bombs had rained down on the city in February 1945. He found an overview of its churches. There were pictures of each of them.

The cathedral, Stadtkirche, was a big structure which had been destroyed during the war. It wasn't the one. It

395

wasn't right at all. The city's other big church was slightly further to the north. Jakobskirche. It was a white church with a black tower divided into three segments — first a hexagonal section with two windows above one another on each side, the lower one slightly bigger than the higher one. The next section was shaped like a little domed cap with a clock. At the very top, the spire, which looked as though it were needle-sharp.

There was no doubt.

It was Jakobskirche in Weimar that Leonard Sheinkman had been able to see from his window, likening it to time itself.

On the other side of the thin wall, Kerstin Holm's increasingly worthwhile — and increasingly awful — conversation with Ernst Herschel in Jena was continuing.

"The Pain Centre?" she said.

"They called it the Pain Centre. They experimented with the brain's pain centre. The cerebral cortex. The objective was for their research subjects to feel the most acute pain possible.

"They developed the procedure gradually. From what we can tell, it started with simple pain experiments up in Buchenwald. The results were so promising that a separate annexe was established, probably under direct orders from Himmler himself. That was when the experimentation really took off. They came to realise that increased blood flow to the brain contributed to an enhancement of pain and started hanging their research subjects upside down as a result. The long wire was a development from that. They were clearly near to a breakthrough of some kind when the Americans reached Weimar. The archives stopped suddenly at the end of March. The Americans arrived in early April. They had probably heard rumours that the end was close, packed up and disappeared into thin air. No one has ever been brought to account for it. In actual fact, we had no idea the institution ever existed before we opened the doors. All other traces of it had been obliterated."

"Have the people responsible been identified?" asked Kerstin Holm. She didn't recognise her own voice.

"Not entirely," said Ernst Herschel. "What we do know has been sent on to the Jewish Documentation Centre in Vienna. Simon Wiesenthal, you know."

"Yes," Kerstin replied in the same peculiar cawing voice. "And what do you know?"

"That there were three officers as well as guard soldiers. All from the SS."

"Names?"

"Only two of the three, I'm afraid."

"What are the names you have?"

"Let me start by explaining the order of command. Two of the three were doctors. SS doctors, if you grasp the full extent of that term. These men were doctors *and* officers. The third wasn't a doctor. He was the boss. The entire institution, the whole Pain Centre, they were his work. His name was Hans von Heilberg.

"Naturally, he made sure to burn all documents relating to himself and his existence is otherwise only sporadically recorded in various war archives. After the war, there isn't a trace of him. We wouldn't have known he existed at all, wouldn't have known that he was in charge of the institution, if he hadn't been treated for a certain complaint by one of the doctors. He had a birthmark that had started bleeding and he was worried it was skin cancer. That was in August 1944. His worries were described by the doctor as 'chronic hypochondria'."

"A birthmark?"

"A birthmark on his throat. According to reports, it was shaped like a rhombus. That's all we know about Hans von Heilberg's appearance."

"And the doctors?"

"We know very little about one of them. He made sure to get rid of all written evidence, but oddly enough he forgot a photograph, so we do at least have a picture of him. It's actually the only picture we have of any of the three."

"And the other?"

"I've been hesitating slightly, and I know you've noticed, Fräulein Holm. He represents a problem for you. For your entire neutral nation. The other SS doctor was Swedish."

"Swedish?"

"We have the most information about him. He wasn't as careful in getting rid of the evidence as the others. Perhaps he didn't think he would survive. Perhaps he was indifferent to it all. His name was Anton Eriksson."

"Jesus," said Kerstin.

"I know that your country has finally started to get to grips with its national legacy from the Second World War, Fräulein Holm. You've unearthed some cannon fodder in the Waffen SS and things like that — but an SS man of that rank isn't something you've come across yet. That was another of the reasons behind my initial reluctance. I asked myself whether I shouldn't put the question to someone higher up first. But now I've said it. Do as you wish with it."

"I will," said Kerstin Holm.

"I'll fax the material over," said Herschel.

They met in the corridor, in line with the thin wall that separated their offices. Each pointed at the other.

"Weimar," they said in unison.

Paul Hjelm and Kerstin Holm went into her office. They quickly recapped their respective discoveries for one another. Then they glanced at a fax which had just arrived. It was about Anton Eriksson. Accompanying it was an extremely blurry, almost completely black photograph of the third man.

"Three men," said Paul Hjelm. "Tormentor 3 seems to have been identified. 'Cruel, sadistic, purple rhombus-shaped birthmark on throat.' Hans von Heilberg. The boss himself."

"This photo doesn't give us much," said Kerstin Holm. "But your summary of tormentor 1 could easily be the Swede, Anton Eriksson. 'Very blond, not German, sorrowful.' It seems most likely that the sorrowful one was the only man not to wipe out all traces of himself. He was probably being eaten up by his conscience even then."

"So should we assume that tormentor 2 — 'ice-cold scientist' — is the unidentified man in the photograph? The fact that he wiped out all other traces of himself surely suggests a certain cool rationality?"

They sat there for a moment, each of them thinking. Still, their thoughts were as one. It was as though nothing, no bones and no cartilage, separated their two brains from one another.

"So what are we looking at here?" Paul Hjelm asked eventually. "How did the Erinyes find out about this method of execution? Why are they using it to kill off pimps? And where the hell does Leonard Sheinkman come into all of this? He should've been executed — he was at the top of the list. But he made it. How?"

Kerstin stepped in. "And why did he never tell anyone about any of this? If he had just told the world that this horrible place existed, all three of them could've been locked up. Or they could've started searching for them right after the war at least. But he kept it quiet for over fifty years instead."

"He turned a new page in his life," said Paul. "He obliterated his past. He didn't want anything to do with it. He just removed it. Like a tumour."

"They must've found out about it from Herschel," said Kerstin, getting to her feet.

"Who?"

"The Erinyes can only have had one single source of information about the hanging upside down and the

400

nail in the brain, and that's the research group in Weimar."

"Ring him back and see who knew about it. Absolutely anyone involved. Who was the first to go into the building? Who did they tell? How did Herschel find out? What happened when he gathered his research group together? Who was involved? Were there any other staff? What happened when the building was completely renovated?"

"You're right," said Kerstin, picking up the receiver.

"But not quite," said Paul. "There are other possible sources. If Sheinkman survived, maybe others did too. The guard soldiers in the Pain Centre, for example. And then at least three others."

"Three war criminals who went underground over fifty years ago," Kerstin nodded.

"Ring anyway," said Paul.

Kerstin spoke with Ernst Herschel. He promised to try to put a list of all possible names together, including how and when the Erinyes might have found out about the method.

"One more thing," Kerstin said into the handset. "Was there any kind of register of the research subjects?"

"Yes," said Ernst Herschel. "Though they're just combinations of letters. No names. No individuals. Just letters. It must've been simplest that way."

"Probably," said Kerstin Holm. "Thanks again for your help. Prepare yourselves for a visit."

"What?" asked the professor.

"We're sending a man," said Kerstin, hanging up.

"Arto?" asked Paul.

"Our well-travelled friend."

And so they began — with a single pair of eyes and four interconnected cerebral hemispheres — to read through the Swedish SS doctor's documents.

CHAPTER
THIRTY-THREE

Odessa was a former beauty. That sounded like a quote from a tourist brochure.

Arto Söderstedt was slightly disappointed that all of his expectations had been confirmed. Each worn-out, vodka-soaked alcoholic he passed — and they weren't few and far between — was a potential robber, and he was constantly being accosted by beggars, primarily children, asking him to buy dog-eared postcards for astronomical prices. The city also had a very particular scent. Like a past-it whore, he thought brutally to himself. Cheap perfume to disguise the decay.

He still hadn't been given the opportunity to cajole the reluctant Eastern European policemen and women without computers into cooperating with him; he was walking around, waiting for them to start work. "A bit later, maybe," a neighbour to the police station had reeled off in muddled German.

He had no real reason to go back to the hotel either. With its combination of extravagance and decay, it stood like a symbol of Odessa. And so he was wandering. He made his way to the water's edge — which wasn't there. Odessa was a port city with a slight quirk: it sat a few hundred metres above the water. The only thing linking the city to the water were those world-famous steps down which the pushchair had bounced in Eisenstein's revolutionary *Battleship Potemkin*. Before those stairs were built in the nineteenth century, there had been no direct link between city and water, between Odessa and the Black Sea.

The city had been powerful once, and it probably still did make a striking impression from down on the water. But walking through it, Söderstedt thought it felt shabby above all else. A relic of a bygone era. Transport to Ukraine's most important port was carried out along other routes these days, of course, but back then, the liveliness of the steps had been clear. It was no coincidence that it had been used as a symbol of capitalist economics in Eisenstein's film.

At least that was how Arto Söderstedt interpreted it.

But now, the steps seemed to be nothing more than a refuge for all kinds of riff-raff, beggars and junkies, and walking down them presented visitors with an immediate health risk. Before Söderstedt ventured down, he nipped over to some shrubbery and broke off a branch. It looked like a walking stick, but in reality it was a weapon. He was ready to defend himself. Not that it could look that way.

He walked down and he walked back up. He counted seventeen more potential attackers, beggars dressed as postcard sellers. In addition to that — despite all attempts to defend himself with the branch — he made it back up with three splashes of vodka on his clothes. Fortunately no vomit.

404

He paused at the top of the steps with the branch in his hand. In the nearest shop window, Uncle Pertti was standing with his hand on his sabre. Arto stared at him, bewitched. Uncle Pertti stared back. Arto dropped the branch. Uncle Pertti dropped the sabre. Arto stuck out his tongue. Uncle Pertti did the same.

The spell was broken.

What did the old devil want? Söderstedt wondered, leaving him behind among the boots in the shop window. Why this obstinacy?

He wandered along the grand old promenade and looked out over the cold, dark surface of the Black Sea, glittering beautifully in the morning sun. He noticed that with each moment that passed, he was becoming more favourably inclined to the city. It had a beauty which wasn't ingratiating, the way the beauty of Italian cities often could be. It was a beauty which didn't try to hide its faults. Instead, it seemed to be saying: here I am, take it or leave it. More or less like Uncle Pertti.

He walked past the famous opera house and university. The buildings really were beautiful. He wasn't even sure that the decay was tragic any more. Perhaps the march of time *should* be preserved in works of art. Perhaps it shouldn't be restored and adorned and tarted up and masqueraded as something it wasn't. Corroded by time — like everything else on earth. Should art really be lifted up and furnished with an eternal value that was, in its very foundation, false? Even if the alternative was obliteration? If time was nothing but a saboteur, a destroyer of eternal values? If that was the case, shouldn't it be withstood?

It was the classic argument of the plastic surgeon . . .

Just as he was starting to feel as though something truly substantial was on the way, he arrived — without really having planned it — back at the police station. This time, the door was open.

He ambled about its decayed old corridors and remarked to himself that he was using the word "decay" a little too often. If this exact corridor had been in Sweden or Finland, would he still have thought of it as decayed? Or was it simply the case that the word was inseparably associated with this particular city? Irrevocably linked to Odessa?

That was when it struck him that Odessa wasn't just a city. It was also an organisation. A particularly unpleasant organisation. Organisation der Ehemaligen SS-Angehörigen. The Organisation of Former SS Members. Founded in 1947 with the sole intention of helping high-ranking Nazis gain new identities in South America and the Middle East. Replaced by the Kameradenwerke in 1952.

He couldn't quite get the context straight, but it was there. He felt it a little more keenly as he knocked on a door bearing Cyrillic letters reading something along the lines of "Commissioner Alexej Svitlytjnyj". The name of the man he was looking for, at least.

Alexej Svitlytjnyj was sitting at his desk and had been forewarned. Just as Söderstedt had suspected, there was no computer on his superbly crafted desk. There was, however, an oddly shaped cigarette hanging from the mouth of the big, composed man in the impeccable Eastern European suit. It looked like one of the suits Soviet leaders used to wear when they stood on a platform above Red Square, waving stiffly to the military parades passing by below. Arto Söderstedt had always suspected that those men had been stuffed and remote-controlled.

Svitlytjnyj was neither, but he was, however, rather apathetic. His English was also surprisingly eloquent.

"I checked with the Ministry of Justice," he said once their introductions were over and done with. "As a representative of Europol, it's perfectly OK for you to access our investigatory materials. But sending it halfway across the world to the Swedish police was a different matter."

"So have you managed to identify the noseless man?" asked Söderstedt.

Svitlytjnyj nodded gravely like an old brown bear.

He looks like a Nevalyashka doll, Söderstedt thought, happy to make use of a long-neglected word from his childhood. Like one of those little plastic dolls with big round heads which teetered back and forth for all eternity when you set them in motion.

"That's correct," Svitlytjnyj eventually said, sluggishly holding out a dog-eared brown folder with a hammer and sickle on the cover. "From the Soviet days," he added with a gesture to the Communist hammer and sickle symbol. "That was another part of the problem when it came to sharing the material."

Söderstedt opened the file and stared down into a forest of Cyrillic letters.

"It's in Russian," he said thoughtlessly.

"No it isn't," said Svitlytjnyj. "It's Ukrainian. A language spoken by seven times more people than Swedish."

"Sorry," Söderstedt replied courteously.

"Turn the page," said Svitlytjnyj. "There's a photograph."

Söderstedt did as he was told. Staring at him was an utterly strange figure with a dark gaze.

The figure had no nose.

"His name was Kouzmin," the commissioner said, taking a deep drag from his cigarette. By this point, there were only about four millimetres of it left. Söderstedt wondered how it would all pan out — would it last another drag?

"Koutjschmin?" he tried.

Svitlytjnyj nodded sideways and made a bobbing motion with his hand.

"Something like that," he said. "Franz Kouzmin. His criminal record isn't particularly extensive. Mostly linked to a long-standing, intense vodka habit. Petty crimes. Break-ins, receiving stolen goods, drunkenness. Hardly a major criminal. He was reported missing by his daughter at the end of September 1981. Apparently he was a widower."

"Does it say anything about his nose?" Söderstedt asked.

"His missing nose," Svitlytjnyj said, getting to his feet; it took him almost thirty seconds. "Might I suggest we carry on in the computer room?"

408

A mystery, Söderstedt thought. The minuscule cigarette had disappeared without a trace. In its place was a freshly rolled, newly lit cigarette. The switch had taken place without him, the seasoned Finnish-Swedish detective, noticing a thing.

"You've got a computer room?" he asked distractedly, getting up.

Svitlytjnyj chuckled and took a long drag.

"You weren't expecting that, were you?" he said.

They went out into the corridor and wandered through all eternity.

"We're busy transferring the old archive over to the new computer system," the commissioner said. "And taking the opportunity to translate it all into English. It takes time. We're up to 'L'. You're in luck."

"What about the nose?" Söderstedt persisted.

"The missing nose," Svitlytjnyj persisted, opening a door.

The room they entered was a hackers' paradise. All the computers seemed to be the latest possible models. Several men and women were tapping away at keys on trendy, lightning-fast terminals. The impression it gave was more American stock-market company than Ukrainian police department.

"You look a bit dumbfounded," Svitlytjnyj said with a smile.

"How can you afford all this?" Söderstedt blurted out undiplomatically.

"Mafia money," the commissioner said with a straight face.

Several others in the room burst into laughter.

"Let me brief you," Svitlytjnyj continued. And so, in peace and quiet — and in perfect English — Arto Söderstedt read the files on Franz Kouzmin.

His twelve-year-old daughter, who had been living in an orphanage at the time, had reported him missing at the end of September, when she had gone for her monthly visit. His wife had died of cancer just two years after the daughter was born, and when his alcoholism worsened, she had been taken away and placed into an orphanage. There were excerpts from an interview with her.

"Dad had just stopped drinking," she had said. "He'd been completely clean for a month. And really, really happy." Though she had no idea why.

OK, Söderstedt thought, checking himself. Kouzmin stopped drinking and was happy, expectant. Like a man going on a trip. A trip to Sweden. He had clearly found something, and that something made him fight a long-standing alcohol problem and board the M/S *Cosmopolit*, bound for Frihamnen in Stockholm.

He read on.

Suddenly, the nose question was solved. He should have guessed. They all should have.

Franz Kouzmin had been adopted by a Ukrainian woman who had taken care of him in Buchenwald, where his parents had died. He had been subjected to a medical experiment related to breathing. An investigation into how important the airways in the nose were for the human ability to breathe.

To answer that question, the SS doctors in Buchenwald had sawn off little Franz's nose.

It turned out it *was* possible to live without one.

Good to know.

Things had become more difficult for him later on in life. But if someone had sawn off my nose, Arto Söderstedt thought, I probably would have turned to alcohol too.

And then he found it.

A name.

He phoned Stockholm.

Jan-Olov Hultin answered. He said: "I was just about to ring you, Arto. You've got to go to Weimar."

Arto Söderstedt simply ignored him.

"Listen carefully to what I'm about to say," he said, focusing on the computer screen in front of him.

"I'm listening," said Hultin.

"Our man without a nose, 'Shtayf' from Södra Begravningsplatsen, was called Franz Kouzmin. That wasn't his birth name, though. He was born to a Jewish home in Berlin in January 1935. His name was Franz Sheinkman."

There was silence at the other end of the line.

"My God," said Hultin.

"You could say that," said Söderstedt.

"Tell me more."

"He was a widower and an alcoholic and had just stopped drinking. He crept out of the Soviet Union in good spirits and set off to Sweden, or more precisely to his father Leonard Sheinkman's house on Bofinksvägen in Tyresö. Somehow, he'd managed to find out where his father was living. It was enough to make him stop drinking. His father thought Franz was dead — dead along with his wife in Buchenwald. But that's not what happened. He wasn't killed, he was subjected to medical experiments; they deliberately sawed his nose off. So, on the evening of the fourth of September 1981, he arrived at his father's house on Bofinksvägen. We don't know what happened when they met, but what we *do* know is that the very same evening, he was stabbed to death and found next to a little lake nearby."

"I see," said Hultin.

"You see what?"

"That you've done a fantastic job. Can you send the files over? Will they allow that?"

"I think so," Söderstedt said, glancing up at the great Alexej Svitlytjnyj. His cigarette was tiny once more, but Söderstedt was forced to admit that he had lost interest in it.

"You can go to Weimar now then," said Hultin. "You need to meet a Professor Ernst Herschel from the history department at the University of Jena. Get there as quickly as you can. We can deal with any further instructions on the way."

"Give me a hint," Söderstedt pleaded.

"The institution where the nail in the brain experiment was developed."

"Ah," Söderstedt replied, hanging up.

Svitlytjnyj sucked the microscopic cigarette butt into his mouth, quickly doused it with a little pooled spit, spat it out and had another immediately ready rolled. He lit it as he leaned forward over the computer and helped Arto Söderstedt navigate the Cyrillic letters on-screen.

And just like that, Franz Kouzmin-Sheinkman's files were sent flying across Europe.

Söderstedt wondered whether he hadn't simply been asked to come to Odessa to admire their computers and spread a little goodwill among the Common European police community.

He said: "I need to copy the files for my own use, too."

He was handed a disk and the computer asked him: "Save Kouzmin?"

"Yes," he answered. With emphasis.

CHAPTER
THIRTY-FOUR

Anton Eriksson was born in 1913, in a small town called Örbyhus to the north of Stockholm. At the age of twenty, he enrolled as a student at the university in Uppsala and, after reading a range of subjects including medicine, German and anthropology, transferred to the grand old university town's most famous independent institution: the State Institute for Racial Biology. The institution had been founded in 1922, the very same year the Swedish Social Democrats had recommended the forced sterilisation of mentally handicapped people on the basis of "the eugenic dangers inherent in the reproduction of the feeble-minded". It was the world's first institution for the study of eugenics and later served as a standard for Kaiser Wilhelm's Institute of Anthropology, Human Heredity and Eugenics in Berlin.

The Kaiser Wilhelm Institute of Eugenics was, in turn, an important precondition for the Holocaust. Though its roots were, of course, much deeper. The early twentieth century had been a time of great change — Sweden was transformed from an agricultural to an industrial society — and in times of upheaval, the need for a scapegoat always arises. The Jews were an obvious choice, since they could just as easily be accused of bolshevism as of capitalism and anti-patriotism — it was simply a matter of choosing which.

Racial thinking of this kind was also linked to the popular science of the time: anthropology and genetics. The Swedish Society for Eugenics had been founded in 1909, and there was also an international society of racial biology which met regularly to discuss how best to produce an *Übermensch*. When they held their grandiose world congress in London in 1912, none other than Winston Churchill had been the chairman. In 1918, a professor from the Karolinska Institut in Stockholm had suggested that a Nobel Institute of Racial Biology should be established, but the time was not yet ripe. In 1921, however, a motion supported by representatives from each of the governing parties was launched, advocating the founding of the State Institute for Racial Biology. The motion was passed by a large majority in Sweden's Riksdag, and the institute opened on New Year's Day, 1922. At its head was Herman Lundborg, with seven staff and an annual budget of sixty thousand kronor.

Herman Lundborg believed that the Nordic race was superior to all others, and as the years went by, he became increasingly drawn to anti-Semitic standpoints. The institute was also influenced by Lundborg's fondness for Germany. He invited a number of Germans to give lectures at the institute, among them Hans F. Günther, who would later become the Nazi ideologue in all matters racial. When the State Institute for Racial Biology held its world congress in New York in 1932, Herman Lundborg was there, as was much of the American upper class, with families like the Kelloggs, the Harrimans and the Roosevelts at the centre of it all. The chairman of the meeting was Ernst Rüdin, a man who would, in just a few short years, be at the fore of Hitler's extensive programme of sterilisation.

By that point in time, the State Institute for Racial Biology in Uppsala had started to stagnate, despite its firmly rooted international reputation. The annual budget had been lowered to thirty thousand kronor and Lundborg was becoming increasingly untenable as head of the institute. In 1936, he was replaced by Gunnar Dahlberg, a man who, to a certain degree, changed the direction of the institute, with its focus shifting from racial biology to human genetics and social engineering. This shift eventually culminated in the now-notorious programme of forced sterilisations carried out on many of Sweden's mentally handicapped citizens.

Anton Eriksson's involvement with the institute came towards the end of Herman Lundborg's tenure. He had a great deal of sympathy for Lundborg's eugenic and anti-Semitic thinking, and when Dahlberg took over Eriksson regarded the change in direction as a betrayal of Lundborg's legacy. Medical and surgical-orientated racial biology was what interested him.

In the material from Weimar, they found a short text written by Anton Eriksson which had been published in the pro-German *Aftonbladet* tabloid in the spring of

416

1936. In the article, Eriksson attempted, using an utterly clinical line of reasoning, to prove the biologically determined inferiority of Jews. As evidence for his thesis, he made use of Herman Lundborg's famous sketches of human profiles.

In early 1937, Anton Eriksson left Sweden to study in Berlin. The last mention of him suggested he was involved with Kaiser Wilhelm's Institute of Eugenics and that he had been admitted to the internal officer training line within the SS.

Then it all went quiet for the talented young man from Örbyhus. Very quiet.

Kerstin Holm and Paul Hjelm read through the file together. They were utterly silent and there was no distance between them.

They could feel Sweden's history changing before their eyes. Who had told them about this when they were at school? Who had told them about their humane, neutral, Nordic country's dark inheritance?

No one.

The black hole in the space-time continuum was starting to fill up.

And the spanner in the works, the fundamental error in their thinking, was fast approaching.

Time was starting to right itself.

Not least thanks to Arto Söderstedt's remarkable new information from Odessa.

They had seen nothing so far which suggested that Anton Eriksson, on his way to becoming an SS doctor, would have felt regret or suffered pangs of conscience over what he had done. To the contrary, he seemed more likely to be the "ice-cold scientist" mentioned in Leonard Sheinkman's diary.

Tormentor number 2.

So why would this rationally driven, methodically working anti-Semite leave behind damning evidence of the Pain Centre in Weimar? No photographs, of course — but plenty of material.

Why?

There was just one plausible explanation.

He had had a sure-fire exit plan.

"When does Leonard Sheinkman's diary end?" Kerstin asked.

"Twenty-first of February 1945," Paul replied.

"And when did the Americans arrive in Weimar?"

"Buchenwald was liberated on the eleventh of April."

Kerstin Holm leaned forward over the table, shoved a portion of snus tobacco beneath her lip and said: "So there's a month and a half between the day Leonard Sheinkman was taken into the operating room to be hung upside down and have a nail driven into his head and the day Weimar was liberated. His brain had hardly been scrambled when he made it out. I mean, he managed to learn Swedish surprisingly quickly, he changed profession from poet to brain specialist surprisingly quickly, and swiftly became a professor and Nobel Prize candidate."

"So what happened during that month and a half between the twenty-first of February, when the diary ends, and the eleventh of April, when the liberation took place?"

418

"Leonard Sheinkman died, of course," said Kerstin Holm. "The Jewish poet from Berlin died an unbelievably painful death in a cellar in Weimar. Right beneath the cultural heart of Europe."

Paul Hjelm got to his feet, went over to the computer and started typing.

"It's been right in front of us the whole time," he said eventually, pointing at the screen. "Qvarfordt's hopeless notes from Leonard Sheinkman's autopsy. The error in our thinking. 'Evidence of cervical spondylosis. Circumcisio post-adolescent. Rheumatoid arthritis, early stage, presenting in the wrists and ankles.'"

"Circumcisio post-adolescent," Kerstin said. "Circumcision as an adult."

"We got lost in the Latin," said Paul.

"In the confusion of tongues," said Kerstin.

They sat in silence for a moment as everything came crashing down on top of them. One by one, the grotesque consequences of their realisation revealed themselves.

Anton Eriksson, the ice-cold Jew-hater and tormentor, had taken part in the experimental torture of the Jewish poet Leonard Sheinkman. The first time had been on 21 February 1945. Perhaps Sheinkman had survived for a couple of rounds, wandering the corridors like a lost soul. Perhaps he had died right away. Either way, he had been long dead when the staff fled the Pain Centre towards the end of March, early April. The ice-cool Eriksson had probably already been aware that the centre's and Nazi Germany's days were numbered back in February. He had probably already picked out a suitable victim with whom to switch identities once the war was over. He had picked Leonard Sheinkman, a man who had been the same age as him.

The Jew-hater became the Jew.

The murderer adopted the victim's identity.

After Sheinkman's death, Eriksson had kept hold of his papers, those which he had with him. The others he acquired anew. He made sure to tattoo Sheinkman's concentration camp number onto his arm, and he had made sure to get circumcised. All bases had to be covered. He had known, not least thanks to Sheinkman's diary which, of course, he had kept, that his wife and son had died in Buchenwald — he had known there was no other family. Perhaps he had even undergone some kind of plastic surgery in order to avoid discovery in Sweden. But it had been ten years and an entire world war since Anton Eriksson had left the country, so the risk of discovery was minimal.

He had arrived in Sweden and completed his language learning in record time — hardly surprising, considering it was his mother tongue. He had also completed his medical education in record time — again, hardly surprising, considering he was already a doctor. He had then become a brain scientist in record time — hardly surprising, considering he had already been experimenting on human brains. And no one had recognised him. He had made it. He had completed his metamorphosis and was now living as a Jew. He went to the synagogue, observed the Sabbath, Passover, Sukkot,

Hanukkah and Yom Kippur, and he married a Jewish woman.

The Nazi had started a Jewish family.

None of this needed expressing.

But one thing did:

"How could he live with it?"

They looked at one another.

"I don't think he could," said Paul Hjelm. "I think he deliberately trained himself to block it all out. I think that Anton Eriksson actually *became* Leonard Sheinkman. I think he even managed to talk himself into thinking he had written that diary."

"But he was reminded of his past *twice*," said Kerstin Holm. "The first time was on the fourth of September 1981. He was nearly seventy by that point, when a newly sober Ukrainian Jew without a nose appeared on the threshold of that lovely house on Bofinksvägen, beaming with joy and claiming to be his son. It was madness. He killed him with a kitchen knife. Two brutal stabs, representing the power of his actions, the entire scope of it all. He took the body out into the woods and dumped it by a nearby lake."

"The second time was when he felt the presence of the Erinyes," Paul Hjelm continued. "That was when it all came back with a vengeance. He was forced to turn the page again. He was forced to read the back of the paper, the side he thought he had wiped clean. It was enough to make him visit Franz Sheinkman's anonymous grave — 'Shtayf'. The gravestone had been kicked over, and by neo-Nazis. It must have felt quite ironic. And just then, while he was at the grave, the

421

Erinyes appeared. The goddesses of revenge from the depths of antiquity. Before they killed him using the very same method he himself had used on countless others in the Pain Centre in Weimar, he talked to them. He had probably been confronted by the weight of his guilt by that point and said something along the lines of 'finally' or 'you took your time'. Just like Nikos Voultsos in Skansen, he took them for real goddesses of revenge. Real Erinyes."

In both cases, there had been plenty to be avenged.

"That still leaves the question of what these two examples of revenge have in common. The prostitutes' revenge on their pimps and the camp victims' revenge on their tormentors. Where's the link between them?"

"We'll have to see what Professor Herschel manages to scrape together in terms of names from Weimar," Paul Hjelm said.

They didn't say much more after that.

Their words felt rather insignificant.

CHAPTER
THIRTY-FIVE

Arto Söderstedt had always wanted to see Weimar. It was one of his private dreams, those that Uncle Pertti's money would help him to realise. Some time in the not so distant future, he would make it there.

In other words, he hadn't been expecting this sudden trip.

He was sitting on the train from Leipzig, where the plane from Odessa had taken him the night before. He had checked in to one Hotel Fürstenhof, fallen asleep without taking even a moment to enjoy the grand old beauty of the building, and hiccuped from pure shock when he was handed the bill by an exquisite blonde he hadn't the heart to argue with. He paid compliantly and hoped that the National Criminal Police accountants wouldn't make too much of a fuss about it. Or did he dare send the bill to Europol in The Hague?

After that, he had wandered along Tröndlinring, bathed in the formidable light of a mild, Central European spring morning, and jumped on board the train to Weimar which had just sped past the border between Saxony and Thuringia in the former GDR.

As places like Bad Kösen, Bad Sulza and Apolda went by, he read the latest message from Hultin, which he had paid a small fortune to the Hotel Fürstenhof in Leipzig to access online. Should the bill for that go to The Hague too? Where exactly did the Common European line for abuse of power lie?

He ignored that thought and started reading.

Leonard Sheinkman wasn't Leonard Sheinkman.

He was a Swedish SS doctor by the name of Anton Eriksson.

Such was the poodle's real core. As Goethe had written in Weimar.

Elsewhere in *Faust*, he had called Leipzig "little Paris", and as the train pulled in to Weimar Hauptbahnhof, Leipzig was undeniably like a metropolis in comparison.

Weimar was nothing more than a tiny little provincial hole.

And yet the place had been European Capital of Culture just the year before. It had also celebrated the 250th anniversary of Goethe's birth.

Still going strong.

A dark-haired woman in her early thirties was waiting on the platform. She was holding a handwritten sign reading "Herr Söderstadt".

It was a step in the right direction, he thought, dragging his unnecessarily heavy luggage over to her and holding out his hand. She gave him a quick, sharp, shy look.

"My name is Elena Basedow," she said in English, her voice unexpectedly deep. "I'm on Professor Herschel's assistant staff."

"Arto Söderstedt," said Arto Söderstedt.

"Not stadt?" she asked, glancing at her handwritten sign.

"Not quite," he said. "More of a small village."

She smiled shyly. "Like Weimar," she said, gesturing with her hands.

"Hopefully," Söderstedt replied awkwardly.

They set off. It was still a glorious Central European spring morning.

"Staff?" he asked. "Does the professor have many assistants?"

"Not exactly," said Elena Basedow. "At the moment, we're purely a research group. The assistants are PhD students. There used to be more of us."

"While you were researching the Pain Centre?"

"Right. There were plenty of volunteer students, right up to autumn 1998. Unpaid history and archaeology students."

"Hmm," said Söderstedt.

They had reached an old Volkswagen Vento just outside the station. Elena Basedow opened the door for him and single-handedly lifted his unnecessarily heavy bag into the boot.

"We're going to go there first," she said, slamming the boot lid with such force that the car jumped. "He's waiting for us there."

Since her words seemed slightly cryptic, Söderstedt asked: "Where?"

"To the Pain Centre. It's been completely renovated now. An IT company took over the building without having any idea what happened there during the war. Not that they'd care . . ."

"But you do," Söderstedt said as the car swung out from the station and began making its way towards the little town centre.

She gave him another quick, shy look.

"Yes," she said. "I do."

"You're Jewish," said Söderstedt.

"I'm a bit of everything," she replied. "I'm part descendant of the Rousseau-influenced eighteenth-century educationalist Johann Bernhard Basedow. Then I'm part Greek. And I'm part Jewish, yes."

"A mix of the best," Söderstedt said, feeling shockingly pure, racially speaking.

She gave him yet another of those quick, shy looks.

"There it is," she said, pointing.

On a secluded little street to the north of the very heart of the town was a building which looked almost plastic, as though it had been iced, covered with a glistening sugary coat. Slightly beyond it, the hexagonal, newly renovated tower of Jakobskirche loomed.

"*I see time,*"

From the cellar windows in the frosted building, the church tower would most likely be visible.

Outside the iced building, where a glossy sign shouted OUD data, a straight-backed, smart-looking man in a suit was waiting. He marched straight over to the passenger door of the Vento and opened it for their guest.

"Professor Ernst Herschel," he said, holding out a hand.

426

At the sight of Arto Söderstedt he froze. It was just for a brief second, but long enough for the detective within Söderstedt to react. Since Herschel's face immediately returned to normal, he decided to wait and see what happened.

It didn't feel especially good.

After all, it wasn't long since he had been told: "I must admit it was something of a shock when you walked into the room."

With that at the back of his mind, he climbed out of the car and looked over to the candied building.

"This is what it looks like now," Ernst Herschel said in a casual tone. "The new times are taking over, airbrushing everything else into golden oblivion."

Then he jumped into the back seat. Söderstedt clambered back in himself. The Vento drove off.

"We're heading south towards the Hochschule für Architektur und Bauwesen," Herschel explained. "I still have my old study there. I'm from the university town of Jena, twenty kilometres to the east. There's no real university in Weimar, but there are some smaller colleges. One of them rented out rooms for our research."

The car passed the enormous castle, which looked as though it belonged somewhere else, in a much bigger town. Or why not an empire?

And then they arrived at the Hochschule für Architektur und Bauwesen. As they wandered up a staircase which seemed as though it was drenched in fine old traditions, Arto Söderstedt wondered what the architecture college staff had to say about the iced building in the vicinity.

427

They came to a cold but elegant study. Elena Basedow set the coffee machine brewing before disappearing out through the doorway.

Assistant staff, Söderstedt thought, sitting down in his assigned seat. Herschel sat down behind the desk.

"I'm very rarely here these days," he said. "The final stages of the Pain Centre work are taking place in the Department of History in Jena."

He held out a list to Söderstedt.

"I just faxed this off to Stockholm. A list of all staff and all conceivable people who, during the research period in Weimar, might plausibly have heard of . . . the nature of the experiments. You can have one too. There you go."

"Thank you," said Arto Söderstedt. "And thank you for your cooperation in general. It's been invaluable."

"Your colleague Kerstin Holm managed to convince me. I must admit, I was initially rather sceptical. I still don't quite understand it all. She said something about a league of some kind, wreaking havoc around Europe with nails like this?"

Herschel opened a drawer in his desk and took out a long, thin, sharp, rusty nail. He handed it to Söderstedt.

"Jesus," Söderstedt said, taking it from him.

It had a heavy legacy, that much was clear. He almost struggled to lift it.

"Yes," he continued as he turned the nail in his hands. "That's right. But we're having real trouble working out who they are."

"The Erinyes," said Ernst Herschel.

428

Söderstedt observed him. Had Kerstin really told him that? Had they got on so well?

Herschel went on:

"According to the legend, they become Eumenides when Athena civilises them. They're brought into a modern society, governed by law. Do you think something similar is going to happen now?"

"Is there a modern society governed by law for them to be incorporated into?" Söderstedt asked.

Herschel stared at him for a moment. Then he started to laugh, loudly and almost savagely.

When the fit was over, he said: "There was one thing I forgot to tell the charming Fräulein Holm. Speaking of a modern society based on law. Do you know what the Pain Centre's three figureheads were given as a salary bonus?"

Söderstedt had no idea.

"Dental gold," said Herschel.

He paused.

"They shared their victims' belongings. Dental gold was the most important source of income. They seem to have collected a considerable amount of it. The more Jews they killed, the more gold they earned. It was an art."

Söderstedt felt sick to his stomach. Eventually, he spoke.

"One thing struck me. You faxed a fairly abundant amount of material on Anton Eriksson but you said you also had files on Hans von Heilberg, the head of the centre. I don't think that material ever made it to Stockholm. It never reached me, at least."

Herschel nodded. "You're right," he said. "I probably only sent the Eriksson material. Here is Hans von Heilberg's file."

It appeared as though on demand.

Söderstedt paused for a moment before looking through von Heilberg's file. He was quite sure of what he would find.

He took a deep breath and dived into the file.

He found it immediately. So simple, so obvious.

"Heilberg, Hans von. Born 18.7.08 in Madgeburg. Father of noble German birth, mother of noble Italian birth. Bilingual."

It didn't seem necessary to read on.

Hans von Heilberg was Marco di Spinelli.

That was that.

Mentally, Arto Söderstedt was already en route to Milan. He pushed the papers back over to the surprised Herschel and was just about to get to his feet when he remembered something.

"Oh, I forgot," he said. "Stockholm, they told me that the photograph of the third man was badly affected by the fax transmission. It would be good if I could see it."

For a moment, Ernst Herschel froze. The exact same movement as he had made before. Marco di Spinelli's voice echoed through Söderstedt: "I must admit it was something of a shock when you walked into the room, Signor Sadestatt. You truly do remind me of someone I knew an eternity ago, back in the beginning of time." And he saw an image, a photograph of an imposing-looking man anchored in a snowdrift, his hand gripping a sabre. The picture wasn't only impressive, it was also familiar.

Strangely familiar.

He sighed deeply as the photograph of the Pain Centre's third man was held out to him. He knew he would see himself.

And sure enough, he did.

The man in the picture was Arto Söderstedt himself.

A shiver passed through him.

"A remarkable likeness," said Ernst Herschel.

Arto Söderstedt jumped to his feet and rushed out of the room.

CHAPTER
THIRTY-SIX

On the plane between Leipzig and Milan, he finally managed to put his thoughts into some kind of order. By then, the worst of the fury and the worst of the horror had abated.

But everything was utterly clear.

There was no escaping it.

He felt as though he had been driven out of Paradise.

In Finland, Finnish SS men enjoyed the same rights as all other war veterans. Since the Finnish Winter War had been fought against the invading Soviet Union, it was natural that members of the resistance had turned to the USSR's enemy, Germany. Many of the fighters from the Winter War had later joined the SS. There were always plenty of commemorations.

Just over a year ago, an international scandal had blown up when the society for the memory of the fallen announced plans to build a memorial for the Finnish and German SS men who had died in battle in Ukraine. Only recently, the Jewish community in Helsinki had protested against a special event. The Finnish veterans had invited their German counterparts to an SS memorial event. This raised all kinds of questions about whether Finland should really be sending official invites to German SS veterans, old German Nazis from the organisation responsible for the systematic elimination of millions of Jews in Europe.

It was all a bit too much for the Jewish community to stomach.

But there was, in other words, nothing unusual in Finnish fighters from the Winter War having links to the Nazi SS. They were officially sanctioned as war veterans by the Finnish government.

Arto Söderstedt's Great-Uncle Pertti Lindrot had been an enthusiastic young provincial doctor who found himself drawn into the Finnish Winter War after the abrupt attack by the Soviet forces. He turned out to have a great aptitude for guerrilla warfare in the winter forests and quickly climbed the ranks. He became a hero after several decisive offences and disappeared without a trace after the Russian victory. According to his own version of events, he had gone out into the Finnish forests like a classic guerrilla fighter. He returned after the war, more or less a broken man. Drank more and more and had trouble keeping his job as a doctor in a variety of increasingly remote backwaters, before eventually returning to Vasa and becoming an eccentric, living that sad life until he turned ninety.

Now Arto Söderstedt knew what Uncle Pertti had really been up to after the Russian victory in the Finnish Winter War.

The young provincial doctor had become an SS officer.

He had been one of those responsible for the Pain Centre in Weimar, and he looked very, very similar to his great-nephew.

Uncle Pertti hadn't liked it. Tormentor number 1, according to Paul Hjelm's notes, had been: "Very blond, not-German, sorrowful." Leonard Sheinkman's words prior to death: "*The kindest of them. He is less German than I, and very blond. He looks so sorrowful. He kills with sorrow in his eyes.*"

Uncle Pertti hadn't liked it, but he had taken the dental gold all the same. And then he had moved on.

Arto Söderstedt had built his Tuscan paradise on a foundation of stolen Jewish dental gold.

He felt his face turn pale.

His paradise had been paid for with the teeth of hundreds of murdered Leonard Sheinkmans.

He had no choice but to run to the plane toilet and throw up. There seemed to be bucketfuls of the stuff. He vomited his disgust, his dread, his regret, his entire ruined conscience.

I'm trampling on their bodies, his vomit screamed. I'm trampling on their bodies to keep my head up above the shit. I can smell the stench, it roared, I can smell the stench and I'm looking out towards the horizon and pretending I think it's beautiful and that it smells of seventeen kinds of basil rather than shit and death and bodies.

But suddenly, the feeling of defeat was transformed. Whatever was rising in him was no longer the bile of self-contempt. It was no longer horror at Uncle Pertti's transformation from war hero to torturer and

434

murderer. It was no longer the repulsion of having a war criminal's — a Nazi's — evil blood coursing through his veins. It was no longer the nausea of having used the war criminal's stolen money.

It was rage.

Pure, simple rage, directed at one person and one person only.

Hans von Heilberg, also known as Marco di Spinelli.

Arto Söderstedt returned to his seat. A moment of turbulence shook the plane.

But the shaking was all his own.

He glanced at his computer screen. On it was a drawing. A drawing of a palace. Through it, a pale, crooked line snaked.

He would bring di Spinelli to account.

It was that simple.

He thought back to his last meeting with Commissioner Italo Marconi. It had ended oddly.

The commissioner had completed his meandering line, twisting this way and that across the drawing. It looked like a child's shaky pencil line on a comic-book labyrinth. Söderstedt had asked: "What do you think Marco di Spinelli did during the war?"

Marconi had put down the pen and fixed his Nordic colleague with his eyes.

"It's obvious," he had said. "He was a Nazi."

Söderstedt had stared back at him, nodded slowly and said: "My God, Italo. You want me to get to him."

"I want you to find out who he really is, yes. You might have more luck than I've had, Arto, with new starting points and fewer rigid restrictions."

"That's not what I mean," Söderstedt had replied. "You want me to go in *via that route*."

Marconi had given him a very quick glance, rubbed his enormous moustache and said, his fingers drumming the drawing: "Theoretically — and I'm only talking theoretically here — it's a classic one-man job. You go in through a vent in the garbage room. That vent opens out onto an alley behind the palace. They empty the rubbish through that vent once a week, using a vacuum pump. The cover on the vent, it's locked with a strong padlock. And you would need to be quick, you would have to move in a very specific way, because the cameras on the opposite wall move in a fixed pattern."

"It sounds completely impenetrable," Söderstedt had said.

"It would be," Marconi had replied, "if you didn't know the movements, weren't familiar with the time frames and didn't have access to a newly copied key."

A brown envelope had been placed on the table; it jingled slightly. Söderstedt had looked suspiciously at it.

"Are you really planning on sticking a blue-eyed Swedish policeman's head into the mouth of the lion in cold blood?"

"That was a lot of clichés in one sentence," Italo Marconi had said with a faint, practically undetectable smile.

"Go on," Arto Söderstedt had replied, his face unmoving.

"It's easier once you're inside the garbage room. You're out of the security cameras' sight anyway. The rubbish is thrown out from three locations within the

436

palace and comes tumbling down into the rubbish bins through wide shafts."

"So let me see if I understand, purely theoretically of course. The rubbish bin, it's covered with a lid?"

"Absolutely correct. A lid with four tubes coming out of it. The rubbish gets sucked out into the alleyway through one of them; that's the one you use to get in. That way, you'll end up in the covered rubbish bin."

"The covered, stinking, pitch-black rubbish bin."

"I can't do anything about the stench and the lid, I'm afraid. But a torch solves the problem of it being dark. When you get into the container, there are three pipes leading up, via three different shafts, to different places inside the palace. The closest of them goes to the kitchen, and that's much too far from the heart of things. The furthest leads to the drawing room of the great hall, and that's too far away as well — albeit in the other direction. The middle shaft, though, it goes to a little kitchenette belonging to di Spinelli's most private rooms. His three personal guards know about it — you've met them already — and possibly his private secretary."

"The one with the glasses," Söderstedt had said.

"Exactly," Marconi had unexpectedly replied. "Marco di Spinelli's secret rooms are where he has had prostitutes all these years. His love nest. Other than through the kitchenette, there's just one door leading to the love nest, and that faces out onto his office."

"I only saw one door in his office and it led to his private secretary's room. The one I came in through."

"This door is behind the sixteenth-century tapestries."

437

"And to get there, you have to climb up thirty metres from the rubbish bin?"

"Seven," Italo Marconi had said. "Seven metres straight up, plus ten or so on a slant at the beginning and the end. Purely theoretically, I'd recommend strong climbing shoes and a thick jumper with reinforced elbows. The lid to the garbage shoot needs to be opened from the inside with a monkey wrench."

"And what the hell do I do then?"

"You?" Marconi had asked, staring at Söderstedt. "Who the hell mentioned you?"

He had paused and sighed before continuing.

"You've managed to do something that no one else has in a long time. You've knocked Marco di Spinelli off balance. I don't know how you did it, but you did. We have to stir things up, and you could be just the thing we've been waiting for. Purely theoretically, that is."

"What about the Erinyes?"

"Well, yes. They're still a much more abstract thing for us. Maybe you can throw a spanner in their plans, too."

When Arto Söderstedt had left Italo Marconi's office that day, he had had absolutely no intention of getting hold of strong climbing shoes and a thick jumper with reinforced elbows, one which provided plenty of grip — that was the kind of thing Viggo Norlander and Gunnar Nyberg got up to, not him.

But things were different now. Back in Leipzig, he had already bought some climbing shoes and a good, thick jumper with reinforced elbows.

And now he understood just how he had managed to throw Marco di Spinelli off balance. It was only partly his doing; his appearance had also played a certain role. He had turned up at the house of Hans von Heilberg — though he hadn't been Hans von Heilberg for fifty years — and had presented him with his companions from the Pain Centre: first, in his own image, Pertti Lindrot; then, in Leonard Sheinkman's image, Anton Eriksson. As they had looked at the time.

Of course he had been thrown off balance.

The two motives for revenge converged in Marco di Spinelli. As Hans von Heilberg, head of the Pain Centre in Weimar, he had murdered and degraded countless people. As Marco di Spinelli, leader of the Ghiottone crime syndicate in Milan, he had also murdered and degraded countless people.

He was a deeply unpleasant man.

The Erinyes themselves also united the two motives for revenge, that much was clear. But how? What they were lacking was a woman who had been struck by the evil of the Ghiottone not once but *twice*. First as Hans von Heilberg and then as Marco di Spinelli.

This woman must also have known that the old professor in Stockholm was not called Leonard Sheinkman, and that the Mafia boss in Milan was not called Marco di Spinelli.

In other words, the leader of the Erinyes was a Jewish-Ukrainian former prostitute with links to the research group in Weimar.

Arto Söderstedt sat still for a moment. He let it all sink in.

Then he nodded and pushed a disk into the laptop. A disk from Odessa.

The Kouzmin file. Franz Kouzmin's tragic life appeared on the screen and Söderstedt filled in the gaps himself.

Kouzmin, Franz. Born Franz Sheinkman to a Jewish home in Berlin, 17 January 1935. Concentration camp in Buchenwald from August 1940. Slave labour in the war industry. His mother was executed in November 1944. His father was moved to the Pain Centre in Weimar, where he died in 1945. The nine-year-old Franz was used as a test subject in medical experiments and his nose was sawn off in January 1945. A Ukrainian woman by the name of Elena Kouzmin took care of and later adopted him, taking him back to her home town: the war-torn Odessa. The family lived in misery. Franz grew up an adopted, Jewish, noseless urchin. Bullied mercilessly at school, he became an alcoholic young. In 1967, aged thirty-two, he married another alcoholic, and in 1969, they had a daughter. His wife died of alcohol-related throat cancer in 1971. In 1974, their daughter was placed in an orphanage.

At some point during the early eighties, Franz had pulled himself together and started searching for surviving relatives across Europe. He found his father's name in the summer of 1981. Living in Sweden. He boarded the M/S *Cosmopolit* in August that same year and headed for Sweden to rekindle his relationship with his father — he probably had the ultimate aim of taking his daughter out of the orphanage. He could vaguely remember his father (judging by what his father had written in the diary) as a good figure from the far-flung past. At 18.25 on 4 September, the M/S *Cosmopolit* docked in Frihamnen in Stockholm. Franz came ashore and climbed into an illegal taxi driven by a Finn called Olli Peltonen. He drove him to Bofinksvägen in Tyresö. Franz knocked on the door of his father's house. His father opened. They didn't recognise one another. That wasn't so strange — nearly forty years had passed since they last met. Beaming with joy, Franz stepped into his father's home. The man he thought to be his father jammed a kitchen knife into his back. What must have passed through his mind in those last few moments of life is impossible to imagine.

Back in Odessa, his daughter had gone to his flat at the end of September. The place was empty. She reported his disappearance to the police. The last words about Franz Kouzmin had been made by his twelve-year-old daughter: "Dad had just stopped drinking. He'd been completely clean for a month. And really, really happy."

That was where his file should have ended. It shouldn't have been possible to say any more about the sad figure of Franz Kouzmin.

But there were still several pages to go.

"Save Kouzmin?" "Yes."

There was *another* Kouzmin. A second file had accompanied the other.

Magda Kouzmin.

His daughter.

Kouzmin, Magda. Born in Odessa to Franz Kouzmin, formerly Sheinkman, and Lizavjeta Kouzmin, née Sjatova, March 1969. Her mother died in 1971, she was in an orphanage from the age of five. Her father died when she was twelve. Early substance abuse. First arrest for prostitution in 1984, at the age of fifteen; some thirty or so more arrests after that, right up to 1997. Abused on twenty or so occasions, hospital treatment required. In 1987, she joined a brothel which provided party officials with prostitutes. Apparently highly appreciated by party officials. Witness statement: "Unbelievably good at her job. I've never known such pleasure." When the Wall came down, the brothel was taken over by the growing Ukrainian mafia which, in 1996, came under the control of an international organisation unknown to the Ukrainian authorities: the Ghiottone. Abused on seven occasions between February 1996 and August 1997. Reported missing along with two other prostitutes by her pimp, Artemij Tolkatjenko, in August 1997. Tolkatjenko moved to Manchester in 1998, and was found murdered near the Old Trafford stadium on 13 March 1999. Magda Kouzmin's fate was unknown.

Magda. Named after her grandmother, Leonard Sheinkman's wife.

Magda. Received a phone call from Lublin while she was in Odenplan metro station in Stockholm.

Magda. Leader of the Erinyes.

Magda. Leonard Sheinkman's grandchild.

In February 1996, Magda's brothel had been taken over by the Ghiottone. The time following this had clearly been a much more hellish time than before. Seven instances of abuse reported to the police meant

442

at least twenty in reality. By August 1997, she had had enough. It couldn't go on any longer. She fled along with two of her colleagues. She was twenty-eight years old and almost destitute. She had two options: die or turn a new page.

She chose to turn a new page — but without forgetting the preceding side. On the contrary, she allowed it to shape her entire future. It became her driving force during her detox and training. Her two former colleagues were by her side the whole time. They trained, deliberately, for an entire year. And then came the time for revenge. They set out on the hunt for their old tormentor, Artemij Tolkatjenko, the Ghiottone pimp from Odessa. He had moved to England by that point, presumably — like Nikos Voultsos a year later — in order to take over another group of prostitutes. They murdered him. Maybe they had even rescued others that first time, recruiting them as new colleagues.

Something had happened. Opportunities were arising. They could see just how much suffering went on within the prostitution business across Europe. They realised they could actually do something about it. They become goddesses of revenge. They became Erinyes.

So why, even that very first time, had they used the execution method from Weimar on their victims? Had Magda Kouzmin already understood the connection between the Ghiottone and the Pain Centre?

Did she already know about Marco di Spinelli?

Something else must have happened between her fleeing in August 1997 and the first murder in 1999.

She had found out what took place in the Pain Centre in Weimar; she had adopted its methods. How had she found out about it? Had she already linked it to what had happened to her father? Probably not. She probably found that out later, perhaps even this year. When she went after the false Leonard Sheinkman.

How had Magda Kouzmin found out about the method before March 1999?

There was only one way. Through Professor Ernst Herschel's research group.

Arto Söderstedt had been given a list by Herschel. He fished it out of his laptop bag. What had Elena Basedow said in Weimar? "There were plenty of volunteer students, right up to autumn 1998. Unpaid history and archaeology students."

Magda had left her life as a prostitute in August 1997. She could hardly have become an unpaid history and archaeology student that quickly. Her circumstances must have been chaotic. She had been on the run from a terrifying mafia organisation and needed to keep her head down. Besides that, she would have needed to detox and come to a decision about her future. That probably wouldn't have been possible until somewhere around the new year, 1997–1998. Unpaid history and archaeology students had been involved until autumn 1998. That narrowed things down to roughly the first half of 1998.

Söderstedt worked through the list. According to Herschel, the voluntary students hadn't been given access to a particularly large amount of information, but there must have been ways of getting round that.

444

She could hardly have pretended to be an established historical researcher.

Which workers had joined during the first half of 1998?

There were seven names listed as having started in spring 1998, disappearing when the building was closed for renovation in the autumn of that year. Of those names, five were women. They were: Steffi Prütz, Maryann Rollins, Inka Rothmann, Elena Basedow and Heidi Neumann.

Arto Söderstedt looked through their names one by one.

He had met Elena Basedow, of course. She was still working on Herschel's so-called "assistant staff". The alert young woman who had come to meet him on the platform in Weimar Hauptbahnhof.

"Herr Söderstadt."

He could cross her off.

But as he looked through the four remaining names, something happened. It was her forename. Magda, after her paternal grandmother. But there were, of course, two grandmothers. The Kouzmin woman, who had taken care of the orphaned Franz Sheinkman in Buchenwald. What had her name been?

Elena Kouzmin.

Arto Söderstedt was motionless.

Elena.

He had met her.

Only a few hours earlier, he had met her.

A wave of ice ripped through him.

The leader of the Erinyes had given him a lift in her car. A Volkswagen Vento. In Weimar.

Elena Basedow was Magda Kouzmin.

The woman who fed Nikos Voultsos to the wolverines, heaved Hamid al-Jabiri like a wheelbarrow across the platform in Odenplan and hung Anton Eriksson aka Leonard Sheinkman upside down from an oak in Södra Begravningsplatsen.

He dialled Ernst Herschel's number and asked: "Elena Basedow, who met me at the station — has she been working for you long?"

"She doesn't work for me."

"What?"

"I came to Weimar yesterday, to go through a few things in my office. I was staying in a hotel overnight. We happened to meet in the evening, and I remembered her from our work on the Pain Centre. In the morning, I asked her whether she couldn't pick you up from the station in my car, since I had a couple of errands to run."

"How was she?" Söderstedt asked.

"What do you mean?"

"How was she in bed?"

"My God."

"I'm serious," said Söderstedt. "How was she in bed? It's important."

There was a moment of silence.

"I've never known such pleasure," said Professor Ernst Herschel.

Söderstedt thanked him and hung up. He sat there for a moment, wallowing in his thoughts.

What had she been doing there?

What additional information had she needed?

He recalled all that had happened between them. It was less than five hours ago. Her gaze on the platform. That first look? A quick, sharp, shy look.

If she — like di Spinelli and Herschel — had recognised Pertti Lindrot in Arto Söderstedt, she had managed to hide it very, very well.

And of course she had.

What was the next step?

It came to him via an agitated woman's voice.

"We're really starting to get tired of asking you now."

Arto Söderstedt looked up and saw a furious air hostess with her hands clamped on her hips.

"Sorry?" he said in confusion.

"The plane landed half an hour ago," the hostess replied.

CHAPTER
THIRTY-SEVEN

Arto Söderstedt was wearing sturdy climbing shoes and a thick jumper with reinforced elbows. In addition to that, he had on a pair of military-green trousers with a large number of pockets.

He had checked in to a hotel in the immediate vicinity of Palazzo Riguardo. Now he was sitting in his room, looking at his watch. 4a.m. He set out into the Milanese night.

Outside, the sky was black. The people of Milan were still enjoying their beauty sleep. He could hear no more than a car or two in the distance. The stars were gleaming from the depths of the heavens; the moon was nothing more than a thin slice.

He crossed a small park and found himself at the end of an alleyway. On one side, the smooth outer wall of a building. On the other, the rear of Palazzo Riguardo, its few solitary windows set high up in the wall.

Söderstedt could see a circular vent with a heavy-looking cover. It was sunk into the thick pink wall of the building.

He watched the two surveillance cameras slowly, slowly rotating on their axes. He waited.

When the cameras reached the outermost points of their motions, he rushed into the alleyway and pressed himself up against the wall opposite the palace. He glanced at his watch and waited. The cameras turned and began to move back, each turning in a different direction.

The key dangling from his hand was trembling slightly.

His eyes were fixed on his watch. Four, three, two, one.

Zero.

He ran. Straight over the alleyway. Key quickly into lock. Vent lid quickly opened. And in he jumped. Into the unknown.

He heard the lid slam shut in the alleyway as he was transported into the palace through a pitch-black, downward shaft. Then he landed in a container with a bang.

He was surrounded by a terrible stench. Rotting fish. He couldn't see a thing and the air seemed thin. He lay on the rubbish like a shapeless lump, desperately trying to breathe calmly. He put the key into a pocket which he fastened shut with Velcro. He groped after another pocket and made out the contours of the small pistol he had found in the envelope from Marconi. "A purely hypothetical pistol, I assume," Söderstedt had said. He let go of it and allowed his hand to wander to yet another pocket. He pulled a small torch out of it and switched it on.

He really was lying on a pile of rubbish. Ants were running back and forth over the remnants of old fish. A couple of small, black worms were wriggling in and out of the eye sockets of a fish head. He could feel a rising wave of nausea he simply had to force back. He had no alternative.

He pointed the bright beam of light up at the roof of the rubbish container. Sure enough, he could make out the mouths of four chutes, each around half a metre in diameter. He found the shaft he had come in through. It was behind him. Slowly, he got to his feet. He could stand, provided he hunched right over. He moved past the first of the chutes in the left-hand corner of the container. At the second, he paused and put his head into the hole. He grabbed the torch and shone it upwards.

The chute turned into a shaft which sloped off to one side at an angle of sixty or so degrees. Beyond that, he could see that it turned sharply upwards. From there, it would be a seven-metre vertical climb.

He just hoped no one would throw anything out from the little kitchenette at four in the morning.

On the other hand, someone might hear him.

The chute was made from metal, probably some kind of aluminium alloy. Any careless movements would, in all probability, echo quite well, even if the pipe was flush against the thick stone walls, dampening the sound.

He also realised that he stank.

They would be able to smell him from a mile away.

Marconi: "Try to take a complete change of clothes. Choose trousers with as many pockets as possible. Purely theoretically, of course."

450

Getting from the container into the chute would be the most difficult thing. Standing with his head inside its mouth, he was up to his shoulders. That meant he needed to jump as high as he could, lock himself into place, get a firm grip with the reinforced elbows and wriggle his way up until he could get a grip with his feet. The angle of the pipe made it slightly easier.

He jumped and locked himself into place. He got a grip with his elbows and wriggled up so that his feet were in place. It worked.

Now he was stuck in the slanting part of the shaft. He shone the torch up, ahead of him. Even this short stretch of pipe felt endless. He had to preserve his strength. He would need it for the vertical climb.

This was simply a prelude.

It took time. He inched slowly, slowly upwards. He knew he was using more energy than he should.

It took him almost fifteen minutes to move those eight or so metres. Once he made it, he sat down in the bend where the chute became vertical and caught his breath. He opened yet another of the pockets in his trousers and pulled out an energy drink. He guzzled it down, shoved it back into his pocket and waited for his breathing to calm down. He felt the energy from the drink reach his bloodstream and his powers were restored.

He shone his torch upwards in the vertical shaft. A huge number of metres above him, seven hundred or so, it looked like, the chute bent once more and continued upwards at a slant.

The final furlong.

He started to haul himself upwards. It was hard work, but he soon found a rhythm to it. He was hitting the sides hard, but despite his efforts, he wasn't making much noise. In the midst of the cross-fire of his quick, echoing breaths, he paused to feel pleased that he wasn't making more noise.

That was when the bag of rubbish suddenly appeared.

He heard the lid of the rubbish chute opening above him, so he was ready. He held his breath and pushed against the walls with all the force he could muster. He waited as the noise grew louder and louder. He strained his neck muscles as hard as he could. And then the bag hit him on the head with a clang.

He could smell the stench.

Leftover shellfish.

Despite the unfortunate circumstances, he managed to think. He didn't want to let the bag move past his head in case it got stuck somewhere next to his face or chest. It would be better to take it up with him, on his head, and then try to get rid of it when he got to the bend. A bend automatically meant more room.

And so he climbed the last three metres with the bag of rubbish on his head like some African woman balancing a barrel of water.

Sure enough, when he came to the bend, he managed to coax the bag down. He wedged himself into the bend with his feet pressed against the vertical wall and held the bag over the abyss.

Did he dare drop it? If they heard it fall now, several minutes after they threw it away, it was bound to catch their attention. But on the other hand, he was quite deep within the walls of the building.

He let it go. It didn't make much noise on its way down to the container.

He swung the torch upwards. Again, the chute was slanting, this time close to seventy degrees. Six or so metres up along the shaft, he could make out the inside of the cover. Only a few minutes ago, it had opened. If it opened again, he would be discovered; they would shoot him and he would fall down into the container like any other piece of rubbish.

They might have managed to fill another bag by this point.

But on the other hand, there wasn't really any going back.

He struggled on, inch by inch. The elbows on his jumper had started to wear away and he could feel the rough stone walls clawing greedily at his increasingly bare skin.

He was so high up now that he could see the lid without straining his neck. He opened the Velcro on the pocket containing the gun. How quickly would he be able to whip it out? he wondered. Without losing his grip and falling headlong into the shaft.

Inch by inch, centimetre by centimetre, closer, closer, closer. His elbows were skinned. He could feel the blood oozing out. And still he continued, inch by inch, centimetre by centimetre, until he reached the lid.

He carefully placed his fingertips on the metal, grabbed a monkey wrench from yet another pocket and clamped it to the inside of the handle mechanism with as much delicacy as he could. His hands were shaking. For a few seconds, they caused the wrench to rattle gently against the handle. Then it was in place.

He took a deep breath and held the monkey wrench utterly, utterly still.

Slowly, he began turning it anticlockwise.

As he turned it, he thought of the consequences. Just fifteen minutes earlier, someone had been here and thrown a bag of rubbish down the chute. How did he know that person wasn't still on the other side of the wall? It was true, he couldn't hear a sound from inside the palace, but it would have been enough if di Spinelli was in his love nest — the room next to the kitchenette. It wasn't his usual bedroom, but maybe he'd had a prostitute there overnight. They might have been eating lobster and drinking champagne. He was just grateful it hadn't been a champagne bottle landing on his head.

He need not have worried.

He opened the lid a fraction of an inch. He could see the outlines of an oven and a stove. Otherwise, nothing.

Suddenly, the lid was torn open and the barrel of a high-calibre gun was jammed into his mouth. The light in the kitchenette came on, blinding him. He was hauled up out of the chute and thrown down to the floor.

"New cologne?" Marco di Spinelli asked.

Someone kicked Söderstedt in the stomach before lifting him up by his hair and throwing him onto a chair. The three bodyguards were standing in a ring around him. One of them shoved his high-calibre pistol into Söderstedt's mouth once more. He thought: Then,

454

back then, when the phone rang in that restaurant on Piazzale Michelangelo in Florence, back then everything had been possible. Then, back then, when the wine had been flowing and he was enjoying the spring breeze as he looked out over the Arno and the whole of Florence was like a man-made paradise in front of him, right then it would have been possible to ignore the phone.

If he had done that, his paradise would still be intact.

A bit boring, perhaps, but boring in a paradisiacal way.

The pistol was yanked out of his mouth. Against the wall behind the bodyguards, Marco di Spinelli was standing, straight-backed. Ninety-two years old and still convinced of the superiority of his genes.

"The bag of rubbish was a nice touch, wasn't it?" he said, wrinkling his nose. "You really do not smell good, Signor Sadestatt."

One of the bodyguards took Söderstedt's little pistol and handed it over to di Spinelli, who looked at it with interest.

"One of those guns the police tend to use when they're avoiding looking like they're policemen. For some reason, they're always the same." He handed the gun back to the bodyguard and said, nonchalantly: "I suppose it was in the envelope."

Arto Söderstedt closed his eyes and understood. He could feel the blood running from his mouth and wondered how many teeth he was missing.

And he realised, with a chilling clarity, that he would never get to meet his new baby.

"You must understand," di Spinelli said, "that we've been filming that irritatingly incorruptible Marconi for years. We followed you to Odessa and to Leipzig and to Weimar and back. You might have hurt yourself."

"Hans von Heilberg," Söderstedt hissed.

"Yes, yes," di Spinelli replied disinterestedly. "But Marconi was right that you did manage to surprise me on your first visit. I'd seen the film from Marconi's office, of course, but you were sitting with your back to the camera so I hadn't seen your face. It surprised me. You also seemed unusually mediocre. Then I realised it was a mask. You weren't unusually mediocre, just mediocre. In a way, that was worse."

"And the Erinyes?" Söderstedt panted.

"Eastern European competition," di Spinelli replied with a shrug. "We have plenty of that these days, but it isn't especially difficult for us to deal with. We'll pick them up soon enough. They usually lose patience. But there's one matter from earlier that we need to straighten out, Signor Sadestatt."

"How is it I'm so similar to Pertti Lindrot, the SS doctor from the Pain Centre in Weimar?"

"Yes, how?"

"You've got nothing to worry about," Söderstedt said. "They're dead, both of them. Pertti Lindrot devoted his life to drinking himself stupid. Anton Eriksson became a Jewish professor and met his end hanging upside down with a metal nail in his brain."

"Well, what do you know," said di Spinelli. "But you haven't answered the question."

"I have no intention of doing so either," Söderstedt replied.

Suddenly, he felt a kind of shifting presence in the palace. He grinned.

"In that case, it's time to relive some old memories," Hans von Heilberg said, picking up a small box, not dissimilar to the kind you would keep expensive old jewellery in. "Of great value to the right collector," he said, removing a long, thin, sharp metal nail from the box. He bent it slightly, like a master fencer bends his rapier before each bout.

Then, suddenly, his three gorillas died.

The nail pinged back and Marco di Spinelli looked down at his three dead lumps of meat in surprise.

Something rushed by the door out towards the love nest. Like an illusion. It was completely empty back there. All he had noticed was a faint movement.

"You move quickly, Magda," Söderstedt said into the nothingness.

The room remained silent and empty. Marco di Spinelli stared towards the mute darkness in the room where, for years, he had received prostitutes. Perhaps there was a glimmer of fear in his steely eyes. He grabbed one of his gorillas' pistols and crept slowly over towards the love nest. He disappeared round the corner.

Söderstedt heard him.

He heard him die.

He didn't scream, that would have been beneath him, but he gave out a wheeze, and that wheeze declared that he had lived too long.

Much too long.

He was dangling from the crystal chandelier in his exquisite office, hanging there like a modern work of art alongside Leonardo and Piero della Francesca's masterpieces and the sixteenth-century tapestries. The faint moonlight was shining in through the window by which the Marquis of Perduto had composed his famous sonnets to Amelia, the girl he had met at the age of eight and never quite managed to forget.

Arto Söderstedt stood alongside him. The little pistol hung from his hand in the same way as Marco di Spinelli hung from his perfect chandelier. Both dangled. There was nothing for Söderstedt to aim his gun at. The room was empty. Elsewhere in the palace, the guards sat playing cards. They were blissfully unaware they were now unemployed.

He squatted down to look at Hans von Heilberg's face. Just like the way in which the man himself had looked at the hundreds of victims whose dental gold had formed the basis of his financial activities in Milan. Activities which, in turn, laid the basis for his criminal empire.

Everything went hand in hand.

Hans von Heilberg's shirt collar had been ripped back. A purple, rhombus-shaped birthmark shone dark against his pale skin.

From his temple, a long, sharp, stiff nail. The steely look in his eyes had been obliterated by the pain.

Time was slowly righting itself once more.

"Are you there, Magda?" Söderstedt asked, looking at di Spinelli's glassy, lifeless eyes.

A faint shifting behind his back confirmed that she was.

They all were.

But when he turned round, he couldn't see a soul.

He smiled.

And then he said, to the room, straight into the incomprehensible: "Thank you."

CHAPTER
THIRTY-EIGHT

It was high summer in Stockholm, the sun low in the unusually deep blue sky. And yet this time, it wasn't at all as though an opera scenographer had tried to imitate nature.

It may not quite have been nature, but at least it was more like nature than before.

Than it had been a few weeks before.

Nature is the terribly awful truth.

The last time Paul Hjelm had been on Bofinksvägen in Tyresö, he had enjoyed a long, deep and open-hearted conversation with Leonard Sheinkman's son. Though in actual fact, Leonard Sheinkman's only son had died, right there, twenty years earlier. The man he had spoken to wasn't Leonard Sheinkman's son at all. He was the mass murderer and Nazi Anton Eriksson's son. He was a Jewish man named Harald Sheinkman who now needed to be brought up to date about the whole sorry state of affairs.

About the fact his father was a Nazi, not a Jew.

About the fact his father was an executioner, not a victim.

About the fact his father hadn't written the yellowed pages of that diary, but stolen it and used it to build a background for himself.

460

About the fact his father had managed to cause the worst pain imaginable by experimenting on guinea pig after guinea pig in a nightmare cellar in Weimar.

About the fact his father had murdered women and children.

How far did the limits of atonement really stretch?

The Pain Centre.

Miles Davis's *Kind of Blue* streamed through the old Audi. That was precisely how Paul Hjelm felt.

Kind of Blue.

He said: "What is it you're going through?"

Kerstin Holm turned to look at him.

Her own crisis had stopped short. The Erinyes were dominating her thoughts now. They didn't leave room for much else.

They dealt out justice, their very own kind of justice. One which consisted of revenge — no more, no less. They took revenge on behalf of unavenged injustices.

So what exactly distinguished them from state-sanctioned death penalties?

She didn't know. At times, they seemed almost fascistic. At times, rightful avengers. Sometimes, they were nothing more than terrorists. Sometimes, they were repressed but utterly vital mythical forces.

One thing was clear: the Erinyes would never become Eumenides. They would never allow themselves to be neutralised by the lightweight society in which they lived.

Because that was what life in the West was — lightweight: easily lived, easily digested, easily fucked. The unbearable lightness of being. An all-American

Existence Light. Filled with chemical sweetener that killed infinitely more quickly than real sugar ever did.

That was the essence of her crisis. Her ... metamorphosis. Even if the word did seem slightly grand. Pretentious, even — and if there was one thing no one wanted to be, it was pretentious. That was where everyone drew the line.

The thing she was searching for was the free zone, that place where the primitive forces had free rein to bubble away undisturbed. That bubble we never fail to pop before it gets too big. The one she could feel the virtual presence of every time she sang with the choir, allowing her voice to rise up towards the high vaulted ceilings and letting the choir's tones surround her like a warm, comforting embrace. Religious? Mmm. But without a sense of the holy, our sense of the *unholy* also withers away. And we need to retain that. Otherwise we die.

That was roughly how it was. But how best to phrase it?

Maybe something like this:

"It's a bit tricky to explain. But don't worry. I'm just brooding, causing myself grief."

Paul Hjelm chuckled. "Story of my life," he said.

They were silent for a moment. The distance between them wasn't especially big. There were no watertight doors keeping them apart. It was all leaking through. No, it wasn't possible to understand someone else completely. But what about yourself?

So what, as Miles Davis was playing.

The image in each of their minds was, at least, the same. Hultin's whiteboard. First, five names. At the bottom, the two who had fled the Ghiottone and Odessa together with Magda in August 1997. Above, three upper-case names in red: Magda Kouzmin, Magda Sheinkman, Elena Basenow. Three names, one woman. Alongside it, an e-fit image put together by Arto Söderstedt and Ernst Herschel. Arto had, in the strictest confidence, told them he suspected Herschel would find it easier to describe her vagina than he did her face, but they managed to put a picture together regardless. A picture of a face and nothing else. They had shown it to Adib Tamir too, and he had confirmed it. That was what she looked like, the bitch who cut Hamid in two.

Arto Söderstedt was fine. He was missing four teeth, wearing peculiar-looking braces and only able to sip Vin Santo through a straw. He was also talking quite strangely. But otherwise, he seemed happier than ever.

It looked doubtful he would ever come home again.

Next to the e-fit of Magda were four photographs, or rather three more e-fits and one proper photograph. They still had just one of the other Erinyes on film, and that was the woman with the mobile phone in Gdynia. Two were the e-fits that Jadwiga from the M/S *Stena Europe* had composed, and the third had been put together by a salesman from a superstore in Bromma to which Jorge, with great finesse, had managed to trace the red-and-purple-striped rope. The salesman could remember selling it to a woman dressed in black. He had assumed she was an Eastern European working girl and started hitting on her. She had paid in the form of 120 kronor and a kick to the groin. That was why he remembered her so well, and she was none of the four they knew of. That meant she was likely one of those who had taken part in the hangings in Skansen and Södra Begravningsplatsen. In Palazzo Riguardo too, in all probability.

Suddenly, the kick to the groin seemed almost gentle. Practically a caress.

There they hung in any case, five sharp female faces with a slight Slavic look to them.

All unidentified apart from Magda Kouzmin.

Europe was now on the hunt for them, and it was all their fault.

The A-Unit's fault.

Neither Paul nor Kerstin were quite sure it was a good thing.

This was a case where plenty of guilty parties had been identified but not a single one had been arrested. Time had somehow set itself right, though; it had caught up with itself. And Jan-Olov Hultin looked fit as a fiddle. Not a stroke in sight. No black hole in the space-time continuum. A newly found sense of clairvoyance, perhaps, but they could live with that. Even Hultin.

They had finally had a response from the phone company in Ukraine. The phone from Odenplan had, on a number of occasions, made calls to two different numbers in Milan. Sometimes they had been to Palazzo Riguardo, presumably threatening calls, and sometimes to a nearby hotel room, where it wasn't entirely implausible to imagine a couple of the Erinyes sitting and waiting, mapping out di Spinelli's entire life. Aside from that, a large number of calls to and from Slagsta. Nothing else of interest.

"Should we go in then?" Paul Hjelm asked. "Should we go in and ruin Harald Sheinkman's life just as he's starting to get back on his feet?"

It was their job.

They both looked up at the beautiful house on Bofinksvägen in Tyresö. Before them, they could see a man without a nose practically skipping up to the house, brushing the roses with his hands and breathing in the scents of the garden through the hole he had in the place of a nose, before reaching its handsome front door and saying to himself: "To think that Pappa did so well when I did so badly. But now, now my life's wounds will heal. As soon as I'm reunited with Pappa, who I loved when we lived in Berlin, who comforted me every night in the terrible Buchenwald. Then I'll return to Odessa and take Magda from that awful orphanage where everyone becomes an addict or a whore, and we'll move here to beautiful Sweden, and finally become a proper family again."

Just a few seconds later, he was dead.

Should Anton Eriksson really be allowed to ruin his own child's life too? Posthumously?

"Like hell," said Kerstin, doing up her seat belt.

"What about the truth?" Paul asked, doing the same.

"Enough's enough."

Paul Hjelm laughed, turned the ignition key and swung out onto Bofinksvägen.

Anton Eriksson could remain the man he had spent half his life believing he was. Professor Emeritus Leonard Sheinkman.

The Nobel Prize candidate.

Hopefully he had, somehow, reconciled with his falsified life before he died.

Paul Hjelm accelerated and turned up the volume.

It was how they felt. Exactly how.

Kind of Blue.

CHAPTER
THIRTY-NINE

And then the thing he had only dreamt of happened.

She came to visit him. "A ray of sunshine," as Anja said later that evening.

She just turned up. Arto was sitting on the veranda, slurping Vin Santo through a straw and enjoying life, and Anja went to open the door.

She came out onto the veranda and said: "It's your colleague from the Italian police."

Could it be Marconi? he wondered. They had already said goodbye.

He turned round and there she was.

She looked just like she had in Weimar. Slightly nervous and clutching a little handbag tightly in her hands.

"Herr Söderstadt," she said cautiously.

His jaw dropped. It really was her.

It was Magda Kouzmin.

It was Magda Sheinkman.

It was Elena Basedow.

He couldn't help but laugh, only for a short, short moment.

She didn't look so violently homicidal. Erinye from 9 until 5.

He asked her to sit down. She thanked him and did so. He didn't know where to begin and apparently nor did she. They sat in silence instead, watching the children run around, their heads bobbing like chess pieces out there among the greenery. Five white-haired and now four black-haired heads. Their group of friends was slowly but surely growing.

"I admire you," she said. "You're living. I'm something else."

"My mother's uncle murdered your grandfather," said Arto Söderstedt.

There were opening lines and then there were opening lines . . .

She turned to him and smiled.

"I guessed he was a relative."

"He only died recently. I inherited his money. All this, it's a false paradise. It's your money. And many, many others'. I still don't know whether I should tell the world that Pertti Lindrot, the war hero, was a real bastard. I don't know — should I sacrifice my children's happiness for that?"

"I don't know," she said. "Pertti Lindrot?"

"Yes. From Finland."

"The third man," she nodded. "We never managed to identify him. It was impossible. Eventually I found out that there was, at least, a picture of him and that Herschel had it in Weimar. I went there and slept with him and copied the photo. Right after that, he asked me to pick up the spitting image of a man I'd just seen in a sixty-year-old photo from the railway station. It was a bit odd."

"I can understand that," said Söderstedt. "He drank himself to death. Slowly but surely. That's the redeeming part of his existence."

"Maybe," Magda Kouzmin said after a moment. "I made sure to check the birthmark on his neck, by the way."

"How did you get into the palace?"

"Same way you did. One after another, nice and calmly. Just a few hours earlier. They had no idea. They were waiting for you, not for us. They'd been following you. They were on to you the entire time."

"How do you know?"

"We were watching them."

"So they were following me and you were following them?"

"Yes. What I want to know is: how did you identify me?"

He looked at her. Was she here on business after all? That didn't feel good.

She could immediately see it in his face.

"Sorry," she said. "It's not my intention to snoop. All I really wanted to ask for was my grandfather's diary."

"It should be yours," said Söderstedt. "But I only have a copy. You can have it."

"Thank you."

And then he told her. Against his better judgement, he told her.

"I found you through your father. That was when I understood the scope of what you'd been through."

"My fate is hardly unique," she said. "It's . . . European."

He chuckled bitterly and said: "My turn to get technical. How did you find out about the method? What made you seek out the research group in Weimar?"

"The Ghiottone took over our brothel in Odessa. That was back when Marco di Spinelli still left his palace. He visited us. He wanted to 'test the girls', he said. He seemed to like me a lot, because he started boasting about his disgusting war crimes in the throes of passion. That was always when he was horniest. He mentioned Weimar one day. There and then, I decided to give him a taste of his own medicine. That was how it all started. Taking out di Spinelli, that was the plan. And the method he described sounded good. About that time, we were constantly being abused by his sleazy henchman, Artemij Tolkatjenko, so once we'd made up our minds, it made sense to start with him. Wherever he was. It turned out he'd gone to England. Manchester. And then we just started seeking out other horrible pimps, that was all. We were always on the way to Marco di Spinelli though."

"So is it over now? The Erinyes will become Eumenides?"

"We'll see," Magda said, smiling shyly. "Once we left Odessa and got on top of the drugs, I went to Weimar to see what he'd been doing there during the war. It was all so secretive, but eventually — using fake grades — I ended up at the Pain Centre, helping out with all the crappy jobs they had. I realised that was where he'd been. And while I was there, I kept looking. I was often alone there at nights. Eventually, I found one of those wires and I started to understand how it worked. I also found some papers from an archive. It was a hell of a shock. The name Leonard Sheinkman was mentioned in connection to some diary. It said that he was dead and that the so-called 'Swede' had taken care of his diary. I realised he was my real grandfather. Dad had told me his name was Sheinkman when he was little and that his father had been taken away from Buchenwald. I burnt the paper and memorised it all. The memories are all I have. What I work with. I found a file about my dad too, later on — just a couple of loose sheets. There were some notes about a ferry headed for Stockholm, and in the phone directory for Stockholm I found a Leonard Sheinkman. My grandfather's name. I realised it must be the so-called 'Swede'. He was pretending to be my grandfather. And he had killed my father. Both my dad and my grandpa. The same man had killed them both."

"You hung him above your father's grave. He was on his way there."

"Oh, I didn't know that," Magda said, looking genuinely surprised. "He'd been going around on the metro for a few days, as though he was on the way somewhere. He was probably catching up with himself and his crimes."

"Speaking of the metro," said Arto Söderstedt. "You said you'd only killed serious criminals, murderers and people who've abused women. Those three thugs in Palazzo Riguardo were also serious criminals, and you knew that in advance?"

"Yes."

"But what about the metro in Stockholm? Odenplan? The person who stole your phone, he was just an immigrant. His name was Hamid al-Jabiri. Did he deserve to be ripped to shreds?"

"No," Magda said unhappily. "That just happened."

"Adrenalin?"

"Probably."

"Can't you see this is all starting to get out of control? Soon, the violence will be an intrinsic value. Soon, you'll be just as speed-blind as the Baader-Meinhof or ETA or the IRA. Everyone will be an enemy. Everyone but you will be worthy of death."

Söderstedt paused and placed his hand on Magda's. He really was trying to express himself clearly. Lives might depend on it.

"Stop this now," he said. "There's no need for it any more. You got di Spinelli. Everyone involved in your grandfather's death is gone. You saved my life and I'm begging you now: stop this. It's dragging us into some other kind of society, and both that society and its opponents are becoming increasingly undemocratic. That's all that will end up happening. The only thing you're really killing is democracy. It's fragile and it's important. Despite everything. So stop it now."

Arto Söderstedt felt like Athena in Aeschylus' Oresteia.

I will not weary of soft words to thee,
That never mayst thou say, Behold me spurned,
An elder by a younger deity,
And from this land rejected and forlorn.

Eventually, the leader of the Erinyes replied: "Lo, I desist from wrath, appeased by thee." And the Erinyes became Eumenides.

But that was poetry.

This was something else.

"I don't think it's possible any more," Magda replied with a faint smile. "Even if I wanted to."

He nodded.

"I tried, anyway," he said.

They sat for a moment longer. The wall between them had risen once more.

"I'll get the diary," he said, getting to his feet.

Magda waited on the veranda. She looked out over the paradisiacal landscape, and no one, absolutely no one in the world, could have known what she was thinking.

He came back and handed her the diary. They parted without a word. He watched as she wandered down the narrow, steep, crooked road to Greve.

Chianti was showing its best side. The sun was playing on her back and made her black clothes almost glow. She disappeared behind the crest of the hill like a piece of glowing coal.

The shadow of her seemed to linger long after she had gone.

It would probably never disappear.

Söderstedt stood there bathed in the scent of nineteen different varieties of basil. A warm wind gently caressed his cheek. The winemakers were pacing slowly back and forth along their vines on the sun-drenched hills. The children were running around increasingly wildly, and black could no longer be distinguished from white, white no longer from black; the clamour of their voices rose in a paean to the luminous wisps of cloud hanging in the clear blue sky.

Everything was wonderful. And everything was false.

He was standing on top of bodies in order to see Paradise.

And he wasn't alone. He was an entire continent.

Anja appeared from her basil-scented landscape like a misplaced marrow. She walked over to him on the veranda and took a sip of his Vin Santo.

"Isn't it wonderful?" she asked.

"Yes," he said, stroking her stomach.

They stood there for a moment.

Eventually, he said: "How's the little rascal doing?"

Anja laughed and hit him with her gardening gloves.

"What is it with you?" she exclaimed. "I'm *not* pregnant."

TO THE TOP OF THE MOUNTAIN

Arne Dahl

After the disastrous end to its last case, the Intercrime team — a specialist unit created to investigate violent, international crime — has been disbanded, their leader forced into early retirement.

The six detectives have been scattered throughout the country. Detectives Paul Hjelm and Kerstin Holm are investigating the senseless murder of a young football supporter in a pub in Stockholm, Arto Soderstedt and Viggo Norlander are working on mundane cases, Gunnar Nyberg is tackling child pornography while Jorge Chavez is immersed in research.

But when a man is blown up in a high-security prison, a major drugs baron comes under attack and a massacre takes place in a dark suburb, the Intercrime team are urgently reconvened. There is something dangerous approaching Sweden, and they are the only people who can do anything to stop it.

BAD BLOOD

Arne Dahl

Now a major TV series

Detective Paul Hjelm and his team receive an urgent call from the FBI. A murderer whose methods bear a frightening resemblance to a serial killer they believed long dead is on his way to Sweden. The FBI hunted him for years, haunted by his signature device: a terrible weapon that squeezed the vocal cords shut. Has he somehow returned from beyond the grave, or is it a copycat killer? And what does he want in Sweden? The team must collaborate with the FBI on a desperate hunt that will take them from rainswept city streets to deserted Kentucky farmhouses.